LOCK

EVERY

DOOR

RILEY SAGER

EBURY
PRESS

This edition published in 2020 by Ebury Press
First published in the UK in 2019 by Ebury Press
First published in the US in 2019 by Dutton, a division of Penguin Random House

3 5 7 9 10 8 6 4 2

Ebury Press, an imprint of Ebury Publishing
20 Vauxhall Bridge Road,
London SW1V 2SA

Penguin
Random House
UK

Ebury Press is part of the Penguin Random House group of companies whose
addresses can be found at global.penguinrandomhouse.com

www.penguin.co.uk

A CIP catalogue record for this book is available from the British Library

ISBN 9781529104424

Printed and bound in Great Britain by Clays Ltd, Elcograf S.p.A.

Penguin Random House is committed to a sustainable future for
our business, our readers and our planet. This book is made from Forest
Stewardship Council® certified paper.

MIX
Paper from
responsible sources
FSC® C018179

FSC
www.fsc.org

To Ira Levin

Ginny gazed up at the building, her feet planted firmly on the sidewalk but her heart as wide and churning as the sea. Not even in her wildest dreams did she ever think she'd set foot inside this place. To her, it had always felt as far away as a fairy-tale castle. It even looked like one —tall and imposing, with gargoyles gracing the walls. It was the Manhattan version of a palace, inhabited by the city's elite.

To those who lived outside its walls, it was known as the Bartholomew.

But to Ginny, it was now the place she called home.

Greta Manville,
Heart of a Dreamer

NOW

Light slices the darkness, jerking me awake.

My right eye—someone's prying it open. Latex-gloved fingers part the lids, yanking on them like they're stubborn window shades.

There's more light now. Harsh. Painfully bright. A penlight, aimed at my pupil.

The same is done to my left eye. Pry. Part. Light.

The fingers release my lids, and I'm plunged back into darkness.

Someone speaks. A man with a gentle voice. "Can you hear me?"

I open my mouth, and hot pain circles my jaw. Stray bolts of it jab my neck and cheek.

"Yes."

My voice is a rasp. My throat is parched. So are my lips, save for a single slick spot of wet warmth with a metallic taste.

"Am I bleeding?"

"You are," says the same voice as before. "Just a little. Could have been worse."

"A lot worse," another voice says.

"Where am I?"

The first voice answers. "A hospital, honey. We're taking you for some tests. We need to see how banged up you really are."

It dawns on me that I'm in motion. I can hear the hum of wheels on tile and feel the slight wobble of a gurney I just now realize I'm flat-backed upon. Until now, I had thought I was floating. I try to move but can't. My *arms and legs are strapped down. Something is pythoned around my neck, holding my head in place.*

Others are with me. Three that I know of. The two voices, and someone else pushing the gurney. Warm huffs of breath brush my earlobe.

"Let's see how much you can remember." It's the first voice again. The big talker of the bunch. "Think you can answer some questions for me?"

"Yes."

"What's your name?"

"Jules." I stop, irritated by the warm wetness still on my lips. I try to lick it away, my tongue flopping. "Jules Larsen."

"Hi, Jules," the man says. "I'm Bernard."

I want to say hello back, but my jaw still hurts.

As does my entire left side from knee to shoulder.

As does my head.

It's a quick boil of pain, going from nonexistent to screaming in seconds. Or maybe it's been there all along and only now is my body able to handle it.

"How old are you, Jules?" Bernard asks.

"Twenty-five." I stop, overcome with a fresh blast of pain. "What happened to me?"

"You were hit by a car, honey," Bernard says. "Or maybe the car was hit by you. We're still kind of unclear on the details."

I can't help in that department. This is breaking news to me. I don't recall anything.

"When?"

"Just a few minutes ago."

"Where?"

"Right outside the Bartholomew."

My eyes snap open, this time on their own.

I blink against the harsh fluorescents zipping by overhead as the gurney speeds along. Keeping pace is Bernard. He has dark skin, bright scrubs, brown eyes. They're kind eyes, which is why I stare into them, pleading.

"Please," I beg. "Please don't send me back there."

SIX DAYS EARLIER

1

The elevator resembles a birdcage. The tall, ornate kind—all thin bars and gilded exterior. I even think of birds as I step inside. Exotic and bright and lush.

Everything I'm not.

But the woman next to me certainly fits the bill, with her blue Chanel suit, blond updo, perfectly manicured hands weighed down by several rings. She might be in her fifties. Maybe older. Botox has made her face tight and gleaming. Her voice is champagne bright and just as bubbly. She even has an elegant name—Leslie Evelyn.

Because this is technically a job interview, I also wear a suit.

Black.

Not Chanel.

My shoes are from Payless. The brown hair brushing my shoulders is on the ragged side. Normally, I would have gone to Supercuts for a trim, but even that's now out of my price range.

I nod with feigned interest as Leslie Evelyn says, "The elevator is original, of course. As is the main staircase. Not much in the lobby has changed since this place opened in 1919. That's the great thing about these older buildings—they were built to last."

And, apparently, to force people to invade each other's personal space. Leslie and I stand shoulder to shoulder in the surprisingly small elevator car. But what it lacks in size it makes up for in style. There's red carpet on the floor and gold leaf on the ceiling. On three sides, oak-paneled walls rise to waist height, where they're replaced by a series of narrow windows.

The elevator car has two doors—one with wire-thin bars that closes by itself, plus a crisscross grate Leslie slides into place before tapping the button for the top floor. Then we're off, rising slowly but surely into one of Manhattan's most storied addresses.

Had I known the apartment was in this building, I never would have responded to the ad. I would have considered it a waste of time. I'm not a Leslie Evelyn, who carries a caramel-colored attaché case and looks so at ease in a place like this. I'm Jules Larsen, the product of a Pennsylvania coal town with less than five hundred dollars in my checking account.

I do not belong here.

But the ad didn't mention an address. It simply announced the need for an apartment sitter and provided a phone number to call if interested. I was. I did. Leslie Evelyn answered and gave me an interview time and an address. Lower seventies, Upper West Side. Yet I didn't truly know what I was getting myself into until I stood outside the building, triple-checking the address to make sure I was in the right place.

The Bartholomew.

Right behind the Dakota and the twin-spired San Remo as one of Manhattan's most recognizable apartment buildings. Part of that is due to its narrowness. Compared with those other legends of New York real estate, the Bartholomew is a mere wisp of a thing—a sliver of stone rising thirteen stories over Central Park West. In a neighborhood of behemoths, the Bartholomew stands out by being the opposite. It's small, intricate, memorable.

But the main reason for the building's fame are its gargoyles. The classic kind with bat wings and devil horns. They're everywhere, those stone beasts, from the pair that sit over the arched front door to the ones crouched on each corner of the slanted roof. More inhabit the building's facade, placed in short rows on every other floor. They sit on marble outcroppings, arms raised to ledges above, as if they alone are keeping the Bartholomew upright. It gives the building a Gothic, cathedral-like appearance that's inspired a similarly religious nickname—St. Bart's.

Over the years, the Bartholomew and its gargoyles have graced a thousand photographs. I've seen it on postcards, in ads, as a backdrop for fashion shoots. It's been in the movies. And on TV. And on the cover of a best-selling novel published in the eighties called *Heart of a Dreamer*, which is how I first learned about it. Jane had a copy and would often read it aloud to me as I lay sprawled across her twin bed.

The book tells the fanciful tale of a twenty-year-old orphan named Ginny who, through a twist of fate and the benevolence of a grandmother she never knew, finds herself living at the Bartholomew. Ginny navigates her posh new surroundings in a series of increasingly elaborate party dresses while juggling several suitors. It's fluff, to be sure, but the wonderful kind. The kind that makes a young girl dream of finding romance on Manhattan's teeming streets.

As Jane would read, I'd stare at the book's cover, which shows an across-the-street view of the Bartholomew. There were no buildings like that where we grew up. It was just row houses and storefronts with sooty windows, their glumness broken only by the occasional school or house of worship. Although we had never been there, Manhattan intrigued Jane and me. So did the idea of living in a place like the Bartholomew, which was worlds away from the tidy duplex we shared with our parents.

"Someday," Jane often said between chapters. "Someday I'm going to live there."

"And I'll visit," I'd always pipe up.

Jane would then stroke my hair. "Visit? You'll be living there with me, Julie-girl."

None of those childhood fantasies came true, of course. They never do. Maybe for the Leslie Evelyns of the world, perhaps. But not for Jane. And definitely not for me. This elevator ride is as close as I'm going to get.

The elevator shaft is tucked into a nook of the staircase, which winds upward through the center of the building. I can see it through the elevator windows as we rise. Between each floor is ten steps, a landing, then ten more steps.

On one of the landings, an elderly man wheezes his way down the stairs with the help of an exhausted-looking woman in purple scrubs. She waits patiently, gripping the man's arm as he pauses to catch his breath. Although they pretend not to be paying attention as the elevator passes, I catch them taking a quick look just before the next floor blocks them from view.

"Residential units are located on eleven floors, starting with the second," Leslie says. "The ground floor contains staff offices and employee-only areas, plus our maintenance department. Storage facilities are in the basement. There are four units on each floor. Two in the front. Two in the back."

We pass another floor, the elevator slow but steady. On this level, a woman about Leslie's age waits for the return trip. Dressed in leggings, UGGs, and a bulky white sweater, she walks an impossibly tiny dog on a studded leash. She gives Leslie a polite wave while staring at me from behind oversize sunglasses. In that brief moment when we're face-to-face, I recognize the woman. She's an actress. At least, she used to be. It's been ten years since I last saw her on that soap opera I watched with my mother during summer break.

"Is that—"

Leslie stops me with a raised hand. "We never discuss residents. It's one of the unspoken rules here. The Bartholomew prides itself on discretion. The people who live here want to feel comfortable within its walls."

"But celebrities do live here?"

"Not really," Leslie says. "Which is fine by us. The last thing we want are paparazzi waiting outside. Or, God forbid, something as awful as what happened at the Dakota. Our residents tend to be quietly wealthy. They like their privacy. A good many of them use dummy corporations to buy their apartments so their purchase doesn't become public record."

The elevator comes to a rattling stop at the top of the stairs, and Leslie says, "Here we are. Twelfth floor."

She yanks open the grate and steps out, her heels clicking on the floor's black-and-white subway tile.

The hallway walls are burgundy, with sconces placed at regular intervals. We pass two unmarked doors before the hall dead-ends at a wide wall that contains two more doors. Unlike the others, these are marked.

12A and 12B.

"I thought there were four units on each floor," I say.

"There are," Leslie says. "Except this one. The twelfth floor is special."

I glance back at the unmarked doors behind us. "Then what are those?"

"Storage areas. Access to the roof. Nothing exciting." She reaches into her attaché to retrieve a set of keys, which she uses to unlock 12A. "Here's where the real excitement is."

The door swings open, and Leslie steps aside, revealing a tiny and tasteful foyer. There's a coatrack, a gilded mirror, and a table containing a lamp, a vase, and a small bowl to hold keys. My gaze moves past the foyer, into the apartment proper, and to a window directly opposite the door. Outside is one of the most stunning views I've ever seen.

Central Park.

Late fall.

Amber sun slanting across orange-gold leaves.

All of it from a bird's-eye view of one hundred fifty feet.

The window providing the view stretches from floor to ceiling in a formal sitting room on the other side of a hallway. I cross the hall on legs made wobbly by vertigo and head to the window, stopping when my nose is an inch from the glass. Straight ahead are Central Park Lake and the graceful span of Bow Bridge. Beyond them, in the distance, are snippets of Bethesda Terrace and the Loeb Boathouse. To the right is the Sheep Meadow, its expanse of green speckled with the forms of people basking in the autumn sun. Belvedere Castle sits to the left, backdropped by the stately gray stone of the Metropolitan Museum of Art.

I take in the view, slightly breathless.

I've seen it before in my mind's eye as I read *Heart of a Dreamer*. This is the exact view Ginny had from her apartment in the book. Meadow to the south. Castle to the north. Bow Bridge dead center— a bull's-eye for all her wildest dreams.

For a brief moment, it's my reality. In spite of all the shit I've gone through. Maybe even because of it. Being here has the feel of fate somehow intervening, even as I'm again struck by that all-consuming thought—*I do not belong here.*

"I'm sorry," I say as I pry myself away from the window. "I think there's been a huge misunderstanding."

There are many ways Leslie Evelyn and I could have gotten our wires crossed. The ad on Craigslist could have contained the wrong number. Or I might have made a mistake in dialing. When Leslie answered, the call was so brief that confusion was inevitable. I thought she was looking for an apartment sitter. She thought I was looking for an apartment. Now here we are, Leslie tilting her head to give me a confused look and me in awe of a view that, let's face it, was never intended to be seen by someone like me.

"You don't like the apartment?" Leslie says.

"I love it." I indulge in another quick peek out the window. I can't help myself. "But I'm not looking for an apartment. I mean, I am, but I could save every penny until I'm a hundred and I still wouldn't be able to afford this place."

"The apartment isn't available yet," Leslie says. "It just needs someone to occupy it for the next three months."

"There's no way someone would willingly pay me to live here. Even for three months."

"You're wrong there. That's exactly what we want."

Leslie gestures to a sofa in the center of the room. Upholstered in crimson velvet, it looks more expensive than my first car. I sit tentatively, afraid one careless motion could ruin the whole thing. Leslie takes a seat in a matching easy chair opposite the sofa. Between us is a mahogany coffee table on which rests a potted orchid, its petals white and pristine.

Now that I'm no longer distracted by the view, I see how the entire sitting room is done up in reds and wood tones. It's comfortable, if a bit stuffy. Grandfather clock ticking away in the corner. Velvet curtains and wooden shutters at the windows. Brass telescope on a wooden tripod, aimed not at the heavens but at Central Park.

The wallpaper is a red floral pattern—an ornate expanse of petals spread open like fans and overlapping in elaborate combinations. At the ceiling are matching strips of crown molding, the plaster blossoming into curlicues at the corners.

"Here's the situation," Leslie says. "Another rule at the Bartholomew is that no unit can stay empty for more than a month. It's an old rule and, some would say, a strange one. But those of us who live here agree that an occupied building is a happy one. Some of the places around here? They're half-empty most of the time. Sure, people might own the apartments, but they're rarely in them. And it shows. Walk into some of them and you feel like you're in a museum. Or, worse, a church. Then there's security to think about. If word gets out that a place in the Bartholomew is going to be empty for a few months, there's no telling who might try to break in."

Hence that simple ad buried among all the other Help Wanteds. I had wondered why it was so vague.

"So you're looking for a guard?"

"We're looking for a *resident*," Leslie says. "Another person to breathe life into the building. Take this place, for example. The owner recently passed away. She was a widow. Had no children of her own. Just some greedy nieces and nephews in London currently fighting over who should get the place. Until that gets resolved, this apartment will sit vacant. With only two units on this floor, think how empty it will feel."

"Why don't the nieces and nephews just sublet?"

"That's not allowed here. For the same reasons I mentioned

earlier. There's nothing stopping someone from subletting a place and then doing God-knows-what to it."

I nod, suddenly understanding. "By paying someone to stay here, you're making sure they don't do anything to the apartment."

"Exactly," Leslie says. "Think of it as an insurance policy. One that pays quite nicely, I might add. In the case of 12A, the family of the late owner is offering four thousand dollars a month."

My hands, which until now had been placed primly on my lap, drop to my sides.

Four grand a month.

To live *here*.

The pay is so staggering that it feels like the crimson sofa beneath me has dropped away, leaving me hovering a foot above the floor.

I try to gather my thoughts, struggling to do the very basic math. That's twelve thousand dollars for three months. More than enough to tide me over while I put my life back together.

"I assume you're interested," Leslie says.

Every so often, life offers you a reset button. When it does, you need to press it as hard as you can.

Jane said that to me once. Back in our reading-on-her-bed days, when I was too young to understand what she meant.

Now I do.

"I'm very interested," I say.

Leslie smiles, her teeth bright behind peachy pink lips. "Then let's get on with the interview, shall we?"

2

Rather than remain in the sitting room, Leslie conducts the rest of the interview during a tour of the apartment. Each room brings a new question, just like in a game of Clue. All that's missing are a billiard room and a ballroom.

First stop is the study, located to the right of the sitting room. It's very masculine. All dark greens and whiskey-colored woods. The wallpaper pattern is the same as in the sitting room, only here it's a bright emerald.

"What's your current employment situation?" Leslie asks.

I could—and likely should—tell her that this time two weeks ago I was an administrative assistant at one of the nation's biggest financial firms. It wasn't much—just a step above being an unpaid intern. Lots of photocopying and coffee fetching and dodging the mood swings of the middle managers I worked for. But it paid the bills and provided me with health insurance. Until I was let go along with 10 percent of the office staff. *Restructuring.* I assume my boss thought that sounded nicer than large layoffs. Either way, the result was the same—unemployment for me, a likely raise for him.

"I'm currently between jobs," I say.

Leslie reacts with the slightest of nods. I don't know if that's a good sign or a bad one. Yet the questions continue as we return to the main hall on our way to the other side of the apartment.

"Do you smoke?"

"No."

"Drink?"

"An occasional glass of wine with dinner."

Except for two weeks ago, when Chloe took me out to drown my sorrows in margaritas. I had five in alarmingly quick succession and ended the night puking in an alley. Another thing Leslie doesn't need to know.

The hallway makes a sudden turn to the left. Rather than follow it, Leslie steers me to the right, into a formal dining room so lovely it makes me gasp. The hardwood floors have been polished to a mirror shine. A chandelier hangs over a long table that can easily seat twelve. This time the busy floral wallpaper is light yellow. The room is situated on the corner of the building, offering dueling views out the windows. Central Park on one side, the edge of the building next door on the other.

I circle the table, running a finger along the wood as Leslie says, "What's your relationship status? While we don't exactly frown on having couples or even families serve as apartment sitters, we prefer people who are unattached. It makes things easier from a legal standpoint."

"I'm single," I say, trying hard to keep bitterness from seeping into my voice.

Left out is how on the same day I lost my job, I returned home early to the apartment I shared with my boyfriend, Andrew. At night, he worked as a janitor in the building where my office was located. During the day, he was a part-time student at Pace University majoring in finance and, apparently, fucking one of his classmates while I was at work.

That's what they were doing when I walked in with my sad little box of things hastily cleared from my cubicle. They hadn't even made it to the bedroom. I found them on the secondhand sofa, Andrew with his jeans around his ankles and his side piece's legs spread wide.

I'd be sad about the whole thing if I wasn't still so angry. And hurt. And blaming myself for settling for someone like Andrew. I knew he was unhappy with his job and that he wanted more out of life. What I didn't know was that he also wanted more than just me.

Leslie Evelyn leads me into the kitchen, which is so huge it has two entrances—one from the dining room, one from the hall. I rotate slowly, dazzled by its pristine whiteness, its granite countertops, its breakfast nook by the window. It looks like something straight out of a cooking show. A kitchen designed to be as photogenic as possible.

"It's massive," I say, awed by its sheer size.

"It's a throwback from when the Bartholomew first opened," Leslie says. "While the building itself hasn't changed much, the apartments themselves have been renovated quite a bit over the years. Some got bigger. Others smaller. This one used to be the kitchen and servants' quarters for a much larger unit below. See?"

Leslie moves to a cupboard with a sliding door that's tucked between the oven and the sink. When she lifts the door, I see a dark shaft and two tendrils of rope hanging from a pulley rig above.

"Is that a dumbwaiter?"

"It is."

"Where does it go?"

"I have no idea, actually. It hasn't been used for decades." She lets the dumbwaiter door slam shut, suddenly back to interview mode. "Tell me about your family. Any next of kin?"

This one's harder to answer, mainly because it's worse than losing a job or being cheated on. Whatever I say could open the floodgates to more questions with even sadder responses. Especially if I hint at what happened.

And when.

And why.

"Orphan," I say, hoping that single word will prevent any follow-ups from Leslie. It does, to an extent.

"No family at all?"

"No."

It's almost the truth. My parents were the only children of only children. There are no aunts, uncles, or cousins. There's only Jane.

Also dead.

Maybe.

Probably.

"Since there's no next of kin, who should we contact in case of an emergency?"

Two weeks ago, that would have been Andrew. Now it's Chloe, I guess, although she's not officially listed on any forms. I'm not even sure she can be.

"No one," I say, realizing how pathetic that sounds. So I add a slightly hopeful caveat. "For now."

Eager to change the subject, I peek through the door just off the kitchen. Leslie gets the hint and ushers me into another hallway, a smaller offshoot of the main one. It contains a guest bathroom she doesn't even bother to show off, a closet, and—the big surprise—a spiral staircase.

"Oh my God. There's a *second floor*?"

Leslie gives a happy nod, more amused than put off by my sounding like a kid on Christmas. "It's a special feature exclusive to the two units on the twelfth floor. Go ahead. Take a look."

I bound up the steps, following the corkscrew curve to a bedroom that's even more picture-perfect than the kitchen. Here the floral wallpaper actually works with the room. It's the lightest shade of blue. The color of a spring sky.

Like the dining room directly below, it's located on a corner of the building. Because this is the top floor, the ceiling slants dramatically to a peak ending at the far wall. The massive bed's been placed so that whoever is in it can gaze out the windows flanking the corner. And just outside those windows is the pièce de résistance—a gargoyle.

It sits on the corner ledge, its back legs bent, front claws gripping the top of the overhang. Its wings are spread so that the edge of one can be glimpsed through the north-facing window and the other through the one pointing east.

"Beautiful, isn't it?" Leslie says, suddenly behind me. I hadn't even noticed her come up the steps. I was too taken with the gargoyle, the room, the whole surreal idea that I could maybe, hopefully get paid to live here.

"Yes, beautiful," I say, too awed by it all to do anything other than repeat her.

"And quite spacious," she adds. "Even by the Bartholomew's standards. Again, because of its original purpose. Once upon a time it housed several servants. They lived here, cooked downstairs, worked a few floors below."

She points out everything I've failed to notice, such as a small sitting area to the left of the steps with cream-colored chairs and a glass coffee table. I cross the room on white carpet so plush I'm tempted to kick off my shoes and see how it feels on bare feet. The wall to the right bears two doors. One leads to the master bath. A quick look inside reveals double sinks, a shower encased in glass, and a claw-foot bathtub. Through the other door is a massive walk-in closet with a mirrored makeup table and enough shelves and racks to fill a clothing store. All of them are empty.

"This closet is bigger than my childhood bedroom," I say. "Scratch that. It's bigger than every bedroom I've ever had."

Leslie, who's been checking her hair in the vanity mirror, turns and says, "Since you've brought up living arrangements, what's your current address?"

Another tricky topic.

I moved out the same day I found Andrew screwing his classmate. Not by choice, mind you. Andrew's name was the only one on the lease. I had never added my own when I moved in. Which technically meant it was never my home to begin with, even though I had lived there for more than a year. For the past two weeks I've been crashing on Chloe's couch in Jersey City.

"I'm between apartments," I say, hoping the situation doesn't sound as Dickensian as it truly is.

Leslie blinks rapidly, trying to hide her surprise. "*Between* apartments?"

"My old place went co-op," I lie. "I'm living with a friend until I can find something else."

"Staying here would be very convenient for you, I imagine," Leslie says tactfully.

In truth, living here would be a lifesaver. It would give me a home base to search for a job and a new place to live. And when it was all over, I'd have twelve grand in the bank. Mustn't forget about that.

"Well then, let's finish up this interview and see if you're the right fit."

Leslie leads me out of the bedroom, down the steps, and back to the crimson sofa in the sitting room. There, I resume my hands-in-lap sitting position, trying hard not to let my gaze drift back to the window. It does anyway, now that late afternoon has brought a deep gold tinge to the sunlight draped over the park.

"Just a few more questions and we'll be done," Leslie says as she opens her attaché case and pulls out a pen and what looks to be an application form. "Age?"

"Twenty-five."

Leslie jots it down. "Date of birth?"

"May first."

"Are there any illnesses or health conditions we should be aware of?"

I jerk my gaze from the window. "Why do you need to know that?"

"Emergency purposes," Leslie says. "Because there's currently no one we can contact if, God forbid, something happens to you while you're here, I'll need a little bit more medical information. It's standard policy, I assure you."

"No illnesses," I say.

Leslie's pen hovers over the page. "So no heart problems or anything of that nature?"

"No."

"And your hearing and vision are fine?"

"Perfect."

"Any allergies we should be aware of?"

"Bee stings. But I carry an EpiPen."

"That's very smart of you," Leslie says. "It's nice to meet a young woman with a good head on her shoulders. Which brings me to my last question: Would you consider yourself to be an inquisitive person?"

Inquisitive. Now there's a word I never expected to hear during this interview, considering Leslie's the one asking all the questions.

"I'm not sure I understand what you're asking," I say.

"Then I'll be blunt," Leslie replies. "Are you nosy? Prone to asking questions? And, worse, telling others what you've learned? As you probably know, the Bartholomew has a reputation for secrecy. People are curious about what goes on inside these walls, although you've already seen that it's just an ordinary building. In the past, some apartment sitters have arrived with the wrong intentions. They came looking for dirt. About the building, its residents, its history. The typical tabloid fodder. I sniffed them out immediately. I always do. So, if you're here for the gossip, then it's best we part ways now."

I shake my head. "I don't care what happens here. Honestly, I just need some money and a place to live for a few months."

That ends the interview. Leslie stands, smoothing her skirt and adjusting one of the bulky rings on her fingers. "The way it usually goes is that I'll tell you to expect a phone call if we're interested. But I see no point in making you wait."

I know what's coming next. I knew it the moment I stepped into that birdcage of an elevator. I'm not worthy of the Bartholomew. People like me—parentless, jobless, borderline homeless—have no place here. I take one last look out the window, knowing such a view will never present itself again.

Leslie finishes her speech. "We'd love for you to stay here."

At first, I think I've misheard her. I give a blank stare, making it clear I'm unaccustomed to receiving good news.

"You're joking," I say.

"I'm as serious as can be. We'll need to run a background check, of course. But you seem like a perfect fit. Young and bright. And I think being here will do you a world of good."

That's when it hits me: I get to live *here*. In the goddamn Bartholomew, of all places. In an apartment beyond my wildest dreams.

Even better, I'll be getting paid to do it.

Twelve thousand dollars.

Happy tears form in my eyes. I quickly swipe them away, lest Leslie think I'm too emotional and change her mind.

"Thank you," I say. "Truly. It's the opportunity of a lifetime."

Leslie beams. "It's my pleasure, Jules. Welcome to the Bartholomew. I think you're going to love it here."

3

"There's a catch, right?" Chloe says before taking a sip of Two-Buck Chuck from Trader Joe's. "I mean, there has to be."

"That's what I thought," I say. "But if there is, I can't find it."

"No sane person would pay a stranger to live in their luxury apartment."

The two of us are in the living room of Chloe's non-luxury apartment in Jersey City, seated around the coffee table that has become our regular dining spot since I started crashing here. Tonight it's scattered with cartons of cheap Chinese takeout. Vegetable lo mein and pork fried rice.

"It's not like it's some kind of vacation," I say. "It's a legitimate job. I have to take care of the place. Cleaning and keeping an eye on things."

Chloe pauses mid-bite, sending noodles slithering off her chopsticks. "Wait—you're not actually going to do this, are you?"

"Of course I am. I can move in tomorrow."

"*Tomorrow?* That's, like, suspiciously fast."

"They want someone there as soon as possible."

"Jules, you know I'm not paranoid, but this is ringing all the alarm bells. What if it's a cult?"

I roll my eyes. "You can't be serious."

"I'm completely serious. You don't know these people. Did they even tell you what happened to the woman who lived there?"

"She died."

"Did they say how?" Chloe says. "Or where? Maybe she died in that apartment. Maybe she was murdered."

"You're being weird."

"I'm being cautious. There's a difference." Chloe takes another gulp of wine, exasperated. "Will you at least let Paul take a look at the paperwork before you sign anything?"

Chloe's boyfriend is currently clerking at a big-time law firm while prepping for the bar exam. After the bar, they plan to get married, move to the suburbs, and have two kids and a dog. Chloe likes to joke that they're upwardly mobile.

I'm the opposite. Sunk so low that I'm currently eating in the same spot where I'll later be sleeping. It feels like in the span of two weeks my entire world has shrunk to the size of this couch.

"I already signed it," I say. "A three-month contract with the possibility that it could be extended."

That last part is a bit of an exaggeration. It was a letter of agreement instead of a contract, and Leslie Evelyn merely hinted that the late owner's nieces and nephews might need more time to agree on what to do with the place. I say it to give the situation a veneer of professionalism. Chloe works in human resources. Contract extensions impress her.

"What about tax forms?" she says.

"What about them?"

"Did you fill one out?"

To avoid answering, I poke my chopsticks into the fried rice, seeking out bits of pork. Chloe yanks the carton from my hand and slams it onto the coffee table. Rice sprays across its surface.

"Jules, you cannot take a job that pays you under the table. That's some shady shit right there."

"It just means more money for me," I say.

"It means it's illegal."

I grab the carton and stuff my chopsticks back into it, defiant. "All I care about is twelve thousand dollars. I need that money, Chloe."

"I told you, I can lend you money."

"That I won't be able to pay back."

"You *will*," Chloe insists. "Eventually. Don't do this because you think you're being—"

"A burden?" I say.

"Those are your words. Not mine."

"But I am one."

"No, you're my best friend going through a rough patch, and I'm happy to let you stay as long as you need. You'll be back on your feet in no time."

Chloe has more faith than I do. I've spent the past two weeks wondering just how, exactly, my life has gone so spectacularly off the rails. I'm smart. A hard worker. A good person. At least I try to be. Yet all it took to flatten me was the one-two punch of losing my job and Andrew being a garbage human being.

I'm sure some would say it's my own damn fault. That it was my responsibility to build an emergency fund. At least three months' salary, the experts say. I would love to backhand whoever came up with that number. They clearly never had a job with take-home pay that barely covers rent, food, and utilities.

Because here's the thing about being poor—most people don't understand it unless they've been there themselves.

They don't know what a fragile balancing act it is to stay afloat and that if, God forbid, you momentarily slip underwater, how hard it is to resurface.

They've never written a check with trembling hands, praying there'll be enough in their account to cover it.

They've never waited for their paycheck to be directly deposited at the stroke of midnight because their wallet is empty and their credit cards are maxed and they desperately need to pay for gas.

And food.

And a prescription that's gone unfilled for an entire week.

They've never had their credit card declined at a grocery store or restaurant or Walmart, all the while enduring the side-eye from an annoyed cashier who silently judges them.

That's another thing most people don't understand—how quick others are to judge. And make assumptions. And presume your financial predicament is the result of stupidity, laziness, years of bad choices.

They don't know how expensive it is to bury both of your parents before the age of twenty.

They don't know what it's like to sit weeping before a pile of financial statements showing how much debt they had accrued over the years.

To be told all their insurance policies have been voided.

To go back to college, shouldering the cost yourself with the help of financial aid, two jobs, and student loans that won't be paid off until you're forty.

To graduate and enter the job market with a lit degree only to be told you're either overqualified or underqualified for every position you apply for.

People don't want to think about that life, so they don't. They're getting by just fine and therefore can't comprehend why you're not capable of doing the same. Meanwhile, you're left all alone to deal with the humiliation. And the fear. And the worry.

God, the worry.

It's always there. A loud hum buzzing through every waking thought. Things have gotten so bleak that I've recently started wondering how far I have left to fall before hitting bottom and what I'll do if I ever reach that point. Will I try to claw my way out, like Chloe thinks I can? Or will I purposefully walk into the howling black void just like my father did?

Until today, I saw no easy way out of my predicament. But now my heavy, hopeless worry has been temporarily lifted.

"I need to do this," I tell Chloe. "Is it unusual? Yes, I will completely admit that it is."

"And probably too good to be true," Chloe adds.

"Sometimes good things happen to good people, right when they need it the most."

Chloe scoots next to me and pulls me into a ferocious embrace, something she's been doing ever since we ended up being freshmen roommates at Penn State.

"I think I'd feel better if it was any building but the Bartholomew."

"What's wrong with the Bartholomew?"

"All those gargoyles, for starters. Didn't they creep you out?"

They didn't. To be honest, I thought the one outside the bedroom window was charming in its own Gothic way. Like a protector standing guard.

"I've heard"—Chloe pauses, seeking an appropriately ominous word—"stuff."

"What kind of stuff?"

"My grandparents lived on the Upper West Side. My grandfather refused to walk on the same side of the street as the Bartholomew. He said it was cursed."

I reach for the lo mein. "I think that says more about your grandfather than it does the Bartholomew."

"He believed it," Chloe says. "He told me the man who built it killed himself. He jumped right off the roof."

"I'm not going to turn this down just because of something your grandfather said."

"All I'm saying is that it wouldn't hurt to be a little cautious while you're there. If something feels off, come right back here. The couch is always open."

"I appreciate the offer," I say. "I do. And who knows, I might be right back here three months from now. But, cursed or not, staying at the Bartholomew is the best way out of this mess."

Not every person gets a do-over in their life. My father certainly didn't. Neither did my mother.

But I now have that chance.

Life is offering me a building-size reset button.

I intend to press it as hard as I can.

NOW

I wake with a start, confused. I don't know where I am, and that terrifies me.

Lifting my head, I see a dim room, brightened slightly by a rectangle of light stretching from the open door. Beyond the door is a glimpse of a sterile hallway, the sound of hushed voices, the light squelch of sneakers on tiled floor.

The pain that had screamed along my left side and in my head is now only a slight murmur. I suspect I have painkillers to thank for that. My brain and body feel gauzy. Like I've been stuffed with cotton.

Panicked, I take stock of all the things that have been done to me while I was unconscious.

IV tube attached to my hand.

Bandage wrapped around my left wrist.

Brace around my neck.

Bandage at my temple, which I press with curious, probing fingers. The pressure sends up a flare of pain. Enough to make me wince.

To my surprise, I can sit up, using my elbows for support. Although it causes a slight push of pain at my side, the movement is worth it. Someone passing by the door notices and says, "She's awake."

A light flicks on, revealing white walls, a chair in the corner, a Monet print in a cheap black frame.

A nurse enters. The same one from earlier. The one with the kind eyes. Bernard.

"Hey there, Sleeping Beauty," he says.

"How long was I out?"

"Just a few hours."

I look around the room. It's windowless. Sterile. Blinding in its whiteness.

"Where am I?"

"A hospital room, honey."

Relief washes over me. The kind of blessed relief that brings tears to my eyes. Bernard grabs a tissue, dabs my cheeks.

"There's no need to cry," he says. "It's not that bad."

He's right. It's not bad at all. In fact, it's wonderful.

I'm safe.

I'm nowhere near the Bartholomew.

FIVE DAYS EARLIER

4

In the morning, I give Chloe an extended hug goodbye before taking an Uber into Manhattan. A splurge while carrying my belongings. Not that I have much. I allowed myself exactly one night to move out of the apartment after I found Andrew and his "friend." There was no crying jag. No screaming loud enough to rattle the walls. I simply said, "Get out. Don't come back until morning. I'll be gone by then."

Andrew didn't argue, which told me everything I needed to know. Even though I never would have taken him back, I was still surprised he didn't at least try to save our relationship. He just left. Where he went, I'll never know. The other girl's place, I assume. So they could pick up where they had left off.

While he was gone, I methodically packed, choosing what could stay and what I couldn't live without. A lot was left behind, mostly things I'd purchased with Andrew and didn't have the energy to fight over. As a result, he got to keep the toaster oven and IKEA coffee table and TV.

At one point during that long, awful night, I considered trashing everything. Just to prove to Andrew that I was also capable of destroying something. But I was too sad and too exhausted to summon such fury. Instead, I settled on shoving every trace of our coupledom into a giant pot on the stove. The photos, the birthday cards, the love notes saved from those first heady months together. I lit a match and dropped it on the pile, watching as the flames rose.

Before I left, I dumped the ashes on the kitchen floor.

Another thing Andrew could keep.

But as I packed for the second time in two weeks, I started to wish I had taken more than just clothes, accessories, books, and keepsakes. I was alarmed by how little I own. My entire life now fits into a suitcase and four fifteen-by-twelve storage boxes.

When the car pulls up to the Bartholomew, the driver gives a low whistle, impressed. "You work here or something?"

Technically, that would be a yes. Yet it sounds better to answer with my unofficial job description. "I'm a resident."

I slip out of the car and gaze at the facade of my temporary home. The gargoyles over the doorway stare back. With their arched spines and open wings, they look ready to hop from their perch to greet me. That duty instead goes to the doorman standing directly beneath them. Tall and bulky, with ruddy cheeks and a Fuller Brush mustache, he's by my side the moment the Uber driver pops the trunk.

"Let me get those for you," he says, reaching for the boxes. "You must be Miss Larsen. I'm Charlie."

I grab my suitcase, wanting to make myself at least a little bit useful. I've never lived in a building with a doorman. "Nice to meet you, Charlie."

"Likewise. And welcome to the Bartholomew. I'll take care of your things. You go on inside. Miss Evelyn is expecting you."

I can't remember the last time I was expected by someone. It makes me feel more than welcome. It makes me feel wanted.

Sure enough, Leslie is waiting in the lobby. She wears another Chanel suit. Yellow instead of blue.

"Welcome, welcome," she says cheerily, punctuating it with air kisses on both of my cheeks. Spotting the suitcase, she says, "Is Charlie taking care of the rest of your things?"

"He is."

"He's a dream, that Charlie. By far the most efficient of our door-men. But they're all wonderful in their own right. If you ever need them, they'll either be outside or right in there."

She points to a small room just off the lobby. Through the door-way, I glimpse a chair, a desk, and a row of security monitors glow-ing blue-gray. One of them shows an angled image of two women paused on the checkerboard tile of the lobby. It takes me a second to realize I'm one of them. Leslie is the other. Looking up, I see the camera positioned right over the front door. My gaze drifts back to the security monitor, which now shows me standing alone as Leslie drifts out of view.

I follow her to a wall of mailboxes on the other side of the lobby. There are forty-two of them, labeled the same as the apartments, beginning with 2A. Leslie holds up a tiny key on a plain ring marked 12A.

"Here's your mail key."

She gives it to me the way a grandmother hands out hard candy—dropping it directly into my open palm.

"You're expected to check the mail every day. There won't be much of anything, of course. But the late owner's family requested that whatever does arrive be forwarded to them. It goes without say-ing that you shouldn't open any of it, no matter how urgent it ap-pears. For privacy's sake. As for your own mail, we recommend getting a post-office box. Receiving personal mail at this address is strictly prohibited."

I give a quick nod. "Understood."

"Now, let's get you up to the apartment. On the way there, we can go over the rest of the rules."

She crosses the lobby again, this time heading to the elevator. Trailing behind her with my suitcase, I say, "Rules?"

"Nothing major. Just a few guidelines you'll need to follow."

"What kind of guidelines?"

We stand by the elevator, which is currently in use. Through the gilded bars, I see cables in motion, slithering upward. The whir of machinery rises from somewhere below. A few floors above us, the elevator car hums as it descends.

"No visitors," Leslie says. "That's the biggest one. And when I say no visitors, I mean absolutely no one. No bringing friends for a tour. No letting family members stay over to save them a hotel booking. And definitely no strangers you might meet in a bar or on Tinder. I can't stress this enough."

My first thought is Chloe, to whom I had promised a tour tonight. She's not going to like this. She'll tell me it's a sign—another alarm bell ringing loud and clear. Not that I need Chloe's help to hear this one.

"Isn't that kind of—" I stop myself, searching for a word that won't offend Leslie. "Strict?"

"Perhaps," Leslie says. "But also necessary. Some very prominent people live here. They don't want strangers walking through their building."

"Aren't I technically a stranger?" I say.

Leslie corrects me. "You're an employee. And, for the next three months, a tenant."

The elevator finally arrives, bringing with it a man in his early twenties. He's short but muscular, with a broad chest and big arms. His hair—black, obviously dyed—flops over his right eye. Small ebony discs rest in both earlobes.

"Well, isn't this marvelous," Leslie says. "Jules, I'd like to introduce you to Dylan. He's another apartment sitter."

I had already intuited this. His Danzig T-shirt and baggy black jeans, frayed at the cuffs, gave it away. Like me, he clearly doesn't belong in the Bartholomew.

"Dylan, this is Jules."

Rather than shake my hand, Dylan shoves his hands into his pockets and gives me a half-mumbled hello.

"Jules is moving in today," Leslie tells him. "She was just

expressing her concerns about some of the rules we have for our temporary tenants. Perhaps you could enlighten her more about that."

"I don't mind them all that much." He has an accent. The thickened vowels and rounded consonants instantly peg him as being from Brooklyn. The old-school section. "It's nothing to worry about, really. Nothing too strict."

"See?" Leslie says. "Nothing to worry about."

"I gotta go," Dylan says, his eyes aimed at the marble floor between his sneakers. "Nice meeting you, Jules. I'll see you around."

He pushes past us, his hands still shoved deep into his pockets. I watch him go, observing the way he walks with his head still lowered. He pauses at the door Charlie holds opens for him, almost like he's having second thoughts about going outside. When Dylan finally does step onto the sidewalk, it's with the skittishness of a deer about to cross a busy highway.

"A nice young man," Leslie says once we're in the elevator. "Quiet, which is what we like around here."

"How many apartment sitters currently live here?"

Leslie slides the grate across the elevator door. "You make three. Dylan's on eleven, as is Ingrid."

She hits the button for the twelfth floor, and the elevator again creaks to life. As we rise to our destination, she goes over the rest of the rules. Although I'm allowed to come and go as I please, I must spend each night in the apartment. It makes sense. That is, after all, what I'm being paid to do. Live there. Occupy the place. Breathe life into it, as Leslie put it during that surreal interview.

Smoking isn't allowed.

Of course.

Nor are drugs.

Another no-brainer.

Alcohol is tolerated if consumed responsibly, which is a relief, seeing how there are two bottles of wine Chloe gifted to me in one of the boxes Charlie's set to deliver to my door.

"You're to keep everything in pristine condition at all times," Leslie says. "If something breaks, contact maintenance immediately. Basically, you need to leave the place looking exactly the way it did when you arrived."

Other than not allowing visitors, none of this sounds unreasonable. And even the no-visitors policy makes more sense now that Leslie's explained the reasoning behind it. I begin to think Dylan is right. I have nothing to worry about.

But then Leslie adds another rule. She mentions it offhandedly, as if making it up on the spot.

"Oh, one last thing. As I mentioned yesterday, the residents here enjoy their privacy. Since some of them have a certain renown, we insist that you don't bother them. Speak only if spoken to. Also, never discuss residents beyond these walls. Do you use social media?"

"Just Facebook and Instagram," I say. "And both very rarely."

For the past two weeks, my social media usage has consisted of checking LinkedIn for potential job leads from former co-workers. So far, it hasn't done me a bit of good.

"Be sure not to mention this place on there. We monitor our apartment sitters' social media accounts, again for privacy reasons. If the inside of the Bartholomew shows up on Instagram, the person who posted it is forced to leave immediately." The elevator shimmies to a stop on the top floor. Leslie throws open the grate and says, "Do you have any other questions?"

I do. An important one, only I'm afraid to ask it for fear of sounding indelicate. But then I think about my checking account, which is now fifty dollars lighter after that Uber ride.

And about how I'll have even less once I buy groceries.

And about the text I got reminding me that my phone bill is past due.

And about the unemployment check I'll be receiving soon and how long that meager two hundred sixty dollars will last in this neighborhood.

I think of all these things and decide I can't care about appearing indelicate.

"When do I get paid?" I say.

"A very good question that I'm so glad you asked," Leslie replies, tactful as always. "You'll receive your first payment five days from now. A thousand dollars. Cash. Charlie will hand-deliver it to you at the end of the day. He'll do the same at the end of every week you're here."

My body practically melts with relief. I was afraid it wouldn't be until the end of the month or, worse, after my three months were up. I'm so relieved that it takes an extra moment for the strangeness of the arrangement to sink in.

"Just like that?" I say.

Leslie cocks her head. "You make it sound like that's a bad thing."

"I was expecting a check, I guess. Something to make it more official and less . . ."

A word Chloe used last night comes to mind. *Shady.*

"It's easier this way," Leslie says. "If you're uncomfortable with the arrangement or having second thoughts, you can back out now. I won't be offended."

"No," I say. Backing out is not an option. "The arrangement is fine."

"Excellent. I'll let you get settled in, then." Leslie holds up a key ring. Attached to it are two keys, one big, one small. "The big one is to the apartment. The small one opens the storage unit in the basement."

Instead of dropping it into my hand like the mail key, she places the key ring in my palm before gently curling my fingers around it. Then with a smile and a wink, she returns to the waiting elevator and is lowered out of view.

Alone now, I turn to 12A and take a deep, steadying breath.

This—right now—is my life.

Here.

On the top floor of the Bartholomew.

Holy shit.

Even more astounding is that I'm getting paid to be here. One thousand dollars every week. Money I can use to erase debt and save for a future that's suddenly far brighter than it was a day ago. A future that's just on the other side of that door.

I unlock it and step inside.

5

I name the gargoyle outside the window George.

It comes to me as I haul the last of my boxes into the bedroom. Standing at the top of the winding staircase, I look out the window, once again drawn to that sumptuous view of the park. Late-morning sunlight pours through, silhouetting the curve of stone wings just beyond the glass.

"Hi, George," I say to the gargoyle. I'm not sure why I choose the name. It just seems to fit. "Looks like we're roommates."

The rest of the day is spent making this deceased stranger's apartment feel like my home. I transfer my underwhelming wardrobe to the overwhelming closet, large enough to hold ten times the amount of clothes, and arrange my meager beauty products on the bathroom counter.

In the bedroom, I personalize the nightstand with a framed photo of Jane and my parents. The picture, taken by fifteen-year-old me, shows them standing in front of Bushkill Falls in the Poconos.

Two years later, Jane was gone.

Two years after that, so were my parents.

Not a day goes by when I don't miss them, but today that feeling is especially acute.

Joining the photo on the nightstand is my battered copy of *Heart of a Dreamer*. The same one I've carried with me for years. The very copy Jane read to me.

"I'm totally a Ginny," Jane said during that first read, referring to the book's main character. "Hopeful, tempestuous—"

"What does that mean?" I had asked.

"That I feel too much."

That definitely summed up Ginny, who experienced everything with a combination of joy and ecstasy. A trip to the Met. An afternoon in Central Park. Tasting real New York pizza. And the reader is swept right along with her, experiencing her lows—being dumped by bad boy Wyatt—and her highs—that kiss atop the Empire State Building with good boy Bradley. It's why *Heart of a Dreamer* has become a touchstone for generations of girls on the cusp of adolescence. It's the life many dream of but few get to experience.

Because Jane first read it to me, she and Ginny have become almost interchangeable in my mind. Every time I read the book, which is often, I imagine it's my sister and not some fictional creation arriving at the Bartholomew, making new discoveries, finding true love.

That's the real reason I love the book so much. It's the happy ending Jane deserved. Not the grim one she in all likelihood received.

Meanwhile, I'm the one who ended up at the Bartholomew. I stare at *Heart of a Dreamer*'s cover, once again not quite believing I'm now inside the same building pictured there. I even spot the window of the very room I'm in. And right next to it is George. Perched on the corner of the building, paws together, wings spread wide.

I touch the image of the gargoyle and feel a pang of affection. Only it's more than that. It's a sense of ownership. For the next three months, George is mine. It's my window he sits outside, and thus he belongs to me.

In a truly just world, he would have belonged to Jane.

With the book in its rightful place, I sit beside George at the bedroom window with my phone and laptop. First, I text Chloe, cancelling the plan for her to visit the apartment tonight. My hope is that a text message and not a phone call will keep her from asking questions and once again expressing disapproval about my current living situation.

No such luck.

Chloe's reply comes literally three seconds after I send the text.

Why can't I come over?

I start to type that I'm not feeling well but think better of it. Knowing Chloe, she'll be at the door in an hour with a gallon of chicken soup and a bottle of Robitussin.

Job hunting, I text back.

All day?

Yeah, I text. Sorry.

So when can I see the place? Paul wants a tour, too.

I have no more excuses at the ready. Sure, I could come up with something on the fly about tomorrow and even the rest of the week, but I can't spend the next three months making excuses. I need to tell her the truth.

You can't.

Chloe's reply is immediate. Why not???

No visitors. Building policy.

I've barely finished sending the text when my phone rings.

"What kind of bullshit is that?" Chloe says as soon as I answer. "No visitors? Even prisons allow visitors."

"I know, I know. It sounds weird."

"Because it *is* weird," Chloe says. "I've never heard of a building telling residents they can't have guests."

"But I'm not a resident. I'm an employee."

"And friends can visit each other at their workplaces. You've been to my office plenty of times."

"Rich and important people live here. Emphasis on the *rich*. And they're big on privacy. I can't really blame them. I'd be, too, if I was a movie star or billionaire."

"You're getting defensive," Chloe says.

"I'm *not*," I reply, even though a definite edge has sliced into my words.

"Jules, I'm just looking out for you."

"I don't need looking after. Nothing bad is going to happen. I'm not my sister."

"Between this no-visitors thing, my grandfather's weirdness, and what Paul has told me about the place, I'm starting to get freaked out."

"Wait—what did Paul say?"

"Just that it's all so secretive," Chloe says. "He said it's next to impossible to live there. The president of his firm wanted to buy there. They wouldn't even let him inside the building. They told him nothing was available but that they could put him on a ten-year waiting list. And then there's the article I read."

My mind is starting to spin. I feel an annoyance headache coming on. "What article?"

"I found it online. I'm going to email it to you. It talks about all the weird stuff that's happened at the Bartholomew."

"What kind of weird are we talking about?"

"*American Horror Story*–level weird. Illnesses and strange accidents. A witch lived there, Jules. An actual witch. I'm telling you, that place is shady."

"It's the complete opposite of shady."

"Then what would you call it?"

"I call it a job." I look out the window, taking in George's wing, the park below, the city beyond it. "A dream job. In a dream apartment."

"That I'm not allowed to see," Chloe adds.

"Is it unusual? Sure. But it's the easiest job in the world. It's practically money for nothing. Why should I give that up? Just because the people who live here are private?"

"What you really should be asking is *why* they're so private," Chloe says. "Because, in my experience, if something seems too good to be true, that's because it is."

The call ends with the two of us agreeing to disagree. I tell Chloe I understand her concerns. She tells me she's happy something good has happened. We make plans to have dinner soon, even though I can't really afford it until next week.

That task out of the way, I go about looking for a job. I wasn't lying to Chloe about that. It's how I plan to spend today—and all the days after it. I grab my laptop and check the latest postings on a half-dozen different job sites. There are plenty of openings available, just not for me. The curse of being your basic office drone. I'm a dime a dozen, and everyone is looking for a quarter.

Still, I make a note of all the jobs that land within my narrow window of qualifications and compose cover letters for each of them. I resist the urge to begin them all with *Please give me a job. Please let me prove myself. Please give me back the feeling of self-worth that's been missing from my life.*

Instead, I write the platitudes all potential employers want to read. Stuff about seeking new challenges, adding to my work experience, reaching my goals. I send them off with my résumé. Three in all, joining the previous four I've sent in the past two weeks.

My expectations of hearing back from any of them aren't high. Lately I've found it best not to get my hopes up about things. My father was the same way. *Hope for the best, prepare for the worst,* he used to say.

By the end, he ran out of hope, and nothing could have prepared him for what lay in store.

With the job search, such as it is, out of the way, I open a spreadsheet on my laptop and try to come up with a budget for the next few weeks. It's frighteningly tight. In the past, I relied on credit cards to get me through lean times. That's no longer an option. All three of my cards are maxed and, at the moment, frozen. All I have to live on is what's in my checking account, a figure that makes my heart sink when I check my balance.

I now have only four hundred and thirty-two dollars to my name.

6

I now have only three hundred and twenty-two dollars to my name. Thanks, wretched cell phone contract that I can't escape for another year.

Unlike the deferments on my student loans or the temporary hardship agreements with the credit card companies, the phone was an expense I couldn't put off. Already I was a week late with the payment and didn't want to risk losing service. Potential employers can't call a phone that's not working. So there it went—another hundred and ten bucks gone in an instant.

I console myself with the fact that an unemployment check will be automatically deposited into my account at the stroke of midnight. It's cold comfort. I'd rather be receiving an employment check for an honest week's work.

Because my current cushy situation doesn't feel honest.

It feels like freeloading.

Never take anything you haven't earned, my father used to say. *You always end up paying for it one way or another.*

With that in mind, I decide to clean, even though the apartment's already sparkling. I start in the upstairs bathroom, wiping down the spotless countertops and spraying the mirrors with glass cleaner. Then it's on to the bedroom, where I dust and sweep the carpet with a sleek vacuum found in the hall closet.

The cleaning continues in the kitchen, where I wipe down the countertops. Then in the study, where I run a feather duster over the desk, the top of which has been cleared of the previous owner's belongings. It strikes me as odd that so much of what she owned remains in the apartment. Her furniture. Her dishes. Her vacuum. Yet anything that could identify her has been removed.

Clothes in the closet? Gone.

Family photos? Also gone, although in both the study and the sitting room are discolored rectangles on the wallpaper where something used to hang.

I look around the study, acutely aware that I've moved from cleaning to snooping. But not in a prurient way. I have no interest in any of the dead owner's dirty secrets. What I'm after is a hint of who she was. If this was the apartment of a CEO or movie star, I want to know who it was.

I search the bookshelf first, scanning the rows of volumes for signs of the dead owner's profession, if not her outright identity. Nothing gives it away. The books are either classics bound in faux leather with their titles embossed in gold or bestsellers from a decade ago. Only one catches my attention—a copy of *Heart of a Dreamer*. Fitting, considering the location.

It's a hardcover, in perfect condition. So unlike my beloved paperback, with its cracked spine and pages that have been so thoroughly turned they're now fuzzy at the edges. When I flip the book over, the author stares back at me.

Greta Manville.

It's not an entirely flattering picture. Her face is made up of harsh angles. Sharp cheekbones. Pointy chin. Narrow nose. On her lips is the barest hint of a smile. It makes her look amused, but in a way no one else would understand. As if she and the photographer had just shared a private joke right before the shutter clicked.

She never wrote another book. I looked her up after Jane read me *Heart of a Dreamer*, eager to find more of her work. Only there was nothing more to be read. Just that single, perfect novel published in the mid-eighties.

I put *Heart of a Dreamer* back on the shelf and move to the desk. Its contents are meager and disappointingly generic. Paper clips and Bic pens in the top drawer. A few empty file folders and old copies of *The New Yorker* in the bottom ones. Definitely no personalized stationery or documents with names on them.

But then I notice the address labels stuck to the magazine covers. All of them bear not only the Bartholomew's address and this apartment number, but a single name.

Marjorie Milton.

I can't help but feel let down. I've never heard of her, which means she was, in all likelihood, your average rich lady—born with money, died with money, now has family squabbling over that money.

Disappointed, I drop the magazines back in the desk and continue cleaning, this time in the sitting room. I hit the biggies—carpet, windows, coffee table—before running a dust mop across the crown molding, my nose mere inches from the wallpaper.

The pattern is even more oppressive up close. All those flowers opening like mouths, their petals colliding. The oval spaces between them are colored a shade of red so dark it flirts with blackness. They remind me of eyes studding the wallpaper.

I take a step back and squint. My hope is that it'll erase the impression that the wallpaper is a series of eyes. It doesn't. Not only are the eyes still there, but the flowers now no longer look like flowers. Instead, those spreading petals take on the shapes of faces.

It's the same with the crown molding. Hidden within the intricate plasterwork are similar wide-open eyes and pinched faces.

The sensible, rational part of my brain knows it's an optical illusion. Yet now that I've noticed it, I can't trick my eyes into returning to what they originally saw. Those flowers are gone. All I can see now are the faces. Grotesque ones with warped noses, mutated lips, elongated jaws that make it look as though they're talking.

But these walls don't talk.

They observe.

Yet something inside the apartment is making noise. I hear it from my spot in the sitting room—a muffled creak.

At first, I think it's a mouse. Only, the Bartholomew doesn't seem like the kind of place that would have mice. Also, it doesn't sound like any mouse I've ever heard. The creak is accompanied by the groan of something that's normally still being forced into motion. It brings to mind rusty cogs and stiff joints.

I follow the sound to its point of origin in the kitchen, at the cupboard between the oven and the sink.

The dumbwaiter.

I throw open the cupboard door, revealing the empty shaft behind it. A cold draft hits me, shivery and crisp. The ropes that hung lazily when Leslie showed me the dumbwaiter during my tour are now taut and in motion. Above, the pulley turns, stopping and starting with each tug of the rope. Each time it moves, it emits a short, shrill squeak.

I peek into the shaft itself, the brisk draft brushing my face. At first I see nothing. Just inky darkness that, for all I know, might stretch to the Bartholomew's basement. Then something emerges from the black, rising to meet me. Soon I can make out the top of the dumbwaiter itself.

Wood.

Thick coat of dust.

Holes on the top and bottom to let the ropes slither through.

The pulley turns and squeaks. The dumbwaiter continues to rise. The draft stirs the dust on top of it, sending up a small puff that makes me back away before it swirls out of the cupboard door like ash from a chimney.

I imagine it in use a hundred years ago. The harried cooks sending down extravagant meals dish by dish as the dumbwaiter shaft filled with the scent of roast chicken, rack of lamb, and fresh herbs. The dumbwaiter's return trip would bring stacks of dirty dishes, soiled silverware, crystal goblets with wine swirling in their bottoms and lipstick on their rims.

It sounds romantic through the soft gauze of time. In truth, it was probably wretched. At least up here, where the servants worked and ate and slept.

When the squeaking of the pulley finally stops, the once-empty space is filled with the dumbwaiter itself. It's a perfect fit. A casual visitor opening the cupboard door wouldn't even know it was a dumbwaiter if not for the ropes. It's a plain wooden box, just like any cupboard.

Resting on the bottom is a piece of paper. Its left edge is slightly ragged, indicating it was torn from a book. Printed on it is a single poem. Emily Dickinson. "Because I Could Not Stop for Death."

I turn the page over and see that someone has written on the back. It's brief. Just three words, the letters large and in all caps.

HELLO AND WELCOME!

Beneath it, in slightly smaller text, is the messenger's name.

Ingrid

I search the kitchen for a pen and paper, finding both in a junk drawer stuffed with rubber bands, ketchup packets, and takeout menus. I write my response—*Hi and thanks*—before placing it inside the dumbwaiter and giving the rope an upward tug with my right hand.

The dumbwaiter shimmies.

The pulley above it creaks.

It's not until the dumbwaiter begins to descend that I realize how big the whole contraption really is. The same size as an adult male, and almost as heavy. So heavy that I need to use both hands to lower it. As it descends, I count how far I think it's traveled.

Five feet. Ten feet. Fifteen.

Just before I hit twenty, the rope goes slack in my hands. The dumbwaiter has been lowered as far as it can go, which by my estimate means to the apartment directly below.

11A.

Home of the mysterious Ingrid. Even though I have no idea who she is, I think I like her already.

7

In the afternoon, I head out to buy groceries, taking the elevator from the silent twelfth floor past levels that are louder and livelier than my own. On the tenth floor, Beethoven drifts from an apartment down the hall. On the ninth, I spy the swing of a door being closed. With it comes a nose-stinging waft of disinfectant.

On the seventh, the elevator stops completely to pick up another passenger—the soap opera actress I saw during yesterday's tour. Today, she and her tiny dog wear matching fur-trimmed jackets.

The actress's appearance leaves me momentarily speechless. My brain fumbles for her character's name. The one my mother loved to hate. Cassidy. That's what it was.

"Room for two more?" she says, eyeing the closed grate across the door.

"Oh, sorry. Of course."

I open the grate and nudge to the side so the actress and her dog can enter. Soon we're descending again, the actress adjusting the hood of her dog's jacket while I think about how my mother would have gotten a kick out of knowing I rode in an elevator with Cassidy.

She looks different up close and in person. Maybe it's the abundant makeup she wears. Her face is entirely covered with foundation, which gives her skin a peachy cast. Or it could be the saucer-size sunglasses she's once again wearing, which cover a third of her face.

"You're new here, aren't you?" she says.

"Just moved in," I reply, debating whether I should add that it's just for three months and that I'm getting paid to be here. I choose not to. If the woman who played Cassidy wants to think I'm a real resident of the Bartholomew, I'm not going to stop her.

"I've been here six months," she says. "Had to sell my house in Malibu to move, but I think it'll be worth it. I'm Marianne, by the way."

I already know this, of course. Marianne Duncan, whose fashionable bitchery on the small screen was as much a part of my adolescence as reading *Heart of a Dreamer*. Marianne holds out the hand not currently occupied by a dog, and I shake it.

"I'm Jules." I look to the dog. "Who's this adorable guy?"

"This is Rufus."

I give the dog a pat between his pert ears. He licks my hand in response.

"Aw, he likes you," Marianne says.

Lower we go, passing two other presences from my first tour— the older man struggling his way down the stairs and the weary aide by his side. Instead of pretending not to stare, this time the man offers us a smile and a trembling wave.

"Keep it up, Mr. Leonard," Marianne calls to him. "You're doing great." To me, she whispers, "Heart trouble. He takes the stairs every day because he thinks it'll prevent another coronary."

"How many has he had?"

"Three," she says. "That I know of. Then again, he used to be a senator. I'm sure that alone caused a heart attack or two."

In the lobby, I say goodbye to Marianne and Rufus and head to the wall of mailboxes. The one for 12A is empty. No surprise there. As I turn away from it, I see someone else entering the lobby. She looks to be in her early seventies and makes no attempt to hide it. No forehead-smoothing Botox like Leslie Evelyn or caked-on foundation like Marianne Duncan. Her face is pale and slightly puffy. Straight gray hair brushes her shoulders.

It's her eyes that really catch my attention. Bright blue even in the dim light of the lobby, they seem to spark with intelligence. We make eye contact—me staring, she politely pretending that I'm not. But I can't help it. I've seen that face a hundred times, staring at me from the back of a book jacket, most recently this very morning.

"Excuse me—" I stop, wincing at my tone. So nervous and meek. I start again. "Excuse me, but are you Greta Manville? The writer?"

She tucks a lock of hair behind her ears and gives a Mona Lisa smile, not exactly displeased to be recognized, but not overjoyed, either.

"That would be me," she says in a Lauren Bacall rasp, her voice polite but wary.

There's a flutter in my chest. My heart beating overtime. Greta Manville, of all people, is right here in front of me.

"I'm Jules," I say.

Greta Manville makes no attempt to shake my hand, instead edging around me on her way to the mailboxes. I make note of the apartment number.

10A. Two floors below me.

"Pleased to meet you," she says, sounding anything but pleased.

"I love your book. *Heart of a Dreamer* changed my life. I've read it, like, twenty times. That's not an exaggeration." I stop myself again, fully aware that I'm gushing. I take a breath, straighten my spine, and say, as calmly as I can, "Do you think you'd be able to sign my copy?"

Greta doesn't turn around. "You're not holding my book."

"I meant later," I say. "Next time we run into each other."

"How do you know there's going to be a next time?"

"*If* we do, I mean. But I do want to thank you for writing it. Reading it is why I moved to New York. And now I'm here. Temporarily, at least."

Greta turns away from her mailbox. Slowly. Not too curious, but enough to study me with those keen, inquisitive eyes. Her lips pucker ever so slightly, as if she's thinking about what to say next.

"A temporary tenant?"

"Yes. Just moved in."

This prompts a slight nod from Greta, who says, "I imagine Leslie went over the rules?"

"She did."

"Then I'm sure she told you about not bothering residents."

I gulp. I nod. Disappointment burrows into my heart.

"She did say residents like their privacy."

"And so we do," Greta says. "You might want to keep that in mind the next time we run into each other."

She shuts the mailbox and edges past me again, our shoulders brushing. I shrink away. In a voice no louder than a murmur, I say, "Sorry for bothering you. I just thought you'd like to know that *Heart of a Dreamer* is my favorite book."

Greta spins around in the middle of the lobby, an armful of mail clutched against her chest. Her blue eyes have turned ice cold.

"It's your *favorite* book?"

I feel the urge to backtrack. The words *One of them* form on my tongue, weak and flavorless. I stop myself. If this is the only time I speak to Greta Manville—and it sure seems like it will be, considering how unpleasant she is—then I want her to know the truth.

"It is."

"If that's the case," she says, "then you need to read more."

The words have the impact of a slap—hot and stinging. I wince. My cheeks turn red. I even sway back on my heels, as if buffeted by a blow. Greta, meanwhile, strides stiff-backed to the elevator, not even bothering to see my reaction.

Knowing she doesn't even care how the insult affects me somehow makes it feel worse.

Like I'm the least important person in the world.

But then I turn toward the front door and see Charlie standing just inside the lobby. While I don't think he witnessed my entire conversation with Greta Manville, he at least saw enough to know why I appear so rattled.

Tipping his cap, he says, "While I'm not allowed to speak ill of the residents, I'm also not supposed to turn a blind eye when one of them is rude. And she was very rude to you, Miss Larsen. I apologize on behalf of everyone at the Bartholomew."

"It's fine," I say. "I've been treated worse."

"Don't let it get you down." Charlie smiles and holds the door open for me. "Now go out and enjoy the beautiful day."

I step outside and see three girls pressed together for a selfie with the gargoyles above the door. One of them raises her phone and says, "Say 'Bartholomew'!"

"Bartholomew!" the other two echo in unison.

I freeze in the doorway until the picture is taken. Giggling, the girls move on, unaware I'm also in the photo. Then again, there's a chance they might not even notice me at all. It's easy to feel invisible on this patch of busy Manhattan sidewalk. In addition to the Bartholomew tourists, I see dog walkers, nannies pushing strollers, harried New Yorkers doing the sidewalk slalom around them.

I join them all at the corner two blocks away from the Bartholomew, waiting for the light to change. The streetlamp there bears a taped flier that's come loose at one edge, the paper flapping like a wind-blown flag. I get glimpses of a woman with pale skin, almond-shaped eyes, and a mane of curly brown hair. Above her photo, in siren-red letters, is one dreadfully familiar word.

MISSING

Memories lurch out of nowhere, leaping on top of me until the sidewalk turns to quicksand beneath my feet.

All I can think about are those first fraught days after Jane vanished.

She was also on a flier, her yearbook photo placed under the word MISSING, which was colored a similarly urgent red. For a few weeks, that picture was everywhere in our tiny town. Hundreds of identical Janes. None of them the real thing.

I turn away, afraid that if I look again it'll be Jane's face I see on the flier.

I'm relieved when the light changes a second later, sending the dog walkers, nannies, and weary New Yorkers into motion across the street. I follow, my footsteps quick, putting as much distance between me and the flier as possible.

8

I now have only two hundred and five dollars to my name.

Grocery stores in Manhattan aren't cheap. Especially in this neighborhood. It doesn't matter that I bought the least-expensive things I could find. Dry pasta and generic red sauce. Off-brand cereal. An economy-size box of frozen pizzas. My only splurge was the handful of fresh fruits and vegetables I bought to keep me from being completely malnourished. It's mind-boggling to me how a few oranges can cost the same as five pounds of boxed spaghetti.

I leave the store with more than a week's worth of meals carried in two sagging paper bags. They're an unwieldy pair, which shift with every step I take. They're heavy, too, a fact I blame on the frozen pizza. I hold the bags high so they can lean against my shoulders for additional support. Even then, I barely make it through the uncaring throng of New Yorkers hurrying past me in all directions. But when I reach the Bartholomew, there's Charlie, who sees me coming and holds the door wide open. He ushers me inside with a dramatic sweep of his arms that makes me feel a bit like royalty.

"Thanks, Charlie," I say through the narrow gap between bags.

"Let me carry those for you, Miss Larsen."

I'm so eager to be relieved of my load that I almost let him. But then I think about what's inside these bulky bags. All those store-brand boxes with their rip-off names and apathetically designed logos. I'd rather Charlie not see them and have the opportunity to judge me or, worse, pity me.

Not that he would.

No decent person would.

Yet the shame and fear are still there.

I'd like to say it's a quirk of my currently dire financial situation, but it's not. This fear stretches back to grade school, when I invited a new friend named Katie to spend the night. Her family was wealthier than my parents. They had a whole house. My family lived in half of one that had been sliced down the middle into two symmetrical units, a fact made glaringly obvious by our neighbor's habit of keeping her Christmas decorations up all year round.

Katie didn't seem bothered by that half of house bedecked in silvery garland and twinkling lights. Nor did she mind the smallness of my room or the budget-conscious mac and cheese we had for dinner. But then morning arrived and my mother placed a box of cereal on the counter. Fruit O's, not Froot Loops.

"I can't eat that," Katie said.

"They're Froot Loops," my mother said.

Katie eyed the box with undisguised scorn. "*Fake* Froot Loops. I only eat the real kind."

She ended up skipping breakfast, which meant I did, too, much to my mother's aggravation. I refused to eat them the next morning as well, even though Katie was long gone.

"I want real Froot Loops," I announced.

This brought a sigh from my mother. "It's the exact same thing. Just with a different name."

"I want the real thing," I said. "Not the poor-people version."

My mother started to cry, right there at the kitchen table. It wasn't subtle crying, either. This was shoulder-heaving, red-faced weeping that left me terrified and confused as I ran to my room. The next morning, I woke to find a box of Froot Loops placed next to an empty bowl. From then on, my mother never bought the generic brand of anything.

Years later, during my parents' funerals, I thought about Katie and those Fruit O's and how much money my name-brand obsession cost over time. Thousands of dollars, probably. And as I watched my mother's casket lowered into the ground, the main thought running through my head was how much I regretted being such a little shit about something as innocuous as cereal.

Innocuous or not, here I am, hurrying past Charlie into the lobby. "I've got them. But I won't say no to being helped with the elevator."

I look across the lobby and see the elevator car descending into its gilded cage. Hoping to catch it before someone on an upper floor can claim it, I dash forward, grocery bags shimmying and Charlie struggling to match my pace. I'm almost at the elevator when I spot a young woman flying down the stairs right beside it. She's in a hurry. Legs churning. Head down. Eyes on her phone.

"Whoa! Look out!" Charlie shouts.

But it's too late. The girl and I collide in the middle of the lobby. The crash sends us ricocheting off each other. The girl stumbles backward. I fall completely, slamming against the lobby floor as both grocery bags spring from my grip. Although a sharp pain shoots through my elbow and down my left arm, I'm more worried about the sight of my groceries scattered across the lobby. Thin sticks of dried spaghetti cover the floor like strands of hay. Nearby is a shattered jar oozing sauce. Oranges roll through the puddle, leaving trails of red.

The girl is by my side in an instant. "I'm so sorry! I can't believe I'm so clumsy!"

Even though she tries to help me up, I remain on the floor, scrambling to shove my groceries back into the bags before others can see them. But the collision has already drawn a small crowd. There's Charlie, of course, who hurriedly gathers the fallen groceries, and Marianne Duncan returning from taking Rufus for a walk. She stands in the doorway as Rufus yaps. The commotion brings Leslie Evelyn rushing out of her office to see what's happened.

Mortified, I try to ignore them all while continuing to collect my groceries. When I reach for one of the rogue oranges, another bolt of pain zaps through my arm.

The girl gasps. "You're bleeding."

"It's just tomato sauce," I say.

Only it's not. I sneak a glance at my arm and see a long gash just below my elbow. Blood streams from the wound in a thick rivulet that goes all the way to my knuckles. The sight makes me so dizzy I momentarily forget about the pain. It comes back only when Charlie yanks a handkerchief from his jacket pocket and presses it to the wound.

Looking around, I see chunks of broken glass scattered across the floor. I can only assume one of them dug into my arm while I was scrambling for the groceries.

"Sweetie, you need to see a doctor," Leslie says. "Let me take you to the emergency room."

That would be a fine idea, if I could afford it. But I can't. Part of my severance package included two more months of health insurance, but even that comes with a hundred-dollar co-pay for an emergency room visit.

"I'm fine," I say, even though I'm starting to think I'm not. The handkerchief Charlie gave me is already crimson with blood.

"You should at least see Dr. Nick," Leslie says. "He'll be able to tell if you need stitches or not."

"I don't have time to go to a doctor's office."

"Dr. Nick lives here," Leslie says. "Twelfth floor. Same as you."

Charlie stuffs the last of my groceries into the mangled bags. "I'll take care of these for you, Miss Larsen. Go on up and see Dr. Nick."

Leslie and the girl help me to my feet, lifting me by my good arm. Before I can protest, they're ushering me into the elevator. Only two of us can fit, which means the girl remains outside the cage.

"Thank you, Ingrid," Leslie says before sliding the grate shut. "I can take it from here."

I stare at the girl through the grate, surprised. This is Ingrid? Although we look to be roughly the same age, she's dressed like someone younger. Oversize plaid shirt. Distressed jeans that reveal pink knees. Converse sneakers with the left laces coming undone. Her hair is dark brown but had previously been dyed blue. A two-inch strip of color fans out across her back and shoulders.

Ingrid catches me staring, bites her bottom lip, and gives me an embarrassed wave, her fingers wiggling.

Inside the elevator, Leslie hits the button for the top floor and up we go.

"You poor girl," she says. "I'm so sorry about this. Ingrid's a lovely girl, but she can also be oblivious to what's going on around her. I'm sure she feels terrible. But don't worry. Dr. Nick will fix you right up."

Soon we're at the door to 12B, Leslie giving it a series of rapid-fire knocks while I continue to press Charlie's blood-soaked handkerchief against my arm. Then the door opens, and Dr. Nick stands before us.

I was expecting someone older but distinguished. Gray hair. Moist eyes. Tweed jacket. But the man at the door is a good forty years younger and a lot better looking than the doctor of my imagination. His hair is auburn. His eyes are hazel, set off by glasses with tortoiseshell frames. His outfit of khakis and a crisp white shirt reveals a tall, trim physique. He looks less like a doctor than an actor playing one on Marianne Duncan's old soap opera.

"What do we have here?" he says, his gaze moving from Leslie to me and my bloody arm.

"Accident in the lobby," Leslie tells him. "Do you think you could take a quick look and see if Jules here needs to go to the ER?"

"I don't," I say.

Dr. Nick gives me a clipped smile. "Maybe I should be the judge of that, don't you think?"

Leslie nudges me gently toward the door. "Go on, sweetie. I'll check on you tomorrow."

"Wait, you're leaving?"

"I need to go. I was in the middle of something when I heard that ruckus in the lobby," Leslie says as she hurries to the waiting elevator and descends out of sight.

I turn back to Dr. Nick, who says, "Don't be nervous. I don't bite."

Maybe not, but the situation makes me uncomfortable all the same. Handsome doctor rich enough to live at the Bartholomew. Eligible girl paid to live right next door. In the movies, they'd banter, sparks would fly, a happy ending would ensue.

But this isn't a movie. Or even *Heart of a Dreamer*. It's cold reality.

I've been on this earth twenty-five years. Long enough to know who I am. An office worker. A girl you might notice at the copier or in the elevator but probably don't.

I'm a girl who read on her lunch break, back when I had a lunch break.

A girl people pass on the street without a second glance.

A girl who has had sex with only three different guys, yet still feels guilty about it because my parents were high school sweethearts who had never been intimate with anyone else.

A girl who has been abandoned more times than I can count.

A girl who catches the attention of the handsome doctor next door only because I've cut myself and am now bleeding on his doorstep. It's the blood that ultimately convinces me to enter Dr. Nick's apartment with an awkward, apologetic smile plastered on my face.

"I'm really sorry about all this, Dr. Nick."

"Don't be," he says. "Leslie was right to bring you here. And please, call me Nick. Now, let's get that arm looked at."

The apartment is almost a mirror image of 12A. The décor is different, of course, but the layout is the same, only flipped. The sitting room is straight ahead, but the study is to the left and the hallway leads to the right. I follow him past a dining room situated on the corner just like the one in 12A. His is more masculine, though. Navy walls. Spiky chandelier that looks like modern art. The table here is round and surrounded by red chairs.

"Although this place has a lot of rooms, I'm afraid an examining room isn't one of them," Dr. Nick says over his shoulder. "This will have to suffice."

He guides me into the kitchen and gestures for me to sit on a stool by the counter. "I'll be right back," he says before disappearing down the hall.

I have a look around in his absence. Our kitchens are roughly the same size and of similar layout, although Dr. Nick's has an earthier vibe. Pale brown tile and countertops the color of sand. The only splash of brightness comes from a painting that hangs over the sink. It depicts a snake with its mouth clamped down on its tail, its long body curled into a perfect figure eight.

I approach the painting, curious. It looks old, the surface spider-webbed with a hundred tiny cracks. But the paint itself remains vibrant, the colors bold and eye-catching. The scales on the snake's back are scarlet. Its belly is seasick green. The one visible eye is a deep shade of yellow. There's no pupil. Just a blank teardrop shape that reminds me of a lit match.

Dr. Nick returns with a first-aid kit and a medical bag.

"Ah, you've noticed my ouroboros," he says. "I picked it up during my travels abroad. Do you like it?"

That would be a definite no. The colors are too garish. The subject matter too grim. It reminds me of a Mexican restaurant Andrew once took me to themed around Día de los Muertos—the Day of the Dead. It had waiters with painted faces and brightly decorated skulls staring from the ceiling. I spent the meal shifting with discomfort.

I do the same once I return to the stool, the snake watching me with his blazing eye. Bright and unblinking, it seems to be daring me to look away. I don't.

"What's its meaning?"

"It's supposed to represent the cyclical nature of the universe," Dr. Nick says. "Birth, life, death, rebirth."

"The circle of life," I say.

Nick gives a quick nod. "Exactly."

I stare at the snake's eye one second longer as Dr. Nick washes and dries his hands, slips on latex gloves, and gently peels the handkerchief from the wound.

"What happened here?" he says, adding, "Wait, don't tell me. Knife fight in Central Park."

"Just two women colliding in spectacular fashion and a broken jar of spaghetti sauce. I'm sure it happens here all the time."

I hold still as he cleans the wound with peroxide, trying not to flinch at the sudden, cold bite of pain. Dr. Nick notices and does his best to distract me with small talk.

"Tell me, Jules, how do you like living in the Bartholomew?"

"How do you know I live here?"

"I assumed that if Leslie brought you to see me then you must be a tenant," he says. "Am I wrong?"

"Partially. I'm a—" I search for the term Leslie had used earlier. "Temporary tenant. Right next door, in fact."

"Ah, so you're the lucky apartment sitter who snagged 12A. You just move in?"

"Today."

"Then let me officially welcome you to the building," he says. "I hope my medical expertise will make up for the lack of a casserole."

"What kind of doctor are you?"

"Surgeon."

I glance at his hands as he attends to my arm. They're definitely surgeon hands, with long, elegant fingers that move with steady grace. When he removes them, I see that the cut looks less severe now that it's been cleaned. Just a two-inch gash that's quickly covered with a rectangle of gauze and sealed in place with medical tape.

"That should do it for now," Dr. Nick says as he peels the latex gloves from his hands. "The bleeding's stopped, but it's a good idea to keep the bandage on until morning. When was your last tetanus shot?"

I shrug. I have no idea.

"You might want to get one. Just to be on the safe side. When was your last checkup?"

"Um, last year," I say, when in truth it's another thing I can't remember. My approach to health care is not seeing a doctor unless I absolutely need to. Even when I had a job, the idea of regular check-ups and preventive visits seemed like a waste of money. "Maybe two years ago."

"Then I'd like to check your vitals, if you'll let me."

"Should I be worried?"

"Not at all. This is just precautionary. The heart can sometimes beat erratically after a fall or loss of blood. I just want to make sure that everything's okay." Dr. Nick digs a stethoscope out of the medical bag and presses it to my chest, just below the collarbone. "Take a deep breath."

I do and get a whiff of his cologne in the process. It has hints of sandalwood and citrus and something else. Something bitter. Anise, I think. It has a similarly sharp tang.

"Good," Dr. Nick says as he moves the stethoscope an inch, and I take another deep inhalation. "You have a very interesting name, Jules. Is that short for something? A nickname?"

"No nickname. Most people think it's short for Julia or Julianne, but Jules is my given name. My father used to say that when I was born, my mother took one look into my eyes and said they sparkled like jewels."

Dr. Nick peers into my eyes. It lasts only a second, but it's still long enough to make my pulse quicken. I wonder if he can hear it, especially when he says, "For the record, your mother was right."

I will myself not to blush, although I suspect it's happening anyway. A noticeable warmth spreads across my cheeks.

"And Nick is short for Nicholas?"

"Guilty as charged," he says while wrapping a blood pressure cuff around my upper right arm.

"How long have you lived at the Bartholomew?"

"I suspect what you really want to know is how someone my age can afford an apartment in this building."

He's right, of course. That's exactly what I want to know. I blush again, this time for being so easily read.

"I'm sorry," I say. "It's none of my business."

"It's fine. I'd be curious, too, if our roles were reversed. The answer—to all your questions—is that I've lived here my whole life. This apartment has been in my family for decades. I inherited it after my parents died five years ago. They were both killed in a car accident while visiting Europe."

"I'm sorry," I say again, wishing I had just kept quiet.

"Thank you. Losing them both so suddenly was hard. And I sometimes feel guilty knowing that if they hadn't died, I'd be living in some Brooklyn walk-up right now, and not in one of the most famous buildings on the planet. In some ways, I feel like I'm also an apartment sitter. Just watching this place until my parents come home."

Dr. Nick finishes taking my blood pressure and says, "One twenty over eighty. Perfect. You seem to be in excellent health, Jules."

"Thanks again, Doc—" I stop myself before I can finish the word. "Nick. I appreciate it."

"It was no problem at all. Not to mention the neighborly thing to do."

He leads me back into the hall, where I get turned around by the opposite layout of the one in 12A. Instead of making a right, I go left, accidentally taking a few steps toward a door at the end of the hallway. It's wider than the others, locked in place with a deadbolt. After a quick spin, I'm back on track, following Nick to the front door.

"I'm sorry for being nosy earlier," I tell him once we're in the foyer. "I didn't mean to bring up bad memories."

"There's no need to apologize. I have plenty of good memories that balance out the bad. Besides, my story isn't uncommon. I think every family has at least one big tragedy."

He's wrong there.

Mine has two.

9

My phone buzzes as I leave Nick's apartment. It's an email from Chloe, which I give a cursory glance while unlocking the door to 12A. The subject line prompts an annoyed sigh.

Scary stuff.

There's no message. Just a link to a website that, when I click on it, brings me to an article with a headline that's ominously blunt.

THE CURSE OF THE BARTHOLOMEW

Rather than read the article, I shove the phone back into my pocket and push into 12A, where I toss my keys into the bowl on the foyer table. Only, my aim is off and the keys end up hitting the edge of the table before clattering onto a heating vent in the foyer floor. An antique grate covers the vent—all cast-iron curlicues with gaps between them wide enough for the keys to tumble right through.

Which they do.

Instantly.

I drop to my hands and knees and peer into the grate, seeing mostly darkness within.

This isn't good. Not good at all. I wonder if losing keys is also against the rules. Probably.

I still have my face pressed to the grate when there's a knock on the door. Charlie's voice rises from the other side.

"Miss Larsen, you in there?"

"I'm here," I say as I lift myself off the floor. Before opening the door, I smooth a hand across my cheek, just in case the grate left any marks on my face.

I whip open the door to see Charlie on the threshold, two large grocery bags in his arms. Unlike the torn and mangled ones from the lobby, these are pristine.

"I thought you might need these," he says.

I take one of the bags and carry it to the kitchen. Charlie follows with the other. Inside are replacements of every item damaged in my collision with Ingrid. New economy-size box of pasta. New jar of sauce. New oranges and frozen pizza. There's even the addition of a bar of dark chocolate. The decadent, expensive kind.

"I tried to salvage what you had bought, but I'm afraid not much survived," Charlie says. "So I made a quick trip to the store."

I stare at the groceries, touched beyond words. "Charlie, you shouldn't have."

"It was nothing," he says. "I have a daughter your age. I hate the thought of her going hungry for a few days. I'd be a terrible father if I let the same happen to you."

I'm not surprised he knows I couldn't afford to replace all the groceries. He saw what I had purchased. All of it implied the tightest of budgets.

"How much do I owe you?"

To my relief, he shoos away the offer like it's a pesky fly. "No need to worry about that, Miss Larsen. It makes up for that unfortunate incident in the lobby."

"Are you referring to the collision or to Greta Manville?"

"Both," Charlie says.

"Accidents happen. As for Greta Manville, I've already shrugged it off." I unwrap the edge of the chocolate bar, snap off a square, and offer it to Charlie. "Besides, everyone else here has been so nice that it was bound to end at some point."

"You're suspicious of nice?" Charlie says as he pops the chocolate into his mouth.

I do the same, talking and chewing at the same time. "I'm suspicious of rich *and* nice."

"You shouldn't be. Most people here are both." Charlie runs his thumb and forefinger over his mustache, smoothing the bristly hairs. "I can only claim to be one of those things, I'm afraid."

"Yes, the nicest. And I feel like I should repay you somehow."

"Just perform a good deed for someone else," he says. "That'll be payment enough."

"I'll do two good deeds," I say, biting my lower lip. "Because it seems I need yet another favor. My keys, um, sort of fell into the heating vent."

Charlie shakes his head, trying to stifle a chuckle. "Which one?"

"Foyer," I say. "By the door."

A minute later we're back in the foyer, me watching as Charlie presses his formidable stomach against the floor. In his hand is a pen-shaped magnet stick, the end of which he lowers through the grate.

"I'm so sorry about this," I say.

Charlie wiggles the stick. "Happens all the time. These grates are notorious. I think of them as monsters. They'll eat up anything that comes their way."

The comparison is apt. The longer I look at the heating vent, the more it resembles a dark maw just waiting to be fed.

"Like keys," I say.

"And rings. And pill bottles. Even cell phones, if one falls at the right angle."

"You guys must get calls about lost toys all the time."

"Not so much," Charlie says. "There aren't any kids living at the Bartholomew."

"None at all?"

"Nope. This place isn't exactly child friendly. We prefer our tenants to be older—and quiet."

Carefully, he removes the stick from the grate. Dangling from the end is my key ring. Charlie plucks it off and gently places it into the bowl on the foyer table. The magnet stick goes back into his jacket's interior pocket.

"If it ever happens again, just grab a screwdriver," he says. "The grate comes off real easy, and you can reach right in."

"Thank you," I say with a sigh of relief. "For everything."

Charlie tips his cap. "It was my pleasure, Jules."

After he leaves, I return to the kitchen and unpack the groceries, overwhelmed not just by his generosity but by the care he took in replacing them. Other than the chocolate, everything in the bags is exactly what I had purchased.

I've just put away the last of the groceries when I hear a telltale creak rise from the cupboard.

The dumbwaiter on the move.

I lift the cupboard door as it rises into view. Inside is another poem. "Remember" by Christina Rossetti.

Seeing it causes a slight hiccup in my chest. My heart skipping a single beat. I know this poem. It was read at my parents' funeral.

Remember me when I am gone away.

Ironic, considering how I long to forget sitting in the front pew of that church my family had never attended, Chloe by my side, a smattering of mourners mute behind us. The poem was read by my high school English teacher—the kind and wonderful Mrs. James, her voice ringing through the silent church as she spoke the opening line.

On the back Ingrid has left me another note.

SORRY ABOUT YOUR ARM

With the same pen and paper I used earlier, I write my response. *It's fine. No worries.*

I put it in the dumbwaiter and send it to 11A, having an easier time this go-round. I'm prepared for both the weight and the distance.

I receive a response five minutes later, most of that time taken up by the dumbwaiter's slow ascent. Inside is a fresh poem. "Fire and Ice" by Robert Frost.

Some say the world will end in fire.

On the back, Ingrid has written not another apology but a command.

CENTRAL PARK. IMAGINE. 15 MINUTES.

10

As instructed, I'm at the Imagine mosaic fifteen minutes later, looking for Ingrid among the usual crowd of tourists and grungy buskers playing Beatles songs. It's a beautiful afternoon. Mid-sixties, sunny and clear. It reminds me of my childhood. Of pumpkins and piles of leaves and trick-or-treating.

It also reminds me of my mother, who adored this time of year. She called it Heather weather, because that was her name.

When I finally spot Ingrid, I see that in her hands are two hot dogs, one of which she holds out to me.

"An apology gift," she says. "For being an idiot. I've always hated those people who look at their phones instead of where they're going. Now I've become one. It's inexcusable. I'm the lowest of the low."

"It was just an accident."

"A stupid, preventable one." She takes a giant bite of her hot dog. "Did it hurt? I bet it hurt. You were bleeding a lot."

She gasps.

"Did you need stitches? Tell me you didn't need stitches."

"Just a bandage," I say.

Ingrid's hand flies to her heart as she exhales dramatically. "Thank God. I *hate* stitches. They say you're not supposed to feel them, but I can. Those wire threads pulling at your skin. Ugh."

She starts to move deeper into the park. Even though a mere minute in her company has left me exhausted, I follow. She's fascinating in the same way tornadoes are fascinating. You want to see how much they're going to spin.

Ingrid, it turns out, spins a lot. Walking a few paces ahead of me, she whirls around anytime she has something to say. Which is about every five seconds.

"I love the park. Don't you?"

Whirl.

"It's, like, this perfect wilderness smack-dab in the middle of the city."

Whirl.

"It's all man-made, you know. Everything is by design, which makes it, I don't know, *more* perfect."

Two whirls this time. Quick, looping ones that leave Ingrid flushed and slightly dizzy, like a child after one too many cartwheels.

She reminds me of a child in many ways. Not just her excitable spirit but also her looks. I can't help but notice our height difference as we stop at the edge of Central Park Lake. I've got about six inches on Ingrid, which means she barely clears five feet. Then there's her thin-ness. She's nothing but skin and bones. In all ways, she looks hungry. So much so that I give her my hot dog and insist that she eat it.

"I couldn't possibly," she says. "It's my apology hot dog. Although I should probably also apologize for the apology hot dog. No one knows what's in these things."

"I just had lunch," I say. "And your apology is accepted."

Ingrid takes the hot dog with a grand curtsy.

"I'm Jules, by the way."

Ingrid takes a bite, chewing a bit before saying, "I know."

"And you're Ingrid in 11A."

"I am. Ingrid Gallagher in 11A, who knows her way around a dumbwaiter. Never thought I'd learn that particular life skill, but here we are."

She plops onto the nearest bench to finish the hot dog. I remain standing, staring at the rowboats on the water and the handful of pedestrians currently crossing Bow Bridge. This is, I realize, the ground-level version of the view from 12A.

"How do you like the Bartholomew?" Ingrid says before popping the last bit of hot dog into her mouth. "It's dreamy, right?"

"Very."

Ingrid uses the back of her hand to wipe away a speck of mustard at the corner of her mouth. "Here for three months?"

I nod.

"Same," she says. "I've been here two weeks now."

"Where did you live before that?"

"Virginia. Before that was Seattle. But I'm originally from Boston." She lies down on the bench, her blue-tipped hair fanning out around her head. "So I guess I don't live anywhere now. I'm a nomad."

I wonder if that's on purpose or out of necessity. A constant flight from poor choices and bad luck. Someone not unlike me. Although, honestly, I see nothing of myself in her.

And then it hits me: I see Jane.

Both share the same rambling, manic-pixie personality that gallops right to the cusp of being too much. I never felt fully balanced around Jane, even though she was my sister and my best friend. But I loved that lack of equilibrium. I needed it to counterbalance the rest of my shy, quiet, orderly existence. And Jane knew it. She'd take my hand and whisk me to the woods on the other side of town, where we'd stand on stumps and do Tarzan yells until our throats hurt. Or into the shuttered headquarters of the town's old coal mine, guiding me through musty offices that had been untouched for years. Or through the back exit of the movie theater, where we'd slip into our seats after the lights went down.

She caused and healed so much. Scraped knees, mosquito bites, broken hearts.

Jules and Jane. Always together.

Until, all of a sudden, we weren't.

"I left Boston two years ago," Ingrid tells me. "I came here to New York. I forgot to mention that earlier. The New York part. The less said about *that*, the better. So it was off to Seattle, where I waitressed a bit. So awful. All those overcaffeinated assholes with their special orders. This summer I went to Virginia and got a job bartending at a beach bar. Then it was back here. Silly me thought it would pan out this time. It didn't. Like, at all. I had literally no idea where to go next when I saw the ad for the Bartholomew. The rest is history."

Just hearing about it all gives me something akin to jet lag. So many places in such a short amount of time.

"And how did you end up at the Bartholomew?" Ingrid sits up and pats the spot on the bench beside her. "Tell me everything."

I take a seat and say, "There's not too much to tell. I mean, other than losing my job and my boyfriend on the same day."

Ingrid displays the same stricken look she had when asking about stitches. "He died?"

"Just his heart," I say. "If he ever had one."

"Why do boys totally suck? I'm starting to think it might be ingrained in them. Like, they're taught at a young age that they can be assholes because most women will let them get away with it. That's the reason I left New York the first time. A stupid, stupid boy."

"He break your heart?"

"Crushed it," Ingrid says. "But now here I am."

"What about your family?" I say.

"I don't have any." Ingrid examines her fingernails, which are painted the same shade of blue as the tips of her hair. "I mean, yes, I had a family. Obviously. But they're gone now."

Hearing that word—*gone*—jolts my heart for a few swift beats.

"Mine, too," I say. "Now it's just me, even though I have a sister. Or had one. I don't really know anymore."

I don't intend to say it. The words simply slip out, unprompted. But I feel better now that they've been spoken. It seems right that Ingrid knows the two of us are in the same boat.

"She's missing?" she says.

"Yes."

"For how long?"

"Eight years." It's hard to believe it's been that long. The day it happened remains so vivid in my memory that it feels like only hours ago. "I was seventeen."

"What happened?"

"According to the police, Jane ran away. According to my father, she was abducted. And according to my mother, she was most likely murdered."

"What's your theory?" Ingrid says.

"I don't have one."

To me, it doesn't matter what actually happened to Jane. All I care about is the fact that she's gone.

And that, if her departure was intentional, she never bothered to say goodbye.

And that I'm mad at her and I miss her, and that her disappearance left a hole in my heart no one will be able to fill.

It was February when it happened. A cold, gray month of constant clouds but little snow. Jane had just finished her shift at McIndoe's, the local pharmacy that sat on the last thriving corner of our town's dour Main Street. She had worked as a cashier there since graduating from high school a year and a half earlier. Saving money for college, she told us, even though we all knew she wasn't the college type.

The last known person to have seen her was Mr. McIndoe himself, who watched from the store's front window as a black Volkswagen Beetle pulled up to the curb. Jane, who had been waiting beneath the pharmacy's blue-and-white-striped awning, hopped inside.

Willingly, Mr. McIndoe told anyone who would listen. There wasn't a struggle. Nor was the person behind the wheel a stranger to Jane. She gave the driver a little wave through the window before opening the passenger door.

Mr. McIndoe never got a good look at the person behind the wheel. He only saw the back of Jane's blue cashier's smock as she entered the car.

The Beetle drove away.

Jane was gone.

In the days following her disappearance, it became clear that none of Jane's friends drove a black Beetle. Nor did the friends of those friends. Whoever was behind the wheel was a stranger to everyone but Jane.

But black Beetles aren't uncommon. Motor vehicle records revealed there were thousands registered in the state of Pennsylvania alone. And Mr. McIndoe didn't think to make a note of the car's plates. He had no reason to. When asked by the police, he couldn't remember a single letter or number. A lot of people in town held that against poor Mr. McIndoe, as if his weak memory was the only thing keeping Jane from being found.

My parents were more forgiving. A few weeks after the disappearance, when it was looking more and more unlikely that Jane would be found, my father stopped by the store to tell Mr. McIndoe there were no hard feelings.

I didn't know this at the time. It was told to me a few years later, by Mr. McIndoe himself, at my parents' funeral.

That, incidentally, was the day I realized Jane would never return. Until then, I had kept a sliver of hope that, if she had simply run away, she might find her way back home. But my parents' deaths didn't go unnoticed. It made the news. And if Jane had heard about it, then I thought she'd surely come back to see them buried.

When she didn't, I stopped thinking she was still alive and quit expecting her return. In my mind, Jane had joined my parents in the grave.

"Even if she's still alive, I know she's never coming back," I say.

"I'm sorry," Ingrid says, adding nothing after that. I've saddened her into silence.

We spend the next few minutes doing nothing but looking out at the lake and feeling the breeze on our skin. It rustles the branches of the trees around us, their golden leaves quivering. Quite a few let go and drift to the ground like confetti.

"Do you really like it at the Bartholomew?" Ingrid eventually says. "Or were you just saying that because you think I do?"

"I like it," I say. "Don't you?"

"I'm not sure." Ingrid's voice has grown quiet and slow. A surprise, considering everything else has been spoken at full volume and thoroughbred speed. "I mean, it's nice there. Wonderful, really. But something about the place seems . . . off. You probably haven't felt it yet. But you will."

I think I already have. The wallpaper. Even though I know it's a pattern of flowers and not faces, something about it unnerves me. More than I care to admit.

"It *is* an old building," I say. "They always feel strange."

"But it's more than that." Ingrid pulls her knees to her chest, a pose that makes her look even more childlike. "It . . . it scares me."

"I don't think there's anything to be scared of," I say, even as that disconcerting article Chloe sent me creeps into my thoughts.

The Curse of the Bartholomew.

"Have you heard about some of the things that have happened there?" Ingrid says.

"I know the owner jumped from the roof."

"That's, like, the least of it. There's been worse. A lot worse."

Rather than elaborate, Ingrid turns around and looks past the treetops, to the Bartholomew looming beyond them. On the northern corner is George, looking down over Central Park West. Seeing him makes my chest swell with affection.

"Do you think it's possible for a place to be haunted, even if there aren't any ghosts there?" she says. "Because that's what it feels like to me. Like the Bartholomew is haunted by its history. Like all the bad stuff that's ever happened there has accumulated like dust and now floats in the air. And we're breathing it in, Jules."

"You don't have to stay there," I say. "I mean, if it makes you so uncomfortable."

Ingrid shrugs. "Where else am I going to go? Plus, I need the money."

There's no need for her to say anything else, a sign that she and I might have more in common than I first thought.

"I need the money, too," I say, in what is surely the understatement of the year. "I couldn't believe how much the job paid. When Leslie told me, I almost passed out."

"You and me both, sister. And I'm sorry for getting all creepy on you just now. I'm fine. The Bartholomew is fine. I think I'm just lonely, you know? I'm on board with all the rules except for the one about not having visitors. Sometimes it feels like solitary confinement. Especially since Erica left."

"Who's Erica?"

"Oh, Erica Mitchell. She was in 12A before you."

I give her a look. "You mean the owner? The woman who died?"

"Erica was one of us—an apartment sitter," Ingrid says. "She was nice. We hung out a little bit. But then she left a few days after I got there. Which was strange, because she told me she had at least two months left."

I'm surprised Leslie never mentioned there had been an apartment sitter in 12A before me. Not that she had any reason to. It's none of my business who lived there. But Leslie had made it sound like the owner had just died, leaving the place suddenly vacant.

"Are you're sure she was in 12A?"

"Positive," Ingrid says. "She sent me a welcome note down the dumbwaiter. When you arrived, I thought it would be fun to do the same thing."

"Did Erica tell you why she left early?"

"She didn't tell me anything. I only heard about it from Mrs. Evelyn a day after she left. I guess she found a new place to live or something. I was bummed because it was nice to have an upstairs neighbor to hang out with." Ingrid's face brightens. "Hey, I have an idea. We should do this every day. Lunch in the park until our time is up."

I hesitate, not because I don't like Ingrid. I do. Quite a bit. I'm just not sure I'll be able to handle her every day. This afternoon alone has left me exhausted.

"Please?" she says. "I've been so bored in that building and there's a great big park to explore. Think about it, Juju. That's what I've decided I'm going to call you, by the way."

"Duly noted," I say, unable to conceal a smile.

"I know it's not perfect. But your name is already kind of a nickname, so that leaves me with limited options. And I know, there's such a thing as bad juju. But there's also good juju. You're the good kind. Definitely."

I highly doubt that. I've had bad juju swirling around me for years.

"But as I was saying, Juju, think of all the fun things we could do." Ingrid begins to count the possibilities on her fingers. "Bird watching. Picnics. Boating. All the hot dogs we can eat. What do you say?"

She gives me an expectant look. Hopeful and needy all at once. And lonely. As lonely as I've felt the past two weeks. Other than Chloe, all my friends seem to have vanished. I don't know if this is my fault or theirs. Maybe I pushed them away without realizing it. Or maybe it's just a natural by-product of my downward spiral. That loss inevitably begets loss. First Jane, then my parents, then my job and Andrew. With each loss, more and more friends drifted away. Maybe Ingrid is the person who'll reverse that tide.

"Sure," I say. "I'm in."

Ingrid claps excitedly. "Then it's settled. We'll meet at noon in the lobby. Give me your phone."

I pull it from my pocket and hand it to her. Ingrid enters her phone number into my list of contacts, spelling her name in all caps. I do the same with her phone, typing my name in appropriately meek lowercase letters.

"I *will* be texting if you try to ditch me," she warns. "Now let's seal the deal with a selfie."

She holds up my phone and squeezes against me. Our faces fill the screen, Ingrid grinning madly and me looking slightly dazed by the encounter. Still, I smile, because for the first time in a long while, things don't seem so bad. I have a temporary place to live and money on the way and a new friend.

"Perfect," Ingrid says.

She taps the phone, and with a click, our pact is complete.

11

I spend my first night at the Bartholomew joyfully confounded over how I ended up here. The evening progresses in a sequence of impromptu steps—a happy dance being made up on the fly.

First, I climb the corkscrew steps to the bedroom, take off my shoes, and revel in the plush softness of the carpet. Walking on it feels like a foot massage.

I then fill the claw-foot tub in the master bathroom, pour in some pricey lavender-scented bubble bath I discover beneath the sink, and soak until my skin is rosy and my fingertips are pruned.

After the bath, I microwave a frozen pizza and plop it, sticky and steaming, onto a china plate so beautiful and delicate that merely touching it makes me nervous. I find a box of matches in the kitchen junk drawer and light the candles in the dining room. I eat sitting alone at one end of the absurd gangplank of a table as the flickering candlelight reflects off the windows.

When dinner is over, I open one of the bottles of wine Chloe gave me and plant myself at the sitting room window, drinking as night descends over Manhattan. In Central Park, the lamps along the paths pop into brightness, casting a ghostly halogen glow over the joggers, tourists, and couples that scurry by. I peer through the brass telescope by the window, spying on one such couple as they walk hand in hand. When they part, it's with reluctance, their fingers extended, reaching out for one final bit of contact.

I empty the glass of wine.

I refill it.

I try to pretend I'm not as lonely as I feel.

Time passes. Hours. When my third glass of wine has been emptied, I retreat to the kitchen and linger there, rinsing the wineglass and wiping down the already-clean countertops. I mull a fourth glass of wine but decide it's not a good idea. I don't want to get stumblingly drunk for the second time in two weeks, even though the occasions couldn't be more different. The first time—when Chloe took me out for those ill-advised margaritas—was a sad drunk, with me weeping between sips. But now I'm oddly happy, content, and, for what feels like the first time in forever, hopeful.

Without thinking, I grab the matches off the counter, swiping one against the box until a flame flares at its tip. I then hold my left hand several inches above the flame, feeling its warmth on my open palm. Something I used to do quite often but haven't tried in ages. There wasn't a need.

Now that old urge has returned, and I slowly lower my hand toward the flame. As I do, I think of my parents and Jane and Andrew and fire chewing the edges of photographs before working its way to the center.

The warmth on my palm soon gives way to heat, which is quickly usurped by pain.

But I don't move my hand. Not yet.

I need it to hurt a little more.

I stop only when my hand twitches against the pain. Self-preservation kicking in. I blow out the match, the flame gone in an instant, a few swirling fingers of smoke the only sign it was ever lit at all.

I light another, intent on repeating the process, when a strange noise rises from the dumbwaiter shaft. Although it's muffled slightly by the closed cupboard door, I can tell the sound isn't the dumbwaiter itself. There's no slow turn of the pulleys, no almost imperceptible creak.

This noise is different.

Louder. Sharper. Clearly human.

It sounds, I realize, like a scream rising up the dumbwaiter shaft from the apartment below.

Ingrid's apartment.

I stand frozen in the kitchen, my head cocked, listening intently for a second scream as the lit match burns its way toward my pinched thumb and forefinger. When it reaches them—a hot flash of pain—I yelp, drop the match, watch the flame wink out on the kitchen floor.

The burn spurs me into action. Sucking on my fingertip to dull the pain, I go from the kitchen to the hallway to the foyer. Soon I'm out of 12A, moving down the twelfth-floor hall on my way to the stairs.

The scream—or at least what I thought was a scream—replays in my head as I descend to the eleventh floor. Hearing it again in my memory tells me checking on Ingrid is the right thing to do. She could be hurt. She could be in danger. Or she could be none of those things, and I'm simply overreacting. It's happened before. All my experiences past the age of seventeen have taught me to be a worrier.

But something about that sound tells me I'm not overreacting. Ingrid had *screamed*. In my mind, there's nothing else it could have been. Especially now that I'm moving through the nocturnal silence of the Bartholomew. All is quiet. The elevator, sitting at one of the floors below, is still. In the stairwell, the only thing I hear is the whisper of my own cautious footfalls.

I check my watch when I reach the eleventh floor. One a.m. Another cause for concern. I can think of several bad reasons why a person would let out a single scream at this hour.

At the door to 11A, I pause before knocking, hoping I'll hear another, happier sound that will ease my mind. Ingrid talking loudly on the phone. Or laughter just on the other side of the door.

Instead, I hear nothing, which prompts me to knock. Gently, so as not to disturb anyone else on the floor.

"Ingrid?" I say. "It's Jules. Is everything okay?"

Seconds pass. Ten of them. Then twenty. I'm about to knock again when the door cracks open and Ingrid appears. She looks at me, eyes wide. I've surprised her.

"Jules, what are you doing here?"

"Checking on you." I pause, uncertain. "I thought I heard a scream."

Ingrid pauses, too. A seconds-long gap during which she forces a smile.

"It must have been your TV."

"I wasn't watching TV. It—"

I stop, unsure if I should be embarrassed or relieved or both. Instead, I'm even more concerned. Something about Ingrid seems *off*. Her voice is flat and reluctant—a far cry from the chatterbox she was in the park. I can see only half of her body through the gap in the door. She's dressed in the same clothes as earlier, her right hand shoved deep into the front pocket of her jeans, as if searching for something.

"It sounded like *you* screamed," I finally say. "I heard it and got worried."

"It wasn't me," Ingrid says.

"But I heard *something.*"

"Or you thought you did. Happens all the time. But I'm fine. Really."

Her face says otherwise. Besides her rictus grin, there's a dark glint in those widened eyes. They seem to burn with unspoken distress. She looks, I realize, afraid.

I move closer to the door, staring directly into her eyes. "Are you sure?" I whisper.

Ingrid blinks. "Yes. Everything's great."

"Then I'm sorry for bothering you," I say, backing away from the door and forcing my own smile.

"It's nice that you were so concerned," Ingrid says. "You're a sweetie."

"Are we still on for tomorrow?"

"Noon on the dot," Ingrid says. "Be there or be square."

I give her a wave and take a few steps down the hall. Ingrid doesn't wave back. Instead, she stares at me a second longer, her smile fading to a grim flat line just before she closes the door.

At this point, there's nothing left for me to do. If Ingrid says she's fine, then I need to believe her. If she says I didn't hear a scream, then I have to believe that, too. But as I climb two sets of steps—one to the twelfth floor, the other to the bedroom of 12A—I can't shake the feeling that Ingrid was lying.

NOW

Bernard leaves.

A doctor enters.

He's older. Snowy hair and strong jaw and tiny glasses perched in front of hazel eyes.

"Hello there. I'm Dr. Wagner." He pronounces it the German way, with a V instead of a W. All his words, in fact, are thickened by an accent that's at once rough and charming. "How are you feeling?"

I don't know enough about how I'm supposed to feel to give a proper answer. I vaguely remember being told I was hit by a car, which I guess should make me feel lucky I'm not dead.

"My head hurts," I say.

"I imagine it does," Dr. Wagner tells me. "You banged it up pretty good. But there's no concussion, which is fortunate."

I touch the bandage on my head again. Lightly this time. Just enough to feel the contour of my skull beneath the fabric.

"Your vitals are good, though. That's the most important thing," Dr. Wagner says. "You'll see some bruising from your thigh to your rib cage. But there are no broken bones, no internal damage. All things considered, it could have been much worse."

I try to nod, the motion stymied by the neck brace. It's heavy and hot. Patches of sweat have formed around my collarbone. I slide a finger behind the brace, trying to wick away some of the sweat.

"*You'll be able to take that off in a little while,*" Dr. Wagner says. "*It's really just a precaution. But for now, I need to ask you a few questions.*"

I say nothing. I'm not sure I'll be able to answer them. I'm not sure the doctor will believe me if I do. Still, I attempt another neck-brace shortened nod.

"*How much do you remember about the accident?*"

"*Not much,*" I say.

"*But you do remember it?*"

"*Yes.*"

At least, I think I do. I recall nothing concrete. Just snippets. I take a deep breath, trying to collect my thoughts. But they're an unruly, unreliable bunch. My skull feels like a snow globe recently shaken, swirling with important bits of information that have yet to land. And I can't grasp one, no matter how much I try.

I recall a screech of tires.

A blast of car horn.

A panicked yelp from somewhere behind me.

Pain. Darkness.

It's the same with my arrival in the hospital. I remember half of it. Bernard and his bright scrubs and being told the unfortunate news about the car. But I can't recall how I got here or what, exactly, I said when I arrived.

I chalk it up to painkillers. They've made me light-headed.

"*Let's try another question,*" Dr. Wagner says. "*A witness said he saw you burst out of the Bartholomew and run right into oncoming traffic. He said you didn't stop. Not even for a second.*"

That I remember.

Even though all I want to do is forget.

"*That's right,*" I say.

The doctor casts me a curious look from behind his tiny frames. "*That's not exactly normal behavior.*"

"*It wasn't exactly normal circumstances.*"

"*It sounds to me like you ran away.*"

"*No,*" I say. "*I escaped.*"

FOUR DAYS
EARLIER

12

I dream of my family.

My mother. My father. Jane, looking exactly like the last time I laid eyes on her. Forever nineteen.

The three of them walk through an abandoned Central Park, the only people there. It's night, and the park is pitch black, all its lamp-posts having been snuffed out. Yet my family gives off their own light, glowing a faint greenish gray as they traverse the park.

I watch their progress from the roof of the Bartholomew, where I sit next to George, one of his stone wings folded around me in a gargoyle semi-embrace.

Out in the park, my parents see me and wave. Jane calls to me, glowing hands cupped around her mouth. "You don't belong here!" she shouts.

As soon as the words reach me, George moves his wing.

No longer hugging.

Shoving.

The stone of his wing is cold against my back as he pushes me right off the roof. Soon I'm falling, twisting in mid-air as I plummet to the sidewalk below.

I wake with a scream in my throat, on the verge of setting it free. I gulp it back down, coughing a few times in the process. Then I sit up and eye George through the window.

"Not cool, dude," I say.

My words have barely faded in the cavernous bedroom when I hear something else.

A noise.

Coming from downstairs.

I'm not even sure it qualifies as a noise. It's more like a sensation. An ineffable feeling that I'm not alone. If someone asked me to describe it, I wouldn't know how. It's not an easily definable sound. Not footsteps. Not tapping. Not even a rustle, although that's the nearest comparison I can think of.

Motion.

That's what it sounds like.

Something moving through space and leaving a slight whisper in its wake.

I slip out of bed and creep to the top of the steps, leaning over them to hear more. I end up hearing nothing. But the feeling—that hair-raising sensation—persists. I am not alone in this apartment.

It occurs to me that it could be Leslie Evelyn, making an early-morning check of the apartment to see if I'm following the rules. I'm sure she has a set of keys to the place. Annoyed, I throw on my tattered terrycloth robe and whisk downstairs. She said nothing about apartment checks. I wouldn't have agreed to that.

Who am I kidding? For twelve grand, I'd agree to almost anything.

But when I get downstairs, I find the apartment empty. The door is locked and deadbolted and the chain remains undisturbed. The noise or presence or whatever the hell you want to call it was just my imagination. The foggy remnants of my nightmare.

Exhausted but too jumpy to go back to sleep, I head to the kitchen to make coffee. Instead of a quick and easy Keurig machine, the apartment has such a high-tech, absurdly complex coffeemaker that I spend several groggy minutes just turning it on. It takes so long that my body is aching for caffeine by the time coffee starts dripping into the pot.

As it brews, I go back upstairs and shower, trying to shake off the nightmare. God, what a strange, awful dream.

There have been others, of course. Not long after my parents died. Nightmares about burning beds and thick smoke and internal organs blackened by illness. Some were so wretched that Chloe had to shake me awake because my cries threatened to wake the entire dorm. But none had ever felt so true, so real. Part of me worries that if I look out the window into Central Park, my family will still be there, glowing their way across Bow Bridge.

So I spend the morning looking at clocks.

The digital alarm clock in the bedroom as I dress for the day.

The clock on the microwave as I pour the coffee that has at long last brewed.

The grandfather clock as I drink said coffee in the sitting room, counting the pairs of eyes in the wallpaper. My tally stands at sixty-four when the clock bongs out the hour. My heart sinks. It's only nine o'clock.

When I was laid off, I was presented with a folder of resources. Job-hunting tips and career counselors and information about student loans in case I wanted to go back to school. Everything I needed to face life as someone who was officially unemployed.

What wasn't in that folder was advice on what to do with all that sudden free time. Because here's something else no one understands unless they've been there: unemployment is boring. Soul-crushingly so.

People have no idea how much of their day is taken up by the act of going to work. The getting ready. The commute there. The eight hours at your desk. The commute home. So much time automatically occupied. Take them away and there's nothing but empty hours stretching before you, waiting to be filled.

Kill time before it kills you.

My father told me that, not long after my mother got sick and he lost his job. It was the peak of his short-lived birdhouse phase, when he spent hours in the garage building them for no discernible purpose. When I asked him why he was doing it, he looked up from the pine plank he had been painting and said, "Because I need one thing in my life I can control."

It's a sentiment that makes sense only in hindsight. At age nineteen, I was confused. As an unemployed adult, I get it. Although finding something to control is hard when my whole existence feels as though it's been hit by a hurricane.

So I kill time by doing another job search, finding no openings I haven't seen before. I do a little light cleaning, even though nothing needs it. I empty trash cans that have hardly anything in them and take the bag to the garbage chute, located in a discreet alcove near the stairwell. I drop the bag inside and listen to it slide all the way down to the basement, where it lands with a soft thud.

Five more seconds wasted.

When the grandfather clock announces noon's arrival, I leave the apartment, spotting no one new on the trip to the lobby. Just the usual suspects coming and going. Mr. Leonard and his nurse struggling up the steps and Marianne Duncan and Rufus in the lobby itself, returning from their walk. Today, Marianne wears a seafoam green cape with a matching turban. Rufus sports a red handkerchief.

"Hello, darling," Marianne says, adjusting her sunglasses as she swans toward the elevator. "It's chilly out there today. Isn't it, Rufus?"

The dog barks in agreement.

Since Ingrid's not there yet, I go to the mailboxes and look to see if anything's been sent to 12A. It hasn't.

I close the mailbox and check my watch.

Five minutes past noon.

Ingrid is late.

When my phone rings in my pocket, I reach for it immediately, thinking it might be her. My stomach tightens when I see who's really calling.

Andrew.

I ignore the call. A second later, a text arrives.

Please call me.

It's followed by a second one.

Can we just talk?

Then a third.

Please????????

I don't reply. Andrew doesn't deserve one. Just like he didn't deserve me.

Only now do I understand that we never should have started dating in the first place. We had nothing in common. But Chloe had just started seeing Paul, and I was feeling lonely. Suddenly there was Andrew, the cute janitor I always saw emptying the office trash as I left work each day. Soon I started saying goodbye to him on my way out. Which led to small talk by the elevator. Which led to conversations that seemed to grow longer with each passing day.

He seemed friendly and smart and just a little bit shy. Plus, his dimples grew more pronounced when he smiled. And he always seemed to be smiling whenever I was around.

Eventually, he asked me out on a date. I accepted. A natural progression ensued. More dates. Sex. More sex. Moving in together. An unspoken understanding that this was how things were going to be from here on out.

I couldn't have been more wrong.

In the days after I left, my feelings toward Andrew veered from hurt to rage to a sense of feeling abandoned yet again. I hated him for cheating on me. I hated myself for trusting him. After that came another, worse emotion—rejection. Why wasn't I enough for him? Why wasn't I enough for anyone? Why do all the people I love keep leaving me?

I take another glance at my phone. Ingrid is now ten minutes late.

It occurs to me that maybe I got our meeting location mixed up and that we were supposed to meet in Central Park instead. I picture Ingrid there now, flirting with one of the buskers at the Imagine mosaic and thinking I had ditched her.

I send a text. Were we supposed to meet in the park?

When two minutes pass without a response, I decide to walk to the park and see. It seems more sensible than texting again. On my way out of the Bartholomew, I look for Charlie to ask if he saw Ingrid leave the building. Instead, I find one of the other doormen—a smiling older man whose name I've yet to learn. He tells me Charlie worked the night shift and called in sick for his shift later today.

"Family emergency," he says. "Something to do with his daughter."

I thank him and move on, crossing to the park side of the street. It's more overcast than yesterday, with a slight chill that foreshadows winter's rapid approach. Definitely not Heather weather.

Soon I'm in Strawberry Fields, where two buskers strum dueling versions of the song on opposite sides of the Imagine mosaic. Both have gained a few easy-to-please onlookers. Ingrid isn't among them.

I check my phone again. Still nothing.

I move on, heading toward the lake and the bench we occupied yesterday. I take a seat and send another text.

I'm in the park now. Same bench as yesterday.

When five more minutes go by without a reply from Ingrid, I send a third text.

Is everything OK?

I realize how overly concerned it sounds. But something about the situation doesn't sit right with me. I think about last night—the scream rising from her apartment, the uncomfortable delay between my knocks and her opening the door, the dark glint in her eyes that seemed to signal something was wrong.

I tell myself I shouldn't be worried.

Yet I am.

I have Jane's disappearance to thank for that. The day it happened is notable for how unconcerned we all were at first. She was nineteen and restless and prone to wandering off on her own unannounced. Sometimes she'd skip dinner without notice and not return until after midnight, smelling of beer and cigarettes consumed in the basement of one friend or another.

When she failed to come home that night, we all assumed that was the case. We ate dinner without her. We watched some stupid movie about aliens on TV. When my parents went to bed, I stayed up to reread my favorite parts of *Heart of a Dreamer.* It was, all things considered, a typical night at the Larsen home.

It wasn't until dawn the next morning that we realized something was amiss. My father woke up to go to the bathroom. On his way there, he noticed Jane's bedroom door was still ajar, the room empty, her bed untouched. He woke up my mother and me, asking if we'd heard Jane come home the night before. We hadn't. After several rounds of awkward, early-morning phone calls to her friends, we finally understood the terrible truth of the situation.

Jane was missing.

In fact, she'd been missing since the previous afternoon, and none of us had immediately thought to check on her. When I look back on our initial lack of concern, I can't help but wonder if Jane would still be here if we had acted sooner or been the least bit worried right away.

Now I worry too much. In college, I drove Chloe nuts by insisting she check in with me throughout the day. On the rare times when she didn't, a twinge of anxiety would form in my gut. I feel one there now about Ingrid—a tiny acorn of worry. It expands slightly when I check my phone again and see that it's now quarter to one.

I leave the park, worry tugging me back to the Bartholomew. On my way, I send another text simply asking Ingrid to please respond. Again, I know I'm overreacting. I also don't care.

Inside the building, I pass Dylan, the other apartment sitter. He's dressed for a jog in the park. Sweats. Sneakers. Electric guitar screeching from his earbuds. I enter the elevator he just vacated and almost press the top button but instead hit the one for the eleventh floor. I tell myself it won't hurt to check on Ingrid. I even come up with reasons for why she was a no-show. Maybe she's sick and not checking her phone. Maybe the battery died and she's impatiently waiting for it to charge.

Or maybe—just maybe—my instincts about last night are right and Ingrid was in some kind of trouble but was too scared to talk about it. I close my eyes and recall the flatness of her voice, that plastered-on smile, the way that smile vanished just before she shut the door.

Once I'm standing outside 11A, I check my phone one last time for a reply from Ingrid. After seeing that there isn't one, I knock on the door. Two gentle raps. As if this is a casual drop-in and not the product of worry sprouting upward from the pit of my stomach.

The door swings open.

Just beyond it stands Leslie Evelyn in another of her Chanel suits. One as red as the wallpaper in 12A. There's a harried look on her face. A strand of hair has escaped her updo and now curls down her forehead.

"Jules," she says, not quite hiding her surprise to see me here. "How's your arm?"

I absently touch the bandage hidden under my jacket and blouse. The cut's so inconsequential that I barely notice it.

"It's fine," I say, glancing over her shoulder into the apartment itself. "Is Ingrid here?"

"She's not," Leslie says with a noticeable sigh.

"Do you know where she is?"

"I don't, sweetie. I'm sorry."

"But doesn't she live here?"

"She did."

I notice her use of the past tense, and my brow furrows.

"She doesn't anymore?" I say.

"That's correct," Leslie says with certainty. "Ingrid is gone."

13

Jane is gone.

That was how my father put it a week after my sister failed to come home. It was almost midnight, and the two of us were alone in the kitchen, my mother having taken to her bed hours earlier. By this point the black Beetle was common knowledge, the police had talked to Jane's friends, and her picture had appeared on every telephone pole and storefront in the county. My father took a sip of the black coffee he'd been mainlining for days and said, simply and sadly, "Jane is gone."

I remember feeling more confused than sad. I still held out hope that Jane would return. At that moment, what I couldn't understand was why she ever left in the first place. I feel that same confusion now as I watch Leslie swipe the rogue curl of hair back into place.

"Gone? She's no longer living here?"

"She is not," Leslie says with a disdainful sniff.

I think of the rules. Ingrid must have broken one. A big one. It's the only reason I can think of for her sudden, shocking departure.

"Did she do something wrong?"

"Not that I'm aware of," Leslie says. "She wasn't kicked out, if that's what you mean."

"But Ingrid told me she'd be here for another ten weeks."

"She was supposed to be."

I'm hit with another kick of confusion. None of this makes sense. "She just *left*?"

"That's right," Leslie tells me. "Swiftly and without notice, I might add."

"Ingrid didn't even tell you she was leaving?"

"She did not. And I really would have appreciated some advance notice. Instead, she just slipped out in the middle of the night."

"Did anyone see her leave? Who was the doorman on duty?"

"That would be Charlie," Leslie says. "But he didn't see her go."

"Why not?"

"He was in the basement at the time. The security camera down there wasn't working properly, so he left his station to try to fix it. When he returned, he found the keys for 11A right in the middle of the lobby. That's where Ingrid dropped them on her way out."

"What time was this?"

"I'm not sure. You'd have to ask Charlie."

"Are you certain she's gone?" I say, thinking out loud. "There's a chance she accidentally dropped the keys in the lobby and didn't notice. Maybe there was an emergency with one of her friends and she had to leave in a hurry. She could be on her way back here right now."

Although my theory is possible, it's also improbable. And none of it explains why Ingrid hasn't texted me back.

It's clear Leslie thinks the same thing. She leans against the doorframe and gives me a look brimming with pity. I don't mind. My parents gave me similar looks after Jane vanished and I'd wake them up with far-fetched theories about where she was and why I was certain she'd return. At seventeen, I was the queen of magical thinking.

"That seems unlikely, don't you think?"

"It does," I say. "But so does Ingrid leaving in the middle of the night without telling anyone."

Leslie tilts her head, the unruly curl on the verge of breaking free again. "Why are you so interested in Ingrid?"

I could give her several reasons, all of them true. That Ingrid was friendly and fun and I liked being around her. That she reminded me of Jane. That it was a refreshing change of pace to know someone other than Chloe who actually wanted to be around me.

Instead, I tell Leslie the biggest cause of my concern.

"I thought I heard a scream last night."

Leslie gives an exaggerated blink of surprise. "In 11A?"

"Yes."

"When?"

"Around one a.m. I came down to check on Ingrid, but she told me I was just hearing things."

"None of the other residents reported hearing anything like that," Leslie says. "Are you sure it was a scream you heard?"

"I-I don't know?"

It shouldn't be a question. I either heard a scream or I didn't. Yet that curl of uncertainty at the end of my sentence means something. It tells me, in its own frustrating way, that maybe what I heard was indeed all in my head.

But then why was Ingrid acting so strangely when she came to the door?

"I'll ask around to see if anyone else heard something," Leslie says. "That kind of thing would be noticed in a building as quiet as this one."

"I'm just worried about her," I say, trying to clarify my concern.

"She left, sweetie," Leslie says dismissively. "Like a thief in the night. Which was my initial thought, by the way. That she was a thief. That's why I'm here. I thought for sure I'd find this place completely cleaned out. But everything is still here. Ingrid took only her belongings."

"And she didn't leave anything behind? Nothing to suggest she'll be back? Or where she went?"

"Not to my knowledge." Leslie steps away from the door. "You're welcome to come in and look."

Just beyond the open doorway I see a hallway and sitting room with a view nearly identical to the one in 12A. The room is neat, modern. No red wallpaper with prying eyes here. Just cream-colored walls enhanced with modern art and furnishings straight out of a Crate & Barrel catalog. In fact, the whole apartment has the look of a display. Furnished but uninhabited.

"Everything's the way it was when Ingrid moved in," Leslie says. "So if she did leave anything behind, it would be in the basement storage unit. I haven't checked there yet because it seems that Ingrid lost the key to it. It's missing from the key ring Charlie found in the lobby."

Which means Ingrid probably never used it. I've certainly had no need to visit 12A's storage unit. All my belongings are in the bedroom closet, which is big enough to hold everything I've ever possessed and still have room for more.

Leslie touches my shoulder and says, "I wouldn't be too worried about Ingrid. I'm sure there's a good reason why she left. And, quite frankly, I'd love to hear it."

As would I. Because, right now, nothing about this makes sense. A renewed sense of worry clings to me as I climb the stairs to the twelfth floor. Back inside 12A, I crash on the sitting room sofa, my brain clouded by confusion. Why would Ingrid want to leave the Bartholomew? Why would anyone?

I glance outside, where fog is quickly settling over the city. The mist skims low across Central Park, making the treetops appear to float like clouds. It's beautiful, in a melancholy way. A view few people can afford. Those who can pay millions for the privilege.

Ingrid had this exact same view, yet she was getting paid for it. Which poses a bigger question: Why did she suddenly abandon the prospect of free rent and twelve thousand dollars? Although she had reservations about the Bartholomew, Ingrid also made it clear that, just like me, she had no money and nowhere else to go. But when she left the Bartholomew, she also left behind an additional ten thousand dollars. Short of a dire emergency, I can't fathom turning down that much cash.

Something about Ingrid's situation had suddenly changed. Quite literally overnight.

I dig my phone from my jacket pocket. Still no word from Ingrid. When I scroll through the texts I sent her, I see that she hasn't read a single one.

Rather than text again, I decide to call, tapping her all-caps name and listening as the call goes straight to voicemail.

"Hi there! Sorry I can't come to the phone right now. Please leave a message after the beep, and I'll call back as soon as I can." A pause. "Oh, this is Ingrid, by the way. In case you didn't already know that."

At last, a beep arrives.

"Hey, Ingrid," I say, trying to keep my tone pitched somewhere between casual and concerned. "It's Jules. From the Bartholomew. Leslie just told me you moved out during the night. Is, um, everything okay? Call or text to let me know."

I end the call and stare at the phone, unsure of what to do next.

Nothing.

That's what Chloe would say. She'd tell me that Ingrid's a stranger. That her business is her own. That I need to focus on getting a job, getting some money saved up, getting my life back in order.

She'd be right on all counts.

I *do* need to find a job. And earn money. And start rebuilding my existence piece by piece.

Yet that acorn of worry I felt earlier is now a full-fledged sapling, with leaf-studded branches stretching into my limbs. Making it grow is the weirdness of last night. That noise that sounded like a scream. Ingrid's unnatural calm. The way she tried to downplay my concern.

I'm fine. Really.

I wasn't convinced last night, and I'm definitely not convinced now. The only thing that will assuage my worry is hearing from Ingrid herself. But in order to do that, I need to first find out where she went.

When Jane went missing, the police gave us a list of steps we needed to follow to make it easier to locate her. Not that it did any good. I'm hoping I have more luck now as I go over those same steps in an attempt to find Ingrid.

Step one: Assess the situation.

Simple. Ingrid left in the middle of the night without telling anyone.

Step two: Think of reasons she might have left.

I'd like to think she left for a positive reason. Something happy. She suddenly found a job or won the lottery or was swept off her feet by one of the buskers in Central Park. But it's not in my nature to be optimistic. Not anymore.

Step three: Think of places she might have gone.

A nonstarter. She could have gone literally anywhere.

Step four: Think of people she might have contacted since going missing.

This one's more doable, thanks to social media. If Ingrid is as much of an oversharer online as she is in real life, all it will take to ease my mind is one status update saying she's back in Boston or got a bartending gig in Alaska. Anything but the unknown will suffice.

I grab my laptop and start searching for Ingrid's social media accounts, beginning with Facebook. That turns out to be more difficult than I expect. I haven't used it in so long that it takes me several minutes and two wrong guesses before I remember my password.

When I finally log in, the first thing I see is my outdated profile pic. A vacation photo. Andrew and me at Disney World. We stand on Main Street, my arm around his waist and his over my shoulder while Cinderella's castle rises behind us.

The picture startles me, mostly because the original was among the photos I set on fire before I moved out. Seeing it again feels like spotting a ghost. It was the only vacation the two of us took together, and even then we couldn't really afford it. But at the time I thought it would be worth the expense. We look happy in the photo. We *were* happy. At least I was. But maybe Andrew was already thinking about finding someone else to screw. Perhaps he already had and I was just blissfully ignorant.

I delete the image and replace it with a blank avatar. That seems like a more appropriate reflection of my current state.

Once that's out of the way, I do a search for Ingrid Gallagher, trying to remember all the places she told me she's lived in the past two years. I narrow the search to New York, Seattle, and Boston, finding two Ingrid Gallaghers. Neither is the Ingrid I'm looking for.

I move on to Twitter, with similar results. Lots of Ingrid Gallaghers. None resemble the one I know.

Next up is Instagram, which I open using the app on my phone.

At last, success.

Ingrid Gallagher has an account.

Her hair is all blue in her profile picture. A too-bright shade that reminds me of cotton candy.

But then I see the photos she's posted and my heart sinks. They're a generic lot. Dimly lit food pictures and oddly angled selfies. The most recent picture is a selfie Ingrid took in Central Park, a bit of the Bartholomew visible over her left shoulder.

It was taken two days ago, probably around the same time I was getting a tour of 12A. Maybe Ingrid was one of the people I spotted in the park during that first, flushed look out the sitting room window. There's even a chance I'm visible in the photo—a dim figure gazing out a twelfth-floor window of the Bartholomew.

Ingrid kept the caption simple—three heart emojis, pink and throbbing.

The photo received fifteen likes and one comment from someone named Zeke, who wrote, cant believe ur back in NYC and havent hit me up.

Although Ingrid never responded, it's heartening to see she knows at least one other person in the city. Maybe she's with him now. I take a closer look at Zeke's profile picture. The Neff cap, scraggly beard, and scuffed skateboard raised conspicuously into the frame tell me all I need to know about the guy.

That impression is reinforced when I click on his own photo gallery. Most of the pictures are selfies. Him shirtless in the bathroom mirror. Him shirtless at Jones Beach. Him shirtless on the street, his jeans slung low enough to show off his boxer shorts. He even took a shirtless picture this morning, snapped in bed as a woman slept next to him. All that can be seen of her is a patch of bare shoulder and long hair spread over the pillowcase.

Blond. No trace of blue. Definitely not Ingrid.

Still, I send Zeke a message just in case she decided to, in his words, hit him up.

> Hi. I'm a neighbor of Ingrid's. I'm trying to get in touch with her. Have you heard from her recently? If not, do you have any idea where she might be? I'm worried about her.

I leave my name. I leave my number. I ask him to call.

After that, it's back to Ingrid's Instagram account, where I hope her older pictures might offer clues about where she could have gone. The photo before the park selfie is a close-up of her fingernails, which had been painted bright green. It was taken five days ago. The caption quotes Sally Bowles from *Cabaret*.

> "If I should paint my fingernails green, and it just so happens I do paint them green, well, if anyone should ask me why, I say: 'I think it's pretty!'"

Seven likes. No responses.

It's the picture before it that truly grabs my attention. Taken eight days ago, it's another close-up of Ingrid's hand. The fingernails are light pink this time. The color of a ripe peach. Her hand rests atop a book. Jutting from its top is the red tassel of a bookmark. Glimpsed in the spaces between her spread fingers is a familiar image—George perched at the corner of the Bartholomew. In addition to that are scraps of a familiar font spelling out an equally familiar title.

Heart of a Dreamer.

The caption Ingrid included is even more surprising.

I met the author!

I've also met the author, and she wasn't too happy about it. Still, this photo seems to suggest that Greta and Ingrid were, if not friends, then at least acquaintances. Which means there's a small chance she might know where Ingrid went.

With a sigh, I grab the last bottle of wine Chloe gave me, leave the apartment, and make my way down the hall to the stairwell.

I'm going to risk breaking another Bartholomew rule and see Greta Manville, no matter how much it's sure to annoy her.

14

My initial knock on the door to 10A is so tentative I can barely hear it over the sound of my thudding heart. So I rap again, using more force. Behind the door, footsteps creak over the floorboards and someone shouts, "I fucking heard you the first time."

When the door finally opens, it's only a crack. Greta Manville peers through it with eyes narrowed to slits. "You again," she says.

I raise the wine bottle. "I brought you something."

The door opens wide enough for me to see her outfit of black slacks and a gray sweater. On her feet are pink slippers. The left one taps with impatience as she eyes the bottle.

"It's an apology gift," I say. "For bothering you in the lobby yesterday. And right now. And for any future times I might do it."

Greta takes the bottle and checks the label. It must be a decent vintage, because she doesn't grimace. I'll need to thank Chloe for not giving me our usual Two-Buck Chuck as a going-away present. Especially now that Greta has drifted away from the door, leaving it open still wider. I pause on the threshold, moving only after her voice drifts out the gaping door.

"You can come in, or you can leave. It makes no difference to me."

I decide to enter, the movement prompting a nod from Greta. She turns and moves wordlessly down the hall. I follow, sneaking glances at the apartment's layout, which is far different from mine. The rooms here are smaller, but there are more of them. A backward look down the hall reveals several doors leading to what I assume are an office, a bedroom, maybe a library.

Although, quite honestly, the entire apartment could be considered a library. Books are everywhere. Filling the shelves of the room opposite the door. Sitting on end tables. Rising from the floor in tilted, towering stacks. There's even a book in the kitchen—a Margaret Atwood paperback splayed facedown on the counter.

"Who are you again?" Greta says as she retrieves a corkscrew from a drawer in the kitchen's marble-topped island. "There are so many of you apartment sitters coming and going that I can't keep track."

"Jules," I say.

"That's right. Jules. And my book is your favorite and so on and so forth."

Greta caps the comment with a mighty pull of the cork. She then fetches a single wineglass, filling it halfway before handing it to me.

"Cheers," she says.

"You're not having any?"

"Sadly, I'm not allowed. Doctor's orders."

"I'm sorry," I say. "I didn't know."

"You couldn't have," Greta says. "Now quit apologizing and drink."

I take an obligatory sip, mindful about not drinking too much too fast. It could easily happen, considering how anxious I am about talking too much, asking too many questions, annoying Greta more than I already have. I take another sip, this time to calm my nerves.

"Tell me, Jules," Greta says, "why did you really stop by?"

I look up from my glass. "Do I need an ulterior motive?"

"Not necessarily. But I suspect you have one. In my experience, people don't arrive bearing gifts unless they want something. A signed copy of their favorite book, for instance."

"I didn't bring my copy."

"A missed opportunity there, wouldn't you say?"

"But you're right. I came here for a reason." I pause to fortify myself with more wine. "I came here to ask you about Ingrid Gallagher."

"Who?" Greta asks.

"She's an apartment sitter. In the unit above you. She left last night. In the middle of the night, actually. And no one knows where she went. And since she mentioned on Instagram that she met you, I thought that, possibly, the two of you were friends and you might know."

Greta gives me a tilted-head gaze, curiosity brightening her blue eyes. "My dear, I didn't understand a single word you just said."

"So you don't know Ingrid?"

"Are you referring to that girl with the ghastly colored hair?"

"Yes."

"I met her twice," Greta says. "Which doesn't qualify as *knowing* someone. Leslie first introduced us as I was passing through the lobby. And by *introduce*, I mean *accost*. I think our Mrs. Evelyn was trying to impress the girl into staying here."

"When was this?"

"Two weeks ago or so, I believe."

This likely would have been during Ingrid's interview tour. The dates match how long she told me she'd been here.

"When was the second time?"

"Two days ago. She came by to see me." Greta gestures to the open bottle on the counter. "*Without* wine. So you have her beat in that respect."

"What was *her* ulterior motive?"

"Now you're catching on," Greta says with an approving nod. "She wanted to ask me about the Bartholomew, seeing how I wrote a book about it. She was curious about some of the things that have happened here."

I lean forward, my elbows on the island counter. "What kind of things?"

"The building's allegedly sordid past. I told her it was ancient history and that if she was looking for gossip, she should try the internet. I don't use it myself, but I hear it's rife with that sort of thing."

"That was it?" I say.

"A two-minute conversation at best."

"And you haven't talked to her since?"

"I have not."

"Are you sure?"

Just like that, Greta's expression darkens again. Her bright-eyed curiosity was like a single ray of sunlight peeking through two storm clouds—fleeting and misleading.

"I'm old, dear," she says. "Not senile."

Chastened, I return to my wine. Murmuring into the glass, I say, "I didn't mean to imply that. I'm just trying to find her."

"She's missing?"

"Maybe." Again, the vagueness of my reply infuriates me. I try to rectify that by adding, "I've been trying to reach her all day. She hasn't responded. And the way she left, well, it concerns me."

"Why?" Greta says. "She's free to come and go as she pleases, isn't she? Just like you are. You're apartment sitters. Not prisoners."

"It's just— You didn't hear anything unusual last night, did you? Like a strange noise coming from the apartment above you?"

"What kind of noise are you referring to?"

A scream. That's what I'm referring to. I don't specifically say it because I want Greta to mention it unprompted. If she does, then I'll know it wasn't just me. That the scream really happened.

"Anything out of the ordinary," I say.

"I didn't," Greta replies. "Although I suspect *you* heard something."

"I thought I did."

"But now?"

"Now I think I imagined it."

Only I don't know if that's possible. Sure, people can hear things that aren't really there, especially the first night in a new place. Footsteps on the stairs. Raps on the window. I heard something myself when I woke up—that slithery non-noise. But people don't imagine random, solitary screams.

"I was awake most of the night," Greta says. "Insomnia. The older I get, the less sleep I require. A blessing and a curse, if you ask me. So if there had been a strange noise coming from upstairs, I would have heard it. As for your friend—"

She slaps her palm against the countertop, the motion sudden, unsettling.

I set down my glass. "Mrs. Manville?"

Greta closes her eyes as her face, already pale, turns ashen. Her whole body tilts. First slowly, then gaining steam until she's leaning at a precarious angle. I rush to her side, keeping her upright while searching for a chair. I find one near the door to the dining room and gently guide her into it.

The movement jostles her back into consciousness. Her head snaps to attention, and life returns to her eyes. She clamps a hand around my wrist, the knuckles knobby with age, purple veins visible beneath tissue-paper skin.

"Dear me," she says, slightly dazed. "Well, that was embarrassing."

I hover over her, not sure what else to do. My body's gained a tremor that runs from head to heel. "Do you need a doctor? I can fetch Dr. Nick."

"I'm not in that dire of shape," she says. "Really, it's nothing. I sometimes get spells."

"Fainting spells?"

"I call them sudden sleeps, because that's what they feel like. An instant slipping away. But then I roar back to life and it's like nothing's happened. Never get old, Jules. It's horrible. No one tells you that until it's too fucking late."

That's when I know it's okay to stop hovering. She's back to her normal, ornery self. Still trembling, I return to the kitchen counter and my glass of wine. No sip this time. I gulp.

"If you'd like, you may ask me one question about that book," Greta says. "You've earned it."

Only one? I have a hundred. But I noticed the pronoun she used. Not *my* book. Or *the* book. It tells me she'd rather talk about anything other than *Heart of a Dreamer*.

"Why did you stop writing?"

"The short answer is because I'm lazy. And unmotivated. Also, I have no financial need to write. My family was wealthy. The book made me wealthier. Even today, it generates enough income to allow me to live very comfortably."

"In the Bartholomew, no less," I say. "Have you lived here long?"

"Are you asking if I lived here when I wrote *Heart of a Dreamer*?"

That's exactly what I'm asking. Being read so easily makes me take another gulp of wine.

"The answer to your *real*, unsolicited question is yes," Greta says. "I was living at the Bartholomew when I wrote it."

"In this apartment?"

Greta gives a quick shake of her head. "Elsewhere."

"Is the book autobiographical?"

"More like wishful thinking," Greta replies. "Unlike Ginny, it was my parents' apartment. I grew up there, moved out after getting married, and moved back in following my divorce. I was aimless and bitter and suddenly had a lot of time on my hands. I decided to fill it by writing what I wished my life to be like. When the book was finished, I moved out again."

"Why?" I ask, still unable to comprehend why anyone would choose to leave the Bartholomew.

"Why does anyone move, really?" Greta muses. "I needed a change of view. Besides, one gets tired of living with their parents. Isn't that why everyone eventually leaves the nest?"

Most people, yes. But not me. I wasn't given a choice.

"Because of how and when the book was written, is that why you hate it so much?"

Greta looks up, affronted. "Who says I hate it?"

"I just assumed you did."

"No, you *surmised*," Greta says. "There's a difference. As for the book, I don't hate it as much as I find myself disappointed by it."

"But it brought you so much success. And it's touched so many people."

"I'm a very different woman now than when I wrote it. Think back to when you were younger. Think about your tastes and behavior and habits. You've changed since then. Evolved. We all do. Which means there are aspects of that younger version of yourself that you'd probably detest now."

I nod, thinking of my mother and store-brand cereal.

"When I wrote that book, I was so in need of fantasy that I failed to do the one thing all good writers are supposed to do—tell the truth," Greta says. "I was a liar, and that book is my biggest lie."

I down the rest of the wine, preparing myself for something I never thought I'd have to do—defend a book to its own author.

"You're forgetting that readers need fantasy, too," I say. "My sister and I used to lie on her bed, reading *Heart of a Dreamer* and picturing ourselves in Ginny's shoes. The book showed us there was life outside our tiny, dying town. The book gave us hope. Even now, after all that hope has been stripped away, I still love *Heart of a Dreamer* and I remain grateful that you wrote it. Sure, the Manhattan in the book doesn't exist in real life. And no, few people in this city end up getting the happy ending Ginny received. But fiction can be an escape, which is why we need idealized versions of New York City. It balances out the crowded, gritty, heartbreaking real thing."

"But what about the real world?" Greta says.

"That sister I mentioned? She disappeared when I was seventeen." I know I should stop talking. But now that the wine has loosened my tongue, I find that I can't. "My parents died when I was nineteen. So, frankly, I've had enough of the real world."

Greta lifts her hand, places her palm to her cheek, and spends a good ten seconds sizing me up. Caught in her stare, I freeze, embarrassed that I've said too much.

"You strike me as a gentle soul," she says.

I've never thought of myself as gentle. Fragile is more like it. Prone to bruising.

"I don't know. I guess I am."

"Then you need to be careful," she says. "This place isn't kind to gentle souls. It chews them up and spits them out."

"Do you mean New York or the Bartholomew?"

Greta keeps staring. "Both," she says.

15

Greta's words stay with me as I climb the stairs from the tenth floor to the twelfth. Not just the part about being chewed up and spit out but the reason Ingrid came to see her. Why would Ingrid be asking about the Bartholomew and its past? Or *allegedly* sordid past, as Greta had deemed it.

It . . . it scares me.

That's what Ingrid had said about the Bartholomew. And I believed her. That little stutter seemed to me like a confession on the verge of being released. As if Ingrid was trying to tell me something she wasn't sure could be said out loud. I dismissed it only because she did, chalking it up to loneliness and her free spirit chafing against the Bartholomew's many rules.

Now I suspect she was more frightened than she let on.

Because departing without warning in the middle of the night isn't how people leave a place when they don't think they're in danger.

It's how they leave when they're terrified.

Stop.

Think.

Assess the situation.

Which is that it doesn't really matter why Ingrid left the Bartholomew. Right now, my concern is finding out where she is and knowing that she's safe. Because I have a worrisome feeling she's not. Call it a post-Jane hunch.

I pause on the eleventh-floor landing to check my phone. Ingrid still hasn't read my texts. Which means she also likely hasn't listened to the voicemail I left. I was hoping she would have responded by now, even if it was just to tell me to stop bothering her. That would be better than nothing.

I shove the phone back into my pocket and am about to continue up the steps when Dylan, the Bartholomew's other apartment sitter, leaves 11B. He's dressed similarly to yesterday. Same baggy jeans. Same black discs in his ears. The only thing that's changed is his T-shirt. Today it's Nirvana.

My presence on his floor clearly surprises him. His eyes widen behind a veil of floppy black hair.

"Hey," he says. "You lost?"

"Trying to find someone, actually," I say. "Did you know Ingrid at all?"

"Not really."

I find that surprising, considering how outgoing Ingrid seems to be. The likely scenario is that Ingrid didn't think Dylan was worth the effort. He's clearly not a fan of small talk. Waiting for the elevator, he stands with his right leg bent at the knee, flexing slightly, like a runner preparing to sprint.

"Not at all? You were neighbors. You never hung out?"

"If saying hi to each other in the elevator means hanging out, then, sure, we hung out. Otherwise, no. Why do you want to know?"

"Because she moved out and I'm trying to reach her."

Dylan's eyes go even wider.

"Ingrid's gone? Since when?"

"Sometime last night," I say. "I was hoping she might have told you she was planning to leave."

"Like I said, we didn't talk that much. She was basically a stranger."

"Then why do you seem so surprised?"

"Because she just got here. I thought she'd have stayed longer."

"How long have you been here?"

"Two months," Dylan says. "Are we about done with the questions? There's somewhere I need to be."

Rather than wait for the elevator, which is in use several floors below, Dylan opts for the stairs. He's either very late for something or extremely eager to be rid of me.

I call after him. "Just one more thing."

Dylan pauses on the landing between the tenth and eleventh floors, looking up at me with his head askance.

"Did you hear any strange noises last night?" I say. "From Ingrid's apartment?"

"Last night?" he says. "No, sorry. Can't help you there."

Then he's off again, speeding around the landing and down more steps before I can ask him another question. I use the stairs as well, slower than Dylan, going up instead of down.

A few floors below me, the elevator grate slides shut with a clang. The sound rockets up the stairwell, startling me. To my right, the cables in the center of the stairwell tighten and the elevator begins to rise. When it comes into view, I see Nick inside, a stethoscope draped around his neck. Seeing me through the elevator window, he gives a friendly wave. I wave back and hurry up the remaining steps to the twelfth floor, which we reach in unison.

"Hey there, neighbor," Nick says as he leaves the elevator. "How's the arm?"

"It's great. Thanks for, you know, fixing it."

I cringe at my tone. Could I be any more awkward? I blame Nick's whole handsome-doctor vibe, which is intimidating. I suspect the wine I had at Greta's is also at fault. It's caught up to me now, making me a little dizzy.

"Making a house call?" I say, gesturing to the stethoscope.

"Yes, unfortunately. Mr. Leonard was having heart palpitations. He swore the big one was coming."

"Is he okay?"

"I hope so," Nick says. "That's not really my specialty. I made him take an aspirin and told him to call 911 if it gets any worse. Knowing him, he won't. Mr. Leonard's a stubborn one. And where are you coming from?"

"The tenth floor."

"Making friends with the neighbors?"

I hesitate, unsure how much I should tell him. "Is that against the rules?"

"Technically, yes. Unless you were invited."

"Then I plead the fifth."

Nick laughs. He's got a nice laugh—a merry chuckle that makes me happy to have caused it. I used to make Andrew laugh all the time. His throaty, trickling laugh was one of the things I liked most about him. I heard it a lot during our first months together. Slightly less after we moved in together. Then it stopped altogether and neither of us noticed. Maybe if we had, things would have turned out differently.

"I won't tell Leslie, if that's what you're worried about," Nick says. "She's the one who insists on those silly rules. Most people here couldn't care less what the apartment sitters do."

"Then I'll confess—I went to visit Greta Manville."

"Now that's a surprise. Greta doesn't strike me as being very social, to put a polite spin on it. How on earth did you manage to charm her?"

"I didn't," I say. "I bribed her."

Nick laughs again, and I realize he's enjoying this conversation. I am, too. I think we might be flirting. I'm not really sure. It's probably just the wine talking. I'm not the kind of girl who flirts with her next-door neighbor.

"It must have been important for you to resort to bribery."

"I needed to talk to her about Ingrid Gallagher."

Nick frowns. "Ah. The runaway."

"So you've heard," I say.

"Word travels fast in this building."

Just like that, I realize Ingrid made a mistake when she approached Greta Manville about the Bartholomew's past. She should have asked someone else. Someone friendly. And handsome. And who has lived here all his life.

"I bet you know a lot about this place," I say.

Nick shrugs. "I've heard some things over the years."

I bite my bottom lip, not quite believing what I'm about to say next. "Would you like to get coffee? Or maybe a bite to eat?"

Nick gives me a surprised look. "What did you have in mind?"

"You pick. After all, you know the neighborhood."

And, I hope, he also knows a lot about the Bartholomew.

16

Instead of going out to eat, Nick suggests retreating to his apartment. "I have leftover pizza and cold beer," he says. "Sorry to be so simple."

"Simple is good," I say.

So is free, considering I don't really have the money to buy my neighbor dinner while fishing for information about the Bartholomew.

Inside 12B, Nick hands me a bottle of beer before returning to the kitchen to heat up the pizza. In his absence, I sip my beer and roam the sitting room, checking out the photographs that fill the walls. Some of them are of Nick looking dapper in a variety of far-off locales. Versailles. Venice. A savannah in Africa lit by the rising sun. Seeing them makes me wonder about the person on the other side of the camera. Was it a woman? Have they traveled the world together? Did she break his heart?

On the coffee table is a leather-bound photo album similar to one my parents owned. It's long gone now, like most of their belongings. I think of the framed photo currently on the nightstand in the bedroom of 12A. It's the only picture that remains of my family, and I'm not even in it. I envy Nick and his entire album of family photos.

The first photograph in the album is also presumably the oldest— a sepia-tinted image of a young couple standing in front of the Bartholomew. The woman has an opaque look about her, thanks to features washed out by too much sun and too little makeup. The man with her is a handsome devil, though. Familiar, too.

I carry the album into the kitchen, where Nick is pulling slices of reheated pizza from the oven. Just behind him, the painting of the ouroboros stares at me with its single, flame-like eye.

"Is this your family?" I ask.

Nick leans in to get a better look at the photograph. "My great-grandparents."

I examine the picture, noticing the ways in which Nick resembles his great-grandfather—same smile, same granite jaw—and the ways he does not, such as in the eyes. Nick's are softer, less hawkish.

"They also lived in the Bartholomew?"

"This very apartment," Nick says. "Like I said, it's been in my family for years."

I continue flipping through the album, the pictures passing in no discernible order. It's a hodgepodge of images in various shapes, sizes, and tints. A color photo of a little boy blowing bubbles—young Nick, I assume—sits beside a black-and-white one of two people huddled together in a snowbound Central Park.

"Those are my grandparents," Nick tells me. "Nicholas and Tillie."

On the next page is a striking photograph of an even more striking woman. Her gown is satin. Silk gloves reach her elbows. Her hair is midnight black and her skin an alabaster white. Her face is made up of sharp angles that, when joined together, merge into something arresting, even beautiful.

She stares at the camera with eyes that are at once foreign and familiar. They seem to pierce the lens, looking beyond it, directly at me. I've seen that look before. Not just in another photograph but in person.

"This woman looks a bit like Greta Manville," I say.

"That's because it's her grandmother," Nick says. "Her family and mine were friends for decades. She lived in the Bartholomew for many years. Greta's whole family has. She's what we call a legacy tenant."

"Just like you."

"I suppose I am. The last in a long line of Bartholomew residents."

"No siblings?"

"Only child. You?"

I glance again at the picture of Greta's grandmother. She reminds me of Jane. Not so much in looks but in aura. I detect restlessness in her eyes. An urge to roam.

"Same," I say.

"And your parents?"

"They died," I say quietly. "Six years ago."

"I'm sorry to hear that," Nick says. "It's tough. I know that from my own experience. We grow up expecting our parents to live forever until, one day, they're suddenly gone."

He transfers the pizza onto two plates and carries them to the round table in the dining room. We sit side by side, positioned so that both of us can look out the window at twilight settling over Central Park. The arrangement gives it the feel of a date, which makes me nervous. It's been a while since I've done anything resembling a date. I had forgotten what it feels like to be a normal single person.

Only nothing about this is normal. Normal people don't dine in rooms overlooking Central Park. Nor is their dinner companion a handsome doctor who lives in one of the most famous buildings in the city.

"Tell me, Jules," Nick says, "what do you do?"

"As in for a living?"

"That's what I was getting at, yeah."

"I'm an apartment sitter."

"I mean other than that."

I take a bite of pizza, stalling. My hope is that Nick will lose patience and move to a different topic. When he doesn't, I'm forced to swallow and admit the sad truth.

"I'm between jobs at the moment," I say. "I was laid off recently and haven't been able to find something else."

"No harm in that," Nick replies. "You could even look at it as a blessing in disguise. What would you really like to be doing?"

"I . . . I don't actually know. I've never given it much thought."

"Never?" Nick says, dropping his slice of pizza onto his plate to punctuate his surprise.

I have, of course. When I was young and hopeful and encouraged to ponder such things. At age ten, I wanted to be a ballerina or a veterinarian, blissfully unaware of the rigors specific to both professions. In college, I chose English lit as my major with the idea that maybe I'd become an editor or a teacher. When I graduated, following Chloe from Pennsylvania to New York with a mountain of debt weighing me down, I couldn't just wait and choose what I wanted to do. I had to take whatever job paid the bills and put food on the table.

"Tell me about you," I tell Nick, desperate to change the subject. "Did you always want to be a surgeon?"

"I didn't have much of a choice," he says. "It's what was expected of me."

"But what would you really like to be doing?"

Nick cracks a smile. "Touché."

"Turnabout is fair play," I say.

"Then I'll rephrase my answer. I wanted to be a surgeon because that's what I was exposed to from a very early age. I come from a long line of surgeons, beginning with my great-grandfather. All my life, I knew how proud they were of their work. They helped people. They saved people on the verge of being lost. It's like they were mystics—bringing people back from the dead. Looking at it that way, I was all too happy to join the family business."

"And business must have been booming if they could afford an apartment in the Bartholomew."

"I'm very fortunate," Nick says. "But honestly, this place never felt special. It is. I know that now. But growing up, it was just home, you know? When you're a kid, you don't realize your situation is different from everyone else's. It wasn't until I went away to college that I realized how unusual it was to grow up here. That's when I finally understood that most people don't get to live in a place like the Bartholomew."

I pick a slice of pepperoni off my pizza and pop it into my mouth. "That's why I can't understand why someone like Ingrid would want to leave."

"I'm surprised you went to Greta," Nick says. "I didn't think they knew each other. Come to think of it, I didn't realize *you* knew Ingrid."

"Only slightly," I say. "You didn't know her at all, did you?"

"We met briefly. Just a quick hello the day she moved in. I might have seen her around the building once or twice after that, but it was nothing substantial."

"She and I made plans to hang out. And now . . ."

"Her sudden departure has you concerned."

"A little," I admit. "The way she left strikes me as weird."

"I don't think it's weird, necessarily," Nick says before taking another sip of his beer. "Apartment sitters have left before, you know."

"Without notice in the middle of the night?"

"Not *quite* like that. But, for one reason or another, they don't think it's the right thing for them to be doing. The person who was in 12A before you did that."

"Erica Mitchell?"

Nick looks at me, surprised. "How do you know about her?"

"Ingrid mentioned her," I say. "She said she left two months early."

"That sounds about right. She was here about a month before telling Leslie she wasn't comfortable with the rules. Leslie wished her well, and Erica moved out. I suspect it was the same with Ingrid. Clearly, she didn't like it here and wanted to leave. Which I understand. The Bartholomew's not for everyone. It can be—"

"Creepy?"

He arches a brow. "Interesting word choice. I was going to say this place can be unusual. Do you really think it's creepy?"

Only the wallpaper, I think.

"Slightly," I say, adding, "I've heard things."

"Let me guess," Nick says. "That it's cursed."

It reminds me of the article, still unread, that Chloe sent me. "The Curse of the Bartholomew." Only Ingrid used a different word to describe this place.

Haunted.

That's how she put it. That the Bartholomew was haunted by its history. Although one could argue the two terms are interchangeable. Both involve dark forces clinging to a place, refusing to leave its residents in peace.

"That and other things," I say. "When I talked about it with Ingrid, she seemed frightened."

"Of the Bartholomew?" Nick says, his voice thick with disbelief.

"I don't know if it was the building itself or something inside it," I say. "But she was definitely afraid. And it's why I think she left. Now I'm trying to find out where she went."

"I wish Ingrid had come to me about this." Nick runs a hand through his hair, more exasperated than annoyed, although I sense some of that as well. Annoyance that anyone could fear the place he's always called home. "I think I could have put her mind at ease."

"So I'm guessing that's a no on the whole curse thing."

"Definitely," Nick says, cracking the faintest of smiles. "Yes, bad things have happened here. But bad things have occurred in every building in this neighborhood. The difference is that when something happens here, it gets conflated by the media and the internet. It's a very private building. That's how the residents like it. But some people mistake privacy for secrecy and fill in the blanks with all kinds of nonsense."

"So you think Ingrid was mistaken?" I say.

"I think it depends on what she heard. This curse nonsense is the result of things that happened decades ago. Long before I was born. Things have been mostly quiet around here."

I catch his word choice. *Mostly.*

"That's not exactly comforting."

"Trust me, there's nothing here to fear," Nick says. "The Bartholomew is generally a pretty happy place. You do like it here, don't you?"

"Of course." I flick my gaze to the expanse of Central Park outside the window. "There's a lot to like."

"Good. Now promise me something. If you get so creeped out that you feel the need to leave, at least come and talk to me first."

"So you can talk me out of it?"

Nick's shoulders rise and fall in a shy shrug. "Or at least get your phone number before you go."

And it's official: he and I really are flirting. I consider the possibility that maybe I'm not the girl I thought I was.

Maybe I'm more.

"My number," I say with a coy smile, "is 12A."

17

Fifteen minutes later, I'm back in my own apartment. Even though Nick showed no signs that I was overstaying my welcome, I felt it best to leave sooner rather than later. Especially once it became clear he had no intention of sharing any of the building's deep, dark secrets. If there are indeed any to share. I got the sense from Nick that he believed the Bartholomew to be as normal—or abnormal, as the case may be—as any other building on the Upper West Side.

Which is why I now sit by the bedroom window, George only a faint outline against the night-darkened sky. With me are a mug of tea, the remainder of the chocolate bar Charlie bought for me, and my laptop, which is open to the email Chloe sent yesterday.

"The Curse of the Bartholomew."

If my theory about Ingrid fleeing because she was frightened is true, then I want to know all the reasons why she might have been scared—and if I, too, should be afraid.

I click the link, which leads me to an urban-legend website. The kind Andrew used to read, with their clickbait tales of alligators in the sewers and mole people in abandoned subway tunnels. This one is a little more professional than most. Clean layout. Easy to read.

The first thing that greets me is a photo of the Bartholomew itself, taken from Central Park on a day that couldn't be more picture-perfect. Blue sky. Bright sun. Autumn leaves aflame. I even see George, the sunlight winking off his wings.

The image stands in stark contrast to the article itself, which drips with menace.

> From the moment it opened its doors to residents, New York City's Bartholomew apartment building has been touched by tragedy. Over its hundred-year history, the Gothic structure overlooking Central Park has witnessed death in many forms, including murder, suicide, and, in its first notable tragedy, plague.
>
> The Spanish flu pandemic that spread like wildfire across the globe in 1918 had already done its worst when the Bartholomew opened to great fanfare in January the next year. Therefore it was a surprise when, five months later, the disease swept through the building, killing twenty-four residents in a span of weeks. Although a few notable names succumbed to illness, including Edith Haig, the young wife of shipping magnate Rudolph Haig, most of the victims were servants, whose close quarters allowed the illness to rapidly spread.

I look up from the screen, unnerved. Because 12A was originally servants' quarters, some of those flu victims could have slept in this very room.

Maybe all of them.

Maybe they even died here.

A horrible thought, made worse by the photo just below that paragraph. It shows several canvas stretchers—seven, at least—resting on the sidewalk outside the Bartholomew, each one occupied by a corpse. Although blankets cover the faces and bodies of the dead, their feet are still visible. Seven sets of bare feet with dirty soles.

A chill passes through me when I think of those feet crossing the spot where I now sit. I do a little shimmy, trying to shake the feeling away. It's no use, for another one arrives when I see the photo beneath it.

It's the Bartholomew's facade again, this time rendered in grainy black and white. A small crowd has gathered on the street—a cluster of parasols and bowler hats. High above them, alone on a corner of the roof, is a man in a black suit. A thin silhouette against the sky.

The building's owner. Moments before his very public suicide.

The text under the photo confirms it.

> After a thorough examination of the premises, doctors determined that the flu deaths were caused by poor ventilation in the servants' quarters. This greatly upset the man who designed and paid for the construction of the building, Thomas Bartholomew, a doctor himself. He became so distraught by the incident that he leapt from the roof of the structure that bore his name. The ghastly act was witnessed by more than a hundred people on a beautiful July day.

There's a link that, when I click on it, takes me to the original *New York Times* article about the suicide. Its headline contains a grim double meaning.

TRAGEDY STRIKES BARTHOLOMEW

I squint at the blurred-by-time newsprint, looking for key details. It was a Sunday afternoon in mid-July, and Central Park was a melting pot boiling over with New Yorkers seeking escape from the summer heat. Some people soon noticed a man standing on the roof of the Bartholomew, like one of its already-famous gargoyles.

Then he jumped.

Witnesses made a point of stressing that fact. This was no accidental fall.

Dr. Bartholomew killed himself, leaving behind a young wife, Louella, and a seven-year-old son.

This is how I work for the next few hours, using the article Chloe sent as a sort of Rosetta stone of Bartholomew history. Each item is accompanied by several links to Wikipedia, news sites, online forums. I click them all, willingly tumbling down a rabbit hole of rumors, ghost stories, and urban legends.

I learn that things settled down after the building's tumultuous start. The twenties and thirties were decades of relative quiet, marked only by a few incidents of note. A man tumbling down the stairs and breaking his neck in 1928. A starlet overdosing on laudanum in 1932.

I learn that the winding stairwell is allegedly haunted, either by the man who fell down the stairs or by one of the servants killed by the flu.

I learn that an unnamed apartment is also rumored to be haunted, presumably by the ghost of the aforementioned Edith Haig.

And I learn that on the first of November in 1944, as World War II neared its bloody end, a nineteen-year-old girl who worked at the Bartholomew was found brutally murdered in Central Park.

Her name was Ruby Smith, and she was the live-in maid of former socialite Cornelia Swanson. According to Swanson, Ruby liked to walk in the park before returning to wake her at seven o'clock each morning. When that didn't happen, Swanson went to the park to look for the girl and found her lying in a wooded area directly across from the Bartholomew.

Ruby's body had been cut open and several vital organs removed, including her heart.

The murder weapon was never found. Neither were Ruby's organs.

The newspapers dubbed it the Ruby Red Killing.

Because there were no defensive wounds or signs of a struggle, the police concluded that Ruby had known her attacker. A lack of blood around the crime scene told them the ill-fated maid hadn't been killed where she was found. But police *did* find blood inside Ruby's small bedroom, located in Cornelia Swanson's apartment. A single red splotch behind the door.

Cornelia Swanson immediately became the police's sole suspect.

Their investigation uncovered an unsavory period from Swanson's past. In the late 1920s, she lived in Paris and became enamored of a self-proclaimed mystic named Marie Damyanov, the leader of an occult group known as Le Calice D'Or.

The Golden Chalice.

This information led police to charge Cornelia Swanson for the murder of Ruby Smith. In the arrest report, police noted the date of the murder—Halloween night.

Cornelia Swanson claimed to have known Marie Damyanov only socially. A close friend of both women stepped forward to say they were more than that. The rumor, he told police, was that the two were lovers.

The case ended up never going to trial. Cornelia Swanson died of an undisclosed illness in March 1945, leaving behind a teenage daughter.

After the Swanson scandal, the Bartholomew fell into another long period of relative quiet. In the past twenty years, there have been two murders. One, in 2004, was a crime of passion in which a woman shot her cheating husband. An option that never crossed my mind. Andrew should consider himself lucky.

The other murder, in 2008, was an alleged robbery gone wrong. The victim was a Broadway director with a thing for male escorts. The alleged perpetrator was, to no one's surprise, one of those escorts. Although he swore he didn't do it, the escort ended up using his shirt to hang himself in his jail cell.

Not counting the inevitable heart attacks and strokes and slow succumbings to cancer, there have been at least thirty unnatural deaths at the Bartholomew. Although that seems like a lot, I also know that bad things happen everywhere, in every building. Murders and health problems and freak accidents. It's absurd to expect the Bartholomew to be any different.

It certainly doesn't feel cursed. Or haunted. Or any other menacing label you could put on an apartment building. It's comfortable, spacious, and, other than the wallpaper, nicely decorated. It's easy to see why Nick and Greta choose to live here. I would certainly stay longer than three months if I could afford to. Which makes it all the stranger that Ingrid chose to leave.

I close the laptop and check my phone. Still nothing from her end.

What bothers me most about Ingrid's silence is that she's the one who threatened to send pestering texts if I was a no-show. Even our first encounter—that messy and humiliating collision in the lobby—happened because she was looking at her phone.

Only now that I think about it, that wasn't our first encounter. Technically, we had met an hour earlier, in a most unusual way.

I rush from the bedroom and twist down the stairs, on my way to the kitchen. Since the dumbwaiter is how Ingrid introduced herself, I can easily see her saying goodbye the same way. And sure enough, when I fling open the door to the dumbwaiter, I find another poem.

Edgar Allan Poe. "The Bells."

Sitting on top of it is a single key.

I pick it up and examine it in the glow of the overhead kitchen light. It's smaller than a regular house key. Just a fraction of the size. Yet I know exactly what it opens. I have a similar key hooked to the ring that currently occupies the bowl in the foyer.

It's for the storage unit.

The very key Leslie said was missing from the others Ingrid had discarded on the lobby floor.

Why she put it in the dumbwaiter eludes me. My only guess is that she left something behind in the storage unit for 11A, possibly with the hope I'd retrieve it and give it to her at a later date.

I shove the key into my pocket, my mind quickly easing. This suggests not a rushed escape from the Bartholomew but a planned departure. All my worry, it seems, has been for nothing. I grab the poem, certain that when I flip it over I'll find an explanation, instructions, maybe plans to meet soon.

The back of the poem contains none of those things.

In fact, one look at what Ingrid wrote sends me plummeting into a deep well of worry.

I read it again, staring at the two words Ingrid had scrawled in a shaky hand.

BE CAREFUL

18

To get to the basement, I have to take the elevator past the lobby and into the depths of the Bartholomew. Compared with the rest of the building, the basement is downright primitive, with walls of bare stone and support beams of concrete. It's cold down here, too. A rush of frigid air hits me as soon as I step out of the elevator. It feels like a warning. Or maybe that's just a side effect of Ingrid's message scraping at my nerves like sandpaper.

BE CAREFUL

It doesn't help that the basement bears a cryptlike quality. Dank and dark. Like it's gone untouched since the Bartholomew rose on top of it a hundred years ago. Yet here I am, palming the key Ingrid left behind and hoping whatever's in that storage unit tells me where she's gone.

Hanging from the support column opposite the elevator is a security camera. The one Leslie said wasn't working when Ingrid left last night. I peer up at it and wonder if I'm being watched. Although I've noticed the bank of monitors in the alcove just off the lobby, I haven't seen anyone looking at them.

I move deeper into the basement. Everywhere I look are cages of steel mesh. One behind the elevator that contains its ancient equipment. Greasy wheels and cables and cogs. Inside another are the

furnace, water heater, and air-conditioning unit. All of them hum—
a ghostly sound that gives the entire basement an air of unwanted
menace.

Another sound joins them. A ragged swish that quickly gets
louder. I spin toward the noise and see a bulging trash bag plummet
into a dumpster the size of a double-wide trailer. Near it is a door of
retractable steel so it can be moved outside for emptying. The entire
area is surrounded by a chain-link barrier.

I'm not surprised. Down here, even the lightbulbs are caged.

I round the dumpster, startling Mr. Leonard's aide, who stands
on the other side. She startles me right back. We both suck in air—
simultaneous gasps that echo off the stone walls.

"You scared the shit out of me," she says. "For a second, I thought
you were Mrs. Evelyn."

"Sorry," I say. "I'm Jules."

The woman nods coolly. "Jeannette."

"Nice to meet you."

Jeannette's dressed for the basement's chill, her purple scrubs covered by a ratty gray cardigan with gaping pockets. One hand rests
just above her ample bosom. Her way of silently telling me just how
much I scared her. She keeps her other hand behind her back in an
attempt to hide the lit cigarette she's holding.

When it becomes clear that I've seen it, she lifts the cigarette to
her lips and says, "You're one of those apartment sitters, aren't you?
The newest one?"

I wonder if she knows this because Leslie told her or if I just look
the part. Maybe the former. Probably the latter.

"I am."

"How long are you in for?" Jeannette asks, making it sound like a
prison sentence.

"Three months."

"Like it here?"

"I do," I say. "It's nice, but there are a lot of rules to follow."

Jeannette stares at me a moment. Her hair's pulled back, which tightens her forehead into an impassive look. "You're not going to narc on me, are you? Smoking's not allowed in the Bartholomew."

"Not anywhere?"

"Nope." She takes another drag. "Mrs. Evelyn's orders."

"I won't tell," I say.

"I appreciate that."

Jeannette takes one last puff before stubbing out the cigarette on the concrete floor. When she bends down to pick it up, a lighter falls from a pocket of her cardigan. I grab it while she drops the butt into a coffee can at her feet and slides it into a corner, where it blends in with the shadows.

"You dropped this," I say, handing her the lighter.

Jeannette stuffs it back into her cardigan. "Thanks. This damn sweater. Stuff's always falling out."

"Before you go, I was wondering if you could help me. One of the other apartment sitters left last night and I'm trying to reach her. Her name is Ingrid Gallagher. She was in 11A."

"Never heard the name."

Jeannette shuffles to the elevator. I follow, pulling out my phone and swiping to the picture of Ingrid and me in Central Park. I hold it in front of her. "This is her."

Jeannette presses the button for the elevator and gives the photo a brief glance. "Yeah, I saw her once or twice."

"Ever talk to her?"

"The only person I talk to lately is Mr. Leonard. Why do you need to find her?"

"I haven't heard from her since she left," I say. "I'm worried."

"Sorry I can't help you," Jeannette says. "But I've got enough to deal with. Sick husband at home. Mr. Leonard convinced he's going to keel over every damn minute of the day."

"I understand. But if you remember anything—or hear something about her from someone else in the building—I'd really appreciate it if you told me. I'm in 12A."

The elevator arrives. Jeannette steps inside.

"Listen, Julie——"

"Jules," I remind her.

"Jules. Right. I don't want to tell you what to do. It's not my place. But it's better to hear it from me and not someone like Mrs. Evelyn." Jeannette brings the grate across the elevator door and stuffs her hands into the pockets of her cardigan. "In the Bartholomew, it's best to mind your own business. I don't go around asking a lot of questions. I suggest you follow my lead."

She hits a button, and the elevator takes off, lifting her out of the basement and out of view.

I follow the string of exposed bulbs inside their red-wire confines to the storage units, which line both sides of a mazelike corridor. Each chain-link door bears the number of its corresponding apartment, beginning with 2A.

It reminds me of a dog kennel. A creepy, too-quiet one.

That silence is broken by my phone, which blares suddenly from deep in my pocket. Thinking it might be Ingrid, I grab it and check the number. Even though it's one I don't recognize, I answer with a distracted "Hello?"

"Is this Jules?"

It's a man calling, his voice lazy and light, with a noticeable stoner drawl.

"It is."

"Hey, Jules. This is Zeke?"

He says his name like it's a question. Like he doesn't quite know who he is. But I do. He's Zeke, Ingrid's friend from Instagram, calling me at last.

"Zeke, yes. Is Ingrid with you?"

I start my way down the corridor, sneaking glances into units as I pass. Most of them are too tidy to be interesting. Just boxes stacked in orderly rows, their contents announced in scrawled marker. Dishes. Clothes. Books.

"With me?" Zeke says. "Nah. We're not that close. We met at a warehouse rave in Brooklyn a few years ago and only hung out a few times since then."

"Have you heard from her today?"

"No. Is she missing or something?"

"It's just really important that I talk to her."

Not even Zeke's slacker voice can hide his growing suspicion. "How do you know Ingrid again?"

"I'm her neighbor," I say. "Was her neighbor, I guess."

In one of the units is a twin bed with rails on both sides and the mattress bent in partial incline. On top of it are several stacks of folded sheets coated with a thin layer of dust.

"She moved out of that fancy building already?" Zeke says.

"How do you know she was living at the Bartholomew?"

"She told me."

"When?"

"Two days ago."

That would have been the same day Ingrid took the photo in the park. The one Zeke commented on.

The corridor makes a sudden turn to the left. I follow it, noting the numbers: 8A, 8B. Inside the one for 8C is a dialysis machine on wheels. I know because my mother used one just like it, back when she was near the end. I went with her a few times, even though I hated everything about it. The disinfectant smell of the hospital. The too-white walls. Seeing her attached to a tangle of tubes as her blood ran through them like fruit punch in a Krazy Straw.

I move past the machine, quickening my pace until I've reached the other side of the building. I can tell because there's another trash chute. A dumpster sits below it, although it's smaller than the other one and, at the moment, empty. To the left of the dumpster is a black door, unmarked.

"What did she say?" I ask Zeke.

"I'm not sure I should tell you anything else," he says. "I don't know you."

"Listen, Ingrid might be in some kind of trouble. I hope she isn't. But I won't know for certain until I talk to her. So please tell me what happened."

The corridor here makes another sharp turn. When I round it, I find myself staring at the storage unit for 10A.

Greta Manville's apartment.

The cage is full of cardboard boxes. Each marked not with its contents but its worth.

Useful.

Useless.

Cheap sentiment.

"She came to see me," Zeke says. "Not unusual. Lots of people come to see me. I, uh, procure things. Herbal things, if you catch my drift."

I do. Color me unsurprised.

"So Ingrid came to buy weed?"

Across from Greta's storage cage is the one for 11A. Unlike all the other storage cages, the only thing inside that chain-link square is a single shoe box. It rests on the concrete floor, its lid slightly askew, as if Ingrid left it there in a hurry.

"That's not what she was looking for," Zeke says. "She wanted to know where she could buy something I don't deal with. But I know someone who does and told her I could be the middleman between them. She gave me the cash; I made the exchange with the supplier and brought it back to Ingrid. That was it."

Fumbling with the phone in one hand and the key in the other, I unlock the cage.

"Who was the supplier?"

Zeke scoffs. "Shit, man. I'm not giving you his name."

I step into the cage and move to the box.

"Then at least tell me what Ingrid bought."

I get the answer twice, both of them arriving in unison. One is from Zeke, who blurts the word over the phone. The other is when I lift the shoe box's lid.

Inside, nestled on a bed of tissue paper, is a gun.

19

The gun sits on my bed, a deep black against the comforter's corn-flower blue. Beside it is the full magazine also found in the shoe box Ingrid left behind. Six bullets, ready to be locked and loaded.

It took all the courage I could muster just to carry the shoe box from the basement to the elevator. I spent the long ride to the twelfth floor in terror, and when I finally did remove the gun and magazine, I used only my thumb and forefinger, holding both at arm's length.

It was the first time I'd ever touched a gun.

Growing up, the only firearm in our house was a rarely used hunting rifle my father kept locked in a gun cupboard. I'm pretty sure I glimpsed it only once or twice during my childhood, and then only fleetingly.

But now I can't stop looking at the weapon whose presence fills the bedroom. Thanks to Google and a soul-deadening number of websites devoted to pistols, I have learned I'm now in possession of a nine-millimeter Glock G43.

During the rest of my conversation with Zeke, I learned that Ingrid told him she needed a gun. Fast. She gave him two grand in cash. He took it to his unnamed associate and came back with the Glock.

"It took an hour, tops," he said. "Ingrid left with the gun. It's the last time I heard from her."

What I still don't know is why Ingrid, who in high school was probably voted Least Likely to Own a Firearm, felt as though she needed one.

And why she bequeathed it to me when she left.

And why she still isn't responding, even after I've sent a half dozen texts, all of which were different versions of WHAT IS GOING ON WHERE ARE YOU WHY DID YOU LEAVE ME A GUN?!?!?!

All I know is that I need to get it out of the apartment. Although Leslie never mentioned it, I'm sure there's a rule at the Bartholomew about apartment sitters possessing firearms. The big question is how. It's not something I can just toss down the trash chute. Nor do I feel comfortable sneaking off to Central Park and tossing it into the lake. And Zeke already balked at my idea of returning it to the man who supplied it.

"No way," he said. "That's not how he operates."

But as much as having the gun here puts me on edge, I'm hesitant to get rid of it until I hear back from Ingrid. She left it behind for a reason.

The fact that Ingrid had it at all brings up a scary prospect. One that completely smashes the idea she left because she was too scared of the Bartholomew's strange past to stay here. A gun is a weapon. Self-defense. You don't need one to protect yourself from a building, even if you somehow think it's haunted. You can't shoot a ghost. Or a curse, for that matter.

But you *can* shoot a person you suspect is trying to do you harm.

I'm suddenly reminded of all the places she said she'd been. Boston and New York, Seattle and Virginia.

Maybe Ingrid wasn't simply restless.

Maybe she was running.

And whoever she was running from had tracked her down, forcing her to flee once more.

My thoughts flash back to last night and those awkward few minutes I spent outside Ingrid's door. Looking back on it, I wonder if everything I had found unusual—the fake smile, the hand digging into her pocket, the single blink when I tried to make eye contact—was her way of telling me something she couldn't say aloud.

That she wasn't fine.

That she needed to leave the Bartholomew.

That saying anything else—even a single word—wouldn't be in either of our best interests.

Now Ingrid is gone, and I can't shake the feeling that I'm partly to blame. If I had been more forceful or nosier, then maybe she would have felt able to confide in me about what was going on.

Maybe I could have helped her.

Maybe I still can.

I return the gun and the ammunition to the shoe box the same way I removed them—cautiously. I then cover the box with its lid and carry the whole thing downstairs to the kitchen, where I shove it in the cupboard under the sink. Better there than in the bedroom, where I'm certain it would keep me up all night.

I check my watch. It's now almost eleven. Roughly ten hours since I found out Ingrid was gone. My family waited about that long to report Jane missing. It was still too late. One of the cops who came to our house even chastised us for taking so long to contact them.

There's always a moment when worry turns to fear, he'd said. *That's when you should have called.*

I'm already there. I crossed that threshold between worry and fear as soon as I found the gun. Which is why I grab my phone, take a breath, and dial 911. I'm connected immediately with a dispatcher.

"I'd like to report a missing person," I say.

"What's the person's name?"

The dispatcher speaks in a dispassionate tone. A calmness that's both soothing and maddening. A little urgency would make me feel better.

"Ingrid Gallagher."

"And how long has Ingrid been missing?"

"Ten hours." I stop, correct myself. "Since last night."

Emotion at last seeps into the dispatcher's voice. One I don't welcome—incredulity.

"Are you sure?" he says.

"Yes. She left in the middle of the night. I didn't hear about it until ten hours ago."

"And how old is Ingrid?"

I say nothing. I don't know.

"Is she a minor?" the dispatcher says, prodding.

"No."

"A senior citizen?"

"No." I pause again. "She's in her early twenties."

More doubt seeps into the dispatcher's voice. "You don't know her exact age?"

"No," I say, adding a hasty, "I'm sorry."

"So she's not a relation?"

"No. We're . . ."

Yet another pause as I think of the appropriate word. I wouldn't call Ingrid a friend, exactly. Or even an acquaintance.

"Neighbors," I say. "We're neighbors, and she's not answering her phone or texts."

"What was her last known location?"

Finally, a question that's easy to answer. "The Bartholomew."

"Is that her residence?"

"Yes."

"Are there signs of a struggle?"

"I'm not sure." A weak, useless answer. I try to make up for it by adding, "I don't think so."

Now it's the dispatcher's turn to pause. When he finally speaks, his voice contains more than doubt and incredulity. There's also confusion. And pity. And just a touch of annoyance to make it clear he thinks I'm wasting his time.

"Ma'am, are you sure she hasn't just gone away for a few days?"

"I was told she moved out," I say.

"That would explain why she's no longer there."

I wince at the dispatcher's tone. The pity's gone. So is the confusion. Only annoyance remains.

"I know it sounds like she just moved out and didn't tell me," I say, "but she left me a note telling me to be careful. And she left a *gun*. Which makes me think she was in trouble somehow."

"Did she ever mention feeling threatened?"

"She told me she was scared," I say.

"When was this?" the dispatcher says.

"Yesterday. And then she left in the middle of the night."

"And you're sure she never said anything else? Maybe on a different occasion?"

"Not to me, but we only met yesterday."

And that's it. I've lost him. Rightly so. Even I can hear how pathetic I sound.

"Miss, I understand that you're worried about your neighbor," the dispatcher says, his voice suddenly gentle, as if he's speaking to a child. "But I really don't know how to help you. You've given me very little information to go on. You're not a family member. And, if you'll pardon me, it sounds like you don't even really know this woman. All I can do is politely ask that you hang up and free this line for callers with real emergencies."

I do. The dispatcher is right. I don't know Ingrid. But I'm not the sad, paranoid woman I sounded like during the call.

Something about this situation is very, very wrong. And I won't know anything more than that until I locate Ingrid. The only thing I do know, made abundantly clear by that dispatcher, is that if I'm going to find Ingrid, I'll have to do it all on my own.

20

Another night, another bad dream.

My family again. They're still in Central Park, occupying Bow Bridge, all of them holding hands and smiling up at me.

This time, though, they're on fire.

I'm once more perched on the roof, nestled inside one of George's open wings. I watch the fire engulf each of them. First my father, then my mother, then Jane. The flames rise to a peak off the tops of their heads. The water below reflects their burning figures, turning three flames into six. When Jane waves to me with a fiery hand, her reflection follows suit.

"Be careful," she calls out as smoke pours from her mouth.

It's thick smoke. Black and roiling and so strong I can smell it from the Bartholomew's roof. Below me, I hear the agitated shriek of a fire alarm echoing through the halls.

I look at George, his beaked face stoic as he stares at my burning parents. "Please don't push me," I say.

His beak doesn't move when he answers.

"I won't."

Then he uses a stone wing to nudge me off the roof.

I wake with a jerk on the crimson sofa in the sitting room, the nightmare clinging to me like sweat. I can still smell the smoke and hear the blare of the fire alarm. It's as if I'm not awake at all but simply caught in another, similar dream. The smoke tickles my nose and throat. I cough.

That's when I understand what's going on.

This isn't a dream.

It's really happening.

Something in the Bartholomew is on fire.

The smell of smoke drifts into the apartment. Out in the hallway, the fire alarm blares. Contained inside that incessant clanging is another sound—pounding.

Someone is at the door.

In between those rattling knocks comes Nick's voice.

"Jules?" he shouts. "You in there? We need to get out of here!"

I fling open the door and see Nick standing there in a T-shirt, sweatpants, and flip-flops. His hair is mussed. His eyes are fearful.

"What's going on?" I say.

"Fire. Not sure where."

I yank my jacket from the coatrack and shove it on, even as Nick starts to pull me out of the apartment. I shut the door behind me because I read that's what you're supposed to do in the case of an apartment fire. Something to do with airflow.

Nick keeps pulling me along, into the hall, where a thin haze of smoke is made more pronounced by the bright strobe of the emergency lights on the wall. I cough twice. Two harsh barks that get lost in the sound of the fire alarm.

"Is there a fire escape?" I say, shouting so Nick can hear me.

"No," Nick shouts back. "Just fire stairs at the back of the building."

He pulls me past the elevator and interior staircase to an unmarked door at the far end of the hall. Nick gives the door a push, but it doesn't open.

"Fuck," he says. "I think it's locked."

He pushes the door again before ramming his shoulder into it. The door doesn't budge.

"We have to take the main stairs," he says before pulling me back the way we came.

Soon we're again at the elevator and stairwell, which now pumps out smoke like a chimney. The sight is so jarring that I come to a halt, immobile with fear, no matter how much Nick tugs my arm.

"Jules, we need to keep moving."

He gives another shoulder-wrenching yank of my arm, and I feel myself pulled unwillingly toward the stairs. Soon we're descending them. Nick moves at a quick, steady pace. I'm more frantic, speeding up then slowing down before being pulled along again.

The smoke is thicker on the eleventh floor—a fog-like, undulating wall. I lift my jacket to cover my nose and mouth. Nick does the same with his T-shirt.

"Go on ahead," he says. "I want to make sure no one else is still up here."

I don't want to go down the rest of the stairs alone. I'm not sure my body will let me. Already I've come to another halt. Dread seems to be riding on the smoke, curling around me, oozing into my pores.

"I'll come with you," I say.

Nick shakes his head. "It's too dangerous. You need to keep going."

I grudgingly oblige, stumbling down the steps to the tenth floor. On the landing, I peer down the hall, squinting against the smoke in search of Greta Manville's apartment. The door is barely visible through the haze. For all I know, she's already made her way out of the building. But what if she hasn't? I picture her in the grip of one of her sudden sleeps, oblivious to the smoke and the screaming alarm.

Just like one of Nick's tugs, the image pulls me down the hall, toward 10A, where I pound on the door. It opens immediately. Greta stands in the doorway, covered in a tent-like flannel nightgown and the same slippers she wore earlier. She's tied a bandanna around her head, which hangs over her nose and mouth.

"I don't need you to rescue me," she says.

Only, she kind of does. When she sets off down the hall, it's at a snail's pace, rivaling me in hesitation. Although in her case I think it's less fear than poor health. Her breath gets heavy before we even reach the stairs. When I try to ease her down the first step, her legs sway like windblown palms.

"That's one," I say.

Which leaves roughly two hundred more steps to go.

I peer down the stairwell, gripped by fear when I see nothing but smoke curling upward.

I cough. Greta does, too, the bottom triangle of her bandanna fluttering.

I grip her hand. We both know we're not going to make it down those steps. Greta's too weak. I'm too terrified.

"The elevator," I say, hauling her back up that one meager step we managed to descend.

"You're not supposed to use an elevator during a fire."

I know that. Just like I knew about closing the apartment door.

"There's no other choice," I snap.

I head to the elevator, dragging Greta in the same way Nick dragged me. I can feel her wrist twisting beneath my fingers, resisting my pull. That doesn't slow me. Fear propels me forward.

The elevator isn't stopped on the tenth floor. Honestly, I didn't expect it to be. Still, I had hoped that maybe, possibly it would be there waiting for us. A stroke of good fortune in a life devoid of it. Instead, I'm forced to pound the down button and wait.

But waiting isn't easy.

Not with the alarm still bouncing off the walls and the strobe lights flaring and smoke still rolling up the steps and Nick now God knows where. I keep coughing and my eyes keep watering, although now it might be real tears and not from the smoke. Fear clangs in my skull. Louder than the alarm.

When the elevator finally arrives, I push Greta inside, close the grate, press the button for the lobby. With a rattle and a shudder, we start to descend.

The smoke is heavier on the ninth floor.

And still worse on the eighth.

We keep descending into plumes far thicker and darker than on the floors above, blowing through the elevator cage in choking drafts. When we reach the seventh floor, it's clear that this is the source of the fire. The smoke here is sharper, stabbing the inside of my throat.

Through the smoke, I see firefighters coming and going along the seventh-floor hall with firehoses that have been carried up the steps so that they spiral around the elevator shaft like pythons.

Just when we're about to move past the seventh floor, I hear something other than the elevator's hum and the shrieking fire alarm and the clomp of firefighter boots on the stairs. It's a sharp bark, followed by the skitter of claws on tile. A furry blur darts past the elevator.

I slam the emergency-stop button. The elevator comes to a quick, quivering halt as Greta gives me a fearful look.

"What are you doing?"

"There's a dog," I say, the words riding on the back of another cough. "I think it's Rufus."

The terrified part of my brain tells me to ignore him, that Rufus will be fine, that I should focus on getting us to safety. But then Rufus barks again, and the noise pierces my heart. He sounds almost as scared as I am. Which is why I pull open the grate. After that comes the thin-barred door, which is more stubborn than it looks. It takes both hands and an extra-hard tug to pry it open.

The elevator itself has stopped three feet below the landing, forcing me to pull myself up onto the seventh floor. I then crawl along the floor to evade the smoke—another of those things-to-do-in-a-fire facts I never thought I'd use.

While crawling, I cough out Rufus's name, the sound lost in all the noise. I peer through the smoke, trying in vain to catch another glimpse of him. He's so small and the smoke is so thick and my eyes are pouring tears. Through that watery haze, I see firefighters stomping into 7C, their voices muffled under helmets and face masks. Through the open apartment door comes a hot glow.

Flames.

Pulsing and bright and painting the hallway a hypnotic orange-yellow.

I climb to my feet, drawn to it. I'm no longer afraid. All I feel now is intense curiosity.

I take a step down the hall, coughing again as I go.

"Jules," Greta calls from the elevator, "grab the dog and let's get out of here."

I ignore her and take another step. Although I suspect I have no choice at all in the matter. I'm being compelled.

I keep walking until there's a noticeable warmth on my face. The heat of the flames caressing my skin.

I close my eyes against the smoke.

I take a breath, sucking it in until I start to cough. Rough, heaving ones that make my body convulse.

Dizzy from the smoke, I experience a jolting moment during which I have no idea where I am, why I'm here, what the fuck I was just doing. But then I hear a bark behind me and I whirl around, spotting a familiar shape hurtling through the smoke.

Rufus.

Panicked and lost.

Him and me both.

Blindly, I drop to the floor again and lurch forward before he can zip past me. I then pull him into my arms, Rufus barking and struggling and pawing my chest in agitation. Rather than crawl back to the elevator, I inch forward on my behind, scooting awkwardly until I reach it. Carefully, I drop the three feet back into the cage and, clutching Rufus in one hand, slam the grate shut with the other. Beside me, Greta shoots me a startled, fearful look before hitting the down button.

Lower we go, into the bottom half of the Bartholomew, the smoke getting lighter the farther we descend. By the time we reach the lobby, it's been reduced to a light haze. That doesn't stop me from coughing. Or wheezing when I'm not coughing.

Greta stays quiet, unwilling to look at me. God, she must think I'm insane. I'd think the same thing if I didn't know the reasons behind my recklessness.

As we leave the elevator and make our way across the lobby, we encounter a trio of EMTs on their way into the building. With them is a stretcher, its wheeled legs folded. One of them looks my way, a question in her eyes.

I manage a nod. One that says, *We're okay.*

They move on, heading up the stairs. We go in the other direction, following the hoses that stretch from the front door. Me and Greta and Rufus. All of us cradled together as we step outside to a street painted red by the siren lights of two fire trucks and an ambulance stopped at the curb. The block itself has been closed to traffic, allowing people, many of them members of the media, to gather in the middle of Central Park West.

As soon as we hit the sidewalk, reporters push forward.

Camera lights swing our way, blindingly bright.

A dozen flashbulbs pop like firecrackers.

A reporter shouts a question that I can't hear because the fire alarm has set my ears ringing.

Rufus, as irritated as I am, barks. This draws Marianne Duncan out of the milling crowd. She's dressed like Norma Desmond. Flowing caftan, turban, cat's-eye sunglasses. Her face is smeared with cold cream.

"Rufus?"

She rushes toward me and lifts Rufus from my arms.

"My baby! I was so worried about you." To me, she says, "The alarm was going off and there was smoke and Rufus got spooked and jumped out of my arms. I wanted to look for him, but a fireman told me I had to keep moving."

She's started to cry. Streaks appear in the cold cream, plowed by tears.

"Thank you," she says. "Thank you, thank you!"

I can only muster a nod. I'm too dazed by the sirens and the flashbulbs and the smoke that continues to roll like a storm cloud in my lungs.

I leave Greta with Marianne and gently push my way through the crowd. It's easy to differentiate residents of the Bartholomew from the onlookers. They're the ones in their nightclothes. I spot Dylan in just a pair of pajama bottoms and sneakers, looking impervious to the cold. Leslie Evelyn wears a black kimono, which swishes gracefully as she and Nick do a head count of residents.

When EMTs emerge with Mr. Leonard strapped to the stretcher and his face covered by an oxygen mask, the crowd breaks into applause. Upon hearing them, Mr. Leonard gives a weak thumbs-up.

By then I'm pulling away from the crowd, on the other side of Central Park West. I walk north a block, putting more distance between me and the Bartholomew. I drop onto a bench and sit with my back to the stone wall bordering Central Park.

I cough one last time.

Then I allow myself to weep.

D r. Wagner looks surprised, and rightly so. His expression is similar to his voice—passivity masking alarm.

"Escaped?"

"That's what I said."

I don't mean to be this standoffish. Dr. Wagner has done nothing wrong. But I'm not ready to trust anyone at the moment. A by-product of living at the Bartholomew for a few days.

"I want to talk to the police," I say. "And Chloe."

"Chloe?"

"My best friend."

"We can call her," Dr. Wagner says. "Do you have her number?"

"On my phone."

"I'll have Bernard look through your things and find the number."

I let out a relieved sigh. "Thank you."

"I'm curious," the doctor says. "How long did you live at the Bartholomew?"

I like the doctor's word choice. Past tense.

"Five days."

"And you felt like you were in danger there?"

"Not at first. But yes. Eventually."

I look to the wall behind Dr. Wagner, at the askew Monet. I've seen the painting before, although I can't remember what it's called. Probably Blue Bridge Over Waterlilies, *because that's what it depicts. It's pretty. From my position on the bed, I can see the curve of the bridge as it arcs over the lily pads and blooms in the water below. But I know that looking at it from another viewpoint would yield a vastly different result. The lines of the bridge wouldn't look quite so clean. The lilies would widen into indistinct splotches of paint. If I were to get up close, the painting would probably look downright ugly.*

The same can be said of certain places. The closer you get to them, the uglier they become.

That's what the Bartholomew is like.

"You felt like you were in danger, so you fled," the doctor says.

"Escaped," I remind him.

"Why did you feel the need to do that?"

I sink back into the pillows. I'm going to have to tell him everything, even though that might not be the best idea. This time, it's not a matter of trust. With each minute that passes, I get the sense that Dr. Wagner only wants to help.

So the question isn't how much to tell him.

It's how much I think he'll believe.

"The place is haunted. By its past. So many bad things have happened there. So much dark history. It fills the place."

Dr. Wagner's brow lifts. "Fills it?"

"Like smoke," I say. "And I've breathed it in."

THREE DAYS
EARLIER

21

I wake just after seven to the same sound I heard my first night here. The noise that's not a noise.

Although this time I no longer think someone's inside the apartment, I'm still curious about what it could be. Every place has its own distinct sounds. Creaking steps and humming fridges and windows that rattle when the wind rushes against them at just the right angle. The key is to find them and identify them. Once you know what they are, they're less likely to bother you.

So I force myself out of bed, shivering in a bedroom made frigid by windows that have gaped open all night. A necessity after the fire. It made the whole place smell like a hotel room in which the previous occupant had smoked a carton of cigarettes.

Padding downstairs in bare feet and flimsy nightclothes, I stop every so often to listen—really listen—to the sounds of the apartment. I hear noises aplenty, but nothing that matches *the* noise. That specific sound has suddenly vanished.

In the kitchen, I find my phone sitting on the counter, blaring out the ring tone specifically reserved for Chloe. Worrisome, considering the two of us instituted a no-calls-until-coffee rule back when we roomed together in college.

"I haven't had my coffee yet," I say upon answering.

"The rule doesn't apply when a fire is involved," Chloe says. "Are you okay?"

"I'm fine. The fire wasn't nearly as bad as it seemed."

The blaze itself was confined to 7C, Mr. Leonard's apartment. It turns out the heart palpitations Nick told me about earlier had returned. Rather than call 911, as Nick strongly recommended, Mr. Leonard ignored the warning signs. Later, while he was cooking himself a late-night dinner, a heart attack arrived. His fourth.

The fire started when Mr. Leonard dropped the pot holder in his hands when the coronary struck. It landed on the stovetop, where it quickly ignited. The fire spread from there, eventually encompassing much of the kitchen while Mr. Leonard crawled to the door in an attempt to get help. He lost consciousness just as the door swung open, fanning the flames in the kitchen and sending gusts of smoke into the upper floors of the Bartholomew.

It was Leslie Evelyn, also a seventh-floor resident, who ended up calling 911. She smelled the smoke, went into the hall to check, and saw the plumes rolling from Mr. Leonard's open door. Because of her quick thinking, the rest of the Bartholomew remained mostly unscathed. Just water damage in the seventh-floor hallway and slight smoke damage to the hallway walls of the seventh, eighth, and ninth floors.

I learned all this once residents were allowed back in their apartments two hours later. Because the elevator can fit only so many people at a time and no one was in the mood to take the stairs, a gossipy crowd formed in the lobby. Some of them I recognized. Most of them I didn't. All of them, save for Nick, Dylan, and myself, were well past sixty.

"I meant emotionally," Chloe says.

A slightly different story. Although I've calmed down since last night, a faint anxiety lingers, just as stubborn as the traces of smoke inside the apartment.

"It was intense," I say. "And scary. And I can't say I slept very well, but I'm fine. This was nothing like what happened at my house. How did you find out about it?"

"The newspaper," Chloe says. "Your picture's on the front page."

I groan. "How bad do I look?"

"Like the chimney sweep from *Mary Poppins.*" I hear the tap of fingers on a computer keyboard, followed by a mouse click. "I just sent you something."

My phone buzzes with an email alert. I open it to see the cover of one of the city's daily tabloids. Filling two-thirds of the front page is a photograph of the Bartholomew's front door, taken just as I emerged with Greta and Rufus. What a strange sight we are. Me still wearing the rumpled jeans and blouse I'd worn all day, and Greta in her nightgown. Both of our faces have been darkened by smoke. By that point Greta had lowered the bandanna, revealing a swath of white skin from nose to chin. Then there's Rufus, sporting a collar that might be studded with real diamonds. We look like extras from three different movies.

"Who's the woman with the bandanna?" Chloe asks.

"That would be Greta Manville."

"The woman who wrote *Heart of a Dreamer*? You, like, adore that book."

"I do."

"Is that her dog?"

"That's Rufus," I say. "He belongs to Marianne Duncan."

"From that soap opera?"

"The very one."

"What a strange alternate universe you've stumbled into," Chloe says.

I glance again at the image on my phone, rolling my eyes at the awful headline the tabloid came up with.

GARGOYLE CHAR-BROIL:
BLAZE AT THE BARTHOLOMEW

"Wasn't there anything else to put on the front page? You know, like real news."

"This *is* news," Chloe says. "Remember, Jules, most New Yorkers see the Bartholomew as the closest thing to heaven on earth."

I move from the kitchen to the sitting room, where I'm greeted by the faces in the wallpaper. A whole army of dark eyes and open mouths. I instantly turn away.

"Trust me, this place is far from perfect."

"So you read that article I sent you," Chloe says. "That's some scary shit, right?"

"It's more than the article that's bothering me."

Concern sneaks into Chloe's voice. "Did something else happen?"

"Yes," I say. "Maybe."

I tell her about meeting Ingrid, our plan to hang out each day, the scream from 11A and Ingrid's insistence it was nothing. I finish with how Ingrid is now gone and not answering her phone and my suspicions that someone caused her to flee.

Left out are all the worrisome parts, specifically the note and the gun. Hearing about those would prompt Chloe to come to the Bartholomew and drag me from 12A. Which I can't afford to do. Receiving my latest unemployment check has left me with slightly more than five hundred dollars in my account. Definitely not enough to help me get back on my feet.

"You need to stop looking for her," Chloe says, just like I knew she would. "Whatever her reason was for leaving, it's none of your business."

"I think she might be in some kind of trouble."

"Jules, listen to me. If this Ingrid person wanted your help, she would have called you by now. Clearly, she wants to be left alone."

"There's no one else looking for her," I say. "If I vanished, you'd look for me. I don't think Ingrid has a Chloe in her life. She has no one."

There's silence on Chloe's end. I know what it means—she's thinking. Choosing her words carefully in an attempt not to upset me. Even so, I know what her response is going to be before she even says it.

"I think this has less to do with Ingrid and more to do with your sister."

"Of course my sister has something to do with it," I say. "I stopped looking for her. And now I can't stop thinking that maybe she'd be here now if I hadn't given up so easily."

"Finding Ingrid won't bring Jane back."

No, I think, *it won't. But it* will *mean there's one less lost girl in the world. One less person who vanished into thin air, never to be seen again.*

"I think you should get away from the Bartholomew," Chloe says. "Just for a few days. Crash at my place this weekend."

"I can't."

"Don't worry about imposing. Paul is taking me to Vermont for the weekend. He booked it last week, when he thought . . ."

Chloe leaves the sentence unfinished. I know what she was going to say. Paul booked it when he thought I'd still be crashing on her couch. I'm not offended. They deserve a weekend alone.

"It's not that," I say. "I'm not allowed to spend any nights away from the apartment."

Chloe sighs—a crackling hiss in my ear. "Those fucking rules."

"No more lectures, please," I say. "You know I need the money."

"And *you* know I'd rather lend you some cash than see you be held prisoner in the Bartholomew."

"It's a job," I remind her. "Not a prison. And don't worry about me. Go to Vermont. Have fun. Go moose watching or whatever it is people do there."

"Call me if you need anything," Chloe says. "I'll have my phone with me the whole time, even though our B-and-B is, like, in the middle of nowhere. Literally in the woods on top of a mountain. Paul already warned me there might not be cell service."

"I'll be fine."

"You sure?" Chloe says.

"Positive."

When the call ends, I remain in the sitting room, staring at those faces in the wallpaper. They stare right back, eyes unblinking, mouths open but silent, almost as if they want to tell me something but can't.

Maybe they're not allowed, just as I'm not allowed to have visitors or spend a night away from 12A.

Or maybe they're too afraid speak.

Or maybe—and this is the most likely scenario—they're just flowers on wallpaper and, like Ingrid's departure, the Bartholomew is starting to get to me.

22

At twelve thirty, there's a knock on my door.

Greta Manville.

A surprise, although not an unpleasant one. It's a nice break from looking for jobs that don't exist and checking my phone every five minutes for a response from Ingrid. Even more surprising is that Greta's dressed for an outing. Black capris and an oversize shirt. Sweater preppily tied around her neck. Slung over her shoulder is a worn tote bag from the Strand.

"To thank you for your assistance last night, you may escort me to lunch."

She says it with benevolent pomp, as if she's bestowing upon me one of life's greatest honors. Yet I detect another emotion lurking in the back of her throat—loneliness. Whether she wanted it or not, I've dragged her out of her cocoon of books and sudden sleeps. I also suspect that, deep down, Greta likes my company.

I loop my arm through hers. "I would be happy to escort you."

We end up at a bistro a block away from the Bartholomew. A red awning covers the door, and fairy lights twinkle in the windows. Inside, the place is bustling with so many locals on their lunch breaks that I fear we won't get a table. But upon seeing Greta, the hostess leads us to a corner booth that's remained conspicuously empty.

"I called ahead," Greta says as she picks up one of the menus left for us on the table. "Also, the owner values loyalty. And I've been coming here for years, since the first time I lived at the Bartholomew."

"How long has it been since you moved back?" I ask.

Greta gives me a stern look across the table. "We're here to have lunch. Not play twenty questions."

"How about two questions?"

"I'll allow it," Greta says as she snaps her menu shut and beckons the nearest waitress. "But let me order first. If I'm going to be interrogated, I'd like to make sure sustenance is on the way."

She orders grilled salmon with a side of steamed vegetables. Even though I assume she's treating, I get the house salad and a water. Frugal habits die hard.

"The answer to your first question," Greta says once the waitress departs, "is almost a year. I returned last November."

"Why did you come back?"

Greta sniffs, as if the answer is obvious. "Why not? It's a comfortable place within close proximity to everything I need. When an apartment opened up, I jumped at the chance."

"I heard it was difficult finding an open apartment there," I say. "Isn't the waiting list huge?"

"That's your third question, by the way."

"But you'll allow it."

"I'm not amused," Greta says, even though she is. There's a noticeable upturn to her lips that she tries to hide by taking a sip of water. "The answer is yes, there is a waiting list. And before you ask the predictable follow-up, there are ways around it if one knows the right people. I do."

When the food arrives, it's a study in contrasts. Greta's meal looks scrumptious, the salmon steaming and smelling of lemon and garlic. My salad, on the other hand, is a bowl of disappointment. Nothing but limp romaine lettuce smattered with tomato slices and croutons.

Greta takes a bite of fish before saying, "Has there been any news regarding your recently departed apartment-sitter friend? What was her name again?"

"Ingrid."

"That's right. Ingrid with the abominable hair. There's still no indication where she went?"

I shrug. Such an ineffectual gesture, when it comes right down to it. All that tiny rise and fall of my shoulders against the booth's vinyl does is remind me how little I really know.

"At first, I thought it was because she was afraid to stay in the Bartholomew any longer."

Greta reacts the same way Nick did—with muted shock. "Why on earth would you think that?"

"You have to admit something feels off," I say. "There are websites, entire websites, devoted to all the bad things that have happened there."

"That's why I avoid the internet," Greta says. "It's a cesspool of misinformation."

"But a lot of it's true. The servants killed by Spanish flu. And Dr. Bartholomew jumping from the roof. That doesn't happen at average apartment buildings."

"The Bartholomew isn't an average apartment building. And because of its notoriety, things that happen there become exaggerated to the point of myth."

"Is Cornelia Swanson a myth?"

Greta, who had been lifting a forkful of salmon to her mouth, halts mid-bite. She lowers her fork, folds her hands on the table, and says, "A word of advice, my dear. Don't mention that name inside the Bartholomew. Cornelia Swanson is a topic no one there wants to discuss."

"So what I've read about her is true?"

"I didn't say that," Greta snaps. "Cornelia Swanson was a lunatic who should have been living in an asylum, not at the Bartholomew. As for all that utter nonsense—that she consorted with that

Frenchwoman and sacrificed her maid in some bizarre occult ritual—it's nothing more than conjecture. What I told you just now is the same thing I said to your friend."

"Ingrid specifically asked about Cornelia Swanson?"

"She did. I suspect she was disappointed by my answer. I think she came looking for all the gory details. But, as I've said, there aren't any to give. In fact, the strangest thing I've seen at the Bartholomew lately is the behavior of a certain young woman who helped escort me from the building last night."

I stab my fork into the salad, saying nothing.

"When the elevator was stopped on the seventh floor, you acted . . . unusual. Would you care to explain what happened?"

I'd noticed the way she watched me once I returned to the elevator with Rufus. I should have seen this lunch for what it really is—an attempt to understand what she had witnessed. Although I don't necessarily need to talk about it, I find myself wanting to. Maybe because Greta wrote *Heart of a Dreamer*, I feel the need to repay her somehow. A story for a story. Only mine doesn't have a happy ending.

"When I was a freshman in college, my father got laid off from the place he had worked for twenty-five years," I begin. "After months of searching, the only job he could get was a night shift stocking shelves at an Ace Hardware three towns away. My mother worked part-time at a real estate office. To make ends meet she got another job waiting tables at a local diner on weekends. I tried to lighten their load by getting two jobs myself. Plus additional student loans. Plus a credit card I never told them about so they wouldn't have to worry about sending me money. That kept us afloat for the better part of a year."

But then, at the start of my sophomore year, my mother was diagnosed with non-Hodgkin's lymphoma, which spread like wildfire to her kidneys, her heart, her lungs. My mother had to quit her jobs. My father cared for her during the day while still going to work at night. I offered to leave college for a semester to help. My father refused, telling me I needed a good education to get a good job. That if I quit, I'd likely never return and end up just like them—two broken people in a broken town.

My mother's medical expenses soared, even though there was no hope of remission. Everything was about keeping her comfortable until the end came. And my father's meager health insurance plan covered only so much. The rest was up to them. So my father took out a second mortgage on the home he had just finished paying off a few years earlier.

I came home every weekend, my mother slightly smaller at every visit, as if she were shrinking right before my eyes. My father was the same way. The stress sapped his appetite until shirts hung like laundry from his clothesline arms. In the evenings, when he was getting ready for work, I'd hear him crying alone in the bathroom. Deep, guttural sobs that couldn't be drowned out by the running sink.

We lived like that for six months. Then the final blow came. The Ace Hardware my father worked at closed its doors. There went his job and health insurance. I was at school when it happened. A sophomore on the verge of flunking out because I was too frazzled with worry and bone-deep exhaustion to focus on my studies.

"Not long after that, my parents died," I say.

Greta gasps. A shocked, sorrowful sound.

I keep talking, too far into the tale to stop now. "There was a fire. It was the middle of the spring semester. The phone rang at five in the morning. The police. They told me there had been an accident and that both of my parents were dead."

Later that day, Chloe drove me home, although there was nothing left of it. Our side of the duplex was a charred ruin.

"Smoke rose from the wreckage," I tell Greta. "It was an awful throat-coating smoke I hoped I'd never smell again. But I did. Last night at the Bartholomew."

The only thing that survived was my parents' Toyota Camry, which had been parked as far from the house as the driveway would allow. Sitting in the driver's seat was a ring with three keys on it. The instant I saw those keys, I knew the fire hadn't been an accident.

One key was for the Camry itself.

The other two opened storage units at a facility a mile outside of town.

One unit contained all my belongings.

The other held all of Jane's.

My father had emptied both of our bedrooms, which told me that even in their darkest hours, my parents still clung to a faint sliver of hope. That Jane would be found. That the two of us could muddle forward together. That things would turn out okay for us in the end.

The storage units would have been enough to tip off investigators, if the insurance policies hadn't already. My father had purchased two in the months before the blaze.

Life insurance for him.

Fire insurance for the house.

So began the investigation that confirmed what I already knew. On the night of the fire, my father and mother shared a bottle of wine, even though she shouldn't have been drinking with her kidneys on the verge of failure.

They also shared a pizza ordered from the very same place they went on their first date.

And a slice of chocolate cake.

And a bottle of my mother's strongest painkillers.

Arson experts concluded the fire began in the hallway just outside my parents' room, spurred on by lighter fluid and some balled-up newspapers. The bedroom door was closed, meaning it took some time for the fire to reach the bed where my parents were found.

They knew this because only my mother died from the overdose.

My father was killed by the smoke.

"I tried to be mad at them," I say. "I wanted to hate them for what they did. But I couldn't. Because even then I knew they did what they thought was right."

I don't tell Greta how when I'm feeling happy, I sometimes get the need to flirt with fire. To feel its heat on my skin. To have the flame singe me just enough to know what it feels like, so that I can understand what my parents went through.

For me.

For my future.

For the sister who has yet to return.

Greta slips her hand over mine, her palm hot, as if she, too, has held it to an open flame.

"I'm sorry for your loss. I'm sure you miss them greatly."

"I do," I say. "I miss them. I miss Jane."

"Jane?"

"My sister. She vanished two years before the fire. There's been no trace of her since. She might have run away. She might have been murdered. At this point, I doubt I'll ever know."

I've slumped noticeably in the booth, my arms at my sides, my body numb. My version of one of Greta's sudden sleeps. If I feel sadness, it's the same simmering grief I always experience. The kind of pain I long ago learned to live with. Talking about my parents and Jane doesn't make that grief feel better or worse. It simply remains.

"Thank you for entrusting me with your story," Greta says.

"Now you know why I prefer fantasy over reality."

"I can't blame you," Greta says. "I also see why you're so keen to find Ingrid."

"I'm doing a terrible job of it."

"If I were a betting woman, which I'm not, I'd wager she went off somewhere with a young man," Greta says. "Or woman. I don't judge when it comes to matters of the heart."

Spoken like the woman who wrote a romance beloved by generations of teenage girls. And even though I want to believe Ingrid is off somewhere enjoying a happily-ever-after, everything I know so far suggests the opposite.

"I just can't shake the feeling she's in trouble," I say. "She specifically told me she had nowhere else to go."

"If you suspect something bad happened, why don't you go to the police?"

"I called them. It didn't go well. They said there wasn't enough information to get involved."

This elicits a sympathetic sigh from Greta. "If I were you, I'd call some of the hospitals in the area. Maybe there was an accident and she required medical treatment. If that doesn't work, I'd look around the neighborhood. If she has no place to go, then there's a chance she's out on the streets. I know it's hard to think someone we know might be homeless, but have you checked any of the city's shelters?"

"You think I should?"

"It certainly couldn't hurt," Greta says with a firm nod. "Ingrid Gallagher might be there, hiding in plain sight."

23

The nearest homeless shelter for women is twenty blocks south and two blocks west of the restaurant. After making sure Greta can get back to the Bartholomew on her own, I go there on the slim chance that she's right and Ingrid is living on the streets.

The shelter is housed in a building that's seen better days. The exterior is brown brick. The windows are tinted. It used to be a YMCA, as evidenced by the ghost of those letters hovering to the right of the main entrance. Also hovering there is a group of women smoking in a semicircle. All of them eye me with suspicion as I approach. A silent message telling me what I already know.

Just like at the Bartholomew, I do not belong here.

I'm starting to think I don't belong anywhere. That it's my lot in life to occupy a limbo all my own. Still, I approach them and smile, trying not to act frightened, even though I am. Which then makes me feel guilty. I have more in common with these women than with anyone at the Bartholomew.

I remove my phone from my pocket and hold it up so they can see the selfie of Ingrid and me in Central Park. "Have any of you seen this girl in the past few days?"

Only one woman in the smoking circle bothers to look. She stares at the photo with hard eyes while biting the inside of her razor-sharp cheeks. When she speaks, her voice is surprisingly soft. I thought she'd sound as weathered as she looks.

"No, ma'am, I haven't seen her. Not around here."

I assume she's the ringleader of this ragtag group, because she nudges the others, compelling them to take a look. They shake their heads, murmur, look away.

"Thanks," I say. "I appreciate it."

Under the watchful gaze of the smokers, I make my way into the building. Just inside the door is an empty waiting area and a registration desk behind a shield of scuffed reinforced glass. On the other side sits a plump woman who studies me with the same disdain as the women outside.

"Excuse me," I say. "I was wondering if you could help me."

"Are you in need of shelter?"

"No," I say. "I'm looking for someone. A friend."

"Has she entered herself into the shelter system?" the woman asks.

"I don't know."

"Is she under the age of twenty-one? Because that means she'd be at a different facility."

"She's over twenty-one," I say.

"If she has children or is currently pregnant, she'd be at one of our PATH shelters," the woman adds. "There are also separate facilities for victims of domestic violence. If she's been on the street awhile, you might find her at a drop-in center."

I lean back, overwhelmed not just by the sheer number of locations and designations but the fact that there's a need for all of them. Once more, it makes me feel fortunate that I found the Bartholomew. It also makes me fear what will happen once I leave.

"No kids," I tell the woman. "Single. No abuse."

That I know of.

The realization blasts into my thoughts like a radio at full volume. Just because Ingrid didn't mention abuse doesn't mean there wasn't any. I again think of the many places she's lived, the endless moving, the gun she bought—possibly when she assumed running was no longer an option.

"Then she'd have come here," the woman says.

I press my phone against the glass so she can see the photo I showed the smokers outside. After a moment's contemplation, she says, "She doesn't look familiar, sweetie. But I'm only here during the day. This place fills up at night, so there's a chance she's here then and I just missed her."

"Is it possible to talk to someone who *is* here at night? Maybe they'd recognize her."

She gestures to a pair of double doors opposite the desk. "There's a few of them still in there. You're welcome to take a look."

I push through the doors into a gymnasium that's been turned into a space for two hundred people. An army of temporary tenants. Identical cots have been spread across the gym floor in untidy rows of twenty each.

I walk among the cots, seeking out the few that are occupied just in case one of them is Ingrid. At the end of the row, a woman sits straight-backed on the edge of her cot. She stares at a nearby set of roll-away bleachers that have been pressed against the wall. Taped to it is an inspirational poster. A field of lavender swaying in the breeze. At the bottom is a quote from Eleanor Roosevelt.

With the new day comes new strength and new thoughts.

"Every day, before I leave for work, I sit and stare at this poster, hoping that Eleanor is right," the woman says. "But so far, each new day only brings the same old shit."

"It could be worse," I blurt out before I can think better of it. "We could be dead."

"Gotta say, I wouldn't mind seeing *that* on an inspirational poster." The woman slaps her thigh and lets out a raucous laugh that fills our side of the gymnasium. "I haven't seen you before. You new?"

"Just visiting," I say.

"Lucky you."

I take that to mean she's been here awhile. A surprise, seeing how she doesn't look homeless. Her clothes are clean and well-pressed. Khaki pants, white shirt, blue cardigan. All of them in better condition than what I'm wearing. My sweater has a hole at the cuff that I cover with my left hand as I hold out the phone with my right.

"I'm looking for someone who might be staying here. This is a recent picture of her."

The woman eyes the photo of Ingrid and me with curiosity. "Her face doesn't ring any bells. And I've been here a month. Waiting for assisted housing to free up. 'Any day now,' they tell me. Like it's a UPS package and not a damn place to live."

"She would have been here in the past day," I say. "If she was here at all."

"Name?"

"Her name is Ingrid."

"I meant *your* name," the woman says.

"Sorry. I'm Jules."

She finally looks up from the photo and, with a gap-toothed smile, says, "Pretty name. I'm Bobbie. Not as pretty, I know. But it's one of the few things that's mine."

She pats the space next to her, and I join her on the cot. "It's nice to meet you, Bobbie."

"Likewise, Jules."

She plucks the phone from my hand to study the photo once more. "She a friend of yours?"

"More like an acquaintance."

"Is she in trouble?"

I sigh. "That's what I'm trying to find out. If she is, I want to help her."

Bobbie sizes me up. Polite suspicion. I can't blame her. She's probably encountered a lot of people with offers of help. Ones with strings attached. As for me, I suspect she sees a kindred spirit, because she says, "I'll keep an eye out for her, if you want."

"I'd appreciate that very much."

"Can you send me the picture?"

"Sure."

Bobbie gives me her phone number, and I text her the photo.

"I'll save your number," she says. "So I can call you if I run into her."

I want her to do more than just call me. I want her to tell me about her life. About the chain of events that led her here. Because we have something in common, Bobbie and me. We're just two women trying to get by as best we can.

"You say you've been here a month?" I say.

"That's right."

"And before that?"

Bobbie gives me another suspicious once-over. "Are you a social worker or something?"

"Just interested in your story," I say. "If you're interested in telling it."

"There's not much to tell, Jules. Shit happens. You know how it is."

I nod. I know exactly how it is.

"My family was poor, you see. Welfare. Food stamps. All that stuff some folks are always trying to get rid of." Bobbie huffs with annoyance. "As if we *like* depending on food stamps. As if we *want* that goddamn brick of orange cheese they give out. I told myself that when I grew up, I wasn't going to let that happen to me. And I managed for a while. But then something unexpected happened, and I had to dig myself a little hole of debt to deal with it. Then to fill in that hole, I had to dig another, this one a little bigger. After a while, there were so many holes that I was bound to fall into one and not be able to get out. It's hard. *Life* is hard. And too damn expensive."

"Have you seen the price of oranges?" I say.

Bobbie laughs again. "Honey, the last time I had fresh fruit, Obama was still in office."

"Well, I hope life gets easier for you very soon," I say.

"Thanks," Bobbie says brightly. "And I hope you find your friend. Doing good deeds—makes this rotten world just a little bit better."

24

When I return to the Bartholomew at three o'clock, Charlie greets me outside, a dark look of concern in his eyes.

"Someone's here to see you," he says. "A young man. He's been here awhile. After an hour, I told him he could wait inside."

Charlie opens the door, and my stomach drops.

There, standing just inside the lobby, is Andrew.

His unexpected—and unwanted—presence makes me see red. Literally. For a second, my vision turns crimson, just like in that Hitchcock movie my dad made me watch once. *Marnie*, it was called. She saw flashes of red like I do now as I march through the door, a scowl on my face.

"What the hell are you doing here?"

Andrew looks up from his phone. "You haven't responded to my calls or texts."

"So you just decided to show up?" A thought occurs to me, momentarily cutting through my anger. "How did you even know I was here?"

"I saw your picture in the paper," Andrew says. "It took me a minute to realize it was you."

"Because it's an awful picture of me."

"I always said you're much prettier in person."

Andrew flashes me his seductive grin. The one that made me weak-kneed when we first met. It's a dazzling smile, and he knows it. I'm sure he used it on the co-ed he was fucking. One flash was probably all it took to lure her into our apartment and onto our couch.

Seeing the grin now leaves my body humming with rage. That's something I've managed to push to the wayside the past two weeks, consumed as I was with worry. But now that he's here, right in front of me, it comes roaring back.

"What the fuck do you want, Andrew?"

"To apologize. I truly hate the way we ended things."

He takes a step toward me. I take several steps back, putting as much distance between us as possible. Soon I'm at the row of mailboxes and digging out the mail key.

"The way *you* ended things," I say as I open the mailbox and peek inside, finding it empty. "I had nothing to do with it."

"You're right. The way I treated you was awful. There's no excuse for it."

I slam the mailbox shut and turn around, seeing that Andrew has followed me. He stands about three feet away. Just out of punching range.

"You should have said all this two weeks ago," I tell him. "But you didn't. You could have apologized then. You could have begged me not to leave. But you didn't even *try*."

"Would that have changed your mind?" Andrew says.

"No." Tears sting my eyes, which pisses me off. The last thing I want is for Andrew to see just how hurt I really am. "But it would have made me feel less stupid for being with you. It wouldn't have made me feel so—"

Unloved.

That's what I'm about to say but stop myself before the word can escape. I fear it will make me look as pathetic as I often feel.

"Were there others besides her?" I ask, even though it's a pointless question. I'm certain there were. I'm also certain it doesn't make any difference now.

"No," Andrew says.

"I don't believe you."

"Honest."

Despite his protests, it's clear he's lying. His eyes shift ever so slightly to the left. It's his tell.

"How many?" I say.

Andrew shrugs, scratches the back of his head.

"Two or three."

Which probably means there were more.

"I'm sorry about all of them," Andrew says. "I never meant to hurt you, Jules. I need you to know that. They meant nothing to me. You did. I loved you. Truly. And now I've lost you forever."

He moves in even closer and attempts to tuck a lock of hair behind my ear. Another one of his surefire moves. He did it right before our first kiss.

I slap his hand away. "You should have thought about that earlier."

"You're right, I should have," Andrew says. "And you have every reason to be angry and hurt. I just wanted to tell you that I regret everything. And that I'm sorry."

He stands in place, as if waiting for something. I think he wants me to forgive him. I don't plan on doing that anytime soon.

"Fine," I say. "You've said your apologies. Now you can go."

Andrew doesn't budge.

"There's something else," he says, growing quiet.

I cross my arms and huff. "What else could there possibly be?"

"I need—" Andrew looks around the lobby until he's certain there's no one else around. "I need money."

I stare at him, stunned. When my legs start to buckle with anger, I try to cover it by taking a step backward.

"You can't be fucking serious."

"It's for the rent," he says, his voice a desperate whisper. "You don't know how expensive that place is."

"I actually do," I shoot back, "seeing how I paid half that rent for a year."

"And you lived there for a few days this month, which means you should give me at least a little money to cover that."

"What makes you think I have any money to give?"

"Because you live *here*." Andrew spreads his arms wide, gesturing at the grandiose lobby. "I don't know what racket you've got going, Jules, but I'm impressed."

Just then, Nick enters the lobby, looking particularly dashing in a fitted gray suit. Even better, he looks rich, which prompts Andrew to eye him with undisguised contempt. Seeing it makes me feel petty. Vindictively so. Which is why I rush to Nick and say, "There you are! I've been waiting for you!"

I pull him into a hug, whispering desperately into his ear, "Please go along with this."

Then I kiss him. More than just a quick peck on the lips. It's a kiss that lingers—long enough for me to feel the jealousy radiating from Andrew's side of the lobby.

"Who's this?" he says.

Nick, thankfully, continues the charade. Casually throwing an arm over my shoulder, he says, "I'm Nick. Are you a friend of Jules's?"

"This is Andrew," I say.

Nick steps forward to shake Andrew's hand. "A pleasure to meet you, Andrew. I'd love to stay and chat, but Jules and I have an important thing to get to."

"Yes," I add. "Very important. I suggest you run along as well."

Andrew hesitates a moment, his gaze switching between Nick and me. His expression is a mixture of insult and injury. I'd like to be the kind of person who doesn't enjoy seeing him hurt. I'm not.

"The door's right there," Nick says, pointing the way out. "In case you're confused."

"Bye, Andrew." I give him the weakest of waves. "Have a nice life."

With one last regretful look, Andrew slips out the door and, hopefully, out of my life. Once he's gone, I pull away from Nick, humiliation burning my cheeks.

"I am *so* sorry about that. I didn't know what else to do. I needed him to leave and couldn't think of a better way to make that happen."

"I think it worked," Nick says while absently touching his lips. They're probably still warm from our kiss. Mine certainly are. "I'm guessing Andrew is an ex-boyfriend?"

We make our way to the elevator, cramming ourselves inside. Standing shoulder to shoulder with Nick, I'm exposed once again to his cologne. That woodsy, citrusy scent.

"He is," I say as we begin our ascent. "Unfortunately."

"It ended badly?"

"That would be an understatement." In the confines of the elevator, I realize how bitter I sound. I wouldn't blame Nick for wanting to stay far away from me after this. No one likes bitter. "I'm sorry. I'm not usually this—"

"Hurt?" Nick says.

"Vindictive."

The elevator reaches the top floor. Nick moves the grate aside, allowing me to exit first. As we walk down the hall, he says, "I'm glad I ran into you. And not just because of the way you greeted me down in the lobby."

"Really?" I say, blushing anew.

"I wanted to know if you'd heard back from Ingrid."

"Not a peep."

"That's disappointing. I was hoping you had."

I could tell Nick about the gun. Or the note Ingrid left that I try not to think about, because thinking about it is too frightening.

BE CAREFUL

Instead, I don't mention them, for the same reasons I didn't tell Chloe. I don't want Nick to think I'm being overly worried, even paranoid.

"I know she's not in the homeless shelter I just returned from visiting," I say.

"That was some smart thinking to look for her there, though."

"I can't take credit. It was Greta Manville's idea."

Nick's brows lift in surprise. "Greta? If I didn't know any better, I'd say the two of you are becoming friends."

"I think she just wants to help," I say.

We reach the end of the hallway, pausing in the wide space between the doors to our respective apartments.

"I'd like to help, too," Nick says.

"But I thought you didn't know Ingrid."

"I didn't. Not very well. But I'm glad she has someone looking out for her."

"I'm afraid I'm not doing a very good job of it," I say.

"Which gives me all the more reason to help," Nick replies. "Seriously, if you need anything—anything at all—let me know. Especially if Andrew comes back."

He gives me a wink and heads to his apartment. I do the same, pausing in the foyer as soon as the door is closed behind me. I feel slightly dizzy, and not just because of Nick. The past twenty-four hours have been so strange it borders on the surreal. Ingrid going missing. The fire. Having lunch with Greta Manville. It's so far from my normal existence that it feels like something Greta herself might have written.

Chloe was right. It is indeed a strange, alternate universe I've stumbled into.

I just hope it's not also something else she told me: that it's all probably too good to be true.

25

I spend the next two hours following Greta's other suggestion and calling the information desks of every hospital in Manhattan. None of them are aware of an Ingrid Gallagher or a Jane Doe matching her description being admitted within the past twenty-four hours.

I'm about to start on hospitals in the outer boroughs when there's another knock on my door. It's Charlie this time, standing in the hall with the largest flower arrangement I've ever laid eyes on. It's so big that Charlie himself is practically invisible behind it. All I see of him is his cap peeking above the blooms.

"Charlie, what will your wife think?"

"Cut it out," Charlie says, a blush in his voice. "They're not from me. I'm just the deliveryman."

I gesture for him to set down the arrangement on the coffee table. As he does, I count at least three dozen blooms. Roses and lilies and snapdragons. Tucked among them is a card.

> *Thank you for saving my beloved Rufus! You're an*
> *absolute angel!—Marianne*

"I heard you were quite the hero last night," Charlie says.

"I was just being a good neighbor," I say. "Speaking of which, how's your daughter? One of the other doormen told me there was some sort of emergency."

"It was much ado about nothing. She's fine now. But it's nice of you to ask."

"How old is she?"

"Twenty."

"Still in college?"

"She plans to go," Charlie says quietly. "Hasn't worked out quite yet."

"I'm sure it will." I take a sniff of the flowers. They smell heavenly. "She's lucky to have a dad like you."

Charlie drifts toward the door, seemingly unsure about whether to leave or not. But then he says, "I heard you were asking about that other apartment sitter. The one who left."

"Ingrid Gallagher. I'm trying to locate her."

"She's missing?"

"I haven't heard from her since she left," I say. "And I just want to know she's okay. Did you ever talk to her?"

"Not really," Charlie says. "I've had more interaction with you in the past five minutes than with her the entire time she was here."

"Leslie told me you were the doorman on duty the night she left but that you never actually saw her leave."

"I didn't. I had to step away from the door to deal with the security camera in the basement. There's a bank of security monitors just off the lobby. It's always a good idea to have another set of eyes watching the place."

"Is the footage saved?"

"It's not," Charlie says, knowing exactly where my thoughts have headed. "Which is why it was necessary for me to check the monitor in the basement."

"What was wrong with it?"

"It was disconnected. A wire in the back had come loose. The camera was still on, but all I saw on the monitor was a blank screen."

"How long were you gone?"

"About five minutes. It was an easy fix."

"Has a camera malfunction ever happened before?" I ask.

"Not on my watch," Charlie says.

"When did you notice it was out?"

"A little after one a.m."

My body freezes. That was around the same time I heard the scream and went to check on Ingrid. Five minutes later, she was gone. Which means Ingrid left immediately after I returned to 12A.

The timing seems too convenient to be a coincidence. In fact, the camera being disconnected just as Ingrid left strikes me as being a distraction.

My first thought is that Ingrid did it herself so that she could leave unnoticed—which would make little sense. There's no rule requiring apartment sitters to remain at the Bartholomew if they don't want to. And Charlie wouldn't have stopped her. He probably would have hailed her a cab and wished her well.

Besides, that would have required Ingrid to gather all her belongings, travel to the basement to disconnect the camera, then go back to the eleventh floor so she could then carry her things all the way down to the lobby. That's a lot of work for something she was well within her right to do, and it surely would have taken more than five minutes. Especially if she arrived at the Bartholomew with a lot of personal belongings.

"Were you on duty when Ingrid moved in?" I say.

Charlie nods.

"How much did she have with her?"

"I can't really remember," he says. "Two suitcases, I think. Plus a couple of boxes."

"Did you see anyone going to the basement before you realized the camera was out?"

"I didn't. I was outside, attending to another resident."

"At that hour? Who was it?"

Charlie straightens his spine, clearly uncomfortable. "I don't think Mrs. Evelyn will like that I'm telling you so much. I want to help, but—"

"I know, I know. The building's big on privacy. But Ingrid's basically the same age as your daughter. If she were missing, you'd be asking a lot of questions, too."

"If my daughter was missing, I wouldn't rest until I found her."

My father had said the same thing once. He meant it at the time. I'm sure of it. But that's the thing about searching. It wears you down. Emotional erosion.

"Don't you think Ingrid deserves the same treatment?" I say. "You don't have to tell me a name. Just give me a little hint."

Charlie sighs and looks past me to the flowers on the coffee table. A hint almost as massive as the bouquet itself.

"She took the dog out a little before one," Charlie says. "I was outside with her the entire time. You know, making sure nothing bad happened. That's not the hour a woman should be on the street alone. Once Rufus did his business, we went back inside. She took the elevator to the seventh floor, and I peeked at the security monitors. That's when I saw the camera in the basement was out."

This means Marianne was in the elevator at roughly the same time Ingrid supposedly left her apartment.

"Thank you, Charlie." I snap off a rosebud from the bouquet and place it in the button hole on his lapel. "You've been a huge help."

"Please don't tell Mrs. Evelyn I said anything," Charlie begs as he adjusts his makeshift boutonniere.

"I won't. I got the feeling from Leslie that it's a sore subject around here."

"Considering the way Ingrid departed, I'm pretty sure Mrs. Evelyn regrets ever letting her stay here in the first place."

With a tip of his cap, Charlie opens the door to leave. Before he can make it all the way out of the apartment, I toss him one last question.

"What apartment does Marianne Duncan live in?"

"Why?"

I flash him an innocent smile. "So I can send her a thank-you note, of course."

I'm certain Charlie doesn't believe me. He looks away, gazing into the hallway. Still, he tosses an answer over his shoulder.

"7A," he says.

26

The seventh floor is as busy now as it was last night. Only instead of firefighters, it's contractors moving through the smoke-stained halls. The door to Mr. Leonard's apartment has been removed and now leans against a hallway wall stippled with smoke damage. Next to it is a section of kitchen counter, its surface covered with burn marks. On the floor, soot spreads across the tile like black mold.

Blasting out of the apartment itself is a cacophony of construction noise. Emerging from the racket are two workers carrying a wooden cupboard with a charred door. They drop it next to the countertop. Before returning to the apartment, one of the workers looks my way and winks.

I roll my eyes and move in the opposite direction, toward the front of the building. At 7A, I give two short raps on the door.

Marianne answers in a rush of perfume-scented air that floats past me and mixes with the smoke smell still lingering in the hall.

"Darling!" she says, pulling me in for a half hug and an air kiss on both cheeks. "I was hoping I'd see you today. I can't thank you enough for rescuing my Rufus."

I'm not surprised to see Marianne carrying Rufus in her arms. What is a surprise is that both of them are wearing hats. Hers is black with a wide, floppy brim tilted so that it casts a shadow over her entire face. His is a tiny top hat held in place with an elastic band.

"I just stopped by to thank you for the flowers," I say.

"Don't you just love them? Tell me you love them."

"They're beautiful. But you really didn't need to go to all that trouble."

"Of course I did. You were a complete angel last night. That's what I'm going to start calling you. The Angel of St. Bart's."

"And how's Rufus doing?" I say. "All better after last night, I hope."

"He's fine. Just a little scared. Isn't that right, Rufus?"

The dog nuzzles the crook of her arm, trying in vain to free himself of the tiny top hat. He stops when a sudden bang echoes up the hallway from 7C.

"Horrible, isn't it?" Marianne says of the noise. "It's been like this all morning. I'm sorry about what happened to poor Mr. Leonard, and I wish him a speedy recovery. I truly do. But it's quite an inconvenience for the rest of us."

"It's been an eventful few days. What with the fire and that apartment sitter leaving so suddenly."

I hope the mention of Ingrid sounds less calculated to Marianne than it does to me. To my ears, it clangs with obviousness.

"What apartment sitter?"

Marianne's face remains obscured by her hat, making her expression unreadable. She reminds me of a femme fatale from the film noirs my father used to watch on lazy Saturdays. Elegant and inscrutable.

"Ingrid Gallagher. She was in 11A. Then two nights ago, she suddenly left without telling anyone."

"I wouldn't know anything about that."

Marianne's voice isn't unkind. On the surface, her tone hasn't changed. Yet I detect a slight cold streak running through her words. She's now on guard.

"I just assumed the two of you had met. After all, you were the first person I met after I arrived." I offer her a shy smile. "You made me feel very welcome here."

Marianne peeks into the hallway, checking to see if anyone else is around. Only one other person is—a workman just outside Mr. Leonard's door, blowing his nose into a red handkerchief.

"I mean, I knew who she was," Marianne says, her voice going so quiet it flirts with being a whisper. "And I knew that she left. But we weren't formally introduced."

"So the two of you never spoke?"

"Never. I think I saw her only a few times, when I was taking Rufus for his morning walk."

"I heard you and Rufus went to the lobby the night she left." Again, it's not the subtlest of transitions. But there's no telling how long Marianne's sharing mood is going to last. "Did you see or hear her go? Or maybe see someone else up and about at that hour?"

"I—" Marianne stops herself, changing course. "No. I didn't."

"Are you sure?"

Being here gives me déjà vu. Marianne has the same say-one-thing-mean-another demeanor Ingrid displayed the night she disappeared. When she answers me with a simple "Yes," the word slides uncertainly off her tongue. She hears how it sounds and tries again, mustering more force. "Yes. I'm sure I saw nothing that night."

Marianne's got one hand on the door now, her gloved fingers flexing against the wood. When she raises her other hand to the brim of her hat, I see that it's trembling. She gives the hallway another up-and-down glance and says, "I need to go. I'm sorry."

"Marianne, wait—"

She tries to close the door, but I desperately slide my foot against the frame, blocking it. I peer at her through the six-inch gap that remains.

"What aren't you telling me, Marianne?"

"*Please*," she hisses, her face still hidden in shadow. "Please stop asking questions. No one here is going to answer them."

Marianne pushes the door against my foot, forcing me to pull it away. Then the door slams shut in another perfume-soaked rush. I stumble backward, suddenly aware of someone else in the hallway with me. Twisting away from Marianne's door, I see Leslie Evelyn standing a few yards down the hall. She's just returned from a yoga class. Lululemon tights. Rolled-up mat under her arm. Thin line of sweat sparkling along her hairline.

"Is there a problem here?"

"No," I say, even though she clearly saw Marianne slam the door in my face. "No problem at all."

"Are you sure? Because it looks to me like you're bothering one of the tenants, which you know is strictly against the rules."

"Yes, but—"

Leslie silences me with a raised hand. "There aren't exceptions to these rules. We thoroughly discussed them when you moved in."

"We did. I was just—"

"Breaking them," Leslie says. "Honestly, I expected more from you, Jules. You were such a well-behaved temporary tenant."

Her use of the past tense stops my heart a moment.

"Are . . . are you kicking me out?"

Leslie says nothing at first, making me wait for the answer. When it arrives—"No, Jules, I'm not"— I let out a grateful sigh.

"Normally I would," she adds. "But I'm taking your past behavior into account. I saw how you helped both Greta and Rufus get out of the building last night. So did the newspapers, apparently. I'd be a cruel person if I made you leave after such a good deed. But what I am is strict. So if I see you bothering Marianne, or any of the residents, again—about anything—I'm afraid you'll have to go. Apartment sitters who don't follow the rules seldom get a second chance. And they never get a third."

"I understand," I say. "And I'm sorry. It's just that I still haven't heard from Ingrid, and I'm worried something bad happened."

"Nothing bad happened to her," Leslie says. "At least not within these walls. She left willingly."

"How do you know that for sure?"

"Because I was in her apartment. There were no signs of a struggle. Nor was anything left behind."

Only she's wrong about that. Ingrid did leave without

something—a Glock that's now stowed under the kitchen sink in 12A. Which means Leslie could also be wrong about Ingrid not leaving other things behind. Even though she didn't arrive with much—two suitcases and a couple of boxes, according to Charlie—it was more than what Ingrid could handle on her own. It would take me at least three trips to move my own meager belongings from 12A.

I apologize to Leslie once more and hurry away, suddenly seized with the idea that some of Ingrid's things could still be in 11A. Shoved in the back of a closet. Under a bed. Someplace where Leslie wouldn't immediately notice them. And among those possibly hidden items could be something indicating not only where Ingrid went but who she was running from.

I won't know with certainty unless I look for myself. Not an easy task. I can think of only one other way inside, and even that requires the help of someone else. Adding to the difficulty is that it needs to be done quickly and quietly.

Because now I have another, unexpected worry to contend with.

Leslie is watching my every move.

27

I really don't think this is a good idea," Nick says.

"You said you wanted to help."

The two of us are in the kitchen of 12A, standing shoulder to shoulder as we stare into the open dumbwaiter. Nick scratches the back of his neck, charmingly uncertain.

"This," he says, "isn't quite what I had in mind."

"You know of a better way to get into Ingrid's apartment?"

"You could —and I know this might sound crazy—just ask Leslie to let you in. She's got a key."

"I'm on her bad side at the moment. She says I was bothering Marianne Duncan."

"And were you?"

I give him a quick rundown of the past hour, from Charlie's flower delivery to Marianne's skittishness to the idea that 11A might still contain some kind of clue regarding what happened to Ingrid.

"With Leslie highly unlikely to cooperate, it's the dumbwaiter or nothing," I say. "You lower me down, I take a look around, you pull me back up."

Nick continues to eye the dumbwaiter with skepticism. "There are, like, a hundred ways in which your plan can go wrong."

"Name one."

"I could drop you."

"I'm not that heavy, and you're not that weak," I counter. "Besides, it's only one floor down."

"Which is far enough to cause serious damage if you fall," Nick says. "Trust me, Jules, this isn't something you should take lightly, even though your bravery is admirable."

I'm not brave. I'm in a hurry. I remember those cops who chastised my family for waiting so long after Jane vanished. They stressed that every minute counts. It's now been more than forty hours since Ingrid disappeared. The clock is ticking.

"I do trust you. Which is why I asked you to help me with this. Please, Nick. Just a quick look. Down and back."

"Down and back," he says, reaching for the dumbwaiter rope and giving it a tug to test its strength. "How much time do you plan on spending between those two steps?"

"Five minutes. Maybe ten."

"And you really think this could help you locate Ingrid?"

"I've tried everything else," I say. "I called hospitals. I went to a homeless shelter. I've asked around as much as I could. I'm running out of options here."

"But what do you expect to find?"

I know what I *don't* expect—another gun, or an even more alarming note written on the back of a poem. But something less sinister and more useful could be lying among the tasteful furnishings of 11A.

"Hopefully something that might hint at where Ingrid has gone," I say. "A piece of mail. An address book."

I'm grasping at straws, I know. Not to mention ignoring the likelihood that nothing belonging to Ingrid remains in that apartment. But if something *is* there, finding it could finally help me locate her, which would put all my questions—and worries—to rest.

"I told you I'd help, so I will," Nick says, shaking his head, as if he can't quite believe he's agreed to this. "What's the plan?"

The plan is for me to climb into the dumbwaiter with my phone and a flashlight. Nick will then lower me into 11A. As soon as I'm out, he'll raise it back to 12A, just in case Leslie keeps tabs on this kind of thing.

I'll then search the apartment while Nick keeps watch on the stairwell landing between the eleventh and twelfth floors. If it looks like someone is approaching, he'll alert me with a text. I'll then leave immediately, using the door, making sure it locks behind me.

We hit our first hurdle as soon as I try to climb into the dumbwaiter. It's a tight fit, made possible only by curling into a fetal position. The dumbwaiter itself starts groaning and creaking as soon as I'm inside, and for a fraught, fearful moment I think it's going to collapse under my weight. When it doesn't, I give Nick a nervous nod.

"We're good," I say.

Nick doesn't look as optimistic. "You sure you want to go through with this?"

I nod again. I don't have any other choice.

Nick gives the rope a tug, freeing it from the locking mechanism on the pulleys above. The dumbwaiter immediately drops several inches. Startled, I let out a whimpered half shriek, prompting Nick to say, "Everything's okay. I've still got you."

"I know," I say.

Even so, I grip the twin strands of rope running through the dumbwaiter. They're on the move, sliding through my clenched fists. One goes up, the other down, reminding me of the cables of the Bartholomew's elevator. I descend farther, the bottom of the cupboard level with my thighs, then my chest, then my shoulders. When it reaches eye level, only a two-inch gap remains. Looking through it, all I can see of Nick is his shirt coming untucked from his jeans as he continues to lower me.

He gives the rope another heave and the gap closes completely, plunging me into darkness.

Only once I'm cut off from Nick and the rest of 12A do I begin to ponder the foolishness of my plan. Nick was right. This is not a good idea. I'm literally inside the walls of the Bartholomew. Any number of bad things could happen.

The rope could snap, sending me falling like a sack of garbage into a dumpster.

The bottom of the dumbwaiter could fall away—a serious possibility, I think, now that it's started creaking and groaning again.

Worse is the idea that it could get stuck, leaving me trapped in a dark limbo between floors. The very thought floods me with claustrophobia so overwhelming I become convinced the dumbwaiter is getting smaller, shrinking ever so slightly, forcing me into a tighter ball.

I flick on the flashlight. A terrible idea. In the sudden glow, the dumbwaiter's walls remind me of the inside of a coffin. It certainly has the feel of one. Dark. Confining. Buried.

I turn off the light. Thrust once more into darkness, I notice the sudden lack of noise around me.

The creaks and groans of the dumbwaiter no longer exist.

When I grab the ropes again, I find them motionless.

The dumbwaiter has stopped.

I'm trapped. That's my first thought. Just like I feared. I nudge the walls with my shoulders, certain there's less room now than there was a few seconds ago.

But then my phone lights up, filling the dumbwaiter with an ice-blue glow.

A text from Nick.

You're lowered.

I elbow the wall to my left, realizing it's not a wall at all.

It's a door.

A cupboard door, to be precise. One that slides upward just like its twin in 12A.

That I never considered the likelihood the door would be closed shows just how little I've thought this whole thing through. By bending my arm and using the flat of my left hand, I manage to raise it just a crack. I then slide my left foot underneath the door to keep it from falling. After contorting my body in ways I'm sure I'll regret later, I'm able to lift the door completely and slide out of the dumb-waiter.

In the darkened kitchen of 11A, I take a moment to stretch, my joints popping. I then text Nick back.

I'm in.

Two seconds later, the dumbwaiter begins to move. Watching its rise, I again question the wisdom of coming down here. So much so that I'm tempted to hop in and let Nick haul me back to the safety of 12A. I ask myself what I truly expect to find here. The answer, if I'm being completely honest, is nothing. Which means I'm risking a lot to be here. If Leslie should suddenly barge in, there goes my twelve thousand dollars and that reset button I so desperately need to press.

But unlike me, Nick isn't wasting any time. The dumbwaiter has already been lifted out of view, leaving me no choice but to close the cupboard door and turn on the flashlight.

There's no turning back now, I'm in 11A. Time to start searching.

I begin in the kitchen, shining the flashlight into every cupboard and drawer, finding the usual assortment of pots, bowls, and utensils. Nothing looks out of place. Nor does anything look like it once be-longed to Ingrid.

The phone brightens in my hand. Another text from Nick.

On the landing now. All is clear.

I continue the search, going through the hallway, the living room, and the study, all of which follow the same layout as 12A. There's even a desk and bookshelf in the study, although they're as devoid of information as the ones directly above them. The desk is empty. The bookshelf mostly is, too, save for a few John Grisham hardcovers and a phone book–thick biography of Alexander Hamilton.

It dawns on me that I have no idea why 11A is vacant. Ingrid never got the chance to mention a previous owner dying or a current resident being gone for an extended period of time. I suppose it could be either of those reasons, although neither would explain why the place looks so uninhabited. I get the feeling I had when peeking inside right after Leslie told me Ingrid had left. That the place seemed less like an apartment than a facsimile of one. Cold, quiet, tasteful to the point of blandness.

I move to the other side of the apartment, the one that doesn't follow the same layout as mine. Where 12A stops at the corner of the Bartholomew, 11A continues down the building's northern side. Here I find a bathroom, glowing white in the flashlight's beam, and two small bedrooms across the hall from each other.

At the end of the hall is the door to the master bedroom. While not as grand as the one on the second level of 12A, it's still impressive. There's a king bed, an eighty-inch flat-screen TV, a master bath, and a walk-in closet. That's where I go first, aiming the flashlight over bare carpet, empty shelves, dozens of wooden hangers holding nothing.

I go to the bathroom next, finding it equally as empty. The cabinets under the sink are bare. In the closet, towels line the shelves, neatly folded.

As I head back into the main bedroom, my phone lights up.

You've been in there awhile, Nick texts. Everything OK?

I note the time glowing at the top of the screen. I've been down here for fifteen minutes. Far longer than I intended.

Finishing up, I text, even though what I should be doing is leaving. There's clearly nothing of Ingrid's left in this apartment. I haven't seen a single box or suitcase or even a remnant that she was ever here at all. But I also don't want to leave without checking every square inch of the place. It took too much effort to get here once. I doubt I'll be able to do it again.

I do a quick check under the bed, sweeping the flashlight back and forth across the carpet.

Nothing.

I go to the nightstand on the left side of the bed.

Nothing.

I then check the one on the right.

Something.

A book, resting like a hotel room Bible at the bottom of an otherwise empty drawer.

A new text arrives from Nick. **Someone's in the elevator. It's moving.**

I text back. **Up?**

Yes.

I aim the flashlight at the book in the drawer. *Heart of a Dreamer.* I'd recognize that cover anywhere. When I pick it up, I find a bookmark with a red tassel tucked among its pages.

I've seen this book—and bookmark—before. In a photo Ingrid posted on Instagram. The same post with the caption boasting how she had met Greta Manville.

This was Ingrid's copy.

I've finally found something else she left behind.

I slide the bookmark from its place and see that nothing about it is personalized. It's as generic as can be. Just an illustration of a cat curled up on a blanket. Ones just like it are sold in every bookstore in America.

My phone glows three times in quick succession, brightening the room like lightning flashes as I start to flip backward through the book, checking for scraps of paper tucked among the pages or notes in the margins. There's nothing until I get to the title page, which bears an inscription written in large, looping letters.

> *Darling Ingrid,*
> *Such a pleasure! Your youthfulness gives me life!*
>
> *Best wishes,*
> *Greta Manville*

My phone lights up again, forcing me to finally check it. I see four missed texts from Nick, each one more frightening than the last.

Elevator stopped on 11.

It's Leslie! Someone's with her.

They're heading to 11A!!

The last text, sent mere seconds ago, makes my heart rattle.

HIDE

I drop the book back into the nightstand drawer and push it shut. Then I rush to the hallway just in time to hear the sound of a key turning a lock, the door opening, and, finally, the voice of Leslie Evelyn filling the apartment.

"Here we are, sweetie: 11A."

28

Leslie and her guest are roaming 11A, their voices low, conversational. So far, they've stayed on the other side of the apartment. The study. The sitting room. Right now they're in the kitchen, Leslie saying something I can't quite make out.

I remain in the master bedroom, where I've stuffed myself beneath the bed. I lie on my stomach, the phone shoved under me to block the glow if Nick texts again. I keep my mouth clamped shut, breathing through my nose because it's quieter that way.

Outside the bedroom, Leslie's voice gets louder, clearer. I can now make out what she's saying, which means she's left the kitchen and is getting closer.

"This is one of the Bartholomew's nicest units," she says. "They're all nice, of course. But this one is extra special."

The person with her is a woman, young and chipper. At least, she's trying to be. I notice a quiver of nervousness in her voice when she says, "It's such an amazing apartment."

"It is," Leslie agrees. "Which means staying here is also a big responsibility. We need someone who'll truly watch over the place."

Ah, so this is an interview for Ingrid's replacement. Leslie wasted no time. It also explains the girl's nervousness. She's trying hard to impress.

"Back to the questions," Leslie says. "What's your current employment situation?"

"I'm an actress," the girl says. "I'm waiting tables part time until I get my big break."

She lets out a nervous chuckle, making light of the idea, as if she doesn't even believe it. I feel bad for her. I'd feel worse if I wasn't hiding in fear, watching their shadows glide along the hallway wall. A moment later they're in the bedroom, Leslie flicking on the overhead light. Like an insect, I shrink farther under the bed.

"Do you smoke?" Leslie asks.

"Only if a role requires it."

"Drink?"

"Not really," the girl replies. "I'm not legal yet."

"How old are you?"

"Twenty. I'll be twenty-one in a month."

They cross the room.

Then approach the bed.

Then stop so close that I can see their shoes. Black pumps for Leslie. Scuffed Keds for the girl. I hold my breath, covering my nose and mouth with my hand for good measure, afraid to make the slightest noise. Even so, my heart pounds so loud in my chest that I'm certain they could hear it if they stopped talking long enough to listen. Thankfully, they don't.

"What's your relationship status?" Leslie asks. "Are you seeing anyone?"

"I, um, have a boyfriend." The girl sounds thrown by the question. "Will that be a problem?"

"For you, yes," Leslie says. "There are certain rules that temporary tenants must follow. One of them is no visitors."

Leslie walks toward the master bath, her pumps vanishing from my field of vision. The girl in the Keds stays a moment longer before reluctantly following her.

"Ever?" she says.

"Ever," Leslie replies from inside the bathroom, the tile giving her voice a watery echo. "Another rule is no nights spent away from the apartment. So if you're approved to stay here, I'm afraid you won't be seeing very much of your boyfriend."

"I'm sure it won't be a problem," she says.

"I've heard that before."

Leslie returns to the foot of the bed, her black pumps mere inches from my face. They're spotless—so polished that I can see my warped reflection in the gleaming leather.

"Tell me about your family," she says. "Any next of kin?"

"My parents live in Maryland. Same with my younger sister. She wants to be an actress, too."

"How lovely for your parents." Leslie pauses. "That's all the questions I have. Shall we return to the lobby?"

"Um, sure," the girl says. "Did I get the job?"

"We'll give you a call in a few days to let you know."

They both leave the bedroom, Leslie flicking off the lights on her way out. Soon I hear the front door close and the key click in the lock.

Even though they're now gone, I wait before moving.

One second.

Two seconds.

Three.

When I do start to move, it's just enough to slide my phone out from under me and check for a text from Nick.

It arrives thirty seconds later.

They're in the elevator.

I crawl out from under the bed and move into the hall on tiptoes, still too frightened to make much noise. At the door, I undo the lock and peek outside, making sure they're really gone. Seeing no one, I lock the door again, close it behind me, and sprint to the staircase.

Nick is still on the landing, his expression changing from fraught to overjoyed when he sees me running up the first set of steps.

"That was nerve-racking," he says.

"You have no idea."

My heart continues to hammer in my chest, making me light-headed. I think the dizziness is from shock that I wasn't caught and immediately booted from the Bartholomew. Or maybe it's because of the way Nick is gripping my hand, his palm hot as he quickly pulls me up the steps to the twelfth-floor landing.

We head straight to his apartment—running, giggling, shushing, both of us riding the high of getting away with something we shouldn't have been doing. Inside, Nick leans against the door, his chest heaving. "Did we just do that?"

I'm also out of breath, answering in huffs. "I . . . think . . . we did."

"Holy shit, we just did that!"

Nick, his hand still holding mine, pulls me into a giddy embrace. His body is warm. His heart beats as fast as mine. Adrenaline leaps off him like an electrical current, passing straight into me until I'm so dizzy the room spins.

I look into Nick's eyes, hoping that will steady me. Instead, I only feel increasingly unmoored. But it's not a bad sensation. Far from it. Caught in a wave of euphoria, I press myself against him until our faces are inches apart.

Then I kiss him.

A quick, impromptu peck that makes me instantly recoil in shame.

"I'm sorry," I say.

Nick stares at me, a flash of hurt in his eyes. "Why?"

"I—I don't know."

"Did you not want to kiss me?"

"I did. It's just—I wasn't sure if you wanted me to."

"Try it again and see."

I take a breath.

I lean in.

I kiss Nick again. Slowly this time. Anxiously. I haven't kissed anyone but Andrew for a very long time, and a silly, girlish part of me worries I've forgotten how. I haven't, of course. It's just as swooningly delicious as I remember.

It helps that Nick's an amazing kisser. An expert. I willingly lose myself in the sensation of his lips on mine, his heart thundering beneath my palm, his hand on the small of my back.

The two of us say nothing as we move down the hallway on swaying legs, kissing against one wall before breaking away and reconnecting a few steps later. I follow him up the spiral steps to his bedroom, his white-hot hand brushing mine.

I pause for a moment at the top of the steps, a meek voice in the back of my brain telling me this is all happening too quickly. I have other things to worry about. Finding Ingrid. Finding a job. Finding some way to gain control of my life.

But then Nick kisses me again.

On my lips.

On my earlobe.

On the nape of my neck as he starts to undress me.

When my clothes fall away, all my worries go with them.

Relieved of them, I let Nick take me by the hand and guide me to his bed.

NOW

D r. Wagner stares at me expectantly, waiting for me to continue. I don't. Mostly because I understand that I am starting to sound crazy.

I absolutely cannot sound crazy.

Not to the doctor. Not to the police, when it's time for the inevitable interrogation. Not to anyone, lest they think I'm the slightest bit unstable and therefore refuse to believe me.

They have to believe me.

"You suggested the Bartholomew was haunted," Dr. Wagner says, trying to keep the conversational ball rolling. "I've always heard those rumors. Urban legends and whatnot. But I also heard all of that was ancient history."

"History can repeat itself," I say.

The doctor's left eyebrow rises, cresting the frame of his glasses. "Are you speaking from experience?"

"Yes. I met a girl on my first day at the Bartholomew. She later disappeared."

I sound calmer now, even though on the inside I'm at full panic. My pulse thrums and my eyelids twitch and more sweat pools inside the brace at my neck.

But I don't raise my voice.

I don't talk faster.

If I edge even the tiniest bit toward hysteria, this conversation will be over. I learned that when I talked to the 911 operator.

"She was there one day, gone the next. It was almost as if she had died."

I pause, giving the statement enough time to settle over Dr. Wagner. When it does, he says, "It sounds to me like you think someone at the Bartholomew was murdered."

"I do," I say, before adding the stinger. "Several people."

TWO DAYS
EARLIER

29

When I wake, it's not George I see outside the window but a different gargoyle. His twin. The one that occupies the south-facing corner. I eye him with suspicion, on the verge of asking him what he did with George.

But then I realize I'm not alone.

Nick is asleep beside me, his face buried in a pillow, his broad back rising and falling.

Which explains the different gargoyle.

And the very different bedroom, which I'm just now noticing.

The previous night comes roaring back. The mad dash from 11A. Kissing downstairs. Then kissing upstairs. Then doing a lot more upstairs. Things I haven't done since before Andrew and I moved in together and sex became routine rather than exciting.

But last night? *That* was exciting. And so unlike me.

I sit up to check the clock on the nightstand.

Ten minutes after seven.

I spent the entire night here and not in 12A. Yet another Bartholomew rule I've broken.

I slip out of bed naked, shivering in the morning chill and feeling suddenly shy. The old me, who went AWOL last night, is returning with a vengeance. I gather my clothes quietly, trying not to wake Nick until after I'm dressed.

No such luck. I've barely slipped on my panties when his voice rises from the bed.

"Are you leaving?"

"Sorry, yeah. I need to go."

Nick sits up. "You sure? I was going to make you pancakes."

Rather than attempt to put on my bra with Nick watching, I simply toss it with my shoes before pulling on my blouse.

"Maybe another time."

"Hey," Nick says. "Why the rush?"

I gesture to the clock. "I didn't spend the night in 12A. I broke one of Leslie's rules."

"I wouldn't worry about that."

"That's easy for you to say."

"Seriously, don't sweat it. The rules are just there to make sure apartment sitters realize this is a serious job."

Nick gets out of bed, displaying none of my shyness. He moves to the window and stretches, showing off a body so beautiful my knees go weak. I have another of those I-can't-believe-this-is-real moments that have happened since I moved into the Bartholomew.

"I do realize that," I say. "Which is why I'm freaking out."

Nick toes a pair of plaid boxers on the floor, deems them acceptable, and slides them on. "I'm not going to tell anyone, if that's what you're worried about."

"I'm worried about losing twelve thousand dollars."

I step into my jeans and give him a quick, close-mouthed kiss, hoping he can't detect my morning breath. Then, with my shoes and bra in hand, I scamper barefoot down the stairs.

"I had a great time," he says as he trails behind me.

"I did, too."

"I'd like to do it again sometime. Any of it." He flashes a grin the devil would envy. "Or all of it."

Heat rushes to my cheeks. "Me, too. But not now."

Nick grips my arm, not letting me leave just yet. "Hey, I forgot to ask. Did you find anything in 11A? I meant to ask last night, but—"

"I didn't give you a chance," I say.

"I was all too happy to be distracted," Nick says.

"I found a book. *Heart of a Dreamer.*"

"Not surprising. Copies of that are everywhere in this building. Are you sure it was Ingrid's?"

"Her name was in it," I say. "Greta signed it for her."

I'd love to tell Nick more. That I'm surprised Greta never mentioned it during our conversations about Ingrid. That I'm worried she's suffering from more than just her sudden sleeps. But I also really, really want to get back to 12A, just in case Leslie Evelyn decides to drop by. After last night, I now expect to see her at every inopportune moment.

"We'll talk later," I say. "Promise."

I give him one last kiss and then rush into the hallway. My first walk of shame. Chloe would say it's about goddamn time, even though I wouldn't have minded going through life without this particular trek. At least it's a short one—a barefoot dash from 12B to 12A.

Once inside, I drop my bra and shoes on the foyer floor and toss my keys toward the bowl. But my aim is off yet again, and the keys end up not just on the floor with everything else but on the heating vent, where they skitter, slide, and drop right through.

Fuck.

Wearily, I head to the kitchen, tripping over a rogue shoe in the process. Since I don't have one of those handy magnet sticks Charlie used, I search the junk drawer for a screwdriver. I end up finding three. I grab all of them, plus a penlight that's also in the drawer.

While I unscrew the grate, I think about Nick. Mostly I think about what he thinks of me. That I'm easy? Desperate? For money, yes, but not affection. Last night was an anomaly, spurred on by adrenaline and fear and, yes, desire.

I harbor no illusions that Nick and I are going to fall in love, get married, and live out our days on the top floor of the Bartholomew. That only happens in fairy tales and Greta Manville's book. I'm no Ginny. Nor am I Cinderella. In less than three months, that clock's going to strike midnight, and it'll be back to reality for me.

Not that I'm far from it. Lying on the floor in yesterday's clothes while reeking of sex is pretty damn real.

But I'm pleased to see that Charlie was right about the grate being easy to remove. I loosen the screws and remove the covering without a problem. The biggest issue comes from the penlight, which flickers until I give it a few good whacks against my palm.

Once it's working properly, I aim it into the vent itself and immediately spot the keys. Surrounding them are other items that have fallen in and been forgotten. Two buttons. A rubber band. A dangly earring that must have been cheap if whoever lived here couldn't be bothered to fish it out.

I grab the keys and leave everything else. Before replacing the grate, I sweep the light across the bottom of the vent, just in case something more valuable has fallen in there. Like cash. A girl's allowed to dream.

Seeing nothing of value, I'm about to turn off the penlight when it catches the edge of something shiny wedged in the corner of the vent. I steady the light and move in for a closer look. Although not cash, it's something just as unexpected.

A cell phone.

Even though Charlie told me it's happened before, I'm still surprised to find a phone at the bottom of the vent. I can understand not bothering to retrieve a cheap earring. But not even someone rich enough to live at the Bartholomew would just abandon their cell phone.

I grab the phone and turn it over in my hands. Although the screen is slightly scratched, it appears to be in good condition. When

I try to turn it on, nothing happens, surely because the battery is dead. It might have been down there for months.

This phone is the same brand as mine. Although the one I have is older, my charger fits it all the same. I go upstairs and plug it into the phone, hoping that after it charges I'll be able to figure out who it belongs to and eventually return it.

While the phone charges, I replace the grate over the vent and then take a shower. Freshly scrubbed and dressed, I return to the phone and see it now has just enough juice to be turned on. When I do, the phone brightens in my hands. Filling the screen is a photograph, presumably of its owner.

Pale face. Almond-shaped eyes. Brown hair in unruly curls.

I swipe a finger across the screen, seeing that the phone itself is locked—a security feature also in use on mine. Without a passcode to unlock it, there's no way of knowing whose phone this is. Or was, seeing how they simply abandoned it in a heating vent.

I swipe back to the first screen, staring again at the woman pictured on it. A realization bubbles up from the deep well of my memory.

I've seen this woman before.

Not in person, but in a different picture. Just a few days ago.

In an instant I'm out of 12A and inside the elevator, which shuttles me to the lobby with its typically excruciating slowness. Outside the Bartholomew, I pass a doorman who isn't Charlie and make a right.

The sidewalk is filled with the usual mix of joggers, dog walkers, and people trudging to work. I pass them all, practically running down the sidewalk until I'm two blocks from the Bartholomew. There, at the corner streetlamp, is a piece of paper hanging on by its last bit of tape.

In the dead center of the page is a photograph of the woman whose phone I found. Same eyes. Same hair. Same china-doll skin.

Above the photo is that red-lettered word that so repelled me the first time I saw the flier.

MISSING

Beneath it is the woman's name.

One I also recognize.

Erica Mitchell.

The apartment sitter who was in 12A before me.

30

I slap the flier flat against the kitchen counter and stare at it, my heart buzzing.

Erica and Ingrid.

Both were apartment sitters at the Bartholomew.

Both are now missing.

That can't be a coincidence.

I take a deep breath and reread the flier. At the top is that awful word spelled out in gaudy red.

MISSING

Below it is the photo of Erica Mitchell, who reminds me more of myself than of Ingrid. We have a similar look. Friendly yet wary. Pretty but not very memorable.

Both of us also occupied 12A. Mustn't forget that.

Running next to the photo is a list of vital statistics.

Name: Erica Mitchell
Age: 22
Hair: Brown
Height: 5'1"
Weight: 110 lbs.
Last seen: October 4

That was twelve days ago. Just a few days after Ingrid moved into the Bartholomew.

At the bottom of the page, also in red, is a number to call if anyone has information regarding Erica's whereabouts.

My parents did the same thing for Jane. Our phone rang a lot those first few weeks. One of my parents always answered, no matter how late it was. But the callers were cranks or desperately lonely or kids daring each other to call a missing girl's number.

I grab my phone and dial. I have no doubt that whoever put up that flier will be very interested to know I found Erica's phone.

The call is answered by a man with a distinctly familiar voice.

"This is Dylan."

I pause, surprise rendering me temporarily mute.

"Dylan the apartment sitter at the Bartholomew?"

Now it's his turn to pause, a good two seconds broken by a suspicious, "Yes. Who is this?"

"It's Jules," I say. "Jules Larsen. In 12A."

"I know who you are. How did you get my number?"

"From the missing poster for Erica Mitchell."

The line goes dead. Another surprise.

Dylan has ended the call.

I'm about to call back when the phone buzzes in my hand.

A text from Dylan.

We can't talk about Erica. Not here.

I text him back. Why not?

Several seconds pass before a series of rippling blue dots appears on the screen. Dylan is typing.

Someone might hear us.

I'm alone.

Do you know that for certain?

I start to type my reply—something along the lines of Paranoid much?—but Dylan beats me to the punch.

I'm not being paranoid. Just cautious.

Why are you looking for Erica? I type.

Why are you calling about her?

Because I found her phone.

My own phone rings suddenly. It's Dylan calling, likely too shocked to text.

"Where did you find it?" he says as soon as I answer.

"In a heating vent in the floor."

"I want to see it," Dylan says. "But not here."

"Then where?"

He gives it only a moment's thought. "Museum of Natural History. Meet me at the elephants at noon. Come alone, and don't tell anyone about this."

I end the call with a queasy feeling in my gut, anxiety gnawing at my insides. Something very wrong is going on here. Something I can't begin to comprehend.

But Dylan seems to understand exactly what's going on.

And it freaks him the hell out.

31

I leave the Bartholomew at the same time Mr. Leonard makes his return. It's a surprise to see him out of the hospital so soon, mostly because he looks like he could use another day there. His skin is pale and papery, and he moves with almost surreal slowness. It requires the assistance of both Jeannette and Charlie to get him out of the cab and across the sidewalk.

I hold the door, taking over Charlie's duty for a moment.

"Thanks, Jules," Charlie says. "I can take it from here."

Mr. Leonard and Jeannette say nothing. Both simply glance at me the same way they did during my tour of the building.

When I get to the American Museum of Natural History, I'm further delayed by the busloads of students swarming the front steps. There are hundreds of them, clad in uniforms of plaid skirts, khaki pants, white shirts under dark blue vests. I nudge my way through them, jealous of their youth, their happiness, their drama and chatter. Life hasn't touched them yet. Not real life.

Once inside the Theodore Roosevelt Rotunda, I pass beneath the skeletal arms of the massive barosaurus and head to the ticket counter. Although the museum is technically free, the woman behind the counter asks if I want to pay the suggested "donation" amount to get inside. I give her five dollars and get a judgmental look in return.

After that bit of humiliation, I enter the Akeley Hall of African Mammals. Or, as Dylan put it, the elephants.

He's already there, waiting for me on the wooden bench surrounding the hall's centerpiece herd of taxidermied elephants. His attempts to appear inconspicuous make him stand out all the more. Black jeans. Black hoodie. Sunglasses over his eyes. I'm surprised museum security isn't hovering nearby.

"You're five minutes late," he says.

"And you look like a spy," I reply.

Dylan removes the sunglasses and surveys the packed hall. The schoolkids have started to ooze into the area, crowding around the surrounding nature dioramas until all that can be seen of the animals are pointed ears, curved horns, giraffe faces staring lifelessly from the other side of the glass.

"Upstairs," Dylan says, pointing to the hall's mezzanine level. "It's less crowded."

It is, but only marginally. After climbing the steps to the second floor, we stand before the only empty diorama. A pair of ostriches guarding their eggs from an approaching group of warthogs. The male's got his head down, wings puffed, beak parted.

"Did you bring Erica's phone?" Dylan says.

I nod. It's in the front right pocket of my jeans. My own phone is in the left. Carrying both makes me feel encumbered, weighed down.

"Let me see it."

"Not yet," I say. "I'm not sure I completely trust you."

I don't like the way he's acting. Everything about Dylan seems jittery, from the way he jingles the keys in his pocket to his constant looking around the hall, as if someone is watching. When he returns his gaze to the diorama, he looks not at the ostriches, which are front and center, but at the encroaching predators. Even though they've been dead and stuffed for decades, he gives them a dark-eyed scowl. I think it's probably intended for me.

"I feel the same about you," he says.

I give him a wry smile. "At least we're on even footing. Now, tell me everything you know about Erica Mitchell."

"How much do *you* know?"

"That she was in 12A before me. She lived there a month before deciding to move out. Now she's missing and you're putting up posters looking for her. Care to fill me in on the rest?"

"We were . . . friends," Dylan says.

I note the pause. "You sure about that?"

We walk to another diorama. This one shows a pair of leopards hidden in a copse of jungle trees. One of them keenly watches a nearby bushpig, ready to strike.

"Okay, we were more than friends," Dylan says. "I ran into her in the lobby on her second day at the Bartholomew. We started flirting, one thing led to another, and we started hooking up on a regular basis. As far as we knew, that wasn't against the rules. But we also didn't broadcast it, just in case it was. So if you're looking for a definitive relationship status, I don't know what to tell you. I don't really know what we were."

I get a flashback to last night with Nick and can instantly relate.

"How long did this go on?"

"About three weeks," Dylan says. "Then she left. There was no notice. She didn't tell me she was leaving—or even thinking about it. One day, she was just gone. At first I thought something might have happened. An emergency or something. But when I called, she never answered. When I texted, she never texted back. That's when I started to get worried."

"Did you ask Leslie what happened?"

"She told me Erica wasn't comfortable with all those stupid apartment-sitter rules and decided to move out. But here's the thing—Erica never once mentioned the rules to me. She certainly never talked about being bothered by them."

"Do you think something changed?"

"I don't know what could have changed overnight," Dylan says. "I left her apartment a little before midnight. She was gone in the morning."

I note the similarities between her departure and Ingrid's. They're hard to miss.

"Did Leslie say she specifically spoke to Erica?"

"I guess she left a note," Dylan says. "A resignation letter. That's what Leslie called it. She said she found it shoved under her office door, along with Erica's keys."

I stare at the diorama, unnerved by the way the leopards are posed. While one of them stalks the bushpig, the other appears to be staring out of the diorama, directly at the people watching from the other side of the glass.

I look away, resting my gaze on Dylan. "Is that when you started looking for Erica?"

"You mean the missing posters? That was a few days after she left. When two days went by and I didn't hear from her, I started to get worried. I went to the police first. That was useless. They told me—"

"That you needed more information," I say. "I got the same thing about Ingrid."

"But they're not wrong," Dylan says. "I don't know enough about Erica. Her birthday. Her address before she got to the Bartholomew. For the poster, I guessed her height and weight. My hope was that someone would recognize her picture and call to tell me they'd seen her. I just want to know she's okay."

We move to another diorama. A pack of wild dogs hunting on the savannah, their eyes and ears alert for prey.

"Have you tried tracking down her family?" I ask Dylan.

"She doesn't have any."

My heart skips a single, surprised beat. "None at all?"

"She was an only child. Her parents died in a car accident when she was a baby. Her only aunt raised her, but she died a couple years ago."

"What about you? You have any family left?"

"None," Dylan says quietly, looking not at me but at the pack of dogs. There are six of them. Their own tight-knit unit. "My mom's dead, and my dad might be. I don't fucking know. I had a brother, but he was killed in Iraq."

Dylan is yet another apartment sitter who doesn't have parents or family nearby. Between him, Erica, Ingrid, and myself, I'm sensing a trend. Either Leslie chooses orphans as some weird act of charity, or she does it because she knows we're more likely to be desperate.

"How much are you getting paid?" I ask Dylan.

"Twelve thousand dollars for three months."

"Same," I say.

"But don't you think that's weird? I mean, who pays that much money to let someone stay in their fancy apartment? Especially when most people would do it for free."

"Leslie told me it was—"

"An insurance policy? Yeah, I was told that, too. But when you add in that, plus all those rules, something about the situation just seems off."

"Then why haven't you left?"

"Because I need the money," Dylan says. "I've got four weeks to go until I collect the whole twelve grand. Once I do that, then I'm out of there, even though I have nowhere else to go. It was the same thing with Erica."

"And Ingrid," I say. "And me."

"One of the things Erica *did* talk about was the Bartholomew and how, well, fucked-up it seems. Have you heard about some of the shit that's gone down there?"

I give a solemn nod, remembering those dead servants lined up on the sidewalk, Cornelia Swanson and her slaughtered maid, Dr. Thomas Bartholomew leaping from the roof.

"I thought Erica was exaggerating." Dylan shakes his head and lets out a quick, bitter chuckle. "That she was being overly worried about the place. Now I think she wasn't worried enough."

"What do you mean?"

"Something weird is going on at the Bartholomew," Dylan says. "I'm sure of it."

The groups of schoolkids have finally found their way upstairs.

They ooze into the space around us, chattering and touching the diorama glass, leaving it riddled with sticky handprints. Dylan pushes away from them, moving to the other side of the room. I join him in front of another diorama.

Cheetahs stalking the tall grass.

More predators.

"Look, will you just tell me what's going on?" I say.

"A few days after Erica disappeared, I found this."

He reaches into his pocket and pulls out a ring, which he drops into my palm. It's a typical Jostens class ring. Gold and gaudy. Just like the ones all my high school classmates had. I never bothered to get one, because even then I thought it was a waste of money. The stone is purple, surrounded by etched letters proclaiming the owner to be a member of Danville High School's class of 2014. Engraved on the inside of the band is a name.

Megan Pulaski.

"I found it behind a couch cushion," Dylan says. "I thought it might have belonged to someone who lived there. Or maybe another apartment sitter. I asked Leslie, who confirmed there was an apartment sitter named Megan Pulaski in 11B. She was there last year. Sounds normal, right?"

"I'm assuming it doesn't stay that way," I say.

Dylan nods. "I Googled the name, hoping maybe I could locate her and mail the ring back to her. I found a Megan Pulaski who graduated from a high school in Danville, Pennsylvania, in 2014. She's been missing since last year."

I hand the ring back to Dylan, no longer wanting to touch it.

"I tracked down a friend of hers," Dylan says. "She created a missing poster just like the one I made for Erica and circulated it online. She told me Megan was an orphan who hasn't been seen or heard from in over a year. The last time they spoke, Megan was living in an apartment building in Manhattan. She never told her the name. She just mentioned it was covered in gargoyles."

"Sounds like the Bartholomew to me," I say.

"It gets weirder," Dylan warns. "A few days ago, I went for a jog in the park. When I got back to the Bartholomew, I saw Ingrid in the lobby. She didn't seem to be coming or going. She just stood at the mailboxes, watching the door. I got the feeling she was waiting for me."

"So you were lying when you told me you didn't really know each other."

"That's the thing; I wasn't. We'd only spoken a few times before that, and one of them was to ask her if she'd heard anything from Erica, because I knew they had hung out a few times."

"What did she say that day in the lobby?"

"She told me she might have learned what happened to Erica," Dylan says. "She said she couldn't talk about it right then. She wanted to go somewhere private, where no one else could hear us. I suggested we meet that night."

"When was this?"

"Three days ago."

My stomach clenches. That's the same night Ingrid vanished.

"When and where were you supposed to meet?"

"A little before one. In the basement."

"The security camera," I say. "You're the one who disconnected it."

Dylan gives me a terse nod. "I thought it was a good idea, seeing how Ingrid was being so secretive. Turns out it didn't matter because she never showed. I didn't find out she was gone until you told me the next day."

Now I know why Dylan had acted so surprised that afternoon. It also explains why he was in such a hurry to get away from me. No one likes to be around a messenger bearing bad news.

"And now I can't stop thinking that Ingrid's missing because she knew what happened to Erica," Dylan says. "When she vanished. *How* she vanished. It's too similar to Erica to be a coincidence. It's almost like someone else learned that Ingrid knew something and silenced her before she could tell me."

"You think they're both . . ."

I don't want to say aloud the word I'm thinking for fear it'll make it be true. I did the same after Jane vanished. We all did, my family tiptoeing around her disappearance with euphemisms. *She hasn't come home. We don't know where she is.* It was finally broken by my father's midnight pronouncement a week later.

Jane is gone.

"Dead?" Dylan says. "That's exactly what I think."

My legs wobble as we move to another diorama. The most brutal of the bunch. A dead zebra being swarmed by vultures. A dozen at least, with more swooping in to snatch whatever scraps are left. Close by are a hyena and a pair of jackals, sneaking into the fray to grab their share.

The frenzied violence of the scene churns my stomach. Or maybe it's Dylan's suggestion that someone in the Bartholomew is killing young women who agree to watch apartments there.

Megan and Erica and now Ingrid.

I stare at the two vultures closest to the glass. They're locked in battle—one bird on its back, taloned feet kicking, the other looming close, wings spread wide.

"Let's say you're right. You honestly believe there's a serial killer in the Bartholomew?"

"I know, it sounds crazy," Dylan says. "But that's what it seems like to me. All three of them were apartment sitters. Then all three disappeared in pretty much the same way."

It makes me think of something my father used to say.

One time is an anomaly. Two times is a coincidence. Three times is proof.

But proof of what? That someone at the Bartholomew is preying on apartment sitters? It's still too preposterous to wrap my head around. Yet so is the coincidence of three young women without families moving out of the building and never contacting their friends again.

"But who could be doing such a thing? And why hasn't anyone else at the Bartholomew picked up on it?"

"Who says they haven't?"

"People there would care if they thought someone had killed apartment sitters."

"They're rich," Dylan says. "All of them. And rich people don't give a damn about the hired help. They're vultures."

"And what are we?"

He gives the diorama one last disdainful look. "That zebra."

"It's insane to—"

On the other side of the hall, one of the schoolgirls lets out a shriek. Not a scared one. A notice-me shriek, designed to get the attention of a nearby group of boys. Still, the sound is so jolting that it takes me a second to regain my composure.

"It's insane to think an entire building would turn a blind eye to kidnapping or murder."

"But you agree that something strange is going on, right?" Dylan says. "Otherwise you wouldn't have listened to me for this long. You wouldn't even be here in the first place."

I continue to stare at the diorama, not blinking, until the whole scene becomes wavy, as if life were slowly returning to those creatures behind the glass. Feathers tremble. Beady eyes move. The zebra takes a single breath.

"I'm here because I found Erica's phone," I remind him.

"And have you seen what's on it?" Dylan asks. "Maybe Erica was in contact with whoever caused her disappearance."

I remove the phone and hold it up for Dylan to see. "It's locked. Do you have any idea what Erica's passcode was?"

"We weren't exactly at the password-sharing stage of our relationship," Dylan says. "Do you know of another way to unlock it?"

I turn Erica's phone over in my hand, thinking. Although I don't know the first thing about hacking into a cell phone, I might know someone who does. Grabbing my own phone, I scroll through the call history until I find the number I'm looking for. I hit the dial button, and a laid-back voice soon answers.

"This is Zeke."

"Hi, Zeke. This is Jules. Ingrid's friend."

"Hey," Zeke says. "Have you heard from her yet?"

"Not yet. But I'm wondering if you could help me. Do you know someone who can hack into a phone?"

There's a cautious pause from Zeke, during which all I can hear are the rowdy schoolkids spilling all around us. Finally, Zeke says, "I do. But it will cost you."

"How much?"

"One thousand. That includes two hundred fifty for me, as a finder's fee. The rest goes to my associate."

I go numb. That's an insane amount of money. Too much for me to afford on my own. Hearing the price almost makes me end the call. My thumb twitches against the screen, ready to hang up on Zeke and not answer if he attempts to call back.

But then I think about Dylan's so-crazy-it-might-be-true theory that a serial killer is living within the Bartholomew's walls. I think about how the apartment sitters who suddenly vanished—Megan, Erica, Ingrid—might have been his victims.

We could be next, Dylan and me.

I think Ingrid knew that. It's why she arranged to talk to Dylan. It's why she left me the gun and the note. She knew that we could also disappear just as suddenly as the others.

To avoid such a fate, we could leave.

Right now.

Flee in the night, just like I hope Ingrid did but am starting to believe she didn't.

Or we could pay a thousand dollars to unlock Erica's phone and possibly get answers about what happened not just to her but to all of them.

"You still there, Jules?" Zeke says.

"Yeah. Still here."

"Do we have a deal?"

"Yes," I reply, wincing as I say it. "Meet me in an hour."

I end the call and stare at the animals in the diorama. The vultures and jackals and hyena. I feel a twinge of pity for them. What a cruel afterlife they have. Dead for decades yet still gnawing, still fighting.

Forever red in tooth and claw.

32

I now have only twenty-seven dollars to my name.

Dylan and I agreed that we should split Zeke's asking price between us. Five hundred from Dylan, five hundred from me.

With the cash stuffed uneasily in our pockets, Dylan and I now sit at the spot in Central Park where we're scheduled to meet Zeke in ten minutes. The Ladies Pavilion. A glorified gazebo with a cream-colored railing and gingerbread trim, the place exudes romance, which must confuse passersby who see Dylan and me inside. Sitting on opposite sides of the pavilion with our arms folded and scowls on our faces, we look like two mismatched people in the middle of a very bad blind date.

"How do you know this guy again?" Dylan says.

"I don't. He's a friend of Ingrid's."

"So you've never met him before?"

"We've only talked on the phone."

Dylan frowns. Not entirely unexpected, seeing how he's agreed to give a substantial chunk of cash to a complete stranger.

"But he knows someone who can hack into Erica's phone, right?" he says.

"I hope so," I say.

Otherwise we're screwed. Me, in particular. Right now, I have nothing. No cash in my wallet. No usable credit cards. Until I get my first apartment-sitting payment in two days, I'm flat broke. Even thinking about it makes me feel faint.

To counter the panic, I look at the sky outside the pavilion. It's an overcast afternoon, the clouds heavy and gray. Heather weather no more. Across from me, Dylan stares at a group of kids scampering up nearby Hernshead, a rocky outcropping that juts into the lake. Although his hoodie and angry-bull build should give him a vaguely thuggish look, his eyes betray him. There's a sadness to them.

"Tell me something about Erica," I say. "A favorite story or fond memory."

"Why?"

"Because it reminds you of what you've lost and what you're trying to get back."

One of the detectives on Jane's case told me that. She had been gone two weeks by that point, and hope was fading.

I told him about the time in seventh grade when a bully named Davey Tucker decided to make my bus ride to school a living hell. Each day as I boarded the bus, he'd thrust his leg into the aisle and trip me as others laughed. This went on for weeks until, one day, I tripped, fell face-first in the aisle, and got a bloody nose. Seeing the blood pouring down my face sent Jane into a rage. She leapt over two bus seats, grabbed Davey Tucker by the hair, and slammed his face into the aisle until he, too, was bleeding. From then on, she was my hero.

"Erica told me a story once," Dylan says, smiling slightly. "About when she was a little girl. There was a mouse in the kitchen, and her aunt set traps everywhere. In the corners. Under the sink. I guess she was hell-bent on killing that mouse. But Erica didn't want it to die. She thought it was cute. So every night, when her aunt was asleep, she'd sneak into the kitchen and use a stick to set off all the traps. That doesn't surprise me. I know she was an animal lover."

"*Is* an animal lover," I say. "Don't use the past tense. Not just yet."

Dylan's smile fades. "Jules, what if we never find out what happened to them?"

"We will," I say, not having the heart to mention the alternative. How you learn to live with a lack of knowledge. How you eventually train yourself not to think about the missing every minute of every day. How the not knowing still gets under your skin and in your blood like an incurable disease.

A lanky man with an unkempt beard appears on the path leading to the pavilion.

Zeke. I recognize him from his Instagram photos.

With him is a short girl with pink hair. She looks young. Barely-in-her-teens young. Her frilly white dress and Hello Kitty purse don't help matters. Nor does the fact that she never looks up from her phone, even as Zeke leads her into the pavilion.

"Hey," Zeke says. "I guess you're Jules."

I nod. "And this is Dylan."

Zeke gives Dylan a wary glance. "Hey, man."

Dylan responds with a brief nod and says, "So can you help us or not?"

"I can't," Zeke says. "But that's why I brought Yumi along."

The girl steps forward and holds out an open palm. "Cash first."

Dylan and I give the money to Zeke, my stomach roiling as the cash leaves my hand. Zeke passes it to Yumi, who quickly counts it before giving him his cut. The rest is shoved into the Hello Kitty purse.

"Now the phone," she says.

I give her Erica's phone. Yumi studies it the way a jeweler does a diamond and says, "Give me five minutes. *Alone*, please."

The rest of us leave the pavilion, making our way to Hernshead. The children who were there earlier are now gone, leaving the whole craggy area to just Zeke, Dylan, and me.

"Hey, is that Ingrid's phone?" Zeke says.

"The less you know, the better," I say.

"Fair enough."

I look over his shoulder to the pavilion, where Yumi sits on the bench I just vacated. Her fingers fly across the phone's screen. I hope that means progress is being made.

"I'm guessing you haven't heard from her?"

"Nah. You?"

"Nothing."

"What do you think happened to her?" Zeke says.

I look to Dylan. Although the headshake he gives is tiny, his message is loud and clear. We need to keep this to ourselves.

"Again, you're better off not knowing," I say. "But if you hear from her, please tell her to contact me. She has my number. She knows where I live. I just want to know she's okay."

Behind Zeke, Yumi emerges from the pavilion. She thrusts Erica's phone back at me and says, "All done."

I swipe the screen and see all of Erica's apps, not to mention her camera, photo gallery, and call log.

"I turned off the lock function," Yumi says. "If it locks up again for some reason, I reset the passcode. It's 1234."

She walks away without another word. Zeke shakes my hand and gives Dylan a strange little salute. "It was a pleasure doing business with you," he says before hurrying to catch up with Yumi.

I watch them leave with Erica's unlocked phone in my hand. I hope that whatever's on it will be worth the high price.

Dylan and I return to the Ladies Pavilion, sharing a bench this time, the two of us crouched over Erica's phone. Both of us know the answer to what happened to her—and, by default, to Ingrid—could be hidden somewhere inside it.

"Part of me doesn't want to know if something bad happened to her," Dylan says as he cradles the phone in his palm. "Maybe it's better to just assume she ran away and that she's living this amazing new life somewhere."

I used to think the same thing about Jane. That she had escaped, trading our sad Pennsylvania town for some far-off locale with blue water, palm trees, and nightly fiestas in a cobblestone square. It was better than the alternative, which was assuming she was murdered within hours of hopping into that black Volkswagen.

Now I'd give anything to know where she is. Grave or tropical villa, I don't care. All I want now is the truth.

"That will change," I say. "You might not think so now, but it's true."

Dylan pushes the phone into my hands. "Then let's rip the fucking Band-Aid off now, I guess."

"Where should we look first?"

"Her call log," Dylan says.

I swipe to the phone's call history, starting with outgoing calls. The first one listed is a number with a Manhattan area code. Seeing it brings a tightness to my chest.

This is the last place Erica called.

I look at the time and date the call was made. Nine p.m., October fourth.

"That's just hours before she vanished," Dylan says.

"Do you recognize it?"

"No."

I dial, my heartbeat knocking at my rib cage as the phone rings once. I hit the speaker button so Dylan can hear the second ring. Still, he presses against me, our shoulders touching.

On the third ring, someone answers.

"Hunan Palace. Takeout or delivery?"

Immediately, I hang up.

Dylan pulls away from me, his hopes dashed. "She ordered us Chinese food that night. I forgot all about that. Fuck."

Undeterred, I scroll through a month's worth of Erica's outgoing calls. Nothing stands out to me. There are a few calls to Dylan. Some made to a woman named Cassie and a man named Marcus. I see another call to Hunan Palace made a week earlier, and a second one to Cassie a few days before that.

The rattle of my heartbeat slows to a disappointed crawl. I'm not sure what I expected. A frantic call to 911, I guess. Or a goodbye call to Dylan.

I move on to Erica's incoming calls. The last one she received was from Dylan.

Yesterday. Three p.m. He didn't leave a message.

But he did the night before, when he called shortly before midnight.

I play the message, watching the clench of Dylan's jaw as he listens to his plaintive voice blare from the phone.

"It's me again. I don't know why I'm calling because it's clear you no longer use this phone. I hope that's the reason and that you're not avoiding me. I'm worried, Erica."

Dylan says nothing as I play the other messages he's left in the past two weeks. In each of them, I note the way his voice wavers between worry and defeat.

It's the same with messages from other people. Cassie and Marcus and a woman who doesn't give her name but sounds vaguely British. Tension tightens their voices. An aural tug-of-war between forced hopefulness and barely contained concern.

Tucked among those messages are ones from less well-meaning sources. Visa calling to remind Erica that she's sixty days late with her payment. Discover calling to tell her the same thing. A man named Keith calling from a collection agency asking where the hell their money is.

"If you don't contact us in the next twenty-four hours, I'm going to call the police," he warns.

That was eleven days ago. How wonderful it would have been if he'd followed through on that threat.

I search the text messages next. Again, Dylan is well-represented. He's sent dozens of them. So many that my index finger cramps up before I get through the past week.

The most recent was sent shortly after midnight, two days ago.

Please tell me where you are.

It was followed a minute later by another.

I miss you.

Two of the people who left voicemails also texted.

Cassie: Haven't heard from you in a while. You OK?

Marcus: Where you been?

Cassie again: Seriously. You OK?? Text me as soon as you get this.

Cassie a third time: PLEASE!

There are even two texts from Ingrid, made the day after Erica disappeared.

Um, where are you?

Are you around? I'm worried.

I swipe back to the main screen, taking inventory of her most-used apps. Missing are the usual suspects. No Facebook, Twitter, or Instagram.

"She didn't—" Dylan catches his use of the past tense and stops to correct himself. "She doesn't believe in social media. She told me it was a huge waste of time."

I go to the gallery of photos stored in the phone, finding a trove of ones snapped inside the Bartholomew. The most recent photo, taken in a bathtub, is a close-up of her toes peeking out of a mound of frothy suds.

It's the claw-foot tub in the master bathroom of 12A. I know because I took a bath there myself during my first night at the Bartholomew. I might have even used the same bubble bath. It makes me wonder if Erica, too, found it beneath the bathroom sink, or if she brought it with her. I hope it's the latter. The idea of me repeating her actions gives me an uneasy chill.

I scroll through the rest of Erica's pictures. It turns out she's an impressive cell phone photographer. She took dozens of well-composed shots of 12A's interior. The spiral steps. A view of the park taken from the dining room. George's right wing kissed by the light of dawn.

It seems she's also a fan of selfies. I find pictures of Erica in the kitchen. Erica in the study. Erica at the bedroom window.

Sitting among the selfies are two videos Erica took. I tap the oldest one first, and her beaming face fills the screen.

"Look at this place," she says. "Seriously. Look. At. This. Place."

The image streaks away from Erica to the bedroom window before swirling around the room itself, the visual equivalent of the dizzy euphoria she must have felt in that moment. I felt the same way. Amazed and fortunate.

After two full spins around the room, Erica returns. Looking directly into the camera, she says, "If this is a dream, don't wake me up. I never want to leave this place."

The video ends a second later, freezing on a shot of her face halfway filling the screen. The other half is a canted angle of the window, George and the city skyline beyond his wing.

I turn to Dylan, who's still staring at the phone with a vacant look in his eyes. I saw that same expression on my father's face shortly after Jane vanished. It never truly went away.

"Are you okay?" I ask.

"Yeah." Dylan then shakes his head. "Not really."

I slide my finger to the second video. The time stamp says it was taken on October fourth.

The night Erica vanished.

Steeling myself with a deep breath, I tap it.

The video begins with blackness. There's a rustling sound as the phone moves, giving a glimpse of darkened wall.

The sitting room.

I'm intimately familiar with those faces in the wallpaper.

The phone suddenly stops on Erica's face, painted gray by moonlight coming through the window. Gone is the giddy, pinch-me grin she displayed in the other video. In its place is quickly building dread.

Like she already knows something bad is about to happen. The image blurs as the phone shakes slightly.

Her hands. They're trembling.

She whispers to the camera. "It's just past midnight, and I swear I heard a noise. I think—I think something's inside the apartment."

I let out a gasp. I know the noise she's talking about. I've heard it as well. That ethereal sound, like the whisper of fabric.

On-screen, Erica looks over her shoulder. My gaze drifts there, too, searching the shadows, expecting to see someone waiting there, watching. When Erica turns back to the phone, she locks eyes with her own image on the screen. She seems unnerved by what she sees.

"I don't know what's going on here. This whole building. It's not right. We're being watched. I don't know why, but we are." She exhales. "I'm scared. I'm really fucking scared."

A noise rises in the background.

A single knock on the door.

Erica jumps at the sound. Her eyes become as wide as silver dollars. Fear sizzles through them.

"Fuck," she whispers. "It's *him*."

The screen suddenly goes black.

The video's abrupt end is jarring. Like a slap to the face. Yanked back to reality, I realize I'm holding my breath and have been since the video started. When I do breathe again, it's a slow exhalation. Beside me, Dylan leans forward, practically doubled over, as if he's about to be sick. He takes a series of quick, shallow breaths.

"Do you have any idea what she's talking about?" I say.

Dylan gulps before answering. "None. If she was feeling threatened by someone, she never told me about it."

That word—*threatened*—makes me think of Ingrid. She definitely felt that way. For proof, one need look no further than the gun in a shoe box under my kitchen sink. I wonder if she grew to feel that way on her own or if Erica warned her. If so, I now understand why Ingrid was so afraid of the Bartholomew. Watching that video has shaken me to my core. It's not just what Erica said that disturbs me. It's the way she looked. Like someone frightened beyond all reason.

"Dylan, I think we're in real danger here," I say. "Especially if we're right and Ingrid vanished because she knew what happened to Erica."

Dylan stays silent, his face pensive, almost passive. Finally, he says, "I think you should stop looking for them."

"Me? What about you?"

"I know how to defend myself."

Of that, I have no doubt. Dylan's got the build of a bodyguard. Big enough to give anyone second thoughts about attacking.

"But I need to know what happened to them," I say.

We have too much in common. Me, Ingrid, Erica, and Megan. All of us adrift, without parents or nearby relatives, somehow finding our way here. Now three of us are gone.

Unless I learn what happened to them, I fear that I might be next.

"This is serious shit we're now dealing with," Dylan says. "You heard what Erica said. Something weird is going on in that building. Maybe we should go back to the police."

"Do you really think they'll help? We have nothing to go on but a vague suspicion that something bad happened to Megan, Erica, and Ingrid."

"I'd say it's more than a suspicion," Dylan says.

"Fine," I concede. "But until we know for certain what's going on, the police aren't going to get involved."

"Then we keep looking." Dylan sighs, almost as if he regrets the words that have just come out of his mouth. "But we need to be careful. And smart. And quiet. We can't risk having what happened to Ingrid happen to one of us."

Dylan steps out of the Ladies Pavilion and turns toward the Bartholomew, staring at what can be glimpsed of it above the treetops. I join him and look up at my own personal section of the Bartholomew. George sits on the corner of the roof, keeping watch. The windows of 12A reflect the white-gray sky. They remind me of eyes. Similar to the ones in the wallpaper.

Wide.

Unblinking.

Staring right back at us.

33

"It's just past midnight, and I swear I heard a noise."

I grip Erica's phone with both hands, mesmerized by her moon-lit face, the fear in her eyes, the quaver in her voice.

"I think—I think something's inside the apartment."

Dylan and I agreed it was best not to head back to the Bartholomew together. All part of being careful, quiet, and smart. We returned fifteen minutes apart, Dylan going first, his hoodie pulled over his head as he hurried away.

I lingered in the park, strolling the path running along the lake. I stared at the rust-colored leaves on the water's surface, the ducks that cut rippling paths through them, the people strolling over Bow Bridge. None of it helped. Nothing erased the fact that something sinister is taking place inside the Bartholomew's gargoyle-studded walls.

Now I'm in 12A, watching Erica's video on a loop. This current viewing is my sixth, and I know what comes next.

First the quick glance over her shoulder, followed by the slow turn back to her phone. Erica then looks at herself on the screen, and alarm shoots into her eyes.

"I don't know what's going on here. This whole building. It's not right."

Not content with just watching the video over and over, I attempt to reenact it. I'm in the sitting room—the same place where it was recorded. I'm even in the exact spot where Erica sat.

The crimson sofa.

Dead center.

An expanse of red wallpaper behind me, looking over my shoulder.

"We're being watched. I don't know why, but we are."

Erica exhales. I do, too.

"I'm scared. I'm really fucking scared."

So am I, which is why I keep watching the video, why I insist on putting myself in Erica's shoes. I'm hoping it will help me avoid whatever fate befell her.

A noise blasts from the phone.

A knock.

The one that makes Erica jump with a start. No matter how many times I replay the video, the sound still gets to me. Even worse is Erica's reaction. That last wide-eyed, frightened utterance.

"Fuck. It's *him*."

When the video cuts to black, I continue to stare at the screen, where Erica's face has been replaced by my own reflection. My expression is more pensive, less frightened. I'm wondering who Erica was talking about at the video's end, if it's the same person she thought was watching, if that watcher was targeting her specifically, or every apartment sitter in the Bartholomew.

Judging from what I saw on the security monitors, it was all of them.

All of *us*, I should say.

I'm now part of this.

Unknown is exactly what part I'm playing. Am I prey, like Erica seemed to be, or an inconvenience, like what Dylan and I suspect Ingrid was?

Maybe I'm both—a person who looked too hard and said too much, putting myself in the middle of something I can't begin to understand.

Yet Ingrid did. Somehow she found out what was going on and tried to warn Dylan. I think she even tried to warn me that afternoon we were together. I see her now, curled up on that park bench, looking years younger than her age as she spoke of the Bartholomew.

It . . . it scares me.

I should have believed her.

I start to watch Erica's video for a seventh time.

"It's just past midnight, and I swear I heard a noise."

As do I.

Two raps on 12A's door—as quick and jarring as gunshots.

My whole body jolts. I suspect I look exactly like Erica does in the video.

The walk from the sitting room to the foyer is slow, cautious, my heart beating double time. The same person who knocked when Erica was making that video could be on the other side of the door. The same person who made her disappear.

It's him.

But when I peer through the peephole, I see not a him but a her.

Greta Manville. Standing at my door with her cardigan and tote bag.

"I had a feeling you intended to check in on me at some point today," she says once I open the door. "I thought I'd spare you the trip and check on you instead."

"That's a pleasant reversal," I say.

Even though I'm holding the door open for her, Greta remains just beyond the threshold, as if waiting for an invitation to enter.

"Would you like to come in?"

Having heard the magic words, she steps inside. "I won't stay long. Never impose. That's a bit of advice many from your generation should heed more often."

"Duly noted," I say before guiding her into the sitting room. "Would you like something to drink? I have coffee, tea, and, well, that's pretty much it at the moment."

"Tea would be lovely. But only a small cup, please."

I retreat to the kitchen, fill the kettle with water, and put it on the stove. When I return to the sitting room, I find Greta roaming its perimeter.

"I'm not being nosy," she says. "Just admiring what's been done to the place. It's less cluttered now."

"You've been here before?"

"My dear, I used to live here."

I look at her, surprised. "Back when you wrote *Heart of a Dreamer*?"

"Indeed."

I knew there were too many similarities for it to be a coincidence. Only someone who's spent hours gazing at the view from the bedroom window would be able to describe it with such accuracy.

"So this really is Ginny's apartment?" I say.

"No, it's *your* apartment. Never confuse fiction with reality. No good ever comes of it." Greta continues to roam, venturing to the spot by the window taken up by the brass telescope. "This is where I wrote the book, by the way. There was a rickety little table right here by this window. I spent hours tapping away on an electric typewriter. Oh, the racket it made! It annoyed my parents to no end."

"How long did they live here?"

"Decades," Greta says. "But it was in the family longer than that. My mother inherited it from my grandmother. I lived here until my first marriage, returning after its inevitable failure to write that book you so adore."

I follow Greta as she moves through the study and then back into the hallway, her index finger trailing along the wall. When the teakettle whistles, we both head to the kitchen, where Greta takes a seat in the breakfast nook. I pour two cups of tea and join her, grateful for her presence. It makes me far less jumpy than I was ten minutes ago.

"How much has the place changed since you lived here?" I say.

"In some ways, quite a bit. In others, not at all. The furniture is different, of course. And there used to be a maid's room near the bottom of the steps. But the wallpaper is the same. What do you think of it? And you can be honest. Don't worry about poking a hole in any nostalgia I might feel for this place."

I look into the teacup, my reflection shimmering atop the copper-colored liquid.

"I hate it," I say.

"I'm not surprised," Greta says as she contemplates me from the other side of the breakfast nook. "There are two types of people in this world, dear. Those who would look at that wallpaper and see only flowers, and those who would see only faces."

"Fantasy versus reality," I say.

Greta nods. "Exactly. At first, I thought you were one of those people who only sees the flowers. Head in the clouds. Prone to flights of fancy. Now I know better. You see the faces, don't you?"

I give her a quick nod.

"That means you're a realist."

"What about you?" I say.

"I see both at once and decide which is more important to focus on," Greta says. "Which I suppose makes me pragmatic. But today, I choose to focus on the flowers. Which is the real reason I stopped by. I wanted to give you this."

She digs through her tote bag, eventually removing a first-edition hardcover of *Heart of a Dreamer.*

"It's signed," Greta says as she hands it to me. "Just as you requested when you first attacked me in the lobby."

"I didn't *attack*," I say, feigning annoyance when in fact I'm touched beyond words.

That feeling—of friendship, of gratitude—lasts only a moment. Because when I open the book and see what Greta wrote on the title page, my blood turns cold.

"You don't like it?" Greta says.

I stare at the inscription, rereading every word. I want to be sure I'm not mistaken.

I'm not.

"I love it," I say, a bit too loudly, hoping the sound drowns out the voice of doubt that's now whispering in my ear.

It doesn't.

"Then why do you look like you're about to be hit with one of my sudden sleeps?"

Because that's how I feel. Like I'm perched on the edge of a great chasm, waiting for the slightest breeze to shove me screaming into it.

"I feel bad, that's all," I say. "You didn't need to go to all this trouble."

"It was no trouble at all," Greta says. "I wouldn't have done it if I didn't want to."

"But you were right to be annoyed with me when we first met. You must get bothered all the time to sign copies. Especially by the building's apartment sitters."

"You're wrong there. I haven't signed a copy for any other person at the Bartholomew. You're special, Jules. This is my way of showing you that."

I try to act flattered, clutching the book to my chest and pretending to be as thrilled as I truly would have been if Greta had done this a day or so ago. In truth, I want this book as far away from me as possible.

"I'm honored," I say. "Truly. Thank you from the bottom of my heart."

Greta continues to give me a concerned look. "Are you sure nothing's wrong?"

"To be honest, I'm not feeling well." Since faking enthusiasm didn't work, I might as well try an excuse that's slightly closer to the truth. "I think a cold is coming on. It always happens when the seasons start to change. I thought the tea would help, but I think what I really need is to lie down for a bit."

If Greta sees through my attempt to get her out of the apartment, she doesn't show it. She simply downs the rest of her tea, hoists the tote bag onto her shoulder, and shuffles out of the kitchen. At the door, she says, "Get some rest. I'll check on you tomorrow."

I force a smile. "Not unless I check on you first."

"Ah, so it's now a contest," Greta says. "I accept the challenge."

With that, she slips out the door, giving me a little wave on her way to the elevator. As soon as she's gone, I close the door and hurry down the hall to the bookshelf in the study. There, I grab the copy of *Heart of a Dreamer* I found my first day here and flip to the title page.

Seeing it creates a strange expansion in my chest. My heart exploding into jagged shards.

I gave Greta an opportunity to tell me the truth, and she refused to take it. I don't know why. Nor do I know what it means.

All I know is that the title page of this book bears not just Greta's handwriting but the exact same inscription she wrote in two other copies. The only difference is the names.

Mine in one.

Ingrid's in another.

And now this.

> *Darling Erica,*
> *Such a pleasure! Your youthfulness gives me life!*
>
> *Best wishes,*
> *Greta Manville*

34

I tell myself it means nothing.

That this is what Greta writes in every copy she signs.

That there are hundreds of women out there with books bearing this very inscription.

That she certainly didn't befriend Erica and Ingrid like she did me. That she didn't invite them in, take them to lunch, tell them about her past, and then what? Kill them? Abduct them?

Of course not.

She's not capable of that. Not physically. Not mentally.

Greta Manville, by virtue of age and infirmity, is harmless.

Then why did she lie? There's nothing suspicious about signing books. Greta's an author. It comes with the territory. If she had simply admitted to signing copies for Ingrid and Erica, I would have thought nothing of it, even with the knowledge that both are now missing. It's her lie that has me freaking out right now.

My hope is that Greta feels a misguided sense of protection. She knows what I've gone through. I've told her all my sad tales. It's likely she pities me and fears that my knowing about the copies signed for the others would make me feel less special. As if thinking I'm her favorite will somehow make up for all the shitty things in my past.

Or maybe Greta knew Ingrid better than she's let on. Erica, too. She was friendly with both, knows they're now missing, and understands that being associated with either of them might drag her unwillingly into a search. It doesn't mean she's involved in their disappearances. Nor does it mean she doesn't care if they're found. She just doesn't have the time, energy, or stamina to look for them the same way I'm doing.

Those two explanations are eclipsed by a third—that Greta is hiding something.

She already told me Ingrid went to see her, allegedly to ask about the Bartholomew's unsettling past. What if that was also a lie? What if Ingrid knocked on Greta's door asking not about the building but about Erica?

It's not as outlandish as it sounds. I ended up on Greta's doorstep seeking information about Ingrid. Which makes it possible she did the same in regard to Erica. Maybe, like I did, she had reason to believe Greta and Erica were friends.

On the flip side, maybe Ingrid *did* ask Greta about the Bartholomew, because she suspected Erica had done the same thing. Iffy but still possible. In order for that logic to hold, I need something to suggest Erica had also been looking into the building's past.

I return to the crimson sofa with Erica's phone, opening the web browser to check her bookmarked sites and browsing history. The bookmarks are typical for a young woman in Manhattan. The MTA schedule, a local weather site, a handful of takeout menus. Her browser history, however, is empty, meaning Erica cleared it. Of course. It was ridiculous of me to expect a browser history filled with incriminating searches about the Bartholomew's dark past.

Rather than close the browser, which I should do, or toss the phone across the room, which is what I want to do, I start a Google search. No, Erica didn't save her browser history, but there's a chance she used the autocomplete function, which automatically types frequently queried topics into the search bar.

I start with the Bartholomew. Just typing in a single *T* brings up a familiar name: Thomas Bartholomew—the doctor who designed and built this place, only to leap from its roof half a year later. Erica was clearly reading up on him.

I click, and the screen is filled with articles about the ill-fated Dr. Bartholomew. The first link takes me to the same *New York Times* article I'd read a few days ago.

TRAGEDY STRIKES BARTHOLOMEW

I go back to the search page and keep scrolling, not stopping until I find something that doesn't seem to address the death of Dr. Bartholomew. Clicking the link, I'm taken to a listing for the Bartholomew in a no-frills directory of Manhattan real estate. It's nothing more than the building's name, address, and a dusting of facts.

Year built: 1919
Number of units: 44
Owner: This building is privately owned and operated by the Bartholomew family. No public records regarding building value, annual profit, and income or estimated price per unit could be found.

I close the web browser and try a different approach, scrolling once more through Erica's old texts. There's little of interest. Just routine exchanges with friends or arranging trysts with Dylan. It's the same with her call log. In the days leading to her disappearance, Erica called only Hunan Palace and Dylan.

But she did receive a call from Ingrid on October third.

The day before she disappeared.

I quickly swipe to Erica's voicemail, bypassing the ones Dylan and I listened to in the park. Just beyond them is a message we didn't get to.

I tap it and hear Ingrid's voice, hushed and worried.

I couldn't stop thinking about what you told me yesterday, so I did a little digging. And you're right. There's something deeply weird going on here. I still don't exactly know what it is, but I'm starting to get really freaked out. Call me.

Erica never called back, which means she either talked to Ingrid in person or thought returning the call wasn't important. I suspect it was the former. Ingrid's message sounds too worried to ignore. Which makes me wonder about not just what Erica told her but what Ingrid discovered afterward. Unfortunately, neither of them is around to provide an answer.

I put down Erica's phone and pick up my own. I then text Ingrid, even though I already know she's not going to respond. I do it out of desperation, on the unlikely chance that, of the dozens of texts I've sent in the past few days, this will finally be the one she sees and replies to.

> If you're out there and can see this, PLEASE respond. I need to talk to you about the Bartholomew and Erica and what you know about both. It's important.

I set my phone facedown on the coffee table, lean back on the crimson sofa, and stare at the wall. Unlike Greta, I can't choose what I see in the patterned wallpaper. They're faces, whether I like it or not.

Right now, they watch me passively, their dark mouths dropped open, as if they're trying to talk, laugh, or sing. Shifting nervously in their gaze, I close my eyes. Silly, I know. Just because I can't see them doesn't mean they can't see me.

My eyes snap open when my phone buzzes on the coffee table. A text has arrived.

I pick it up, shock turning my body cold when I see who it's from. Ingrid.

> Hi, Jules. Please don't be worried. I'm fine.

Relief rushes through me. It starts at my hands and feet before coursing into my limbs, warm and glorious.

I was wrong. About everything. Ingrid isn't dead or kidnapped.

And if there's a logical explanation for her absence, then there are possibly ones for what happened to Erica and Megan.

What I need to know now, though, is what that explanation is.

I send three texts in response, my still-warm fingers flying over the screen.

> Where are you?

> Are you OK?

> What is going on?

A minute passes with no response. After two more go by, I start to pace back and forth across the sitting room. I occupy myself by counting my steps. I get to sixty-seven before three blue dots appear on the phone's screen, rippling like a tiny wave. Ingrid typing her reply.

> In Pennsylvania. A friend hooked me up with a waitressing job.

I've been worried, I write. Why didn't you call or text back?

This time, a reply comes immediately.

> I left my phone on the bus. It took days to get it back.

I wait for more, expecting a flurry of texts as exuberantly descriptive as the way Ingrid talked. But when her response arrives, it's the opposite. Staid, almost dull.

> Sorry for any confusion.

> Why did you leave without telling me?

I didn't have time, Ingrid texts back. Short notice.

But that makes no sense. I was at Ingrid's door literally minutes before she left. All she did was simply confirm our plans to meet in the park.

Then it hits me—this isn't Ingrid.

All the relief I felt minutes ago is gone, replaced with a sharp-edged chill that sends pinpricks of dread across my skin.

I'm communicating with the person who made Ingrid disappear.

My first thought is to call the police and let them sort everything out. But Dylan and I have both already gone to the police, with disappointing results. In order for them to get involved, I need more than a hunch that this isn't Ingrid.

I need proof.

Call me, I type.

The reply is instantaneous. Can't.

Why not?

Too noisy here.

I need to be careful. My suspicion is starting to show. Rather than reply, I grip the phone, my thumbs poised just above the screen. I need to think of a way to get whoever this is to definitively reveal they're not Ingrid—without realizing they're doing it.

What's my nickname? I finally type.

On the screen, the blue dots appear, disappear, then appear again. Ingrid-but-not-Ingrid is thinking. I watch the dots come and go while hoping against hope that when an answer does appear, it will be the correct one.

Juju.

The nickname Ingrid gave me in the park that day.

I want *this* to be the truth instead of the dreadful-but-likely scenario that's been in my thoughts ever since talking to Dylan.

The answer finally arrives, announcing itself with a buzz.

Trick question. You don't have a nickname. Jules is your
real name.

I yelp and throw the phone. A quick, frantic toss. Like a fire-
cracker. The phone hits the floor and does a single flip before landing
facedown on the sitting room carpet. I collapse onto the crimson sofa,
my heart dripping like hot candle wax into the pit of my stomach.

There's only one person who knows that.

And it's definitely not Ingrid.

It's Nick.

35

My phone buzzes again, the sound muted by the carpet.

I stay where I am. I don't need to see this new text to know the truth. I have my memory.

Me sitting in Nick's kitchen, my wounded arm freshly clean, him making small talk, asking me if Jules was a nickname.

Most people think it's short for Julia or Julianne, but Jules is my given name.

Other than Chloe and Andrew, he's the only person in recent memory who's been told the story behind my name. How stupid I was, basking in Nick's attention, enjoying that zap of attraction when he looked into my eyes.

The phone buzzes again.

This time I move, approaching it with caution. Like it's something that can sting. Rather than pick it up, I flip the phone onto its back and read the texts I've missed.

Jules?

You still there?

I'm still staring at the words when there's a knock on the door. A single, startling rap that makes me look up from the phone and gasp.

A second knock arrives. As nerve-jangling as the first.

Nick's voice follows. "Jules? Are you home?"

It's him.

Just on the other side of the door.

Almost as if he's been summoned by my suspicion.

I don't answer the door.

I can't.

Nor can I say anything. A single tremulous word from me will tip him off that I know. About everything.

I turn and face the door, noting the way it's framed by the sitting room archway. A door within a door.

Then I see the chain dangling from the doorframe.

Just below it is the deadbolt, also in an unlocked position.

In the center of the doorknob itself, the latch lies flat.

The door is completely unlocked.

I leap to my feet and rush toward the foyer, trying to make as little noise as possible. If I don't answer, maybe Nick will go away.

Instead, he knocks again. I'm in the foyer now, inching closer to the door. The sound—so loud, so close—prompts a startled huff.

I press my back against the door, hoping Nick can't sense my presence. I can certainly feel his. A disturbance of air mere inches away.

Nick could charge right in if he wanted to. One twist of the doorknob is all it would take.

Luckily, he only talks.

"Jules," he says. "If you're there and can hear me, I just want to apologize for this morning. I shouldn't have brushed off your concern about not being in your apartment all night. It was cavalier of me."

With my left hand, I reach out to touch the doorknob, my fingers sliding over the unlocked latch at its center.

"Anyway, I also want you to know that I had a really great time last night. It was amazing. All of it."

I grasp the latch between my thumb and forefinger. Holding my breath, I turn it upward, my left arm twisting at an odd angle. Pain pinches my knuckles.

Then my wrist.

Then my elbow.

I keep turning the latch, millimeter by millimeter.

"As for what happened, well, I don't want you to think I usually move so fast. I was—"

The lock slides into place with a noticeable click.

Nick hears it and stops, waiting for me to make another sound.

Beside me, the doorknob turns.

He's testing the lock, moving the knob back and forth.

After another breathless second, he resumes talking.

"I was caught up in the moment. I think we both were. Not that I regret it. I don't. It's just, I want you to know I'm not that kind of guy."

Nick departs. I hear his footsteps retreating. Still, I remain at the door, not moving, afraid he'll suddenly return.

But I heard what he had to say.

He isn't that kind of guy.

I believe him.

He's someone else entirely.

36

I pace the sitting room, crossing back and forth in front of the windows. Outside, night settles over Central Park with silent swiftness, coating it in darkness. Bow Bridge has become a pale strip over black water. A single person strolls across it, oblivious to the fact that she's being watched.

Like I used to be. Just a day or two ago.

I envy her ignorance. I wish I could go back to that blissful state. But there's no coming back from what I know.

I keep pacing from one wall to another, confronted by faces in the wallpaper no matter which direction I turn.

Those faces.

They know what Nick is.

They knew it all along.

A serial killer.

I know how improbable that sounds. I know it's crazy. That I'm even considering the idea terrifies me.

Yet a pattern has emerged. Of girls coming here. All of them desperate and broke and without family. Then they disappear without warning or explanation. It's a scenario that's been played out at least three times.

I know what I need to do—call the police.

And say what?

I have no proof that Nick did anything to Ingrid, Erica, or

Megan. Even though I'm certain he has Ingrid's cell phone, it doesn't mean the police will think he's guilty of anything. And there's no one else who can help me convince them. There were no other witnesses to the conversation Ingrid and I had in the park. No one but her knows the nickname she bestowed upon me that day.

But staying here could be a point of no return. The beginning of my end. My mother swallowing the last of those pills. My father striking a match outside the bedroom door. Jane climbing into that Volkswagen Beetle.

I'll leave and go to Chloe's. Back to her couch. To a place where I'll be safe.

I grab my phone and text Chloe.

> I need to get out of here.

I pause, breathe, type more.

> I think I'm in danger.

I put down the phone, resume pacing, return to the phone five minutes later. Chloe hasn't read my text yet. So I call her, reaching her voicemail. It isn't until I hear her recorded greeting that I remember she's out of town. Off to the Vermont wilderness with Paul. And me without a key to her apartment, which I returned the morning I left for the Bartholomew.

So Chloe's out.

That leaves no one.

Literally no one else I can turn to.

Loneliness settles over me like a shroud. I'm shocked by how isolated I am. No family. No Andrew. No co-workers who'd be willing to help me out in a pinch.

But I'm wrong.

I have Dylan.

I call him next, again getting only voicemail. I consider leaving a message but decide against it. I'll sound crazy. No matter how hard I try, it'll seep through. It's better to say nothing than to risk sounding insane.

Not getting a message might entice him to call back.

A crazy one would do the opposite.

My only choice now is to grab my things, go to a hotel, and spend the weekend there until Chloe returns.

It's a good plan. A smart one. But it all falls apart as soon as I check my bank balance and am reminded of the five hundred dollars I spent to unlock Erica's phone.

The twenty-seven dollars left in my account won't get me a night anywhere. Even if I did find a motel that cheap somewhere in Jersey, all my credit cards are maxed *and* frozen. I have no way of getting any spending cash, nothing left for food or an emergency.

Nothing can happen until I get paid for a week of apartment sitting. One thousand dollars. Scheduled to be hand delivered by Charlie two days from now.

There's no other way around it.

In order to leave, I need to stay.

I look across the hall to the foyer and the front door. The deadbolt and chain are in place, right where I left them after Nick departed. They're going to stay that way.

I move into the kitchen, drop to my hands and knees, open the cupboard beneath the sink. There, sitting innocuously between dishwasher soap and trash bags, is the shoe box Ingrid left behind.

I carry the box back to the sitting room and place it on the coffee table. Lifting the lid, I see the Glock and magazine exactly the way I left them. I remove both, surprised by how easy it is to slide the ammo clip into the gun itself. The two connect with a click that makes me feel, if not strong, then at least ready.

For what, I have no idea.

With nothing else to do but wait, I take a seat on the crimson sofa and, gun in my lap, stare again at the wallpaper.

It stares back.

Hundreds of eyes and noses and gaping mouths.

A few days ago, I had thought those open mouths meant they were talking or laughing or singing.

But now I know better.

Now I know what they're really doing is screaming.

NOW

D r. Wagner gives me a look that's one part shock, two parts disbelief. "That's an alarming accusation."

"You think I'm lying?"

"I think you believe it happened," Dr. Wagner says. "That doesn't mean it's real."

"I'm not making it up. Why would I do that? I'm not crazy." There's a feverishness to my words. A simmering hysteria that's crept in despite my best efforts. "You have to believe me. At least three people have been murdered there."

"I read the news," the doctor says. "There haven't been any murders at the Bartholomew. Not for a very long time."

"That you know of. These didn't look like murders."

Dr. Wagner runs a hand through his leonine hair. "As a physician, I can assure you it's very difficult to disguise murder."

"He's a very smart person," I say.

Bernard, the nurse with the kind eyes, pokes his head into the room.

"Sorry to interrupt," he says. "I saw this and thought Jules might like to have it in the room with her."

He holds up a red picture frame, the glass spiderwebbed with cracks. One shard has fallen out, the space gaping like a missing tooth. Behind the skein of cracks is a photograph of three people.

My father. My mother. Jane.

I was carrying it when I ran from the Bartholomew. The only possession I thought worth saving.

"Where did you find it?"

"It was with your clothes," Bernard says. "One of the medics gathered it up at the scene."

That frame wasn't the only thing I was carrying. I had something else with me.

"Where's my phone?" I ask.

"There was no phone," Bernard says. "Just your clothes and that picture."

"But it was in my pocket."

"I'm sorry. If it was there, no one found it."

Worry expands in my chest. Like a ball of dough. Rising. Growing. Filling me up.

Nick has my phone.

Which means he can find all the information on it and delete it. Not only that, he can read my texts, see who I've contacted, learn what I've told them.

There are others.

People who now know what I know.

Including, I realize with a rib-shuddering gasp, Chloe.

I think of those texts I sent Chloe and how much they've put her in jeopardy.

I need to get out of here. I think I'm in danger.

Now our roles are reversed. Now it's Chloe who's in danger. When Nick can't find me, he'll go looking for Chloe. Maybe he'll pretend to be me, just like he pretended to be Ingrid. He'll lure her in. And God knows what will happen to her when he does.

"Chloe," I say. "I need to warn Chloe."

I try to slide out of bed, the pain in my body rumbling awake. It's so bad that I double over and gasp for breath. It's hard to take in air, thanks to the damn neck brace. I tear it off and drop it on the floor.

"Honey, you need to get back in bed," Bernard says. "You're in no condition to be walking around."

"No!" My voice—alarmingly crazed, even to me—rings off the white walls. Gone is any pretense of calmness. I'm now panic personified. "I need to talk to Chloe! He'll be looking for her!"

"You can't leave this bed. Not like this."

Bernard swoops toward me, his hands on my shoulders, pushing me back into bed. I try to fight him off, my legs kicking, arms flailing. The IV in the back of my hand feels like a jellyfish sting. When I flail again, the IV tube goes taut. The metal stand by the bed tilts, falls, clatters against the floor.

The nurse's eyes darken into something distinctly unkind. "You need to calm down," he says.

"She's in danger!" I'm still kicking, still writhing. Bernard pins me against the bed, where I thrash beneath his weight. "You have to believe me! Please!"

I feel a pinch on my upper left arm, there and gone in an instant. Looking to the other side of the bed, I see Dr. Wagner with a syringe and the needle that's just been plunged into my flesh.

"This will help you rest," he says.

I now know for certain he doesn't believe me. Worse, he thinks I'm crazy. Once again, I'm on my own.

"Help Chloe."

My voice has gone quiet. The sedative kicking in. My head lolls onto the pillow. When Bernard backs away from me, I realize I can no longer move my limbs.

I make one last plaintive whisper before the sedative fully takes hold. "Please."

I sink against the bed like someone plunging into a warm pool, descending deeper and deeper until I'm so far gone I wonder if I'll ever emerge.

ONE DAY
EARLIER

37

My family is dancing across Bow Bridge. I sit in my usual spot next to George. Watching them. Wishing I could dance with them. Wishing I was as far away from this place as possible.

The park is silent except for the sound of my family's shoes beating against the bridge floor as they twirl across it in single file. My father is first. My mother's in the middle. Jane takes up the rear.

As they dance, I notice that their heads are lit from within by tiny flickering flames. Like jack-o'-lanterns. Tongues of fire lick from their mouths and leap in their eyes. Yet they can still see me. Every so often, they look up at me with those fiery eyes and wave. I try to wave back, but something's in my hands. I haven't noticed it until now. I've been too distracted by my parents and sister and the flames. But now the thing in my hands takes precedence over the carnival far below.

It's heavy, slightly wet, hot like the lit matches I sometimes hold to my palm.

I look down.

Sitting within my cupped hands is a human heart.

Shiny with blood.

Still beating.

I wake up screaming. The sound blasts from my lungs, the sound reverberating off the walls. I clamp a hand over my mouth, just in case another scream is on its way. But then I remember the dream, gasp, and pull my hand away, checking it for blood and slime that aren't really there.

I look from my hand to my surroundings. I'm in the sitting room, sprawled across the crimson couch. The faces in the wallpaper are still staring, still screaming. The grandfather clock ticks its way toward nine a.m., the sound filling the otherwise silent room.

When I sit up, something slides from my lap onto the floor.

The gun.

I slept with it all night. Apparently, that's my life now. Sleeping in my clothes on a thousand-dollar sofa while cradling a loaded gun. I suppose I should be frightened by what I've become. But there are more pressing things to be afraid of.

The gun goes back into the shoe box, which is in turn put back in its hiding place under the sink. Like a fickle lover, I no longer want to look at it now that I've held it all night.

Back in the sitting room, I grab my phone, desperately hoping to see that Chloe or Dylan called me during the night. They didn't. All I see are the texts I sent Chloe.

> I need to get out of here.

> I think I'm in danger.

The fact that Nick has Ingrid's phone can mean only one thing: he also killed her. A horrible thought. With it comes gut-squeezing grief that makes me want to lie down on the floor and never get up again.

I resist because I'm in the same situation she was. A person who might know too much. A person at risk. The only question now is how much *Ingrid* knew about Nick.

Erica told her something. Of that I'm sure. She shared her suspicion that something was amiss at the Bartholomew, and Ingrid started digging around. The voicemail Ingrid left confirms it.

I grab Erica's phone from the coffee table, where it sat all night, and replay the voicemail.

I couldn't stop thinking about what you told me yesterday, so I did a little digging. And you're right. There's something deeply weird going on here. I still don't exactly know what it is, but I'm starting to get really freaked out. Call me.

I close my eyes, trying to form a timeline of events. Erica vanished the night of October fourth. Ingrid left this message the day before. If what she said in her voicemail is correct, then Erica had revealed her concerns about the Bartholomew the day before that, on October second.

Quickly, I scroll through Erica's texts, checking to see if I missed something she sent to Ingrid on that date. There's nothing. I return to the call log, doing the same for her outgoing calls.

And that's when I see that Erica had missed another call from Ingrid.

The time was shortly after noon.

The date was October second.

Ingrid had even left another voicemail.

Hey, it's Ingrid. I just got the message you sent down the dumbwaiter. Which is super cool, by the way. It's, like, old-timey email. Anyway, I got it and I'm confused. Am I supposed to know who Marjorie Milton is?

I stop the message, play it again, listen intently.

Am I supposed to know who Marjorie Milton is?

I play it a third time, Ingrid's voice sparking a memory. I know that name. It was read rather than heard. In fact, I saw it in print inside this very apartment.

I cross into the study, where I fling open the bottom desk drawer. Inside is the stack of magazines I found on my first day here. All those copies of *The New Yorker*, each marked with an address and a name.

Marjorie Milton.

The former owner of 12A.

Why Erica would feel the need to tell Ingrid about her is a mystery. Marjorie Milton is dead. And I'm pretty sure neither Ingrid nor Erica ever met the woman. Both arrived long after her demise.

I'm on the move again, winding up the stairs to the bedroom window where both George and my laptop sit. I flip it open and Google Marjorie's name. Dozens of results appear.

I click on the most recent article, dated a week ago.

CHAIRWOMAN RETURNS
TO GUGGENHEIM GALA

The article itself is pure society-page fluff. A museum fund-raiser held last week in which businessmen and their trophy wives spent more per plate than what most people make in a year. The only item of note is a mention that the event's longtime coordinator was back after serious health issues forced her to miss last year's gala.

It includes a photo of a seventy-something woman wearing a black gown and a proud, patrician smile. The caption below the picture gives her name.

Marjorie Milton.

I check the article's date again, making sure it is indeed from last week.

It is.

Which means only one thing.

Marjorie Milton, the woman whose death opened a spot in the Bartholomew for at least two apartment sitters, is alive.

38

I look at my watch and sigh.

Seven minutes past two.

I've entered the third hour of sitting on the same bench just outside Central Park. I'm hungry, tired, and in dire need of a bathroom. Yet sitting here is preferable to being back at the Bartholomew. At this point, anything is.

The park itself is behind me. In front of me, directly across the street, is the apartment building where Marjorie Milton currently resides.

Like much of what I know about Mrs. Milton, I found her address online. It turns out that in Manhattan even the filthy rich are sometimes listed in the White Pages.

Other things I've learned: That her friends call her Margie. That she's the daughter of an oil executive and the widow of a venture capitalist. That she has two sons who, no surprise, grew up to become an oil executive and a venture capitalist. That she has a Yorkie named Princess Diana. That in addition to chairing pricey museum fund-raisers, she also gives generously to children's hospitals, animal welfare groups, and the New-York Historical Society.

The biggest thing I learned, though, is that Marjorie Milton is alive and well and has been since 1943.

Some of this information, such as where she lives, was discovered before I left the Bartholomew. But most was gleaned while I was on the bench, the hours ticking by as I searched the internet from my phone.

I'm here in the hope that Marjorie will eventually come outside to take Princess Diana for a walk. According to a *Vanity Fair* piece about her that ran three years ago, it's one of her favorite things to do.

Once she does, I'll be able to ask not only why she left the Bartholomew, located a mere ten blocks south of her current address, but why the people still living there claim that she's dead.

While I wait, I continually check my phone for responses from Chloe and Dylan that have yet to arrive. Finally, at half past two, a wisp of a woman in brown slacks and a teal jacket emerges with a leashed Yorkie by her side.

Marjorie.

I've now seen enough photos of her to know.

I leap from the bench and hurry across the street, approaching Mrs. Milton as soon as Princess Diana stops to pee in the topiary by the neighboring building's front door. When I get a few steps behind her, I say, "Excuse me."

She turns my way. "Yes?"

"You're Marjorie Milton, right?"

"I am," she says as Princess Diana tugs at the leash, eager to mark the next topiary. "Do we know each other?"

"No, but I live at the Bartholomew."

Marjorie looks me up and down, clearly pegging me as an apartment sitter and not a permanent resident. My clothes are the same ones I've been wearing since yesterday, and it shows. I haven't showered. I haven't put on makeup. Before leaving to stake out her building, I did the bare minimum. Comb through my hair, brush across my teeth.

"I don't understand how that's any concern of mine," she says.

"Because you also lived there," I reply. "At least that's what I've been told."

"You were misinformed."

She's in the midst of turning around and walking away when I reach into my jacket and produce a copy of *The New Yorker* that's been rolled up inside it. I tap the address label.

"If you want people to believe that, then you should have taken your magazines with you when you left."

Marjorie Milton glares at me. "Who are you? What do you want?"

"I'm the person living in the apartment you used to own. Only I was told you were dead, and I'd really love to know why."

"I have no idea," Marjorie says. "But I never owned that apartment. I simply stayed there for a brief time."

She resumes walking, the Yorkie trotting several feet in front of her. I trail behind them, not content with the answers I've been given.

"How long were you there?"

"That's none of your business."

"Apartment sitters are disappearing," I say. "Including the one who was in 12A after you and before me. If you know something about that, then you need to tell me right now."

Marjorie Milton halts, surprising Princess Diana, who trots forward a few paces before being choked by the tightened leash. The dog is forced to take a few backward steps while her owner spins around to face me.

"If you don't leave me alone this instant, I'll give Leslie Evelyn a call," Marjorie says. "And trust me, you don't want that. I lived there, which you know already, but I won't say anything else."

"Not even if people are disappearing?" I say.

She looks away from me, ashamed. Quietly, she says, "You're not the only ones with rules."

Then she's off again, Princess Diana pulling her along.

"Wait," I say. "What kind of rules?"

I grab the sleeve of her jacket, trying to keep her there, desperate for one single bit of useful information. When Marjorie pulls away from me, the sleeve stays in my hands. Her arm slides out of it, and the jacket falls open, revealing a white blouse underneath. Pinned to it is a tiny brooch.

Gold.

In the shape of a figure eight.

I let go of the jacket. Marjorie stuffs her arm back into it and pulls it closed. Before she does, I get one last look at the brooch, seeing that it's not an eight at all.

It's an ouroboros.

39

Two hours later, I'm in the main branch of the New York Public Library, one of many occupying the Rose Main Reading Room. The library itself is bright and airy. Late-afternoon sun slants through the arched windows. Puffy pink clouds adorn the murals on the ceiling. Hanging from it are chandeliers that cast circles of brightness onto the long tables aligned in tidy rows.

I'm gripped with unease as I contemplate the stack of books in front of me. A sense of darkness closing in. I wish it was because of the books themselves. Old, dusty volumes about symbols and their meanings. But this ominous mood has been with me since the moment I glimpsed Marjorie Milton's brooch.

The snake eating its tail.

Exactly like the painting in Nick's apartment.

I said nothing to Marjorie after I saw it. The brooch and its possible meaning left me speechless. I simply backed away, leaving her standing with her dog on the sidewalk. I kept walking, as if the simple act of putting one foot in front of the other would somehow help everything make sense.

The disappearances and Nick and Mrs. Milton's short-lived stay at the Bartholomew. They're all connected. I'm certain of it. An ouroboros of a most sinister nature.

Which is why I ended up at the library, striding to the help desk and saying, "I need as many books on symbology as you can find."

Now a dozen titles sit in front of me. I hope at least one of them will help me understand the meaning behind the ouroboros. If I can learn that, then maybe I'll have a better idea of what's going on at the Bartholomew.

I grab the top book from the stack and flip to the index, looking for entries about the ouroboros. I do the same with the others until twelve open books are fanned out across the table. The arrangement provides a gallery view of the ouroboros in all its many incarnations. Some are as simple as line drawings. Others are elaborate etchings embellished with crowns and wings and symbols within the serpent's circle. Hexagrams. Greek letters. Words written in unknown languages. The sheer volume and variety overwhelm me.

I grab one of the books at random—an outdated symbology textbook—and read its entry.

> The ouroboros is an ancient symbol depicting a serpent or dragon forming a circle or figure eight by eating its own tail. Originating in ancient Egypt, the symbol was adopted by the Phoenicians and then the Greeks, where it gained the name used today—Ouroboros, which is roughly translated as "he who eats the tail."
>
> Through this act of self-destruction, the serpent is in essence controlling its own fate. Eating itself—which will bring death—while also feeding itself, which brings life. On and on and on for all eternity.
>
> A symbolic representation of coming full circle, the ouroboros became associated with many varied beliefs, most notably alchemy. The depiction of a serpent devouring itself symbolizes rebirth and the cyclical nature of the universe. Creation rising from destruction. Life rising from death.

I stare at the page. Key words emerge from the pack, standing out as if they were bold red and underlined.

Creation rising from destruction.

Life rising from death.

All of it an unbroken circle. Going on and on forever.

I snatch another book and leaf through it until I come to an image of a card from a tarot deck.

The Magician.

It depicts a man in red-and-white robes standing at an altar. He lifts a wand toward the heavens with his right hand and points to the ground with his left. Sitting above his head like a double halo is a figure eight.

An ouroboros.

There's another, different one around his waist. A snake holding itself in place by biting its own tail.

The altar contains four objects—a staff, a sword, a shield adorned with a star, and a goblet made of gold.

I lean in closer, studying first the shield, then the goblet.

Upon closer inspection, I realize the star in the shield isn't just any star. Its interconnected lines form five distinct points, all of them surrounded by the circle of the shield itself.

A pentagram.

As for the golden cup, it looks less like a goblet and more like something ceremonial.

A chalice.

Seeing it next to the pentagram strikes a bell deep in the recesses of my memory. I leap from the table, leaving the books thrown open across it. Back at the information desk, I summon the same exasperated librarian who helped me earlier. He cringes when he sees me.

"How many books do you have on Satanism?" I say.

The librarian's cringe becomes a wince. "I don't exactly know. A lot?"

"Give me all of them."

By five thirty I have, if not all of them, then at least a damn good sampling. Sixteen books now sit in front of me, replacing the symbology texts that have been swept aside. I sort through this new stack, flipping to their indexes, scanning the names in the hope one stands out from all the rest.

One eventually does, in a scholarly text titled *Modern Deviltry: Satanism in the New World*.

Marie Damyanov.

I remember it from the article I read about the Bartholomew's tragic past. All those dead servants and rumored ghosts and Cornelia Swanson's alleged murder of her poor maid. One of the reasons Cornelia seemed so guilty was because she had once consorted with Damyanov, an occult leader.

Le Calice D'Or.

That was the name of her group of followers.

The Golden Chalice.

I flip back a hundred pages, locating a telling passage about Marie Damyanov.

> While times of strife cause many to seek solace in their faith, it also forces others to consider the option of appealing to a satanic messiah, especially during eras marked by extreme warfare or plague. Damyanov believed that after forming the heavens and the earth, God abandoned his creations, allowing chaos to reign. To endure this chaos, Damyanov advised her followers to appeal to a mightier deity—Lucifer—who could be summoned not with prayers but with blood. Thus began rituals in which young women would be cut, their blood caught in a golden chalice and poured over an open flame.
>
> Years later, some of Damyanov's disillusioned followers hinted at more horrific practices in letters to friends and confidantes. One wrote that Damyanov claimed the sacrifice of a young woman during a blue moon would summon Lucifer himself, where he would grant those present with gifts of good health and immense fortune. The author of

the letter then went on to admit that he never witnessed such an act, saying it was most likely a tale created to sully Damyanov's reputation.

After Damyanov was arrested for indecency in late 1930, Le Calice D'Or disbanded. Damyanov herself faded from public view. Her whereabouts after January 1931 are unknown.

I reread the passage, my sense of unease intensifying. I try to recall details of the Cornelia Swanson case. Her maid's name was Ruby. I remember that. The Ruby Red Killing. She was cut open, her organs removed. Something like that is hard to forget. As is the fact that the murder took place on Halloween night. I can even remember the year: 1944.

I grab my phone and find a website that gives you the lunar cycle for every month in any given year. It turns out that on Halloween in 1944, the sky was brightened by the second full moon of the month.

A blue moon.

My hands start to shake, making it difficult to hold the phone as I do a new internet search, this time for a single name.

Cornelia Swanson.

A flurry of articles appears, pretty much all of them about the murder. I click on one and am greeted by a photo of the infamous Mrs. Swanson.

I stare at the picture, and the world goes sideways, as if the library has suddenly tilted. I grip the edge of the table, bracing myself.

Because the photo I'm looking at is one I've seen before. A sharp-featured beauty in a satin gown and silk gloves. Flawless skin. Hair as dark as a moonless night.

I saw it in the photo album in Nick's apartment. Although he identified the woman, he never used her name.

But now I know it.

Cornelia Swanson.

And her granddaughter is none other than Greta Manville.

40

I text Dylan from inside the library.

Call me ASAP! I found something!

When five minutes tick by and he doesn't respond, I decide to call him. A theory is forming. One I need to share with someone else, if only so they'll tell me I'm being crazy.

But here's the thing: I'm not being crazy.

Right now, insanity would be a blessing.

Outside, I lean against the base of one of the library's stone lions and dial Dylan's number. The call again goes straight to his voice-mail. I leave a message, urgently whispering into the phone.

"Dylan, where are you? I've been looking into some of the people living at the Bartholomew. And they're not who they say they are. I think—I think I know what's going on, and it's some scary shit. Please, please call me back as soon as you get this."

I end the call and stare up at the sky. The moon is out already—full and bright and hanging so low it's bisected by the spire of the Chrysler Building.

As kids, Jane and I loved full moons and how their light would stream in through her bedroom window. Sometimes we'd wait until my parents went to sleep and stand in the ice-white glow, as if bathing in it.

That memory is tainted now that I've read what members of the Golden Chalice allegedly did during full moons. Just like the Bartholomew, it's another piece of my past with Jane sullied.

I turn around, about to head back inside the library, when a ring bleats from the phone still white-knuckled in my hand.

Dylan calling me back at last.

But when I answer the phone, it's an unfamiliar voice I hear. A woman, her tone tentative.

"Is this Jules?"

"Yes."

A pause.

"Jules, it's Bobbie."

"Who?"

"Bobbie. From the shelter."

And then I remember. Bobbie, the kind and funny woman I spoke with two days ago.

"How are you?"

"I'm hanging in there. New day, new thoughts. All that Eleanor Roosevelt bullshit. But as much as I like to gab, this isn't a social call."

My pulse, which was just starting to settle down, revs up again. Excited blood pumps through my veins.

"You found Ingrid?"

"Maybe," Bobbie says. "A girl just came in. She looks a lot like the girl in that picture you gave me. But there's a chance it's not her. She looks more ragged now than in the photo. In all honesty, Jules, she looks like something dead the cat just dragged in."

"Did she say she was Ingrid?"

"She doesn't talk much. I tried to buddy up to her, but she wanted none of it. The only thing she told me is that I could go fuck myself."

That doesn't sound like Ingrid. Then again, I have no idea what she's been through in the past few days.

"What color is her hair?"

"Black," Bobbie says. "A dye job. A crappy one, too. She missed a spot in the back."

I grip the phone tighter. "Can you see her right now?"

"Yeah. She's sitting on a cot, legs pulled to her chest, not talking to anyone."

"That spot she missed in her hair—do you see any color there?"

"Let me look." Bobbie's voice becomes muted as she pulls away from her phone to get a better view. "Yeah, there's some color there."

"What is it?"

I hold my breath, preparing for disappointment. Considering the way my life has gone, I've come to expect it.

"It looks to me like a spot of blue," Bobbie says.

I exhale.

It's Ingrid.

"Bobbie, I need you to do me a favor."

"I can try."

"Don't let her leave," I say. "Not until I get there. Do anything you can to keep her there. Hold her down if necessary. I'll be there as soon as I can."

Then I'm off, rushing down the library steps and turning onto Forty-Second Street. The shelter is ten blocks north and several long cross blocks west. Through a combination of jogging, speed walking, and willfully ignoring traffic lights, I make it there in twenty minutes.

Bobbie is waiting for me outside. Still dressed in her work khakis and cardigan, she stands at a noticeable remove from the circle of smokers I saw two days ago.

"Don't worry, she's still inside," she tells me.

"Has she talked more?"

Bobbie shakes her head. "Nope. Still keeps to herself. She looks scared, though."

We enter the building, Bobbie's familiar presence allowing me to bypass the woman at the desk behind the scuffed glass. Tonight, the converted gymnasium is far more crowded than the afternoon of my first visit. Nearly every cot has been taken. Those that aren't occupied have been marked with suitcases, trash bags, grungy pillows.

"There she is," Bobbie says, pointing to a cot on the far side of the gym. Sitting on top of it, knees pulled to her chest, is Ingrid.

It's not just her hair that's changed in the past three days. Everything about her is darker, dirtier. She's become a shadow version of her former self.

Her hair, now the color of tar save for that patch of telltale blue, hangs in greasy strings. Her shirt and jeans are the same ones she had on the last time I saw her, although they're now stained from days of wear. Her face is cleaner but raw and weathered, as if she's spent too much time outdoors.

Ingrid looks my way, recognition dawning in her bloodshot eyes. "Juju?"

She leaps off the cot and runs toward me, pulling me into a strong, scared embrace.

"What are you doing here?" she says, showing no sign of letting me go.

"Looking for you."

"You left the Bartholomew, right?"

"No."

Ingrid breaks the embrace and backs away, eyeing me with palpable suspicion. "Tell me they didn't get to you. Swear to me that you're not one of them."

"I'm not," I say. "I'm here to help."

"You can't. Not anymore." Ingrid collapses onto the nearest cot, her hands covering her face. Her left one trembles, out of control. Even when she grasps it with her right, it still shakes, her dirt-streaked fingers twitching. "Juju, you need to get out of there."

"I plan to," I tell her.

"No, *now*," Ingrid says. "Run away as fast as you can. You don't know what they are."

Only, I do.

I think I've known for a while but wasn't able to completely comprehend it.

But now all the information I've gathered in the past few days is starting to make sense. It's like a photograph just pulled from a chemical bath. The image taking shape, emerging from the blankness, revealing the whole ghastly picture.

I know exactly what they are.

The Golden Chalice reborn.

41

At Ingrid's insistence, we go someplace secluded to talk.

"I don't want anyone to hear us," she explains.

At the shelter, that means commandeering the men's locker room of this former YMCA. Outside, Bobbie stands guard at the door, blocking anyone who might try to enter. Inside, Ingrid and I stroll past rows of empty lockers and shower stalls that have been bone dry for years.

"I haven't showered in three days," Ingrid says, staring with longing at one of the stalls. "The closest thing has been a whore's bath at Port Authority, and that was yesterday morning."

"Is that where you've been all this time?"

Ingrid drops onto a bench across from the showers. "I've been everywhere. Port Authority. Grand Central. Penn Station. Anywhere there are crowds. Because they're looking for me, Juju. I know they are."

"But they're not," I say.

"You don't know that for certain."

"I do, because—"

I stop myself before the rest of the sentence emerges.

Because I'm the only one who's been looking for you.

That's what I was about to say. But I now know that's a lie. They've been looking for her, too.

Through me.

Rather than search themselves, they had me do it. It's why Greta Manville suggested places for me to look. Why Nick lowered me down in the dumbwaiter to search 11A, hoping I'd find something of use. It's probably even why he slept with me. To endear himself, keep me close, learn everything I had discovered.

I assume he didn't pretend to be Ingrid via text until after they realized I knew something was amiss. By that point, they were prepared to cut their losses as far as Ingrid was concerned.

"If you were so scared of being found, why didn't you take a bus or train out of the city?"

"That's kind of difficult when you don't have any money," Ingrid says. "And I've got next to nothing. My meals have been fished out of trash cans. I had to shoplift this stupid hair dye. What little money I do have came from panhandling and stealing coins from fountains. So far I have, like, twelve dollars. At this rate, maybe I'll have enough to leave the country after a decade. Because that's what we have to do, Juju. Go someplace where they'll never be able to find us. It's the only way to escape them."

"Or we could go to the police," I suggest.

"And tell them what? That a bunch of rich bitches at the Bartholomew are worshipping the devil? Just saying it sounds ridiculous."

As does hearing it out loud, even though it's exactly what I think is happening. They post discreet ads in newspapers and online, luring people to the building with the promise of money and a place to stay. People like me and Ingrid and Dylan.

Each of us entered the Bartholomew willingly. But once we were there, the rules kept us trapped.

"How did you figure it all out?"

"It was Erica who started it," Ingrid says. "We went to the park, just like you and I did, and she told me she found out that the person who was in 12A before her wasn't dead, which is what she'd been told. That freaked her out a little. So I did some research into the Bartholomew and learned about some of the weird stuff that happened there. That freaked Erica out *a lot*. So when she left, I assumed it was because she felt too creeped out to stay there anymore. But then Dylan came by asking if I'd heard from her. And that's when I suspected something else was going on."

Her story is a lot like my own. Her new friend went missing; she started to think something weird was going on and decided to look into it. The only difference was that she learned about Greta Manville's relationship to Cornelia Swanson much sooner than I did.

"I met Greta in the lobby during my interview with Leslie," Ingrid says. "And I thought it was cool to be in the same building as an author, you know? At first, I thought she was nice. She even gave me a signed copy of her book. But when I read about Cornelia Swanson and noticed their resemblance, I knew what was up."

"You asked her about it," I say. "She told me."

"I guess she left out the part about threatening to get me kicked out if I ever talked to her again."

That detail went unmentioned, even when Greta told me about her life at the Bartholomew. My apartment used to be her apartment, which means that at one point it belonged to Cornelia Swanson.

It's the same apartment where she murdered her maid.

Only it wasn't just a murder.

It was a sacrifice.

Fulfilling the promise of the ouroboros.

Creation from destruction.

Life from death.

Ruby might have been the first, but I have a heart-sickening feeling that Erica was the last. I try not to think about how many others there have been in between then and now. There'll be plenty of time to dwell on that later. Right now, I need to focus on one thing—extricating myself from the place in a way that will cause the least amount of suspicion.

"What happened after you talked to Greta?"

"I knew I didn't want to stay there, that's for damn sure." Ingrid stands and makes her way to the row of sinks along the wall. She turns on the tap and starts splashing her face with water. "At that point, I had two thousand dollars in apartment-sitting money. Enough to get me far away from that place. But I also knew there'd be a lot more money coming if I stayed."

The cash. Dangled in front of us at the end of each week. Yet another way the Bartholomew trapped us. It certainly kept me there another night.

"I decided to stay," Ingrid says. "I didn't know for how long. Maybe another week. Maybe two. But I wanted to feel safe, so I—"

"Bought a gun."

Ingrid looks at me in the mirror above the sink, her brows arched. "So you found it. Good."

"Why did you leave it there in the first place?"

"Because something happened," Ingrid says, her voice getting quiet. "And if I tell you what it is, you're totally going to hate me forever."

I join her by the sink. "I won't. I promise."

"You will," Ingrid says, now using a damp paper towel to clean the back of her neck. "And I totally deserve it."

"Ingrid, just tell me."

"That gun cost me everything I had. That two grand I had saved up? Gone, like that." She snaps her fingers, and I can see the chipped remains of her blue nail polish. "So I asked Leslie if I could get an advance on my apartment-sitting money. Nothing huge. Just a week's pay early. She told me that wasn't possible. But then she said that I could have five thousand dollars—not a loan or an advance, but five grand with no strings attached—if I did one little thing."

"What was it?"

Ingrid stalls by examining a strand of her black-as-pitch hair. When she looks in the mirror, there's disgust in her eyes. As if she hates every single thing about herself.

"To cut you," she says. "When we crashed in the lobby, that wasn't an accident. Leslie paid me to do it."

I recall that moment with vivid clarity, like it's a movie being projected right there on the bathroom wall. Me burdened with my two grocery bags. Ingrid rushing down the stairs, her eyes on her phone. Then the collision, our bodies ricocheting, the groceries falling, me suddenly bleeding. In the chaotic aftermath, I didn't have time to give too much thought as to how my arm had been cut.

Now I know the truth.

"I had a Swiss army knife," Ingrid says, unable to look at me. "I held it against my phone, with just the tip of the blade exposed. And right when we crashed, I sliced your arm. Leslie told me it shouldn't be a big cut. Just enough to draw blood."

I back away from her. First one step. Then another.

"Why . . . why would they need you to do that?"

"I don't know," Ingrid says. "I didn't ask. By then, I had my suspicions about what she was. What *all* of them are. And I guess I thought it was some kind of test. Like they were trying to convert me. Enticing me to join them. But at the time, I was too desperate to ask questions. All I could think about was that five thousand dollars, and how much I needed it to get away from that place."

I keep moving away from her until I'm on the other side of the bathroom, sinking into an open stall and dropping onto the toilet seat. Ingrid rushes toward me and drops to her knees.

"I'm so sorry, Juju," she says. "You have no idea how sorry I am."

A bubble of anger rises in my chest, hot and bilious. But it's not directed at Ingrid. I can't blame her for what she did. She was broke and desperate and saw an easy way to make a lot of money. If our roles were reversed, I might have done the same thing, no questions asked.

No, my anger is reserved for Leslie and everyone else in the Bartholomew for exploiting that desperation and turning it into a weapon.

"You're forgiven," I tell Ingrid. "You did what you needed to do to survive."

She shakes her head and looks away. "No, I'm a shitty person. Truly awful. And right after it happened, I decided I needed to leave.

Five thousand dollars was more than enough for me. I didn't want to stay there and see how much lower I could sink."

"Why didn't you tell me all of this that day in the park?"

"Would you have believed me?"

The answer is no. I would have thought she was lying. Or, worse, deeply disturbed. Because no one in their right mind would believe there was a group of Satanists occupying a building like the Bartholomew. That, of course, is how they managed to go undetected for so long. The preposterousness of their existence is like a shield, deflecting all suspicion.

"And you certainly wouldn't have forgiven me for hurting you like that," Ingrid says. "In my mind, the best thing I could do was try to warn you by giving you some idea about what was going on there. I hoped it would, I don't know, scare you enough to leave. Or at least make you think twice about staying."

"Which it did," I say. "But does this mean you really did run away?"

"Yes, but not the way I wanted to," Ingrid says, talking so fast now that I can barely keep up. "That night, I was all packed and ready to leave. I put that note in the dumbwaiter, trying to do everything I could to get you to leave. I left the gun for the same reason. Just in case, God forbid, you needed to use it. I didn't leave immediately, because Leslie told me she'd be by at some point in the night to give me the five thousand dollars I was promised. Also, I had arranged to tell Dylan everything I knew, just in case it could help him find out what happened to Erica. My plan was to get the cash from Leslie, meet Dylan in the basement, grab my things, and give the keys to Charlie on the way out. That didn't happen, obviously."

"What went wrong?"

"They came for me," Ingrid says. "Well, *he* did."

My thoughts flash back to that video of Erica.

It's him.

"Nick," I say.

Ingrid shudders at the name. "All of a sudden, he was there."

"At the door?"

"No," she says. "*Inside* the apartment. I don't know how he got in. The door was locked. But there he was. I think he had been there for hours. Hiding. Waiting. But the moment I saw him, I knew I was in danger. He looked mean. Like, truly scary."

"Did he say anything?"

"That I shouldn't struggle."

Ingrid pauses, and I suspect she's replaying that moment in her head the same way I saw our collision in the Bartholomew's lobby. She starts shaking again. Not just her hands, but her entire body—an uncontrollable tremble. Tears pool in her eyes as she croaks out a single, mournful sob.

"He told me it would be easier that way," she says as the tears break free and stream down her cheeks. "And I knew . . . I knew that he was planning to kill me. He had a weapon with him. A stun gun. I screamed when I saw it."

And I heard that scream as I stood in the kitchen of 12A. Which means others probably heard it, too. Including Greta, who lives directly below that apartment. I suspect no one said anything because they knew what was happening.

Ingrid was being led to slaughter.

"How did you get away?"

"You saved me." Ingrid wipes her eyes and gives me a warm, grateful smile. "When you came to the door."

"Nick was there?"

"Right behind me," Ingrid says. "I didn't want to answer the door, but when we heard it was you, Nick told me I had to open it or you'd get suspicious. He had the stun gun pressed against my back the entire time, just in case I tried to warn you. He told me he'd paralyze us—me then you."

That explains everything. Why it took Ingrid so long to open the door. Twenty seconds, by my count. Why she had opened it only a crack. Why she wore that obviously fake smile and told me she was fine.

"I knew something was wrong," I say, surprised by my own tears, which spring forth suddenly now that Ingrid's have stopped. "I wanted to help you."

"But you *did*, Jules. I had pepper spray in my pocket. A tiny bottle attached to my key ring. Nick appeared so fast I didn't have time to reach for it. Then you came to my door. And you talked to me just long enough for me to reach into my pocket and grab it."

I remember that vividly. The way her right hand had been plunged into the pocket of her jeans, grasping for something.

"After you left, I begged him not to hurt you," Ingrid says. "Then I hit him with the pepper spray. After that, I ran. I didn't take anything with me. There wasn't any time. I had to leave everything behind. My phone. My clothes. Money. The only thing I had were the keys, which I threw onto the lobby floor because I knew I wouldn't be able to come back."

The locker room door opens, and Bobbie pokes her head inside.

"Ladies, you're going to need to wrap this up," she says. "I can't stay out here all night. It's getting packed out here, and someone's going to take my cot if I'm not in it soon."

Ingrid and I make our way out of the locker room into a shelter even more crowded than when we left it. Bobbie is right. All the cots have now been claimed. Many are occupied by people sleeping or reading or just staring off in silence. A few serve as makeshift social hubs, where groups of women sit in clusters to laugh and converse. It's a loud and bustling place, which makes me understand why Ingrid stuck to bus and train stations. There's safety in numbers.

For the two of us.

But there's still one apartment sitter left at the Bartholomew. And he's all alone.

That realization prompts another thought. One so awful it makes my heart beat like a snare drum in my chest.

I pull out my phone and swipe through my search history, returning to the lunar calendar I looked at earlier.

I type in this month.

I type in this year.

When the results appear, I gasp so loud it makes others in the shelter stop and stare. Ingrid and Bobbie close in around me, concerned.

"What's wrong?" Ingrid says.

"I need to go." I pull away from them, heading to the exit. "Stay with Bobbie. Trust no one else."

Ingrid calls after me. "Where are you going?"

"The Bartholomew. I need to warn Dylan."

In a matter of seconds, I'm out of the gymnasium, then out of the building, then out on the street, where the moon still glows bright and round.

It's a full moon.

The second one this month.

A blue moon.

42

I take a cab back to the Bartholomew, even though I can't afford it. My wallet is empty.

So is my bank account.

But speed is the most important thing right now. I've allowed myself twenty minutes to get back to the Bartholomew, collect what I can, meet up with Dylan, and then get the hell out of there. No explanations. No goodbyes. Just in and out, dropping my keys in the lobby before I'm out the door.

Already I'm behind schedule. Traffic on Eighth Avenue is a slow crawl north. In five minutes, the cab's traversed only two blocks. I sit in the back seat, fear and impatience forming a potent combination that has my entire body buzzing. My hand shakes as I grab my phone and call Dylan.

One ring.

The cab, which has been idling at a red light, surges forward the moment the light turns green.

Two rings.

We zip past another block.

Three rings.

Another block goes by. Sixteen more to go.

Four rings.

After zooming across one more block, the cab screeches to a halt at a red light. I'm thrust forward, barely avoiding the plexiglass barrier between the back seat and the front. The phone drops from my trembling hands.

It keeps ringing, the sound distant and tinny on the cab floor. The ringing stops, replaced by Dylan's outgoing voicemail message.

"This is Dylan. You know what to do."

I snatch the phone from the floor, practically shouting into it.

"Dylan, I found Ingrid. She's safe. She doesn't know where Erica is. But you need to get out of there. Right now."

In the front seat, the cabbie looks up and gives me a curious glance in the rearview mirror. Arched brows. Creased forehead. Already he's regretting picking me up. He'll regret it even more in a minute.

I look away and keep shouting into my phone, the words tumbling out.

"I'm on my way there now. If you can, meet me outside. I'll explain the rest after we leave."

I end the call as the light changes and the cab speeds forward again, hurtling us through Columbus Circle at a dizzying pace. On the right, the buildings fall away, replaced with the tree-studded expanse of Central Park.

Thirteen blocks to go.

I send Dylan a text.

CALL ME.

I immediately send another, more urgent one.

YOU'RE IN DANGER.

We zip by one more block. Twelve more remain.

I tell myself to stay calm, stay focused.

Don't panic.

Think.

That's what will get me out of this mess. Not panicking. Panic only breeds more panic.

But thinking—calm, rational thought—will work wonders. Only, rational thought is impossible after I check my watch. Ten minutes spent in this cab and I'm not even halfway there.

Time to bail.

When the cab stops at the next light, I throw open the passenger door and leap out. The driver starts shouting at me, words I can't make out because I'm too busy scrambling past cars in other lanes on my way to the sidewalk. Behind me, the cabbie honks his horn. Two quick, angry honks followed by a lengthy one that follows me up the block.

I still hear it as I run across the street.

Eleven blocks to go.

I keep running, my pace quickening to a full sprint. Most people hear me coming and step out of the way. Those who don't are shoved aside.

I ignore their hard stares and angry gestures as I pass. All I can focus on is getting to the Bartholomew as fast as possible and, once I'm there, leaving just as quickly.

Stay calm.

Stay focused.

Get in.

Get out.

As I run, I make a list of what to grab once I'm back in 12A. The photograph of my family. That's my main priority. The photo fifteen-year-old me took of Jane and my parents that now sits in a frame next to the bed. Everything else can be replaced.

I'll also grab my phone charger, my laptop, some clothes. Nothing that can't fit into a single box. There won't be enough time for a return trip. Not with the minutes ticking by and the blocks passing slowly, even though I'm running as fast as I can.

Five more blocks.

Four more.

Three more.

I reach the end of another block and cross the street against the light, barely skirting past an oncoming Range Rover.

I keep running. My lungs are on fire. So are my legs. My knees scream. My heart pounds so hard I worry it might burst right through my rib cage.

I slow down once I near the Bartholomew. An unconscious winding down. Approaching the building, I scan the sidewalk, looking for signs of Dylan.

He's not there.

Not a good sign.

The only person I see is Charlie, who stands at the front door, holding it open, waiting for me to come inside.

"Evening, Jules," he says, a good-natured smile widening beneath his bushy mustache. "You must have been busy. You've been out all day."

I look at him and wonder how much he knows.

Everything?

Nothing?

I'm tempted to say something. Ask for his help. Warn him to leave just as quickly as I'm about to. It's a risk I can't take.

Not yet.

"Job hunting," I say, forcing my own smile.

Charlie tilts his head in curiosity. "Any luck?"

"Yes." I pause, stalling. Then it comes to me. My perfectly rational excuse for leaving. "I got a job. In Queens. But because the commute is so far, I won't be able live here anymore. I'll be staying with friends until I can find a place."

"You're leaving us?"

I nod. "Right now."

When Charlie frowns, I can't tell if his disappointment is genuine or as fake as my smile. Not even after he says, "Well, I for one hate to see you go. It's been a pleasure getting to know you."

He continues to hold the door, waiting for me to enter. I hesitate, taking a quick glance at the gargoyles that hover over the front door.

At one point, I thought they were whimsical. Now, like everything else about the building, they terrify me.

Inside the Bartholomew, all is quiet. There's no sign of Dylan here, either. No sign of anyone. The entire lobby is empty.

I hurry to the elevator, my body resisting every step. By now I'm moving only through sheer force of will, commanding my stubborn muscles to step into the elevator, close the grate, press the button for the eleventh floor.

The elevator rises, lifting me higher into a building that's eerily silent. On the eleventh floor, I push out of the elevator and move quickly down the hall to Dylan's apartment.

I knock on Dylan's door. A quick trio of raps.

"Dylan?"

I knock again. Harder this time, the door shaking beneath my fist.

"Dylan, are you there? We need to—"

The door swings away, leaving my fist swiping at nothing but air before dropping to my side. Then Leslie Evelyn appears. Filling the empty doorway. Wearing her black Chanel suit like armor. Wielding a fake smile.

My heart, which has been pounding like thunder in my chest, suddenly stops.

"Jules." Leslie's voice is sickly sweet. Honey laced with poison. "What a pleasant surprise."

I start to feel myself leaning to the side. Or maybe I'm not and it only feels that way. Shock leaving me reeling, unmoored, adrift. I can think of only one reason why Leslie would be in Dylan's apartment.

I'm too late.

Dylan's been taken.

Just like Megan and Erica and God knows how many people before them.

"Can I help you with something?" Leslie says, her eyelids fluttering in mock concern.

My mouth drops open, but no words come out. Fear and shock have stolen my voice. Instead, I hear Ingrid's voice, blasting like a siren into my thoughts.

Run away as fast as you can.

I do.

Away from Leslie. Down the hall. To the stairwell.

Rather than down, I go up. I have to. Others might be waiting for me in the lobby.

My only option is 12A. If I can get there, then I can lock the door, call the police, demand that an officer come and escort me from the building. If that doesn't work, there's always Ingrid's gun.

So I start to climb, even though my knees throb and my hands shake and shock has left me numb.

Up the stairs.

Counting them as I go.

Ten steps. Landing. Ten steps.

Finally on the twelfth floor, I hurry down the hall, winded and aching. Soon I'm inside 12A, almost weeping with relief.

I slam the door behind me and secure it.

Lock. Deadbolt. Chain.

I slump against the door for a sliver of a second to catch my breath. Then it's down the hall, up more stairs, going slower this time.

In the bedroom, I go straight to the nightstand and grab the framed photo of my family. Everything else is expendable. This is all I need.

With the picture tucked under my arm, I descend the winding steps one last time. Soon I'll be in the kitchen, calling the police, digging out the gun, cradling it in my lap until help arrives.

At the bottom of the steps, I move into the hallway and stop.

Nick is there.

He stands straight-backed just beyond the foyer, blocking any attempt I might make to leave. Something's in his hand, held behind his back where I can't see it.

His face is expressionless. A blank slate onto which I project a hundred fears.

"Hey there, neighbor," he says.

43

"How did you get in here?" I say.

A wasted question. I already know. Behind Nick, in the study, part of the bookshelf sits away from the wall. Beyond it is a dark rectangle. A passageway connecting one apartment to the other. If I searched it, I'm sure I would find a small set of steps in the wall leading to both 11A and 11B.

Nick could have entered 12A anytime he wanted. In fact, I think he did. That noise I heard early in the mornings. The soft swishing sound, like socks on carpet or the train of a dress sliding across a table leg.

That was Nick.

Coming and going like a ghost.

"Where's Dylan?" I'm so frightened I no longer recognize my voice. Pitched high and tremulous, it sounds like someone else. A stranger. "What have you done to him?"

"Didn't Leslie tell you? He moved out."

Nick smirks as he says it. A slight, scary upturn of his lips. I see it and know for certain that Dylan is dead. Nausea rushes through me in a fast and furious wave. I grip my stomach, certain I'd be throwing up right now if it wasn't completely empty. All I can do is gag.

"Please let me leave." I swallow hard, gasping for breath. "I won't tell anyone what's going on here."

"And just what do you think is going on?" Nick says.

"Nothing," I reply, as if that clear lie is all it will take to convince him to let me go.

Nick gives a sad shake of his head. "You and I both know that's not true."

He takes a step forward. I do the opposite, taking two backward.

"Let's make a bargain," he says. "If you tell me where Ingrid is, then maybe—just maybe—we'll take her and spare you. How does that sound?"

It sounds like a lie. One as obvious as mine.

"I guess that's a no," Nick says when I don't answer. "That's a shame."

He takes another step and reveals what's been held behind his back.

The stun gun, a blue spark dancing across its tip.

I sprint down the hall, cutting right, into the kitchen. Once inside, I drop to my knees, sliding across the floor, aiming for the cupboard under the sink. I fling open the door and grasp at the shoe box, knocking it onto its side, the lid askew.

The box is empty.

I'm hit with a blast of memory. Me texting Ingrid about the gun. A text, I now realize, she never saw.

Other than me, Nick is the only one who knows about that text.

Behind me, his voice rises from the hallway.

"I admire your survival instincts, Jules. I do. But having a gun in the apartment is far too dangerous. I had to remove it and put it in a safe place."

He rounds the corner and steps into the kitchen. He's in no hurry. There's no need to be. Not when I'm trapped like this. Alone and defenseless. Armed with nothing but a framed photo of my family, which I hold out in front of me like a shield.

"This doesn't have to end violently, you know," Nick says. "Offer yourself up peacefully. It's easier that way."

I search the kitchen, desperately looking for a weapon. The wood block of knives on the counter is too close to where Nick is standing, and the utensil drawer is too far away from me. He'll be on me the moment I make a move for either.

Still, I have to try something. No matter what Nick says, going in peace is not an option.

To my right is the closed cupboard tucked between the oven and sink. I fling it open, revealing the dumbwaiter behind it. Nick moves as soon as I start to clamber inside. I'm halfway into it by the time he reaches me, the stun gun sparking. I kick at him. Wildly. Savagely. Screaming as my foot connects with his chest.

Through eyes half-closed with fear, I see another blue crackle of the stun gun. I kick again, aiming higher, at his face, his glasses crackling beneath my heel.

Nick yelps and reels backward.

The stun gun blinks out and clatters to the floor.

I pull my leg into the dumbwaiter, suddenly reminded of how small it really is. Using both hands, I give the rope a tug. A second later, the dumbwaiter plummets and I'm thrown into darkness.

I try to keep hold of the rope as the dumbwaiter drops, but it's moving too fast, zipping over my palms, slicing into them. I pull my hands away and clamp my knees against the rope, hoping it will slow my descent.

I can't tell if it's working. It's too dark, and the dumbwaiter is too loud, creaking under my weight. A line of heat forms at my knees. Friction burning through the denim of my jeans. I part my knees and scream again, the sound consumed by the noise of the dumbwaiter as it smashes into the apartment below.

The impact blasts through my entire body. My head snaps backward. Pain shoots up my spine. My limbs smack against the sides of the dumbwaiter.

When it's all over, I wait in the darkness, aching and scared and wondering if I'm too injured to move. Because I *am* injured. Of that there's no doubt. Pain rings my neck, hot and throbbing. A noose of heat.

But I can lift the dumbwaiter door and crawl out, careful not to jar my battered body. As I slide onto the kitchen floor of 11A, I'm surprised to see I can walk, albeit slowly. Pain hobbles every step.

I grit my teeth and push through it, moving out of the kitchen and into the foyer, where I fling open the door.

Out of 11A, the pain lessens with each step. Fear, I think. Maybe adrenaline. It doesn't matter which, if it gets me down the hallway faster.

As I approach the elevator, I see that—miracle of miracles—it's still stopped on the eleventh floor. The door sits open, as if waiting for me. I run toward it, suddenly aware of motion to my left.

Nick.

Coming down the steps from the twelfth floor, the stun gun zapping. His glasses dangle from one ear, the frames slanted across his face. The right lens is shattered. Blood oozes from a cut below his right eye, like crimson tears.

I throw myself into the elevator and pound the button for the lobby.

Nick reaches the elevator as the outer door closes. He thrusts his arm between the bars, stun gun sparking like St. Elmo's fire.

I reach for the interior grate and slam it into his arm, pinning it against the door.

I pull back and do it again.

Harder this time.

So hard that Nick jerks his arm away, the stun gun falling from his hand.

I slam the grate into place, and the elevator begins to carry me downward. Before I sink beyond the eleventh floor, I see Nick take to the stairs.

Tenth floor.

Nick is flying down the steps. I can't see him yet, but his shoes slap against the marble, echoing down to me.

Ninth floor.

He's getting closer. I get a glimpse of his feet crossing the landing between floors before the elevator slides out of view.

Eighth floor.

A scream for help balloons in my lungs. I keep it inside. I already know that, just like Ingrid's, it will go ignored.

Seventh floor.

I spot Marianne standing on the landing, watching. No makeup. No sunglasses. Her skin a sickly yellow.

Sixth floor.

Nick speeds up after passing Marianne. He's in full view now. A churning blur streaking across the landing, descending almost at the same speed as the elevator.

Fifth floor.

I bend down and scoop up the stun gun, surprisingly heavy in my hand.

Fourth floor.

I press the button on the side of the stun gun, testing it. The tip sparks in a single, startling zap.

Third floor.

Nick continues to keep pace with me. I rotate in the elevator car, watching out the windows as he moves. Ten steps, landing, ten more steps.

Second floor.

I stand with my hand on the grate, ready to fling it open as soon as the elevator stops.

Lobby.

I burst out of the elevator just as Nick starts down the staircase's final ten steps. I've got roughly ten feet on him. Maybe less.

I cross the lobby in frantic strides, not daring to look back. My heart pounds and my head swims and my body hurts so much that I can't feel the stun gun in my hand or my family's photo still tucked under my arm. My vision narrows so that all I can see is the front door ten feet from me.

Now five.

Now one.

Safety's just on the other side of that door.

Police and pedestrians and strangers who'll have to stop and help.

I reach the door.

I push it open.

Someone shoves me away from the door. A large, hulking presence. My vision expands, taking in his cap, his uniform, his mustache.

Charlie.

"I can't let you leave, Jules," he says. "I'm sorry. They promised me. They promised my daughter."

Without thinking, I fire up the stun gun and jab it into his stomach, the tip buzzing and sparking until Charlie is doubled over, grunting in agony.

I drop the stun gun, push out the door, zoom across the sidewalk and into the street.

Charlie calls out behind me, "Jules, look out!"

Still running, I risk a glance behind me and see him still doubled over in the doorway, Nick by his side.

There's more noise. A cacophony. The honk of a horn. The screech of tires. Someone, somewhere screams. It sounds like a siren.

Then something slams into me and I'm knocked sideways, flying out of control, hurtling into oblivion.

NOW

When I wake, it's with jolting suddenness. My eyelids don't flutter open. There's no lazy, dry-mouthed yawn. I simply go from darkness to light in an instant, feeling the same way I did before I went to sleep.

Panicked.

I understand the situation with neon clarity. Chloe is in danger. Ingrid, too, if they ever find her. I need to help them.

Right now.

I look to the open door. The room is dark, the hallway silent. Nary a whisper or sneaker squeak to be heard.

"Hello?" *Thirst has distorted my voice, turning it into an ungainly croak.* "I need—"

To call the police.

That's what I want to say. But my throat seizes up, cutting me off. I force out a cough, more to get the attention of a nurse than to revive my voice.

I try again, louder this time. "Hello?"

No one answers.

The hall, for the moment, appears to be empty.

I search the table by the bed for a phone. There isn't one. Nor is there a call button with which to summon a nurse.

I slide out of bed, relieved to discover I can walk, although not very well. My legs are wobbly and weak, and my entire body is gripped with pain. But soon I'm out of the room and into a hallway that's shorter than I expected. Just a dim corridor with doors leading to two other rooms and a small nurses' station that's currently empty.

There's no phone there, either.

"Hello?" I call out. "I need help."

Another door sits at the end of the hall, closed tight.

It's white.

Windowless.

And heavy, a fact I learn when I try to pry it open. It takes an extra tug and a pain-flaring grunt to finally get it to budge.

I pass through it, finding myself in another hallway.

One I think I've seen before. Like all my recollections of late, it's vague in my mind. A half memory made hazy by pain and worry and sedatives.

The hallway turns. I turn with it, rounding the corner into another hall.

To my right is a kitchen done up in muted earth tones. Above the sink is a painting. A snake curled into a perfect figure eight, chomping on its own tail.

Beyond the kitchen is a dining room. Beyond that are windows. Beyond them is Central Park colored orange by the setting sun, making it look like the whole park is on fire.

Seeing it sends a stark, cold fear pulsing through me.

I'm still in the Bartholomew.

I have been the whole time.

The realization makes me want to scream even though my throat won't allow it. Fear and thirst have clenched it shut.

I start to move, my bare feet smacking the floor in worried, hurried steps. I get only a few feet before a voice rises from somewhere behind me.

Hearing it opens my throat, despite the thirst and fear. A scream erupts from deep inside me, only to be pushed back by a hand clamping over my mouth. Another hand spins me around so I can see who it is.

Nick.

Lips flat.

Eyes angry.

To his right is Leslie Evelyn. To his left is Dr. Wagner, a needle and syringe in his hand. A bead of liquid quivers on the needle's tip before he jabs it into my upper arm.

Everything instantly goes woozy. Nick's face. Leslie's face. Dr. Wagner's face. All of them blur and waver like a TV on the fritz.

I gasp.

I let out another scream.

Loud and pitiable and streaked with terror.

It careens down the hall, echoing off the walls, so that I'm still hearing it when everything fades to nothingness.

ONE DAY
LATER

44

I dream of my family in Central Park, standing in the middle of Bow Bridge.

This time, I'm with them.

So is George.

It's just the five of us on the bridge, looking at our reflections in the moonlit water below. A slight breeze blows through the park, forming ripples on the water and making our faces look like funhouse-mirror versions of their true selves.

I stare at my reflection, marveling at how it wobbles and wavers. Then I look at the reflections of the others and notice something strange.

Everyone is holding a knife.

Everyone but me.

I turn away from the water and face them. My family. My gargoyle.

They raise their knives.

"You don't belong here," my father says.

"Run," my mother says.

"Run away as fast as you can," Jane says.

George says nothing. He simply watches with stoic stone eyes as my family lurches forward and begins to stab me.

TWO DAYS
LATER

45

I wake slowly. Like a swimmer uncertain about surfacing, pulled against my will from dark waters. Even after I regain consciousness, sleep lingers. A fog curling through me, languorous and thick.

My eyes stay closed. My body feels heavy. So heavy.

Although there's pain in my abdomen, it's distant, like a fire on the other side of the room. Just close enough that I can feel its heat.

Soon my eyelids move, flickering, fluttering, opening to the sight of a hospital room.

The same one as before.

No windows. Chair in the corner. Monet hanging from the white wall.

Despite the fog in my head, I know exactly where I am.

The only thing I don't know is what will happen to me next and what's already happened.

My body refuses to move, no matter how much I try. The fog is too heavy. My legs are useless. My arms are the same. Only my right hand moves—a weak flop against my side.

Turning my head is the most movement I can muster. A slow turn to the left lets me see the IV stand by the bed, its thin plastic tube snaking into my hand.

I can also tell that the bandage around my head is gone. My hair slides freely across the pillow when I roll my head in the opposite direction. That's where the photo of my family sits, my wan reflection visible in the cracked frame.

The sight of that pale face sliced into a dozen slivers causes my right hand to twitch. To my surprise, I can lift it. Not much. Just enough to get it to flop onto my stomach.

I move my hand across the hospital gown. Beneath the paper-thin fabric is a slight bump where a bandage sits. I can feel it on the upper left side of my abdomen, slightly below my breast. Touching it sends pain flashing through my body, cutting the fog enough for me to really feel it. Like a lightning strike.

With the pain comes panic. A confused horror in which I know something is wrong but I can't tell what it is.

My hand keeps moving down my side, slow and trembling. Just to the left of my navel is a different dreadful rise. Another bandage.

More pain.

More panic.

More smoothing my hand over my stomach, fingers probing, searching for yet another bandage.

I find it in the center of my lower abdomen, several inches below my navel. It's longer than the others. The pain gets worse when I press down on it. A gasp-inducing flare.

What did you do to me?

I think it more than say it. My voice is a dry croak, barely audible in the room's dim silence. But in my head it's a full-throated sob.

At my stomach, the pain burns with more intensity. This fire is no longer distant. It's here. Roaring across my gut. I clutch it with my one working hand. My thoughts continue to scream. My weakling voice can only moan.

Outside the room, someone hears me.

It's Bernard, who rushes in, his eyes no longer kind. When he glances my way, he looks not at me but past me. I moan again, and he disappears.

A moment later, Nick enters the room.

I let out another mental howl.

Get away from me! Please don't touch me!

My voice can't make it past that first word. A hoarse, haggard "Get."

Nick removes my hand from my stomach and places it gently at my side. He feels my forehead. He strokes my cheek.

"The surgery was a success," he says.

A single question forms in my thoughts.

What surgery?

I attempt to ask it, sputtering out half a syllable before the mental fog returns. I can't tell if it's exhaustion or if I've once again been injected with something. I suspect it's the latter. Sleep threatens to overtake me. I'm back to being a swimmer, this time sinking into the murky depths.

Before I go under, Nick whispers in my ear.

"You're fine," he says. "Everything is fine. Right now, we only needed the one kidney."

THREE DAYS LATER

46

Hours pass. Maybe days.

It's hard to tell now that my existence has been reduced to two modes—asleep and awake.

Right now, I'm awake, although the fog makes it difficult to know for sure. It's so overpowering that everything has the feel of a dream.

No, not a dream.

A nightmare.

In this maybe-nightmare state, I hear voices just outside the door. A man and a woman.

"You need to rest," the man says.

I note the accent. Dr. Wagner.

"What I need is to see her," the woman says.

"That's not a good idea."

"Ask me if I give a damn. Now push me in there."

That's followed by a hum. Rubber wheels on the floor. Someone in motion.

Because of the fog, I can't recoil when a hand, leathery and rough, clasps my own. My eyelids part just enough to see Greta Manville, looking frail and small in a wheelchair. Her skin clings to her bones. Veins zigzag beneath the papery whiteness. She reminds me of a ghost.

"I didn't want it to be you," she says. "I need you to know that."

I close my eyes and say nothing. I don't have the strength.

Greta senses this and fills the void with more chatter.

"It was supposed to be Ingrid. That's what they told me. During her interview, they asked for her medical records and she handed them over. Lo and behold, she was a potential match. But then she left and there you were. Another match. I had no choice in the matter. It was you or certain death. So I chose life. You saved me, Jules. I will always be grateful for that."

I open my eyes again, just so I can glare at her. I see that she's wearing a hospital gown similar to mine. Light blue. The same color as the bedroom wallpaper in 12A. Near the collar, someone has pinned a golden brooch just like the one Marjorie Milton was wearing.

An ouroboros.

I pull my hand away from hers and scream until I fall back to sleep.

47

I wake.

I sleep.

I wake again.

Some of the fog has burned away. Now I can move my arms, wiggle my toes, feel the painful intrusion of the IV and catheter that invade my body. I can even tell that someone's in the room with me. Their presence pokes through my solitude like a splinter through skin.

"Chloe?" I say, hoping against hope that all of this has been a nightmare. That when I open my eyes I'll be back on Chloe's couch, heartbroken about Andrew and worried about finding a new job.

I'd settle for that kind of worry.

I'd embrace it.

I say her name again. A wish repeated. If I keep saying it, maybe it will come true.

"Chloe?"

"No, Jules, it's me."

It's a man, his voice at once familiar and unwanted.

I open my eyes, my vision blurred by whatever it was they gave me. In that watery haze, I see someone in the chair beside the bed. He comes into focus slowly.

Nick.

He wears a new pair of glasses. Basic black instead of tortoiseshell. Beneath the frames, a wicked bruise circles his right eye. The spot where my foot connected with his face. I'd do it again to his other eye if I could. But all I can do now is lie here, a prisoner to his gaze.

"How are you feeling?" he says.

I remain silent and stare at the ceiling.

Nick places a plastic tumbler full of water and a small paper cup on the tray beside the bed. Inside the paper cup are two chalky white pills the size of baby aspirin.

"I brought you something for the pain. We want you to be comfortable. There's no need to suffer."

I continue to stay quiet, even though I *am* in pain. It burns through my abdomen—a fierce, throbbing agony. I welcome it. That pain is the only thing distracting me from fear and anger and hate. If it goes away, I'll descend into a dark swamp of emotion from which I might never escape.

Pain equals clarity.

Clarity equals survival.

Which is why I break my silence to ask the question I didn't have the strength to utter yesterday.

"What did you do to me?"

"Dr. Wagner and I removed your left kidney and transplanted it into a needy recipient," he says, avoiding using Greta's name, as if I don't already know it's her. "It's a common procedure. There were no complications. The recipient's body is responding well to the organ, which is excellent. The older the patient, the more common it is for their body to reject a transplanted organ."

I muster the strength to ask another question. "Why did you do it?"

Nick gives me a curious look, as if no one has ever asked him that before. I wonder how many people in this same predicament have squandered that opportunity.

"Under normal circumstances, we prefer that donors know as little as possible. It's better that way. But since these aren't normal circumstances, I see no harm in trying to clear up some of your *misconceptions.*"

He hisses the word with clear distaste. As if it's my fault that he's being forced to say it.

"In 1918, the Spanish flu came out of nowhere, killing more than fifty million people worldwide," he says. "To put that in perspective, the Great War going on at the same time killed almost seventeen million. Right here in America, more than half a million people died. As a doctor, Thomas Bartholomew was on the front lines of this particular war. He saw it strike down friends, associates, even family members. The flu didn't discriminate. It was ruthless. It didn't care if you were rich or poor."

I remember that horrible picture I saw. The dead servants lined up on the street. The blankets over their corpses. The dirty soles of their feet.

"What Thomas Bartholomew couldn't understand was how a millionaire could succumb to the flu as easily as a piece of tenement trash. Shouldn't the wealthy, by virtue of their superior breeding, be less susceptible than people who have nothing, come from nothing, *are* nothing? He decided his destiny was to build a facility where important people could live in comfort and splendor while he kept them safe from many of the ailments that afflicted the common class. That's how the Bartholomew was born. This building was willed into existence by my great-grandfather."

A memory forces its way into my pain- and drug-clouded mind. Nick and me in his dining room, talking over pizza and beer.

I come from a long line of surgeons, beginning with my great-grandfather.

Another memory quickly follows. The two of us in his kitchen, having my blood pressure checked, Nick distracting me with small talk. After I told him the story behind my name, he shared the obvious fact that Nick was short for Nicholas. What he didn't tell me— not then, not ever—was his last name.

Now I know it.

Bartholomew.

"My great-grandfather's dream didn't last very long," Nick says. "His first task was to find a way to protect the residents in case the Spanish flu ever flared up again. But things went very wrong, very quickly. Some of the same people he was trying to protect got sick. Some even died."

He doesn't mention the dead servants. He doesn't need to. I know what they were.

Test subjects.

The unwilling participants in a mad doctor's experiment. Infect the poor to heal the rich. Clearly, it didn't go as planned.

"When it looked like the police might get involved, my great-grandfather felt he had no choice but to end the investigation before it could even begin," Nick says. "He took his life. But an ouroboros never dies. It's simply reborn. So when my grandfather left medical school, he chose to continue his father's work. He was more careful, of course. More discreet. He shifted the focus away from virology to prolonging life. With wealth comes power. Power earns you importance. And the truly important people in the world deserve to live longer lives than those who are beneath them. That's especially true as we face another epidemic."

Telling his tale has left Nick energized. Beads of moisture shine along his hairline. Behind his glasses, his eyes gleam. No longer content to sit, he gets up and starts moving about the room, passing the Monet and the open door and then coming back again.

"Right now, at this very moment, hundreds of thousands of people wait for organ transplants," he says. "Some of them are important people. Very important. Yet they're told to just get in line and wait their turn. But some people can't wait. Eight thousand people a year die waiting for a life-saving organ. Think about that, Jules. Eight thousand people. And that's just in America alone. What I do—what my family has always done—is provide options for those who are too important to wait like everyone else. For a fee, we allow them to skip that line."

What he doesn't say is that letting so-called important people move to the front of the line requires an equal number of unimportant people.

Like Dylan.

Like Erica and Megan.

Like me.

All it takes to get us here is one small ad. Apartment sitter needed. Pays well. Call Leslie Evelyn.

After that, we simply disappear.

Creation from our destruction.

Life from our deaths.

That's the meaning behind the ouroboros.

Not immortality, but a desperate attempt to spend a few more years eluding the Grim Reaper's inevitable grasp.

"Cornelia Swanson," I say. "What was she?"

"A patient," Nick says. "The first transplant attempt. It went . . . badly."

So Ingrid and I had it all wrong. This isn't about Marie Damyanov or the Golden Chalice or devil worship. There is no coven. It's just a group of dying rich people desperate to save their lives no matter the cost. And Nick is here to facilitate it.

I roll onto my side, the pain shrieking through my body. It's worth it if it means I no longer have to look at him. Still, I can't resist asking a few more questions. For clarity's sake.

"What else are you going to take?"

"Your liver."

Nick says it with shocking indifference. Like he doesn't even consider me a human being.

I wonder what he was thinking that night in his bedroom, when I let him kiss me, undress me, fuck me. Even in that moment, was he appraising me, taking stock of what my body offered, wondering how much money I would make him?

"Who's going to get it?"

"Marianne Duncan," he says. "She's in need of one. Badly."

"What else?"

"Your heart." Nick pauses then. The only concession to my feelings. "That's going to Charlie's daughter. He's earned it."

I figured there had to be a reason people like Charlie willingly worked at the Bartholomew. Now I know. It's a classic quid pro quo, exploited by the upper classes for ages. For doing their dirty work, the little folks will get something in return.

"And Leslie? Dr. Wagner?"

"Our Mrs. Evelyn is a believer in the Bartholomew's mission," Nick says. "Her late husband benefitted from a heart transplant during my father's tenure. When he died—years later than was expected, I might add—she offered to keep things running smoothly. And, of course, she'll be first in line if she should ever need my services. As for Dr. Wagner, he's simply a surgeon. A damn good one who lost his license more than twenty years ago after showing up for surgery drunk. My father, in need of assistance due to growing demand, made him an offer he couldn't refuse."

"I pity you," I tell Nick. "I pity you, and I hate you, although not as much as you hate yourself. Because you do. I'm sure of it. You'd have to in order to do what you're doing."

Nick pats my leg. "Nice try. But guilt trips don't work on me. Now take your pills."

He grabs the paper cup and holds it out to me. I have just enough strength to knock it out of his hand. The cup drops to the floor, the pills bouncing into the corners.

"Please, Jules," Nick says with a sigh. "Don't become a problem patient. We can make the rest of your time here comfortable or extremely unpleasant. It's up to you."

He leaves quickly after that, letting the pills remain on the floor. The cleanup job falls to Jeannette, who enters the room a minute later dressed in the same purple scrubs and gray cardigan she wore when we first spoke in the basement.

She places new pills on the tray. When she bends down to pick up the ones on the floor, her cigarette lighter slips from her pocket and joins them. Jeannette curses under her breath before scooping it all up.

"Take the pills or get the needle again," she says while shoving the lighter back into her pocket. "Your choice."

It's not much of a choice, considering they share the same purpose, which is more than to simply ease my pain.

It's sedation.

Sustained weakness.

So when it comes time for the next donation, I'll go quietly, without fuss.

Staring at the pills, those two tiny eggs in a white-paper nest, I can't help but think of my parents. They, too, had a choice—to continue fighting a battle they had no chance of winning or to willingly wrap themselves in the sweet embrace of nothingness.

Now I face a similar decision. I can fight back and inevitably lose, making what little time I have left, to use Nick's words, extremely unpleasant. Or I can make the same choice my parents did.

Give up.

Succumb.

No more pain. No more problems. No more worry and heartache and constant wondering about Jane's fate. Just a deep, painless slumber in which my family waits for me.

I turn to their photo on the bedside table, their faces crisscrossed by cracks in the glass.

Shattered frame. Shattered family.

I look at them and know which choice to make.

I grab the paper cup and tip it back.

FOUR DAYS LATER

48

They keep the door closed. It's also locked from the outside. During my rare bouts of wakefulness, I hear the click of the lock before anyone enters. Which is often. People are always coming and going. A veritable parade stomping through my drug-induced slumber.

First up is Dr. Wagner, who checks my vitals and gives me my pills and a breakfast smoothie. I dutifully put the pills in my mouth. I don't touch the smoothie.

Next are Jeannette and Bernard, who wake me with their chatter while they change my bandages, replace the catheter, swap out the IV bag. From their conversation, I gather that this is a small operation. Just the two of them, Nick, Dr. Wagner, and a night nurse who's in big trouble after I managed to slip out unnoticed.

There are apparently three patient rooms, all of them currently occupied—a rarity, to hear Jeannette tell it. I'm in one. Greta's in another. The third is occupied by Mr. Leonard, who only days ago received a new heart.

Although they never mention Dylan by name, I know where that heart came from. Just thinking about it beating inside frail and ancient Mr. Leonard's stitched-up chest makes me shove a fist in my mouth to keep from screaming.

When I do eventually fall asleep again, it's with tears in my eyes.

They're still there when I'm startled awake I-don't-know-how-many hours later by Greta Manville. The door unlocks, and there she is, no longer in a wheelchair but moving around with the help of a walker. She looks healthier than the last time I saw her. Not as pale, and more robust.

"I wanted to see how you're doing," she says.

Even though I'm half-comatose from the little white pills, enough anger courses through me to produce two words.

"Fuck you."

"I'm not proud of what I've done," Greta says. "What my entire family has done, starting with my grandmother. I know you know about that, by the way. You're smart enough to have figured it out by now. Then my parents. Kidney disease runs in the family. Both of my parents needed transplants. So when I needed one as well, I returned to this place, knowing its purpose. And its sins. You judge me harshly, I know. I deserve to be judged. Just as I deserve your hatred and your desire to see me dead."

The fog parts. A rare moment of clarity, fueled by anger and hatred. Greta is right about that.

"I want you to live as long as possible," I say. "Years and years. Because each day you're alive means one more day you have to think about what you've done. And when the rest of your body starts to fail you—and it will, very soon—I hope that small piece of me that's inside you keeps you alive just a little bit longer. Because death isn't good enough for you."

I'm spent after that, sinking into the mattress like it's quicksand. Greta remains by the bed.

"Go away," I moan.

"Not yet. There's a reason I'm here," she says. "I'm being released to my apartment tomorrow. It'll be more comfortable for me there. Dr. Nick says being in my own place will speed up my recovery. I thought you'd want to know."

"Why?"

Greta shuffles to the door. Before closing it behind her, she takes one last look at me and says, "I think you already know the answer."

And I do, in a hazy, half-conscious way. Her departure means there'll be room for someone else.

Maybe Marianne Duncan.

Maybe Charlie's daughter.

Which means I won't be here by this time tomorrow.

49

I sleep.

I wake.

Bernard—he of the bright scrubs and no-longer-kind eyes—arrives with lunch and more pills. Because I'm too dazed to eat, he uses pillows to prop me up like a rag doll and spoon feeds me soup, rice pudding, and what I think is creamed spinach.

The drugs have made me oddly chatty. "Where are you from?" I say, slurring my words like someone who's had one too many drinks.

"You don't need to know that."

"I know I don't *need* to. I *want* to."

"I'm not telling you anything," he says.

"At least tell me who you're doing this for."

"You need to stop talking."

Bernard shovels more pudding into my mouth, hoping it will shut me up. It does only for as long as it takes me to swallow.

"You're doing it for someone," I say. "That's why you're here and not at, like, a regular hospital, right? They promised to help someone you love if you work for them? Like Charlie's doing?"

I'm given another mouthful of pudding. Rather than swallow, I let it drip from my lips, talking all the while.

"You can tell me," I say. "I won't judge you. When my mother was dying, I would have done anything to save her life. *Anything.*"

Bernard hesitates before answering in a soft murmur, "My father."

"What does he need?"

"A liver."

"How much time does he have left?"

"Not much."

"That's a shame." The sentence comes out mushy. A single, smushed word. *Thassashame.* "Does your father know what you're doing?"

Bernard scowls. "Of course not."

"Why?"

"I'm not answering any more of your questions."

"I don't blame you for not wanting to give false hope. Because you might be right here one day. Someone rich and famous and *important* will need a kidney. Or a liver. Or a heart. And if there's no one like me around, they'll take it from you."

I lift my hand and wave it around, weakly pointing in his general direction. After a second, it plops back onto the bed because I'm too weak to hold it up any longer than that.

Bernard drops the spoon on the tray and pushes it aside. "We're done here."

"Don't be mad," I say, slurring a bit. "I'm just saying. That deal you made? I don't think it's gonna stick."

Bernard thrusts the tiny paper cup at me, his hands shaking. "Shut up and take your pills."

I pop them into my mouth.

50

Hours later, I'm roused from my deep slumber by Jeannette, who unlocks the door before carrying in more food and yet more pills.

I look at her, groggy and dazed. "Where did Bernard go?"

"Home."

"Was it something I said?"

"Yes." Jeannette slides the tray in front of me. "You talk too much."

Dinner is the same as lunch. More soup. More creamed spinach. More pudding. The pills have made me surly, uncooperative. Jeannette has a hard time scooping even the slightest bit of soup into my mouth. I outright refuse to open my mouth for the spinach.

It's the rice pudding my pill-addled body craves. Willingly I open wide when Jeannette dips the spoon into it. But as she's bringing it toward my mouth, I change my mind. My jaw clamps shut, and I suddenly turn away, pouting.

The spoon hits my cheek, sending pudding splatting onto my neck and shoulder.

"Look at this mess," Jeannette mutters as she grabs a napkin. "Lord forgive me, but I can't say I'll be sad to see you go."

I lie completely still as she leans over me to mop up the spilled pudding. Sleep is already threatening to overtake me again. I'm almost completely unconscious when Jeannette nudges my shoulder.

"You need to take your pills," she says.

My mouth falls open, and Jeannette drops the pills into it, one at a time. Then I'm asleep, closed fists at my sides, riding the narcotic fog until my mind is empty and blissful and at peace.

When I hear the door's lock click into place, I wait. Breathless. Counting the seconds. After a full minute has passed, I stuff my fingers into the far reaches of my mouth and fish out the pills. They emerge softened and slimy with saliva.

I sit up, wincing with pain, and lift my pillow. Beneath the case, in the pillow itself, is the small tear I created yesterday after talking to Nick. I shove the spit-slick pills into it, where they join the others. Eight of them in total. A whole day's worth of little white pills.

I replace the pillow and lie back down. I then unclench my fist and examine the cigarette lighter I snatched after it fell from Jeannette's cardigan pocket while she cleaned me.

It's made of cheap plastic. The kind you can pick up at a gas station for a dollar. Jeannette probably has two more sitting in her purse.

She won't miss this one.

51

I toss the blanket aside and slide my legs over the side of the bed, even though it hurts to move, hurts to breathe. Three sets of stitches pull at the skin of my abdomen.

Before placing my feet on the floor, I pause.

I'm not sure standing's a good idea. Even if it is, I'm not sure I can. I am, for lack of a better word, in shambles. My legs tingle from disuse. The back of my hand is bleeding from when I plucked out the IV. Removing the catheter was even worse. Soreness pulses through my core, a counterpoint to the pain roaring along my stomach.

Yet I attempt to stand anyway, sucking in air to steel myself against the pain before pushing off the bed. Then I'm up, somehow standing on these weak, wobbling legs.

I take a step.

Then another.

And another.

Soon I'm staggering across the room, the floor seeming to rock back and forth like a ship's deck on a stormy sea. I sway with it, lurching from one side to the other, trying to stay upright. When the floor doesn't stop moving, I grip the wall for support.

But I keep walking, my joints crackling, as if I'm a freshly hatched chick, now shedding eggshell. The sound follows me all the way to the door, where I try the handle and discover it is indeed locked.

So it's back to the side of the bed, where I grab the photograph of my family. I press it against my chest with one hand while gripping Jeannette's cigarette lighter in the other.

With a flick of my thumb, there's a flame, which I touch against the fitted sheet in the center of the bed. It ignites in an instant—a fire-ringed hole that grows exponentially. The flames soon reach the top sheet, and that, too, starts to burn. It's the same with the mattress. Expanding circles of fire spreading into each other and then outward, all the way to the pillows, which pop into flame.

I watch, squinting against the smoke, as the entire bed is engulfed. A rectangle of fire.

Then, just as I had hoped, the fire alarm starts to blare.

52

It's Dr. Wagner who enters the room first, drawn by the fire alarm's literal siren's call. Jeannette follows right behind him. They unlock the door and burst inside. Jeannette screams when she sees the flames on the bed now threatening to make the leap to the walls and ceiling.

Because they're too focused on the fire, neither of them sees me standing just behind the recently opened door.

Nor do they see me slip out of the room.

By the time they turn around to notice me, it's too late.

I'm already closing the door behind me and, with a quick turn of my wrist, locking them inside.

53

I walk as fast as I can, which isn't very fast at all. Pain hobbles me—a fierce, stabbing ache that keeps me gasping. Still, slow walking is better than not being able to walk at all.

Behind me, Dr. Wagner and Jeannette pound on the door from inside my room. In between their frantic knocks I hear the sounds of Dr. Wagner coughing and Jeannette shrieking.

To my left is a darkened doorway. Inside I see Mr. Leonard, dead to the world despite the racket coming from the room next door. Surrounding him is all manner of monitoring equipment, their lights disconcertingly festive. Like a strand of Christmas bulbs.

I make my way to the nurses' station, where I allow myself to pause for just a second to catch my breath. Just beyond it is another hospital room and the short corridor I took the first time I left this place. The corridor ends at a door that leads directly into Nick's apartment. From there, I need to make it down the twelfth-floor hallway to the elevator. In my condition, taking the stairs isn't an option.

I push off the nurses' station and am on my way to the corridor when the door at its end starts to open. I duck into the room to my left and press myself against the wall by the open doorway, hoping I haven't been spotted.

Outside, I hear the rapid click of heels.

Leslie Evelyn.

While waiting for her to pass, I scan the darkened room.

That's when I see Greta.

She sits up in bed, startled, staring at me in fear.

Her mouth drops open, on the knife's edge of a scream.

One sound from her could give me away, which is why I stare back, my eyes saucer-wide, silently begging her to stay quiet.

I mouth a single word.

Please.

Greta's mouth stays open while Leslie hurries past the door. She waits a few more seconds before finally speaking.

"Go," she says in a hoarse whisper. *"Hurry."*

54

I wait to move until Leslie pushes open the door two rooms down. Smoke pours from the room, gray and heavy, filling the nurses' station. I use it as cover while heading down the corridor. With each passing step, the pain seems to calm. I don't know if it's actually going away or if I'm just getting used to it. It doesn't matter. I just need to keep moving.

And I do.

To the corridor's end.

Through the door left open by Leslie.

Into Nick's apartment.

I close the door behind me, remembering how heavy it is, using a shoulder to nudge it back into place. When the door is finally closed, I spot the deadbolt in its center.

I slide it shut.

Satisfaction swells in my chest, although I harbor no illusions that Leslie and all the rest are now trapped. Surely there's another way out of there. But it will certainly delay them, and I need all the time I can get.

I hobble onward, exhaustion, pain, and adrenaline dancing through me. It's a heady mix that makes me dizzy.

When I reach Nick's kitchen, the whole place seems to be spinning. The cabinets. The counter with its wooden knife block. The doorway to the dining room and the night-darkened park outside the windows.

The only thing not spinning is the painting of the ouroboros.

It undulates.

Like it's about to slither right off the canvas.

The snake's flickering-flame eye watches me as I shuffle to the knife block on the counter and grab the biggest one.

Having the knife in my hand chases away some of the disorientation. Like the pain, it lingers, but at a level low enough to push through. I need to escape this place. I owe it to my family.

I look at the photograph still clutched to my chest. When faced with the decision to take those pills, I saw their faces and knew what my choice had to be.

To fight.

To live.

To be the one member of my family who doesn't vanish forever.

I keep going, out of the kitchen, back into the hallway, where thin strands of smoke have started to make an appearance. Here the noise of the fire alarm is distant yet audible. A system separate from the rest of the building.

The sound fades slightly as I head down the hallway. At the other end is Nick's study, the bookcase at the far wall still open. Beyond it is 12A. The study. Then the hallway. Then a way out.

Doors within doors within doors.

I stagger toward them, oblivious to the smoke, the pain, the exhaustion, the dizziness. My sole focus is the bookcase in the study. Reaching it. Passing through it. But as I approach the open bookcase, I feel a sudden heat at my back.

I whirl around to see Nick standing in a corner of the study.

In his hands is Ingrid's gun.

He lifts it, aims it my way, and pulls the trigger.

I close my eyes, wince, try to spend my last second on earth thinking about my family and how much I miss them and how I hope there's some way to see them in the afterlife. In that fraught, fearful darkness, I hear a metallic click.

Then another.

Then two more.

I open my eyes and see Nick continuing to pull the trigger of the unloaded gun. Like it's a toy and he's just a kid playing cowboy.

I don't try to run. In my condition, I won't get very far. All I can do is lean against the bookcase and contemplate Nick as he smiles, pleased with himself.

"Don't worry, Jules," he says. "I can't shoot you. You're too valuable."

Nick takes several steps toward me, the gun now lowered.

"Over the years, my family has received a lot of money for people like you. It's ironic, I know. That you, who's so worthless on the outside, is worth so much on the inside. And that people who on the outside offer so much have inside of them things so useless that they must be replaced. You think that what we do here is murder."

I glare at him. "Because it is."

"No, I'm doing the world a service."

Roughly ten feet separate us now. My grip tightens around the knife's handle.

"Think about the people who come here," Nick says. "Writers and artists, scientists and captains of industry. Think of all they give to the world. Now think of yourself, Jules. What are you? What do you offer? Nothing."

He takes two more steps, closing the gap between us.

I lift the knife, barely aware of what I'm doing until it's pressed against my neck. The blade's edge creases the flesh beneath my chin. My pulse hammers against the steel.

"I'll do it," I warn Nick. "Then you'll really be left with nothing."

He calls my bluff.

"Go ahead," he says with a blithe shrug. "There'll be someone else to take your place. You're not the only desperate person out there, Jules. There are thousands in need of shelter and money and hope. I'm sure we can find your replacement tomorrow, if need be. So go ahead. Slit your throat. It won't stop us."

He takes two more steps. One slow, the other a startling leap toward me.

I thrust the knife forward until it makes contact with Nick's stomach.

There's a pause. A breath of resistance as the blade runs up against flesh and muscle and internal organs. It passes in a flash and all that flesh, all those muscles, all those organs give way as the knife continues onward, sinking deeper into his stomach. So deep that my hand doesn't stop moving until the edge of it is pressed against Nick's shirt.

I gasp.

So does Nick.

The sounds are simultaneous. Two shocked, shuddering inhalations that fill the room.

I gasp again as I yank the knife away.

Nick doesn't.

He can only moan as blood soaks his shirt, the fabric changing from white to red in seconds. Then Nick hits the floor. A swift, uninterrupted drop.

I back away from him and the blood that's quickly spreading across the floor. That backward shuffle takes me through the bookcase passage into the study of 12A. There I do another shoulder nudge to close the bookcase. Before it lumbers into place, I take one final, fleeting glance into Nick's apartment. He's still on the floor, still bleeding, still alive.

But probably not for long.

I let the bookcase fall back into place without a second glance.

Almost free.

Inside 12A, all traces of my existence are gone. The apartment looks just as it did when I first set foot inside it. Uninhabited. Devoid of life.

But it's also a trap.

I know that now.

I should have known it then.

This perfect apartment with its perfect views inside a perfect building. It was all designed to be as enticing as possible to someone like me, who started out poor and stayed that way. What's worse is that this isn't a recent development. It's always been the sole purpose of the Bartholomew. The only reason the building exists is to serve the rich and trap the poor.

Those servants laid out like firewood. Cornelia Swanson's maid. Dylan and Erica and Megan and all those other men and women without families who were lured here with the promise of a reset button for their sad lives.

They deserve closure.

Even more, they deserve vengeance.

Which means only one thing.

This whole fucking place needs to be burned to the ground.

55

I start with the study, pulling books at random from the shelves to form a pile in the middle of the floor. When I'm done, I grab the copy of *Heart of a Dreamer* Greta signed for Erica and hold the lighter to a corner of its dust jacket.

Fire tears across the book.

I drop it onto the pile and walk away.

In the sitting room, I remove the cushions from the crimson sofa. One is shoved under the coffee table, where I use the lighter to set it ablaze.

In the dining room, I repeat the process—place a cushion under that ridiculously long table, light it, leave.

In the kitchen, I stuff the cushion into the oven and crank up the heat.

Sitting on the table in the breakfast nook is another copy of *Heart of a Dreamer*. I turn to the page Greta signed for me and, with a flick of my thumb, light it up. I wait for a flame to bloom before dropping it down the dumbwaiter shaft.

After that, it's up to the bedroom, with me climbing the spiral steps as fast as my battered body will allow. On the nightstand is one final copy of *Heart of a Dreamer*. My real copy, first read to me by Jane as we lay on her bed.

I scoop it up and carry it back downstairs.

By the time I've reached the foyer, the apartment has filled with smoke. Already the fires have grown out of control. A glance down the hall reveals flames crawling across the floor of the study. In the sitting room, tongues of fire lick at the underside of the coffee table while smoke rises from its surface. A light crackling sound in the dining room tells me the table there is meeting a similar fate.

Satisfied, I open the door and leave 12A for the last time.

I keep the apartment door open as I move down the hallway, letting smoke billow out behind me. At the elevator, I press the down button. While waiting for it to arrive, I go to the nearby trash chute. I then flick the lighter and hold it just below the final copy of *Heart of a Dreamer.*

My hand resists bringing the flame any closer.

This isn't just some random copy of the book.

It's my copy.

Jane's copy.

But I also understand that she'd want me to do it. This isn't the Bartholomew of her dreams. It's a shadow version of that fantasy realm. Something dark and rotten to its core. If Jane knew the truth about the Bartholomew, I'm sure she'd despise it as much as I do.

Without another moment's hesitation, I place the book against the lighter's white-hot flame. As fire leaps across its cover, I drop the book down the trash chute, where it hits the dumpster below with a soft sizzle.

The fire alarm in the rest of the building goes off just as the elevator reaches the twelfth floor. I step into it, ignoring the shrieking alarm, the flashing emergency lights, the smoke rolling out of 12A in sinuous waves.

I simply descend, staring at the elevator floor, where blood drips from beneath my hospital gown. My stitches have come loose. Warm liquid oozes from one of the wounds, and a blossom of red appears in the front of the gown.

On my way down, I see that the residents have already started to evacuate. They move down the stairs in rushed packs. Rats scurrying from the sinking ship. Between the sixth and seventh floors,

Marianne Duncan sits on the landing, jostled by others coming down the staircase. Tears stream down her face.

"Rufus?" she all but screams. "Come back, baby!"

Our eyes lock for a moment, hers yellowed from jaundice, mine aflame with vengeance. I give her the finger as the elevator sinks to the next floor.

None of the retreating residents try to stop my descent. All it would take is a press of the elevator button on a lower floor. But they see the look on my face and the blood-stained knife in my hand and instinctively stay away.

I'm the kind of girl you don't want to fuck with.

As the elevator comes to a stop in the lobby, I spot a small, dark shape streaking down the steps. Rufus, also making his escape. I yank open the grate and step out of the elevator, lowering my aching body just enough to scoop him up. He shivers in my arms and lets out a few sharp yaps that I hope are loud enough for Marianne to hear several floors above us.

Together, we approach the door. Charlie is there, helping the Bartholomew's population of old and infirm get outside. He sees me and freezes, shocked, his arms dropping to his sides. This time, he doesn't try to stop me. He knows it's all over.

"I hope your daughter gets the care she needs," I tell him as I pass. "Do the right thing now, and maybe one day she'll forgive you."

I continue on, limping out of the Bartholomew as police and fire trucks start to arrive. It's a firefighter who spots me first, although it's hard not to. I'm a bleeding girl in a hospital gown with bare feet, a frightened dog, a cracked family photo, and a blood-slicked knife.

Immediately, I'm swarmed by cops, who pry the knife from my hand.

I refuse to give them Rufus or the picture of my family.

I'm allowed to keep hold of them as I'm wrapped in a blanket and guided first to a waiting patrol car and then, when it arrives, to an ambulance. Soon I'm on a stretcher, being carried to the ambulance's open back doors.

"Is anyone else inside hurt?" a cop asks me.

I give a weak nod. "A man on the twelfth floor—12B."

I'm then loaded feetfirst into the ambulance with two EMTs. Through the open rear door, I get a tilted view of the Bartholomew itself. I look to the northern corner where George sits, stoic as ever, even as flames start to leap in the window just behind his wings. I'm about to give him a whispered goodbye when I notice movement on the other side of the roof.

A dark figure emerges from the smoke, stumbling toward the roof's edge.

Even though he's so high up and the heat of the fire causes the air around him to shimmer, I can tell it's Nick. He has a towel pressed to his stomach. When a smoke-filled breeze kicks up, the towel flutters, flashing bits of red.

Two more people join him on the roof. Cops. Although their guns are drawn, they show no signs of using them. Nick has no place to run.

Still, he continues to stagger along the roof. The smoke pouring from 12A has gotten thicker, darker. It blows across him in malevolent strands, bringing him in and out of my vision.

When the smoke clears, I see that he's reached the edge of the roof. Even though he must be aware of the cops following his path, he ignores them. Instead, he looks outward, surveying the park and the city beyond it.

Then, like his great-grandfather before him, Nicholas Bartholomew jumps.

SIX MONTHS LATER

56

Lo mein or fried rice?" Chloe says as she holds up two identical cardboard containers of Chinese food.

I shrug. "You pick. I'm fine with either."

The two of us are in her apartment, which has, for the time being, become my apartment. After I was released from the hospital, Chloe handed me the keys and moved in with Paul.

"But what about rent?" I had asked.

"I've got it covered for now," she said. "Pay me what you can when you can. After what you went through, I refuse to make you sleep on the couch."

Yet the couch is where I am at the moment, sitting next to Chloe as we open our takeout containers. Lunch instead of dinner. Joining us this afternoon is Ingrid, fresh from her new job at a midtown Sephora. Although she's dressed in black, her nails are a vivid purple. The bad bus station dye job is long gone, replaced with a relatively demure strawberry blond with a few pink streaks that frame her face.

"Rice for me, please," she says. "I mean, I like the taste of lo mein better, but the texture's so icky. It reminds me of worms."

Chloe grits her teeth and hands her the container. If they gave out Nobel Prizes for patience, she'd certainly be in contention for one. She's been a saint since the moment I was released from the hospital with a clean bill of health. I haven't heard her complain once.

Not about the reporters who spent a full week camped outside the building.

Not about the nightmares that sometimes leave me so shaken that I call her in the wee hours of the morning.

Not about Rufus, who yaps at her every time she enters the apartment.

And certainly not about Ingrid, who's here more often than not, even though she now shares an apartment with Bobbie in Queens. Chloe knows that Ingrid and I are now bound together by what happened. I've got Ingrid's back. She's got mine. As for Chloe, she looks out for us both.

The two of them first met while I was being held against my will in the Bartholomew. When I never came back to the shelter, Ingrid went to the police, claiming I was taken by a coven living at the Bartholomew. They didn't believe her.

The police didn't think anything was amiss until Chloe, returning from Vermont early after eventually receiving the texts I had sent, also contacted them. A friendly cop put the two of them in touch. After Chloe went to the Bartholomew and was told by Leslie Evelyn that I had moved out in the middle of the night, the police got a search warrant. They were on their way to the building just as I was setting fire to 12A.

The fire ended up doing less damage than I intended. Yes, 12A was burnt beyond repair, but the blaze in the basement was contained by the dumpster. Still, it was enough damage to make me worry that I could face criminal charges. The detective working the case remains doubtful that will happen. I was in shock, fearing for my life, and not in my right mind.

I'll agree the first two are true. As for the third claim, I knew exactly what I was doing.

"Even if you are charged," the detective told me, "there's not a judge in this whole city who won't dismiss it. After hearing what went on there, I'm tempted to torch the place myself."

From my understanding, that's the consensus across the country.

Because what took place at the Bartholomew was so insidious in its efficiency.

People in need of a life-saving organ were tipped off, usually by a former Bartholomew resident. They then used a dummy corporation to purchase an apartment, paying up to a million more than its market value.

There they waited. Sometimes for months. Sometimes for years. Waiting for an apartment sitter who'd be a suitable donor of whatever it was they needed. After the surgery, the resident spent a few more weeks in the Bartholomew to recuperate. The body of the apartment sitter, meanwhile, was quietly removed via a freight elevator in the rear of the building and taken to a crematorium in New Jersey with Mafia ties.

Records found in Leslie Evelyn's office indicate that, over the span of forty years, more than two hundred Bartholomew residents received organs harvested from one hundred twenty-six unwilling donors. Some were runaways, and some were homeless. Some had been reported missing, and some had no one in their lives to realize they were ever gone.

But now everyone knows their names. The NYPD published the full list online. So far, thirty-nine families know the fates of their long-missing relatives. Although it's not happy news, it's closure, which is why I don't blame myself for sometimes wishing Jane's name was on that list.

Bad news is better than no news.

Almost everyone involved was brought to justice, thanks to Charlie. He took my advice and did the right thing, providing police with valuable information about how the Bartholomew operated, who worked there, who lived there, who died there.

Those who managed to escape during the fire were slowly but surely rounded up, including Marianne Duncan, the other doormen, and Bernard. All of them copped to their respective roles in the enterprise and were sentenced accordingly. Marianne began her ten-year stint in prison yesterday. She's still waiting for a new liver.

The legal fallout extended to former employees and residents, including an Oscar winner, a federal judge, and the wife of a diplomat. Marjorie Milton hired the best defense lawyer in Manhattan to represent her—until it turned out he had also used the Bartholomew's services. Both eventually entered guilty pleas. The tabloids had a field day.

Even more shocking was the participation of Mr. Leonard. Also known as Senator Horace Leonard from the great state of Indiana. Since he was in no condition to be evacuated during the fire, he was simply left there. Police found him crawling across the floor of the room next to mine. He probably would have died were it not for Dylan's heart pumping in his chest.

Although he won't be sentenced until next month, even his own attorneys expect him to get life in prison. Thanks to Dylan's heart, that could mean a lot of time behind bars.

Then again, Mr. Leonard could always kill himself, which is what Dr. Wagner did after Leslie freed him and Jeannette from the burning room. Once the three of them escaped out a back exit of the Bartholomew and went their separate ways, he spent two days at a Sheraton in Flushing, Queens, before putting a gun to his temple and pulling the trigger.

Jeannette went the opposite route, going home and sitting with her husband until the police arrived.

Leslie Evelyn was apprehended at Newark Liberty International Airport as she was about to board a flight to Brazil. Because she was the only major player left alive, prosecutors pummeled her with charges ranging from human trafficking to aiding and abetting to tax fraud.

After she received multiple life sentences, I sent her a list of rules she needed to follow in prison. At the top was this: *No nights spent away from your cell.*

I didn't sign the letter. She knows damn well who it came from.

Out of everyone I encountered at the Bartholomew, only one person is neither dead nor facing years in prison.

Greta Manville.

She was nowhere to be found when cops stormed the Bartholomew. The police searched her apartment and the basement storage cage, finding them mostly intact. The only thing that looked amiss was an empty box in the storage cage marked with a single word—*Useful*.

Whatever was inside must have been very useful indeed, for Greta made a clean getaway. No one has seen or heard from her since, a fact that messes with my emotions more than it should. While I have a burning desire to see her brought to justice, I also know that I never would have escaped without her help.

Then there's the fact that she literally has a piece of me with her everywhere she goes. I wasn't lying when I told her I hoped she lived a long, long time. Otherwise it would all be such a waste.

As for me, I'm still adjusting to my new existence as a celebrity victim—two words, by the way, that should never be used together. Yet that's what I was called during those few weeks when I was a media darling. Everyone was talking about the plain, quiet girl with no job and no family who took down an evil criminal enterprise. Chloe took a two-week leave of absence from work to help me deal with all the interview requests. I did the bare minimum. A few phone interviews. Nothing in person. Definitely nothing on camera.

I told the reporters exactly what happened, without embellishment. The truth is bizarre enough. I ended each interview by talking about Jane, imploring anyone with the slightest bit of information to please come forward, anonymously if necessary.

So far, there have been no new leads.

Until there are, I'll keep trying, hoping for the best but planning for the worst.

But people have been generous in other ways. My former boss called to tell me my old job was waiting for me if I ever wanted to return. I politely declined. The day I was released from the hospital, Andrew showed up with flowers. He didn't stay long or say very much. He just told me he was sorry. I believe him.

Then there's the GoFundMe page Chloe set up to help pay for my medical expenses. Although I wasn't keen on the idea of accepting charity, I didn't have a choice. When your sole possession is a broken picture frame, you come to terms with relying on the kindness of strangers.

And people have truly been kind. I've received so many clothes that Bobbie and I started handing things out at the homeless shelter. Same thing with shoes and phones and laptops. Everything I lost has been replaced threefold.

That's in addition to the money I've received. More than sixty thousand dollars in five months. The amount got to be so high that I begged Chloe to close the account. It's more than enough money, especially considering that on Monday I'll be starting a new job at a nonprofit group that tries to help people locate missing loved ones. They asked if I wanted to work for them after I used some of my GoFundMe money to make a donation in Jane's memory. I said yes. The office is small. The salary is even smaller. But I'll get by.

I'm feeding Rufus a barbecue sparerib when I notice the time. Quarter after one.

"We need to go," I tell Ingrid.

Ingrid brushes rice from her lap and jumps to her feet. "We definitely don't want to be late for this."

"Are you positive you want to do this?" Chloe says.

"I think we need to," I tell her. "Whether we want to or not."

"I'll be here when you get back," she says. "With wine."

On the walk to the PATH station, I get a few strange looks from passersby. I'm finally being noticed, for all the wrong reasons. On the train itself, I spot a girl reading *Heart of a Dreamer*. Not my first sighting since word got out that Greta Manville was involved with the Bartholomew's dark doings. The book is suddenly back in vogue, returning to bestseller lists for the first time in decades.

The girl catches me watching and does a double-take of recognition. "Sorry," she says.

"Don't be," I say. "It's a really good book."

Ingrid and I reach the Bartholomew just before two, finding the block closed off to cars. The crane and wrecking ball have already arrived, parked in the middle of Central Park West like some giant metal beast. A temporary fence has been erected around it, presumably to deter onlookers.

It doesn't work. The park side of the street is mobbed. Many are from news outlets, their cameras aimed at the building across the street. Others are the morbidly curious who want to boast that they were there when the infamous Bartholomew was demolished. Rounding out the pack are well-meaning but misguided protestors who lift signs that read SAVE THE BARTHOLOMEW.

Despite its age and notoriety, the building had never been granted historical status from the city. The Bartholomew family wanted it that way. Historical designation meant more oversight—something they needed to avoid.

With Nick dead and without historical status, the Bartholomew became just like any average building in Manhattan—available to buy and, if the new owner saw fit, demolish. Which is what the real estate conglomerate that bought it immediately decided to do. Unlike the protestors, they're fully aware no one in their right mind would buy an apartment that had been used in an organ transplant black market.

Now the Bartholomew faces its final minutes, and half the city has come out to watch it die.

Ingrid and I push our way into the fray. We go unnoticed, thanks to the accessories we donned after emerging from the subway. Knit caps and sunglasses and jackets with the collars pulled up around our necks.

I peer through the chain-link fence at the Bartholomew, which stands as solemn and silent as a mausoleum. It's the first time I've laid eyes on it in six months. Seeing it again brings a fearful chill that shoots through my bones even after I tighten my jacket.

Missing from the northern corner of the roof is George. At my request, he was removed and put into the care of the nearby

New-York Historical Society. City officials were happy to oblige. The plan is to put George on display as a monument to the people who died there. I hope it happens. It might be nice to visit him.

The crowd around us goes silent as a worker climbs into the cab of the crane. Once he's in place, an alarm sounds. So loud I feel it in my chest.

I start to cry, the tears sudden and unstoppable. Most of them are for those who never left the Bartholomew. Dylan especially, but also Erica, Megan, Ruby, and so many more.

I cry for my family.

Jane, who may or may not still be out there.

My parents, who had been beaten down by life until they simply gave up.

But a few of those tears, I know, are reserved for me. Younger, more hopeful me, who saw the Bartholomew on a book cover and believed the promises it offered were real. That girl is gone now, replaced by someone wiser and harder but no less hopeful.

Ingrid sees the tears streaming out from beneath my sunglasses and says, "Are you okay?"

"No," I say. "But I will be."

Then I wipe away the tears, grip Ingrid's hand, and watch the wrecking ball swing.

ACKNOWLEDGMENTS

For me, the most difficult part of finishing a book is this page right here. It's quite hard trying to thank a group of people when you already know words aren't enough to express your gratitude. Still, an attempt must be made. To that end, here's a heaping helping of thanks.

To Maya Ziv, my amazing US editor, and everyone at Dutton and Penguin Random House who have worked so hard on my behalf. You are everything an author could want and more. I would be lost without our Dream Team.

To everyone at Ebury, my UK publisher, for keeping things running smoothly across the pond. My UK editor, Gillian Green, deserves a special shoutout for calling this book "positively Hitchcockian," which is probably the nicest compliment I've ever received.

To my agent, Michelle Brower, and everyone at Aevitas Creative Management for always having my back. I'm so proud to be among your list of authors, and I am so grateful for everything you do.

To the friends and family who continue to cheer me on from the sidelines, especially Sarah Dutton. Thank you, old friend.

To the readers who have embraced my books in the past three years.

To the bloggers and Instagram users who have been so generous with both their praise and their photography skills.

Finally, to Mike Livio, whose patience and understanding continue to astound me on a daily basis. None of this would be possible without you.

ABOUT THE AUTHOR

Lock Every Door is the third thriller from **Riley Sager**, the pseudonym of an author who lives in Princeton, New Jersey. Riley's first novel, *Final Girls*, was a national and international bestseller that has been published in more than two dozen countries, won the ITW Thriller Award for Best Hardcover Novel, and is currently being developed into a feature film by Universal Pictures. Sager's second novel, *The Last Time I Lied*, was a *New York Times* bestseller.

Read more gripping thrillers from Riley Sager

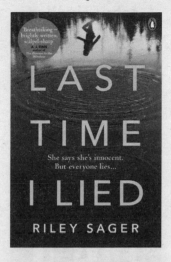

And don't miss Riley Sager's debut thriller

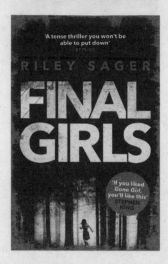

Three girls. Three tragedies. One unthinkable secret.

The media calls them the Final Girls – Quincy, Sam, Lisa –
the infamous group that no one wants to be part of. The sole
survivors of three separate killing sprees, they are linked
by their shared trauma.

But when Lisa dies in mysterious circumstances and Sam shows
up unannounced on her doorstep, Quincy must admit that
she doesn't really know anything about the other Final Girls.
Can she trust them? Or can there only ever be one?

All Quincy knows is one thing: she is next.

Out Now

Keep reading for an exclusive preview

PINE COTTAGE
1 A.M.

The forest had claws and teeth.

All those rocks and thorns and branches bit at Quincy as she ran screaming through the woods. But she didn't stop. Not when rocks dug into the soles of her bare feet. Not when a whip-thin branch lashed her face and a line of blood streaked down her cheek.

Stopping wasn't an option. To stop was to die. So she kept running, even as a bramble wrapped around her ankle and gnawed at her flesh. The bramble stretched, quivering, before Quincy's momentum yanked her free. If it hurt, she couldn't tell. Her body already held more pain than it could handle.

It was instinct that made her run. An unconscious knowledge that she needed to keep going, no matter what. Already she had forgotten why. Memories of five, ten, fifteen minutes ago were gone. If her life depended on remembering what prompted her flight through the woods, she was certain she'd die right there on the forest floor.

So she ran. She screamed. She tried not to think about dying.

A white glow appeared in the distance, faint along the tree-choked horizon.

Headlights.

Was she near a road? Quincy hoped she was. Like her memories, all sense of direction was lost.

She ran faster, increased her screams, raced toward the light.

Another branch whacked her face. It was thicker than the first, like a rolling pin, and the impact both stunned and blinded her. Pain pulsed through her head as blue sparks throbbed across her blurred vision. When they cleared, she saw a silhouette standing out in the headlights' glow.

A man.

Him.

No. Not Him.

Someone else.

Safety.

Quincy quickened her pace. Her blood-drenched arms reached out, as if that could somehow pull the stranger closer. The movement caused the pain in her shoulder to flare. And with the pain came not a memory but an understanding. One so brutally awful that it had to be real.

Only Quincy remained.

All the others were dead.

She was the last one left alive.